C000061434

THE DARK S...

Would you dumb down to fit in?

Simon escapes the ridiculous Riverside University of London by exchanging with its American partner – the University of Sunshine Bayside, only to wake up to the wokest of woke colleges. Virtues are punished as vices, conformity trumps originality, and minds are melded – one falsehood at a time. Being good at his job is his first mistake. In election year, politicians, terrorists, spies, publicists, journalists, and bluffers compete to make an example of him in their fight for a new global society.

The professor is about to be taken to school...

BRUCE OLIVER NEWSOME teaches at the University of San Diego. He has held standing faculty positions at the University of Pennsylvania, University of California Berkeley, and the Defence Academy of the United Kingdom. Bruce earned a doctoral degree in International and Strategic Studies, a masters degree in Political Science, and a bachelors with honors in War Studies. He is the author of more than a dozen books in history and social science. He advocates for science and free speech on YouTube and Twitter as the "Risky Scientists." Bruce is a proud citizen of both Britain and America, and is fluent in both languages. As an academic, he often considered registering his sense of humor as a disability. He thought the same of his objectivity. As a male, his preferred pronoun is "he."

The Dark Side of Sunshine

a social and political satire

by

Bruce Oliver Newsome

The Dark Side of Sunshine
A social and political satire

by Bruce Oliver Newsome, Ph.D.
www.BruceNewsome.com

Find bonus chapters, photographs, and videos at:
www.patreon.com/bruceolivernewsome

Published by: Perseublishing, PO Box 181802, Coronado, California 92178, United States of America

Copyright © 2020 Bruce Oliver Newsome, Ph.D.

All rights reserved. No part of this publication may be reproduced or stored in a retrieval system or transmitted, in any form or by any means, electronic, mechanical, photocopying, recording or otherwise, without prior permission in writing from the author.

This is a work of fiction. Names, characters, businesses, places, events and incidents are either the products of the author's imagination or used in a fictitious manner. Any resemblance to actual persons, living or dead, or actual events is purely coincidental.

FIC052000   FICTION / Satire
FIC016000   FICTION / Humorous / General
FUP   FICTION / Satirical fiction and parodies

1st paperback edition

ISBN: 978-1-951171-11-7

Cover images by: Jennifer Catlin; and Mohamed Mahmoud Hassan (https://freeimagesandillustrations.blogspot.com/?m=1)

Chapters

1. Riverside

"Sinner! What murder and mayhem are you conspiring? You warmonger!"

Simon braced for the slap on the back, but could not arrest the hot flush that lifted the hair on his head. He turned into Ricky Docker's face – a web of purple capillaries straining against the skin, close and above, large and saggy. Simon smoothed his hair, continued the motion, pointed unconvincingly at the window, and inhaled, but his eyes stuck on the foggy, rainy view.

"And, furthermore, I don't know what sort of impression you're trying to make, pondering the outside. Everybody can see you! And closing your office door. Nobody can see you! A new lecturer in international relations should be less interested in the world, more interested in his department. As for your interests – conflict! You're so conflictual! Frankly, I think your only hope is to defect to my domain. Everybody knows I'm a good person, because I do human rights."

Simon wondered why he never sensed Ricky's approach, but his mind was busy, and when his mind was busy he resented outer stimuli and inner feelings. He refocused through the window on the countless little impacts upon the river. The rest of London was washed without color or perspective. Simon struggled to re-imagine the warm breeze from sun-kissed slopes, when a wave of humidity hit him from the radiator. Injury lingered on his back, while Ricky continued in a self-satisfied mix of joviality and menace.

"Where were you yesterday?"

"I was researching."

"Impossible – I didn't see you."

"I was in the archives."

"How pretentious! As if that talk about rigor and objectivity isn't suspicious enough! And, furthermore, the archives are free! What about your research grant? How is the department supposed to pay its overhead if you lecturers don't submit their research grants?"

Simon deliberated earnestly, but Professor Docker advanced again.

"You missed the meeting about countering extremism on campus."

"I didn't know!"

"Well, we told the government you were there, because we put you in the proposal – because you're conflictual."

"Oh, thank you."

"And, furthermore, try spending less time with our other junior colleague. She's a girl – she told me. Try to be less heterocentric. We can reach only one conclusion. Of course, I'm only saying all this for your own good, because I'm a good person."

Ricky drew breath and extracted a hip flask from the pocket of his greasy, hairy jacket. "Come on – it's time for elevenses. You can justify yourself there."

The Riverside University of London, in a surprisingly old-fashioned way, had a Senior Common Room – what the Americans would call a "faculty lounge," Simon excitedly reminded himself, although he could not remember how he knew that.

One table was besieged by impatient elders. Their youngers hurried to arrange a dented stainless-steel urn of tea, a vacuum flask of milk, a dirty basket carrying packets of sugar, a rusty platter of biscuits, and a stack of crazed white plates.

Ricky Docker strode into the throng as if it had gathered in his honor. He was one of those misshapen, variegated old bluffers that every university department seems to have. He saw himself as the life of the party but expected to be treated as a serious academic. He ranked as full professor, and attended every day, but never seemed to teach. On the outside of his office, he posted a long resumé of his career, which included twenty years as chair of the Senior Common Room, chair of an "international conference" in Paris two decades ago, visiting lectureships at unfamiliar foreign universities, and editorship of "a highly regarded" series of publications, but he himself authored no books. His resumé concluded: "He has an international reputation as a scholar and has been an inspiration to students for over 30 years." Alongside this yellowing piece of paper, he posted lewd cartoons from obscure satirical magazines.

Simon habitually walked to the opposite wall, to the "pigeonholes" (in the old-fashioned parlance that still prevailed). Pigeonholes were assigned in alphabetical order, so each pigeonhole shifted whenever teaching staff changed, once a month or so. Simon went searching for the letters "S.I.N.R.," which were pressed into a piece of sticky-backed plastic by a hand-held machine that was still going strong, like the lady who wielded it, since the 1980s.

Sleepy, self-assured eyes passed in front of Simon, then stopped, expressionless, but uncomfortably close. Simon knew to speak first.

"Good morning, Joan."

"Hello Simon."

She paused long enough for him to feel compelled to speak again. "I thought we had a date in the archives…"

"You have a letter."

"Oh."

Her silence provoked him further.

"Thank you, Joan."

"No worries, Simon."

"Are you well?"

"I am brilliant."

"How was the conference on feminist international relations theory?"

"There's nothing more empowering than a room full of people who agree with you."

"I'm jealous."

"You should consider changing your focus. It's entirely inclusive. Of course, a man can never be a feminist because he's never experienced sexism, but you know what I mean because you and I are young, and everybody else here is so old they're bigots."

Joan ambled to the tea urn, smiled generally, and was invited to go first.

Simon held in two hands an envelope that was unmistakably foreign in design. The letter's unfamiliar typesetting occupied his mind longer than the realization of the paragraph that mattered.

"I say! I've been accepted!"

Nobody paid any attention.

"I'm going to America."

The silence was deafening.

Professor Sir Barry Liddell pushed out of the scrum, stirring a cup of tea slowly, his elbows stuck out like sharp handles on the sides of a lumpy teapot. "I do America," he said quietly.

Dorian Floorman straightened in his chair indignantly, then

addressed the ceiling: "Well, as everyone knows, I wrote the leading book on the special relationship. That should give you everything you need to know." He waited a few seconds without response, then sought Simon's gaze: "It's in the bookstore: 'The Anglo-American Relationship Through the Next Millennium'."

"As a Scot, I find that offensive," came a shrill voice from the outlying chairs.

"As a Celt, I agree," said another.

Dorian Floorman rose higher: "I've said many times that the second edition will be called 'The British-American Relationship'."

"It should be called 'European-American Relationship'," said a voice behind Simon. "You nationalist dinosaur."

Ricky Docker paused in front of Dorian Floorman's chair, stirring his tea with the mouth of his flask: "F.Y.I: change the title, pretend it's a new book." He tapped the side of his nose, and nodded curtly.

Professor Sir Barry Liddell had not moved: "You can't go to America. Your job is to teach."

Simon held up the letter: "It's a teaching exchange. I was invited to apply."

"No, you weren't."

"Everybody was invited – the email…"

"That was not for lecturers. It was for professors."

"It was sent to everybody," Simon insisted, with childish despair.

Ricky Docker looked startled: "Of course, I was far too busy with invitations from outside the colonies."

A faltering voice emerged from the chairs facing the window: "It's quite right that a lecturer of international relations should dabble in some international relationship himself – err, or herself, as the case may be…"

"Them-self," added someone, helpfully.

"Indeed, err, themselves, by teaching internationally, even if it is America."

A shrill voice interrupted. "Why would anyone want to go to America? It has no culture."

"Oh, you don't want to go to America! They don't have any public healthcare! I had the most awful experience in New York last year."

Simon turned with genuine interest: "Why? What happened?"

"The doctor saw me the very same day! I wasn't ready for that!"

"I see."

Professor Sir Barry Liddell pondered his next move. He liked to drink his tea facing the entrance, from what he called "a strategic position." Sir Barry loved the semantic frame "strategy." He would exclaim the term, while his usually lethargic body spasmed from his right shoulder, as if he were swinging a scythe: "Napoleon knew that he would need to defeat Britain or lose the war. That, ladies and gentlemen, was his STRATEGY!...Hitler knew that he would need to defeat Britain or lose the war. To win the war – that was Churchill's STRATEGY!...Tony Blair won his first wars because he took my advice on STRATEGY!...Tony Blair lost his other wars against my advice on STRATEGY!"

Once, Simon happened to be visiting the library when it was the backdrop to a televised interview, marking the anniversary of the end of some war or other: Simon could never decipher which, because, for 15 minutes, Barry Liddell mumbled in his usual way, looking downwards, frowning, sometimes reaching for a book so that he could read out what he had written better. The only statement that was broadcast was his animated conclusion: "That is the essence of STRATEGY!" The journalist made up the rest, with the preface: "The eminent Professor Sir Barry Liddell believes that..."

Now, Sir Barry was looking downwards as he stirred his tea, frowning, his untrimmed eyebrows sticking upwards and outwards, the big ears glowing in front of the strip lights, a few wisps of hair reaching for each other atop his head. That pose had seemed inspiring and prototypical at the annual conference on "Lessons from Past Grand Strategies for Future Change," but the same pose lost its mystique among the disinterested members of the Senior Common Room.

Suddenly, Sir Barry looked up with triumph. "As the head of Department, I need to approve everything."

"It was sent from the Director's office."

"You shouldn't take any notice of him."

"His email said the university would fund a temporary replacement."

Docker could not contain himself. "Oh! Nobody can argue with that."

Sir Barry waited for Docker to complete his rushed departure, then sat down facing the scrum: "You shouldn't go. You'll regret it." He stirred his tea and looked at the door again. "If you are STRATEGIC, you could come and go as you please, like Ricky Docker, once you're promoted to professor, of course, say, 30 years from now. In 15 years, you might make Senior Lecturer, like Dorian Floorman. That is the essence of STRATEGY."

Dorian Floorman sat up energetically again: "You'll find America very difficult. Very few people understand America. But if you understand the special relationship…" Floorman stopped speaking, nodding to himself, waiting for a response that never came. "Of course, if their department is run by a Roosevelt, you'll need to be a Churchill, but if it's run by a Bush, you'll need to be a Blair." He nodded at the ceiling, and bit on a biscuit.

"Of course," said Sir Barry acidly, "I told Tony that myself, before your book was published."

Dorian Floorman was suddenly unrestrained. "What young Simon needs is a department of liberal institutionalists who naturally co-operate across borders."

"He needs rational liberal institutionalists, who know that the British know better. At least, the Americans know me that way."

"Let's assume that the department is full of institutionalists…"

"Let's assume that the department is rational…"

"You cannot reduce institutions to unitary actors!"

"It's an assumption."

"A bad assumption!"

"Let's imagine you're on a desert island…"

"Oh, not this again!"

"I'll assume that you would model everybody on the island – their motivations, skills, and assets."

"Of course."

"Why? Just assume that everybody rationally works as one. And assume they have a boat."

Floorman and Liddell reprised their argument, while the shrill voices took their opportunity.

"You can't teach Americans – they're dogmatic!"

"They steal our best academics."

"They take our failed academics."

"They steal our foreign academics."

"That's imperialism!"

"Exactly! Americans are racist."

"And they're foreign."

"You don't want to teach racists!"

"You can't join the Great Satan!"

Simon exclaimed in desperation: "It's Sunshine University!"

The shrill voices restarted in a lower octave: "Ooh! That's a wonderful university!"

"I made my first pilgrimage in 1967."

"Did you know, the city is a nuclear-free zone?"

"That's why it gave birth to free speech!"

"The first free speech by foreigners, anyway."

Joan passed close in front of Simon, gazing languidly into his eyes: "Don't worry Simon. It can't be as foreign as a British university."

2. Riverside's Director

Neil Daly prided himself as a sociable academic, the face of the university, someone who could mix easily in the private and the public sectors, a welcoming face between awkward academics and bullish donors. Every morning, as he was driven past "The Dear Leader of the Holy Socialist People's Republic School of Business," he would look up at the words carved in stone above the grand entrance and say to himself, "That's as good as my name up there."

That was a reminder to call Sharon to expect him in five minutes. The best part of his day started once the car turned between the School for Human and Social Agendas (formerly known as Humanities and Social Sciences) and the Centralized Collaboration Cottage (formerly known as the Director's Tower). He liked to hear the car door open, while he was gathering his coat and newspaper. He liked to slide sideways between the car and the loading dock. He liked to race the security guard to the service lift. He liked to hear the frantic jingle of the keys that unlocked the button to the top floor. He liked to take the time to thank the guard with proletarian familiarity, before hurrying off along the quiet, dim corridor to the bright, open doorway.

"Good morning, Director Daly," said Sharon, with the pressed lips that experienced visitors realized as a smile. She exchanged a cup and saucer for his coat and newspaper.

"Thank you, Sharon. What would I do without the world's best co-executive assistant for egalitarian excellence?"

"That's an idea, Director Daly," said Sharon, keeping her lips pressed together. She hung his coat, placed the rolled-up newspaper in the bin, then opened the door connecting their offices.

Behind her, he sipped his tea, raised the biscuit from the saucer, and gazed out of the window above her desk. He sighed. "You know, Sharon, if only everybody spent every morning reading that newspaper from front to back, the world would be a harmonious place."

"That's an idea, Director Daly," said Sharon, looking into the corridor, watching a wispy ball of hair and dust drift ever closer to the threshold, sometimes falling back, but coming more than going, like a nervous rat, until it rolled behind the filing cabinet with newfound confidence.

Neil Daly sighed again. "It takes regular engagement with the news of the world, in entirety, every day, to remind us to check our privileges and keep ourselves humble!" He took a deep breath, nodded, smiled, and bit gently on his lower lip. He placed the cup on her desk, put the last piece of biscuit in his mouth, brushed the crumbs off his lapel, and walked into his office.

She closed the door behind her, then stood looking out of the window above his desk. As he struggled with his seat, he returned to his theme. "Not just any newspaper, of course, but one with a conscience, with a mission. There's no enlightenment in objective reporting."

He took hold of the computer's monitor with both hands and shuffled his chair closer. "A newspaper that reports not just the news, but the arts too. That rubbish from an upturned bin that won the Churner Prize last year taught me more about the tragedy of modern urban life than any scientific study."

"That's an idea, Director Daly."

"It's not just the visual and performing arts. I read the book reviews first, so I know what to think before I read the book." He stuck his head out like a tortoise and stabbed at the keyboard. "People just don't realize how early my day starts, long before I get to their emails. Why, I'm already reading the newspaper when the car comes for me at eight-thirty! At the coffee shop, I finish every page, as long as it takes – not just the business pages, mind you, but the sports pages too, so I can hold a conversation with the most uneducated member of staff. I don't turn on my phone until I'm in the car. Then I take my elevenses early just to be sure to get to their damned emails by ten-thirty." He squinted at the clock on the wall behind him. "What does that say?"

"Ten-thirty-eight."

"There you go! I've been at it for more than two hours already." He looked up at her attentively. "Perhaps you could make that known, Sharon."

"That's an idea, Director Daly."

He continued to look at her: "The whole story of self-less dedication, from eight-thirty, mind you."

"That's an idea, Director Daly."

He turned back to the computer, deleting emails with noisy slaps and taps that prompted Sharon to take up her notepad and write: "Order computer peripherals."

"Good girl! Write it down – the whole story, mind you! Don't forget to note the time I spend on email – before the lunch meetings. Then I spend all my lunchtime talking up this university – sometimes late into the evening. I don't get a lunch break like everybody else. I bet they don't realize that," he said, stabbing the keyboard with particular emphasis on the final word.

Sharon wrote down: "Finance director: shift hospitality budget into marketing."

"Don't forget to remind everybody that the deal in the desert took me three days of hard negotiating, not counting two days on the Dear Leader's yacht just to get there, and another two days back, a day in Corfu each way, and a tourist flight with no first-class seats. And I had to spend all day on the following Monday just deleting emails."

Sharon drew an arrow from "finance director" to the next line: "Shift Corfu from travel to outreach."

He looked up again. "I wasn't aware that his son was going to be admitted. You can remind everybody of that too."

Sharon wrote down: "Admissions Office: training in reputational risk."

She clasped her notebook in front of her waist: "Director Daly, that reminds me. The Dear Leader's Son has written to you again personally, asking for a teaching position, noting that some of the other doctoral students in his year continued into teaching positions."

If ever a tortoise could look moody, Neil Daly would give the best impression. He stopped stabbing, but said nothing.

Sharon continued: "He added that he was sure the International Criminal Court would drop charges against a teacher at such an enlightened university. But just in case, he requested that you allow him to teach by video link. He says he can't trust a former imperialist and slave-trading nation to comply with international law."

"Please remind the Dear Son that since the Dear Leader was overthrown, this university had to return the Dear Leader's Foundation for International Charity, Trade, and Teaching."

Sharon wrote: "Cut teaching positions in Liberal Studies."

Neil Daly started to stab again. "All these academics can do is send emails, wasting my time. Do they know how much money I could be bringing in to this university if I wasn't doing this?"

Sharon wrote: "Remove Director's email address from weekly newsletter." Then she spoke: "I could take over your account again."

"No, Sharon! Donors expect their correspondence to remain private and confidential."

Neil Daly stuck his neck out further and squinted. "What should I make of this? 'Dear Director Daly, Professor Sir Barry Liddell sends his regards, and requests that you confirm that the exchange teaching offer does not apply to…' Sharon, what does this acronym mean? S-I-N-R."

"It must be a name. See? The pronunciation is bracketed afterwards – 'Sinner'."

"Oh no! That looks foreign – so foreign, it's missing vowels, and its pronunciation needs to be bracketed! That's the worst kind of foreign! We all know that code: 'Don't piss off this one, walking lawsuit for racial discrimination.' Well, not on my watch! I've got another year to go, so screw you, whoever sent this! Who sent this?"

Sharon moved closer and read out: "'Richard Docker, call me Ricky, I hate Richard. We met at the all-faiths Christmas Party'."

"Did we?"

"I can check."

"Oh, I get it now! Barry Liddell made a nobody do it, that's how bad this is! So Barry thinks he's going to make me deny this opportunity to a litigious foreigner, because I wouldn't read the email properly, I'd just reply, 'Oh sure, Barry, whatever you say Barry. You advised the prime-minister, Barry. The prime minister asked you to write the official history of his wars, Barry. The prime minister asked you to prove the legality of his wars, Barry. The prime minister appointed you to the public inquiry into his wars, Barry.' Well, Barry Liddell didn't count on my eagle eyes this time, did he, Sharon?"

"That's an idea, Director Daly."

"Sharon, I've got an idea! You get hold of the Inter-University Exchange Council; and you order them to get this foreigner out to whatever damned university he wants, as quickly as possible."

"Or 'she,' Director Daly."

"You're right! It could be a woman! What if it's transgender? The email doesn't even specify the gender – that means it's transgender! Could this day get any worse?" He clutched the monitor with both hands and looked at Sharon desperately. "Give it a travel fund, excuse it from teaching for a year after return, just get it out of here, Sharon!"

"Yes, Director Daly. Forward the email to me. I'll email Ricky to tell him that his email came to me while you were out and after the decision had been made, then I'll call the Exchange Council to confirm the travel."

"Oh, Sharon! You have a heart as big as mine."

3. London home

Mr. and Mrs. Hart had inherited the house from one of their parents. Simon did not want to appear nosy, but suspected that Mrs. Hart had grown up in it.

Mrs. Hart liked the family to sit together for breakfast, except she would excuse herself early to clean the room around them. Then she would work her way through the hall and the kitchen to the window overlooking the garden, where she would sit with a mug of tea, pondering what she would do with the little lawn and its three borders once the weather brightened.

Mr. Hart liked to remain at the head of the dining table, looking out on the street, spreading papers all over the surface. Every few seconds, he would shift suddenly in the creaky chair, letting out a puff or a sigh, adjusting his enormous glasses from the front of his nose to the back, or vice versa, and knocking the curtain of flab under his chin with the back of his hand. Eventually, with a flurry, he would gather everything up into a battered briefcase that was once branded as "diplomatic." In the hall, he would struggle to attain a coat and umbrella with childish ineptness, while calling out urgently, "Darling! Darling!" as if gathering his wife to escape the apocalypse. "I must go darling! I really must go, otherwise I'll be late." She would come quickly, but otherwise calmly. They would kiss two or three times, then he would turn away from her saying, "I am so sorry, darling, I must go, I have so much to do." Simon understood that Mr. Hart worked in insurance, and had once been wealthy and fancy-free, but pandemics and lockdowns had wiped out his company's reserves. Now he was managing risk for a minor hauler. Mrs. Hart would wish him a lovely day, close the door gently behind him, and return to the window by the garden.

They were older parents with just one child. Simon called her Jennifer. They called her Jenny Wren. On sunny weekends, she sat in the garden with lemon juice in her hair, but fretted about damage. She was the most earnest teenager that Simon had ever met. Her greatest adventure to date was the daily commute to school, yet Simon saw little of her. She often took dinner at a schoolfriend's home. At home, she said little, but listened gratefully. She went to bed early. She got up later than her mother wanted, and often left the front door ajar, while she rushed to catch the same train as her friends. Mrs. Hart was always the most urgent and anxious about the journey.

Simon did not need to leave for work so early, but after a little reading and writing in his room, he would feel guilty to be denying Mrs. Hart the full pleasures of the house. Upon guilt, he would leave quickly, with little to gather – having stored most of what he needed in his office. Simon liked to time his return thirty minutes before the scheduled dinner, lest he disturb her preparations. If he needed anything from his room during the day, his dilemmas were painful. If he could not avoid it, he would telephone her on some other pretext, before warning her that he would be picking something up "in about an hour." He always sensed that she was pleased to be told, but disappointed anyway. She was frightfully well spoken, and often seemed to be poised to lead a government ministry or a financial department, but Simon saw her only at home.

Dinner was always a pantomime, which Simon at first found entertaining, but soon wished to accelerate. Mr. Hart had suffered a heart attack some months before Simon took a room, and was under medical instructions to avoid dairy products, but he liked bread and butter with every meal. He would slice off some butter, while Mrs. Hart said, "Darling! Think of your cholesterol." Mr. Hart would retort, "Oh, Darling! It's just a little piece. Look! Look how small it is!" He would spread it with artistic relish, and eat it with less care. "Eat some more vegetables, darling," Mrs. Hart would counsel. Mr. Hart would comply, before lubricating them with butter, when Mrs. Hart would lean forward with anguish, and hiss, "That's really enough, darling, you don't need that," or some variation thereof. Mrs. Hart's responses were quite varied, but Mr. Hart's script was predictable, down to the theatrical delivery. Simon initially played along by laughing gently, until he realized that Mrs. Hart fixated with stifled panic, as if Mr. Hart would fall off his chair at the next mouthful. Once his fingers were empty, she would deflate in her chair, having eaten little, leaning on one buttock, with her arms folded and a strained expression. This was the most emotional he ever saw her. Simon wondered why she did not remove butter from the table before dinner, but everything seemed to have its place.

Simon often wondered whether he was the last person in London with a traditional boarding arrangement. His friends had split into groups to search for houses in the outer zones, or apartments in the inner zones. All would sign a lease, then fight over who got the master bedroom at the back of the building. The front room would normally be reserved in common, except sometimes one person slept on the couch and paid a reduced share of the rent. In converting houses into apartments, landlords might convert every room into a bedroom, except a tiny kitchen and tinier bathroom, over which half a dozen people would fight every morning. Sometimes, Simon visited friends sharing a room – men he knew on the same rugby team, men who fretted about what to do if a girl suddenly wanted to come home, men who would take sleeping bags to the common room so that a mate could be alone with his girlfriend, on expectation that the mate would return the favor. They all dreamed of meeting a girl who had inherited a home or could afford the mortgage without tenants. In the morning, these bleary men would arise from a chaos of fabrics, sports equipment, and detergents, put on expensive suits and ties, and commute to work indistinguishable from those who owned mansions.

Mr. and Mrs. Hart were the last homeowners on Crimson Street. The other houses had been converted to flats by private landlords or purchased by the council for provision to hard shirking families. Mrs. Hart saw contractors replacing windows, heaters, roofs, or doors, whenever the safety standards or risk managers rotated. Those same contractors would give quotes that she could not afford. Sometimes Simon wondered if her regular perusals of the garden were really musings on how she could keep the house going.

Simon thanked himself he had chosen academia over commerce. He was poorer in salary, but richer in time, so he could choose to commute, shop, and seek healthcare when his friends could not. Simon lived in London because he had grown up in the countryside watching his elders commute for longer days than farmers worked in summertime. He often said, with knowing pretension, that he thought that an academic should live within the same community as his students. It was a fashionable thing to say; he had said it when he was interviewed; and he was sure it had helped.

He was sure of it when a letter arrived from the Inter-University Exchange Council, confirming his appointment at the University of Sunshine, with a generous travel fund. He had not realized that a travel fund was available, but most university communications are obtuse.

He wanted to think ahead – realistically and openly. Yet he found himself regressing to fantasies that preceded his doctorate: ivory towers, cloisters, vows of silence, tall libraries, punting, communal dining, solving equations with chalk in hand, discovering a scrap of paper in an archive like the missing piece of a jigsaw puzzle, heroically focusing all one's mental power on an unsolved theory, a good-natured debate with respected friends, the pondering of distant horizons, and realizations in the bath.

He informed his parents, but neither his achievements not their aging had mellowed their investment in the heir over the spare. Simon's last task was to persuade Mrs. Hart to pose in the little garden. He put his arm around her far shoulder. She leaned away, clasped her hands, and smiled meekly. Jenny Wren snapped the photograph. He promised to send a copy.

Only Jenny followed him to the door, silently, until he was outside: "I almost forgot your letters, here. Perhaps, by next year, you will be posting me an invitation to the University of Sunshine!"

On the train, he opened a good luck card of Jenny Wren's own design. Then he opened a formal warning from Sir Barry Liddell: Simon was expected to return after the autumn term to a full teaching load. Sir Barry added, in his own hand: "I know the University of Sunshine very well from my own radical youth; I have a great deal of influence there; and I am often invited back. Our world is a small one."

4. Jimmy Pons

Simon passed a dozen open cubicles before he found a wooden door. Through a small, partially frosted window, a man was looking at him with mouth open, while playing with papers, with sudden urgency. The man leaned to each side in exaggerated struggle with the view, straightened in his chair as if to look taller, then beckoned Simon to come in.

"Hello, Professor Pons. I am Dr. Ranald."

Pons turned back to his desk, picked up more papers, tapped their edges on the table, put them down reluctantly, then returned to look at Simon. In motion, Jimmy Pons was a blur of discordant shapes and colors. At rest, some regions emerged from the mess: clumpy hair, scruffy beard, a shirt that inclined up and over his belly, trousers that concertinaed on the floor, and bulky running shoes.

"Yes?"

"I am the exchange professor."

"Simone?"

"It's pronounced 'Simon'."

"You're not a woman?" asked Pons, with disappointment.

"No. I'm the exchange professor from London."

Pons opened a drawer and pulled out a package. "Simon."

"Yes, Simon."

Pons repeated "Simon" several times. "Ranald?"

"Yes."

"I assumed you would have more color, coming from a city of color, with that name."

"I think it's a Scottish name."

Professor Pons perked up: "Scots are colonial victims too. Call me Jimmy. Take a seat. Welcome to Bayside. How was your flight?"

"Long, not socially distanced, and passive-aggressive – but aren't they all?"

"How do you like the beautiful University of Sunshine?"

"I haven't seen much yet. I got to the hotel after dusk last night, and all I've seen today are the streets leading here, rather filthy streets actually. Perhaps I lost my way."

"I always thought Simon was a French name. It never occurred to me as Scottish!"

"No. I think it's English."

"You don't sound Scottish."

"No. I don't think I am Scottish."

Jimmy's face crumpled with dissonance. He could not tell whether this young man meant to be amusing or patronizing, so he took up the file again: "From London, and you teach P.A.W. Studies."

"Yes. We pronounce it 'poor studies'."

"Poverty and Want Studies?"

"Peace and War Studies."

"Oh, that's why you were sent here! This is Peace and Extremism Studies."

"Indeed."

"PAX Studies – it's Latin for 'peace,' you know."

"Yes, I thought so. I remember some Latin from school."

Again, Jimmy looked uncomfortable. "What can you teach?"

"I teach PAW's introductory course on war."

"We don't teach war here – only peace."

"Well, I teach a course on counter-terrorism and counter-extremism."

"Well, counter-extremism is fine, but 'counter-terrorism' is Islamo-phobic."

"I could call it 'Counter-Extremism'."

"What sort of extremism?"

"Any extremism."

"No, we have a course on right-wing extremism already. What else can you teach?"

"International security…"

"What's your bias?"

"My anchoring, if anything, would be European security."

"I established this department in opposition to Eurocentrism."

"I see. I teach a course on the causes of war."

"That sounds theoretical."

"It does review some theories."

"No, we don't want anything theoretical. We stick to the facts."

Simon was quiet a while. "Well, that's all I have."

"I want you to teach the course on methods."

"That is important." Simon took up his pen expectantly.

"Yes. We've never made it a requirement before. Julie needed something to teach. Poor Julie was denied funding for this year." Simon's eyebrows rose involuntarily, to which Jimmy reacted quickly: "It wasn't her fault – the institution doesn't understand her unique contribution." He ended with a knowing look. Simon's expression did not change. Jimmy leaned forward a little. "You're familiar with the paternalism of university administrations. She's a woman!"

Simon could not voluntarily relax his eyebrows, so he felt compelled to speak before he could consider his response: "Actually, you're the first man I've met here."

"Exactly!" Jimmy leaned back in his chair and pressed his fingertips together, with a look of triumph. "I hired them all! I hired Julie when no-one else would, and I'm keeping her! I'm gathering the grant money to bring her back."

"I see," said Simon. Jimmy held his gaze with slight nods of the head, but said nothing. "Well, err, I wish her well."

"Don't worry, I will make sure of it." Jimmy was ready to explain some cunning strategy, if only Simon would give the pretext.

"So then: methods?"

"Yes, you will teach methods each semester – that's now a core course."

"I don't mind if somebody else want to teach it."

"Nobody wants to teach it. You'll teach it every semester. It will be large this semester, because of the backlog."

"Backlog?"

"Yes, Julie was denied funding last year too."

"Oh dear! What sort of methods?"

"Don't worry about that. Here, take Julie's syllabus."

"Is this the cover sheet?"

"No, that's it. How do you want to be named?"

"Well, in my department I am conventionally listed as 'Dr. Ranald'."

"That's 'oh so formal'!" Jimmy attempted to copy Simon's accent, rocking from side to side with each syllable, sitting straight up in his seat, with a pursed smile. He slumped back in his seat, exhausted but delighted.

"I'm also known as 'Dr. Simon Ranald'."

"Do you have any other names?"

"Ian."

"That's worse!"

"Nigel."

"Oh please!"

"I am known as 'Sinner' – after my initials."

"That's Christian-centric – it would make other faiths un-comfortable."

"Hmm – well, that's all the names I have."

"Let's put 'Ranald'."

"Thank you, I preferred 'Dr. Ranald' anyway."

"'Doctor' is too conventional: that's why I don't have a doctorate."

"Just 'Ranald'?"

"Yes, and try not to make it sound so British – your names, your accent, your color. Try not to be so – so – imperialistic! Remember, most of our students are born of imperialized cultures, including all the Americans. And glorifying imperialism is a dismissible offense around here."

5. Jimmy's swagger

"My name is Dr. Simon Ranald, and this is the first class in methods for PAX students."

Simon looked up. The silence was skeptical.

"Methods are now a requirement for your major, in line with the social sciences…"

The peace was shattered by the brutal decapitation of a can of energy drink. The opener shifted in the seat as if testing its durability.

"Why don't you introduce yourselves to each other? Say, from the back, across there, and forward."

This they were eager to do. The first student chose to give names and preferred pronouns, so everybody followed suit: "she and her," "he and him," "zee and zem," "ee and em," "per and per." Simon urgently wrote on a page, while he drew a map of the seats.

"Well, my intent today is just to show you the syllabus, then you can decide whether you want to come back next week. I imagine that you're still selecting courses, but we have much to cover: we'll start lectures next week, so I'd prefer you to decide by then. If you're still unsure, you should come to my office hours, in between times."

One student stood up. Simon put his finger on the appropriate pronoun, when "ze" said, "I heard a lot of 'should'." Then "ze" walked out.

A second student stood up: "I sense a lot of expectations." She too walked out.

A third student raised her hand: "Why are you here?"

"Well, I wanted to try a new opportunity," he said honestly. Then he wanted to relate. "And America is the land of opportunity, after all."

"That phrase has been censured by the Student Council as counter-revisionist." She gathered her things and departed.

Another student stood up: "The predominance of males in this room is a micro-aggression." She followed her friends.

Simon asked if anyone else wanted to leave, then explained the topics each week, the assignments, and his office hours. He asked for questions, then reminded everyone that he would see them next week if they chose to stay enrolled.

Only one student approached the lectern: "Dr. Ranald? Hi! I'm

Nicole. I am so pleased you're offering this course, I am really looking forward to it – this will be easy for me, because I am an English lit. major, and I love writing, and I plan to write a narrative about my struggle against extremism, to counter the conventional narrative."

Simon was hesitant. "Well, thank you for saying so, but this might not be the best course for you, as I won't be teaching narratives, so much as theories and evidence, as I said."

"Oh, I understood all that – a scientist's narrative." Then she rushed to another class before he could correct her.

Simon followed, but found Jimmy waiting in the corridor: "Come on, Simon, I'll take you for a beer." Jimmy swaggered in a way that Simon took for a parody of masculinity. He was about to laugh politely, when he realized his mistake.

Jimmy was a difficult conversationalist on the move, as he greeted students energetically, forgot Simon's conversation, and demanded repetition. At each request, Simon turned his face to address directly, then stumbled on the broken paving.

Jimmy suddenly pointed across Simon's front: "I helped to set up that building." Whenever Jimmy finished talking about himself, he smiled with his mouth closed and his bottom lip forced out.

They passed a Victorian building, marked with the university's brand, next to a larger sign, which Simon read out loud: "Safe space for undocumented: in this building we have no walls." Simon continued to speak out loud: "Well, I bet you didn't set up that sign."

Jimmy replied with his greatest passion so far: "What do you mean?"

"Well, this building has walls, literally."

"Don't take literalness too literally, Simon." He smiled with his bottom lip forced out. Then he realized something else with triumph. "We teach literature, not literalness." He reset his bottom lip.

Simon did not know what to say. Jimmy took him into the most salubrious hotel at the bottom of the hill, sat at the bar, ordered beers, and spun on the stool to face the window. "Now, Simon. I am a caring employer. Whatever you need…"

"Well, now you mention it, I need advice on somewhere to stay – longer term. I have been staying in a cheap hotel, pending some faculty housing."

"There isn't any. Faculty housing would be privileged."

"I'd settle for student housing."

"Not even freshers can be guaranteed student housing."

"So how does one find housing?"

"The students use the campus service."

"May I use it?"

"No! That would be privileged."

"May I ask how you found somewhere to live?"

"I married a rich old woman and moved to the peninsula!" Jimmy smiled, but he was not joking. He continued to watch the street, one arm stretched along the bar.

Simon stopped making conversation. Jimmy seemed intent on getting buzzed, which became obvious halfway down his first pint. "You know, Simon, when I retire, I'm going to sit on a beach in Costa Rica with girls bringing me cold beer." He paused to relish the image. "Young girls!" His face broke into a huge smile. His eyes widened, returned to normal, and sparkled. "I'd pick the ones I want that day, and say to the rest, 'Unlucky girls, come back tomorrow'."

Simon knew then, if he had not known already, that he did not want to be alone with Jimmy Pons.

Jimmy suddenly turned towards him. "Simon, I've had some complaints."

"Oh dear!"

"Yes, I've been told you've assigned a lot of reading."

"But I just finished the first class."

"The students texted me during class. Is it true?"

"Well, only two books for the semester."

"Oh no, that's far too many. The students aren't used to that. You see, they're used to learning in less prescriptive ways, less structured ways, more creatively. You know what I mean?"

"Not really."

Jimmy turned towards the bar and placed his palms on its shiny surface. "Here the students expect their lecturers to tell them what not to read."

"That's not what I'm used to."

"Of course, I understand." Jimmy smiled, before speaking slowly, emphasizing each alternate syllable like the high note in a staccato rhythm: "That's the institutional way you're used to!" He paused, slapped the bar, and leaned back.

"Well, what do you think I should do?"

Jimmy flew through a soaring monologue of triumphs, of the many students whose lives he had changed, the self-gratification of guiding young minds to think as he thought.

Occasionally, Simon asked what Jimmy had assigned in his syllabus, what textbooks he would recommend, how he structured the topics across weeks, but Jimmy always urged him to "escape structures," to "find the students' inner voices," before he raced into another anecdote, which always started with "a beautiful young girl, full of promise," and ended with a life changed.

"I remember one girl, a beautiful young girl, full of promise. She wanted to write her thesis about the Middle East. I said, 'No, you need to write about your people.' She was from Hawaii, you see, although she didn't see herself that way. She desperately wanted to write about the Middle East, but I kept saying, 'No, find your people, support your people, find your people's voice!' Finally, I told her I would not grade her thesis if she wrote about the Middle East, so she wrote a compelling narrative about the Hawaiian people. I changed her life." He nodded and smiled.

"If everything is narrative, where are the facts?"

"Exactly! Everything is a narrative."

A long pause followed. "Jimmy, I think I need to leave for another appointment."

"Of course, I think my work here is done."

"So, what should I put in the syllabus?"

"Nothing! Find your voice!" Jimmy smiled smugly, then added darkly, "Nobody stays in my program if they can't find their voice."

6. The cottage

Simon spent the weekend online, searching for furnished apartments. Few were available, so he resolved to visit them all. He started under the red awning of his grotty hotel, curbed by blinding reflections, noise, and fumes, on the busiest street between the Bay and the campus. From there, all routes led uphill, where he escaped to quiet streets, gardens, parks, and grand houses. Alas, the tenancies on offer were revealed as a couch in a mansion occupied by dozens of students already, a janitor's closet on a roof, a tent in a garden, a disabled bus in a driveway, a treehouse, and a garden shed. He walked on, discovering the neighborhoods, the views across the Bay, the spectacular variations in temperature and humidity, and the names of the cities that merged together into metropolitan sprawl.

By Sunday, he had switched from respondent to advertiser: "Quiet visiting professor needs a room or apartment for the semester." After invitations to consider what he had already seen, he was offered a "cottage." This was the only offer he visited on Monday.

He walked north, away from campus, further uphill, past boring blocks of apartments, until a faux Tudor courtyard of apartments marked a dramatic change. He saw interesting gardens, discrete mansions, small parks on the side of steep slopes, and well-designed schools. He found the desired street, where the mansions were founded on huge boulders. His target was the largest of all.

The owner introduced herself as Vonessa: "Don't forget the 'o' – it's an Irish name; we love the British Isles here. You're so lucky to be brought up with that heritage."

"Indeed – probably the last generation to be so lucky."

"Come in! You'll see, we keep it alive here." She led him through a huge room of books and wood, talking all the way.

"You'll love this area. We're within walking distance of the gourmet ghetto, you know? Well, let me tell you: overlooking the bay, all the authentic working-class flavors of the world, organic, slow food, locally sourced. So, you're supporting both the environment and the working class, you see? My husband and I used to go for dinner at Chez Radical for our anniversary. After all the years we lived here, we found that at one anniversary we'd be booking a table for the next, that's how popular it became! You should take your sweetie, but book now, for next year; and you need to put a hundred dollars down, to secure the reservation."

"I don't think I have a hundred dollars – or a sweetie."

"Well, that might change – I know lots of ladies. They went for the jocks and not the nerds, and now they want a professor."

"They must be mistaken."

"Oh, I get it: education is all consuming. That's why I moved here, to put the kids through the high school, and the university, although actually they chose colleges in the mid-west. They're all working in agriculture – actually, agri-tech: plotting water use and yields, you know? Still, it's very working class, and obviously the communities are all working class. I am an actress – well, sometimes, maybe once a month: aspiring – change of career, after divorce – fifth year A.D. I also sing and dance – always have. Actually, I have an audition coming up with one of your British actresses. I'm a bit nervous about it, just because, well, she's been hired all the way from Britain, so she must be good, right?"

"She might just be British."

"Actually, you could help me if I needed to go for a part speaking British."

"Anything to keep it alive."

She repeated the words as he had pronounced them. "I used to be a lawyer, you know, on the peninsula – but I always did a lot of *pro bono* work, for the trade unions, including yours. And my husband volunteered on the medical malpractice cases – he's a physician. We used to receive the cases right here actually. We always thought the kids should see the working class up close and personal, live in a working-class city, go to working-class schools."

Vonessa showed him towards the rear, showed him the seam where she had knocked two duplexes together, guided him through a large kitchen, instructed the cleaners in Spanish, showed him the dining room that was too good to use, stepped down into an enormous sunroom, and stepped out into the garden. The "cottage" was what he would call a summer house – with a square plan, log walls, one glass door, a wooden floor, a table and a chair in the left corner, and a kitchen on the right below a sliding ladder up to a bunk.

"It's not much. I keep it for my daughter and son-in-law to visit. She's gone off it — it's too rustic for her, she says. But her husband doesn't mind. Well, boys are dirtier, aren't they? That reminds me, the dog likes to come to the door, but he won't come in: he just likes biscuits — that's why we keep a little bucket of biscuits, just there — see, just one, to let him know he's a good boy. The cat will likely come in, if the door is open, so if you don't like cats, keep it closed. Gardeners come every Wednesday morning, and she doesn't like them, so she'll likely scratch to get in. I know, it's not much, but I thought, when I saw your ad., you sounded desperate, and I like to help education."

"It's delightful. I'd take it, if you'd let me."

He moved in the next evening, as the sun was setting. The garden was damp, cool, and musty. The squirrels scampered across the roof to roost in the redwoods that towered above. He went to bed early, turned out the lights, and admired the twilight through the quiet sway of the trees.

The morning was foggy enough for the trees to drip with water. He explored the hill before a deserved breakfast. He read potential textbooks and adjusted his syllabus, before realizing another visit to the library. "Dress in layers," advised Vonessa. By late morning, the sun was burning through: he uncovered his flimsy shirt, but did not resent restoring his coat in the cool of the underground library.

The way back in the evening seemed dissimilar. The main street was hot and crowded with people seeking food. Some sat to eat and talk under road-signs marked "KEEP OFF THE MEDIAN," as cars raced by on both sides. Others dropped to eat cross-legged wherever they grew weary on the sidewalk.

Simon turned up the high road, further into the Gourmet Ghetto. Across the sidewalk stood a man with four large dogs on one lead: he looked loftily into the distance with drooping eyelids, as one dog defecated, and the rest spread out disconsolately.

Simon again took the high road. Across a large lawn ran a young cat with cries of affection. As he offered his hand, he heard a distant banging, from a window at the top of the mansion. There a woman pointed angrily and mouthed the word, "Bad."

Simon continued to the end of the street, to find the high road.

He could see the top of the ridge that he had reached at dawn, so he bore towards it, in search of the quieter streets, the longer ways around, the luxuriant gardens, the interesting architecture. He remembered one lawn peppered with flowers, but found a child dancing on them, encouraged by its parents: "Oh, Dawnfire, you're so creative. They're nicer flowers than at home, aren't they?"

Simon turned the corner to keep on the high road. He wondered how high he should aim before he could bear how low he had started. The Bay stretched away below, then seemed to climb towards an indistinct horizon level with his eyes.

At the next corner, his eyes traced the ways up, until his elbow was struck by the arms of a woman wildly illustrating her spoken words. She held her wrist and said to her friend: "That man hit me."

Simon took the high road. He itched to run, but the way ahead steepened up to the next junction. He stepped on the level and moved easier, until he heard a car screech to the stop sign behind him. With rising acuity, he heard a quiet monologue to his side, moving at his speed. He turned to see the driver leaning across the passenger seat, speaking as if rapping a song, quietly and repetitively: "I will mess you up. I can mess you up, have no doubt. I can mess you up easily. I can mess you up stoned. I can mess you up drunk. I can mess you up."

Simon was late to realize he was the subject, until the car sped through the stop-sign and swung around. Simon felt lost and compulsive: he ran through the planters blocking the most precipitous way down. He imagined his whole body cart-wheeling into the Bay. He tried to forget his imagination, for one more block - block after block. The housing grew denser, the slope eased, and he could see the main street, until a police car braked across his path.

"Stop where you are! What's your hurry? Where are you going? What are you running from? Do you have anything in your pockets? Are you armed? Are you carrying anything sharp? Are you in the habit of hitting women?"

The questions recycled quicker than he could answer, until he was sitting on the back seat of the police car, handcuffed, alone, perversely calmed by the slight reverberations from the closure of the door behind him. The world outside seemed remote, patchy, and filtered, as if he were watching a drama. Another police car pulled up, then a third. Six policemen visibly relaxed in the downtime between taking and transferring a responsibility. Perversely, Simon wanted to stay where he was – the quietest, coolest, cleanest, staunchest place he had yet known in Bayside. He saw himself deep in the lowest and quietest basement of the library. He seemed a stranger in his own memory.

He was still replaying when the door opened. "We got our first independent witness. She called in to report a man matching your description running away from a dangerous driver. Her statement began with you stepping around those two ladies. You got lucky. Don't do it again."

Simon relayed this drama to Vonessa, at length, trying to make sense to himself as much as to her, but with less detail or understanding than he should have realized in the moment.

She looked upon him kindly but with some disappointment. Her immediate reaction was fluent: "You should have stuck to the working-class districts." She sighed before her final words on the subject: "You've got to be careful with the police. It's not their fault, they're just systemically racist. And foreign is almost as good as a race. You don't want to get kicked out of this country."

7. Joe Karolides

At the start of the teaching week, Simon opened an email from the "Service for Disabilities Accommodation for Inclusivity" or "DAFI."

One of the students in your class has a disability demanding a reduced-distraction environment (where auditory and visual stimuli are reduced) for quizzes and exams. You should accommodate this disability. If you have any questions, ask your department chair. Do not discuss the student's accommodations with the student.

Simon replied with an email asking for the name of his department chair, but an automatic reply stated that the "DAFI does not accept correspondence at this email address."

Simon searched online for PAX, but found only PAX students running their own social media. They suggested that he might be a spy for the Dean of Liberal Studies. He contacted the Dean's office, which directed him to the World and International Studies Program, with the reminder that the Teaching Program was different to the Research Program, even though both were known as "WISP."

Simon was rewarded with an appointment on Thursday morning, inside a yellow neo-Gothic building that fronted on the sunny side of the clock tower. Its castellated roof gleamed against the dark background of redwood trees and buildings, on a rapidly rising slope. The main entrance opened to an reception desk but no humans. Two corridors ran away at right angles, along a mezzanine, above the Ethnic Studies Library. Below, he saw a poster entitled "This library is color-blind, inclusive, and non-aggressive," next to a cartoon of a rising fist, entitled "Fight White Power!"

The flimsy grey cubicles seemed endless, until he found the only open door. Inside sat a man with good posture. He sat side-on, but quickly looked up and smiled.

"Welcome to Bayside."

"Thank you Professor Karolides."

"Dr. Karolides, but call me Joe."

"Joe, thank you."

"Please sit down. Nice shoes! May I suggest you don't wear them outside the office? I ruined three pairs in my first year – dog mess, human mess, who knows. Yes, really! It just doesn't come out of leather."

"Well, I have some running shoes and some hiking boots."

"Boots – you need the support on these sidewalks."

"You're right!"

Joe took care to look through his spectacles without using them as a barrier. "What can I do for you?"

"Well, I seem to be an exchange lecturer within your department."

"This is a program."

"So, what is PAX?"

"It's one of our majors."

"Then, Jimmy Pons is not a department head?"

"No. Surely Jimmy explained this to you?"

"No. Then, Jimmy Pons reports to you?"

"Not exactly – we work together: all the majors must conform to some requirements from WISP; each major head can choose the rest."

"I don't think I have encountered such an arrangement before."

"I am glad you found me, Simon. We needed to meet. You should come to the program's reception on Wednesday, to meet the director and the other major heads."

"You're not the director?"

"No, I am the co-director. Professor Juncker is the director."

"Can I meet him now?"

"No, he sits in the geography department."

"So, you run the program – and Professor Juncker approves everything?"

"I really spend most of my time disapproving of things. Professor Juncker gets to approve things. I am good at saying 'no'; and soothing lecturers who can never be professors."

"I've seen that too."

"It's not what I imagined when I got into education."

"No, me neither, but you seem to know it better."

"It's a sham really. We validate the instructors so that they can validate the students."

"Indeed! Then the students validate us."

"So that the institution appears valid to their recruiters."

"Indeed."

"Right."

Simon was amused and delighted but did not know what to say next.

"What has Professor Pons got you teaching?"

"Methods."

"Let's raise that to the programmatic level. I can't find time to teach the senior thesis anymore, and you could help by absorbing that requirement. How many students have enrolled?"

"Well, it seems to change every day."

"Yes, it would. You see, students are allowed to add or drop for the first third of the semester." Joe smiled at one corner of his mouth. "You've got less time to drop students for yourself, so I'd advise you to take advantage of that quickly."

"I see. Well, I had more than fifty students when I last checked."

"That's far too many for methods – I'll have our administrator cap it at twenty, and defer the rest to next semester. How are you teaching methods?"

"Actually, Professor Pons asked me to teach them creatively."

"How would you like to teach them?"

"As a social scientist."

"Meaning?"

"I would teach them to stop talking about narratives and start talking about theories and evidence."

"You should. Teach them. And I'll open a slot for you to teach another programmatic course – a functional course, an elective. Meantime, we'll find a cubicle for you here, one with bookshelves. Come to the reception next Wednesday. We have other majors that could make use of you. But the Director should approve my decision, so, make a good impression."

8. Reception

Simon stepped on to the wiry grey carpet. Blinking on the sunny side of the building, he walked around the corridors to the other side, to find his cubicle – the last cubicle: three soft panels held together by plastic fasteners, against an internal wall. He closed the flimsy door and waited for the panels to stop vibrating. He sat down at the desk. In the gloom, he struggled to see where to plug in the computer. "This will keep me humble," he said out loud, before looking up at the huge gap between the panels and the ceiling.

Simon gave himself ten minutes to get to the second week's class. He was early. He watched the clock tick to ten minutes past the hour, before raising his voice: "Now, let's get started: I understand that on 'Bayside time' students have ten minutes' grace to get from one class to the next. I remembered this week, but please remind me next week. Now, we'll all go by the same clock – yes, that one; no, not your phones, not your computers, because I don't allow electronic devices during my classes."

He gave them a break of five minutes after the first hour, another after the second hour. At ten minutes before the top of the third hour, he closed his lecture and urged them to their next class. As he was walking in the bright sunshine admiring the yellow Gothic building, he suddenly realized that he had let the students go ten minutes early, and none had told him.

Simon opened his emails: DAFI demanded that he allow a new student to use a laptop computer. Simon emailed the student to clarify how he wanted to be accommodated, then wrote to the DAFI director as politely as his mood allowed:

> You accommodated this student on the same day that I informed him I was banning electronic devices. He tells me that he needs a laptop to "multitask" (his word) with games and email (his admission) in order to maintain his "morale" (his word). Now, do you still think this student has a disability that warrants him using a laptop in class for extra-curricular purposes, to the distraction of other students who are present for curricular purposes?

Simon received an automated reply, reminding all staff that questioning a student's disabilities could be considered discriminatory by the university's code of conduct, the state's criminal code, and the civil courts.

He went to the reception on the terrace outside Joe's office. It jutted over the stream, like the stern of a yacht, within a concrete balustrade painted in mild yellow. The redwoods were almost within touching distance. Between the trees, Simon could see the nondescript building in which he had visited Jimmy Pons. In the foreground, Simon realized the vestige of the natural environment. It must have seemed the right setting for a largely agricultural university in a largely agricultural state.

Simon grazed the buffet, stood aside, and searched the faces. Clearly, students predominated, but none that he knew; they were younger and more inquisitive. Simon considered the dominant apparel: blue, with a stylized representation of a yellow sun, surrounded by the legend "Golden Suns." The terrace seemed vast and bright, although mostly shaded. The guests preferred to place their plates on the balustrade, lean back, and face in. Some gathered in the brightest corner, turned towards the sun, took off layers, and complained about global warming. Others gathered in the shaded corner, turned their backs on the breeze, and put on layers. He realized two microclimates within a dozen yards.

Joe placed a hand on his shoulder, and introduced him to the WISP's administrator – Alison, who smiled flatly, stooped with an ambiguous mix of humility and weariness, and spoke quietly but authoritatively. "You'll find WISP an easy place to work. We employ mostly PAX students – they're trained in conflict resolution and counter-extremism, you see. The people who can't get along with that – well, something must be wrong with them. That's the test." She sucked in her lips and cheeks, and nodded cruelly.

Simon did not know what to say, so Alison talked about herself: having lost her mother over the summer, she was now caring for her father in the evenings, after working a full day, paying for a carer to visit her father during the day. She paused: "I'm sorry – I must have sounded self-indulgent there. Of course, I realize that the terms 'father' and 'mother' are problematic, because they genderize the act of parenting."

She introduced him to the two full-time PAX faculty. Prisha Pradesh had been hired in the previous year, by Jimmy Pons, but, after she brought a husband and four children to a reception, he agreed that she should transfer her office to WISP. Earnest Keeper had been hired by Jimmy Pons more than four years ago, and moved to WISP soon thereafter, after being discovered socializing without Jimmy. Prisha taught courses on conflict resolution and Indian politics; Earnest taught courses on international law and Korean politics.

"So, the commonality that surprises me is: you both specialize in Asia."

"Not really," said Earnest, "but Asian Studies is WISP's biggest major, and needs more courses, and PAX is shrinking."

"And my parents are Indian," said Prisha. She participated with her head upright, her eyes wide open, with an expression between surprise and encouragement.

Earnest listened with his eyebrows raised, his head tilted back and to the side. He tilted in and sharpened his expression when speaking. "And I taught English as a second language in Korea before coming here."

"Then, on those grounds, I could qualify to teach European Studies," mused Simon, seriously.

They laughed. Prisha looked surprised, apologetic, encouraging, and exasperated at the same time: "Our students are mostly Asian; and prefer their professors to show Asian expertise."

Earnest leaned in to speak quietly: "Especially if one looks European!"

Alison stepped in: "Caucasian-American!"

"That too. After my lecture on human trafficking in Southeast Asia yesterday, a student stayed behind to reprimand me for presuming to speak on behalf of victims of color, given that I was white."

"Caucasian-American!"

"Yes, she was Caucasian-American."

"Are you Caucasian-American?"

"Honestly, I'm not sure anymore.

"Don't presume that I'm more popular," said Prisha. "Most of my students really want to hear about China." She talked without changing expression, except to allow for short intakes of breath like laughs between clauses: "I heard, the other day, students referring to

U.S.B. as University of Sino-Bayside!"

"I've got another one for you," said Earnest, "I heard that the biggest lobby against affirmative action in this state is the Chinese-American Council. I didn't think many students knew that, until I heard some students referring to U.S.B. as Unaffirmative Students are Better."

Alison stepped in gravely. "I was in a meeting when someone joked that we should be renamed University of Shanghai-Beijing." Her nodding never stopped, although she added: "How racist!"

"That reminds me," said Earnest. "I heard that DAFI is considering foreignness as a disability."

"Well, that reminds me," said Simon anxiously. "DAFI just told me I have a student with a disability who will need three times as much time to complete his exams than the other students, but I planned a mid-term exam for a whole three-hour class, so that would entitle him to nine hours."

"Just stop giving exams – assign papers only; then you can ignore most accommodation letters."

Alison warned Earnest about perceptions of prejudice, when Joe steered Simon towards a stranger. "Yes, that's right, thank you Joe: I am Hattie Maddux: I am the founder, director, and enabler-in-chief of Asian Studies: the fastest growing major on campus! Everybody's pivoting to Asia! Prisha and Earnest work for me. And Jewel Lighter is my latest hire." Jewel Lighter stepped out of Hattie's shadow, raised a hand, barely smiled, and never spoke.

"So, you're the new teacher of methods." Hattie Maddux leaned forward to impress, while Simon leaned away from her foul breath and yellow teeth. "Oh! I predicted you. Let me tell you: Bayside is investing in undergrad. education, and everything is changing, it's a major upheaval." Jewel Lighter kept staring at Simon, and took out a notebook.

"What's changing?"

"Well, practically everything. The President of the whole University System is sending regular explicit directives to that effect."

"To what effect?"

"Everything!"

"I have not seen anything except short emails about how admirable we all are."

"Exactly: that is natural, sensible, leadership by a new President – she is encouraging us. And I can read between the lines whatever she cannot make explicit. We want more money for instructors to develop courses together – because we all know how bad individualism is for teaching. We'll get more funding if we take more students." Then she leaned in and added with exaggerated effort: "As if we need more students."

Simon gagged, turned away, and found himself in the correct posture to take more food, which he could not stomach.

"Are you alright? Well, let me tell you. You can expect everything to change, although I shouldn't say what."

"Then please don't."

"Change comes to those who want it. What's the matter? You look depressed again."

"That sounds circular."

"It is what it is, Simon."

A tall man uncertainly called for everybody's attention. "As a Luxemburger, I am not good at starting with a joke, so I won't," then he laughed. "My name is Professor Guillaume Juncker, but call me Will. For those of you who don't know me, I am the director of WISP. I am sorry that I have not met most of you, but I have come from a reception at the geography department."

He lent forward, raised his eyes, pulled back the corners of his mouth, and sucked his bottom lip under an equine over-bite, before speaking again. He spoke slowly, without apparently closing his lips or inflecting, except to drop his head with each self-deprecation, until his face was almost parallel with the ground. He raised his head but lowered his eyes again, and thus restarted the cycle. Simon kept thinking of Vonessa, which puzzled him, because she had the posture of a dancer, until he pictured Vonessa reading her lines in front of the kitchen window, with unwavering affectations whatever the character.

By then, Will had stopped talking: all that Simon could remember was that everybody was valued, and his door was always open. Will asked the faculty to introduce themselves and their courses. Since Simon had only one course to mention, he felt inadequate. His moment passed quickly, which was both relieving and degrading. As the group returned to disparate conversations, Joe brought Will over. Simon would remember only that he was appreciated for "travelling so far to help us out." Will moved on, drifting aimlessly in a sea of shorter people, neither striking nor discrete, neither engaging nor withdrawing.

"I can always tell who doesn't fit in!"

"I beg your pardon?"

"That's a dead giveaway too." The stranger was thoroughly amused.

"I don't understand."

"That's so cute! Look, you're adorable. Hi, I'm Grace."

"My name is Simon. How do you do?"

"Adorable!"

"Do you work in WISP?"

"No, I came here for the free food."

"You're a student?"

"No, I'm an objectivist!" She was good-looking; she was well-dressed; and she smelt nice too. She didn't fit in.

"So, what's your connection with WISP?"

"My connection is that I was hungry when it had free food! I have an app for that. Let me show you – more users, more tips. It's immoral not to take what's available."

"So, what's your connection to Bayside?"

"My sister is with some man who is in some job here, and they're having a baby, probably tonight, if she keeps her promise. She's taking forever! I could have stayed at work longer. I don't know when to book my return flight. At this rate, I'll be here through the weekend. What are you doing this weekend?"

"I don't know yet."

"What do you do for fun?"

"I don't know. I suppose I work a lot."

"You're an objectivist too!"

"I mean, some of my work is fun: I teach to get paid; I research whatever is wanted by the people who promote me; then in whatever free-time I have left, I get to research what interests me – and that's what I enjoy."

"Any day is a good day if you're making money."

"Oh, it's not profitable."

"We need to work on that."

"Well, that's presumptuously generous of you."

"Do you want to show me around?"

"You could probably show me around. I arrived just a few days ago."

"I've never been here before – I've been avoiding this place for years, on principle. I won't patronize anywhere that forces you to recycle. That's fascism. At home, I mix all my trash, just for balance. Do you have any friends here?"

"No."

"Don't you like ladies?"

"I don't know – I've never met one."

"You're funny! I'll tell you what: I'll give you my number, and you can call me. I won't be here long, so we need to be quick."

Joe waited patiently for the interloper to depart: "Simon, this is Aimee Pharisees, the chair of Middle Eastern Studies."

"That's an unusually focused major."

"Not if you're Middle Eastern."

"Are you?"

"No, political science. I went to Israel for my junior year. Then I came back to Bayside, was taught constructs of identity, and realized we're all the same if only we could smash traditional constructs, so I started the course on 'Jews and Muslims.' Of course, I realize that Middle East Studies is a traditional construct, but the English language is so limiting. The English messed up everything there."

"Perhaps I could teach a course on the British in the Middle East."

"I refer to that travesty in every class."

"Do you have a course on Egypt?"

"No. I teach that in Africa Studies – I went there once."

"Do you include Turkey?"

"Turkey is in Europe."

"Iran?"

"Iran isn't part of Arabia."

"So, you study Saudi Arabia?"

"No! Our Saudi sponsors wouldn't like that."

"The Gulf states?"

"They're not really states."

"Yemen?"

"It's practically Saudi Arabia."

"Iraq?"

"It's practically Iran."

"Syria?"

"It's practically Turkey."

"Jordan?"

"Jordan is my brother's name."

"Palestine?"

"As I said: I teach a course on Jews and Muslims."

"Perhaps I could teach a course on Europe-Middle East relations."

"Again, as I've said: I teach a course on Jews and Muslims. I wonder why you are here."

9. Asian relations

Joe knocked on Simon's wobbly cubicle: "You made quite an impression on her."

"Who?"

"Hattie."

"Oh, I don't think I did."

"Yes, she wants you to teach a course on Asian relations."

"I don't specialize in Asia."

"That doesn't matter. She's got a syllabus for you. It would be a good way to get you embedded here."

Coming from Joe, Simon did not think he could refuse. "That's my task for the weekend then."

Simon's routine was settled. He rose early to climb anonymously in the fog. Returning to the cottage, he found the cat desperate to join him. Simon reassured her from the shower, and again while he ate, before settling down at the desk with everything he needed. Little Lola took his lap, lay on her side, kneading his belly while gazing lovingly into his eyes, until she dropped her chin, sighed, rumbled, and snored. He worked quietly, weighed down with the heavy responsibility of the light cat. Squirrels scampered from tree to roof to tree, except to pause on a branch to peer with reflective black eyes at the unfamiliar. Once Lola was up, he let her return to the house, while he walked to the library, in search of books that he would need to read before writing his lectures.

He awoke on Monday morning unsettled by the absence of fog and cat. He wondered if he had slept late, until he realized that what seemed like midday was dawn without marine layer. Vonessa warned him of Bayside's second summer. "The leaves have turned, but here we go again. It seems to start earlier each year. Resign yourself to it for the next few months." He spent the rest of the day in the basement of the library.

The next day, he taught the students of methods how to argue logically. That evening, he received an email from DAFI ordering him to accommodate "cultures for whom logic is western-centric."

Instead, he prepared for his first class on Asian Relations.

"Good morning, this bright Thursday. I am Dr. Simon Ranald, and this is the introduction to Asian Relations, where you'll be learning logical approaches to non-Western cultures. And, logically, since the late start for this course was not your fault, you'll still get credit for a full course unit."

Simon showed the syllabus, then released the students to ponder whether the culture and logic of his course suited them, or to approach him with any further questions.

"Hi, I'm Aurelia. Hi! I'm in your methods course too!"

"Yes, I recognize you: hello."

"I liked your methods so much, I decided to enroll in this course, as soon as I received the email." Her countenance was sleepy, but her gaze was restless, moving right and left, until she or her subject stopped speaking, when she would give a confirmatory nod and smile.

"Thank you, that's complimentary. You'll find the courses complementary – in the sense that you can practice the methods in this course."

"Oh, I hadn't thought of that. Can I write about Asia in the methods course?"

"You cannot submit the same content for grade in both courses, but, yes, you may cross-fertilize."

"Hey! I wouldn't use that phrase around here – somebody could accuse you of sexual harassment."

"Cross-fertilize?"

"Shh!"

"Oh dear! Are you offended?"

"No. I warned you – so you know I'm cool."

"How very confusing."

"I'll recruit my friends – they're cool too."

"Please do. I'd like good students to bring good students: that makes my job easier."

"Perhaps you'd like to speak directly to them, at my sorority?"

"I don't think faculty belong in a sorority."

"It's not that sort of sorority – it's an academic sorority: it accepts only pledges with a certain GPA." Simon continued to look skeptical. She rose to the challenge: "I have a perfect GPA."

"I don't think I've ever met a perfect GPA."

"Well," she said, stepping closer, conspiratorially, "I have a trick for that: I take every course pass-fail, except the intro. courses where I know I'll get A-grades." Her eyes rose; she nodded with her mouth open and her chin sticking out – with a smile that widened her eyes.

"I've never heard of pass-fail."

"Your transcript shows a pass as long as you get a passing grade. And you'd need to be an idiot to get an 'F' – an effing idiot!"

"I've never seen an 'F'."

"Exactly!" Her chin rose and jutted, and she nodded vigorously.

"So, all the other grades are passing grades?"

"Yes. And I've rarely seen a grade lower than B."

"What if the student didn't show up at all?"

"Unless they're stupid, they could still turn in something for every assignment, and get a grade."

"What if they didn't turn in anything?"

"Then they'd be incomplete, which still isn't a fail!"

"So, why would anyone not choose pass-fail?"

"EXACTLY!"

Simon tapped a finger on his lips and frowned at the ground. Aurelia panted and looked to the sides like a delighted child.

"Aurelia, thank you – thank you for informing me. I feel embarrassed to have been ignorant of such important information."

"I think you should come to my sorority. I bet you'd hear lots of important information. My sisters are smart," she said seriously; then she nodded credibly.

"But I am not a sister."

"You don't need to be. We have a student-professor dinner this week." Simon tapped his finger to his lips again. She pondered his manner, then continued: "I wasn't going to invite anyone, but I could."

"I shouldn't be out on a school night."

"The dinner is this weekend."

"I'm quite fussy about food – the frats always smell of barbecues."

"We have great food – lots of seafood and home-grown vegetables for smarter sisters."

"The weather's rather warm for hot dinners."

"We have great air conditioning; and we're off campus."

"I'd show up sweaty after the walk."

"We have a shuttle bus for sisters after dark – it could pick you up if you're in the city."

"Okay, Aurelia, you've got me."

***

He returned to his office, where Hattie Maddux was waiting. "Hey Simon. I'll take you for lunch, at the Women's Faculty Club."

"Can I enter the Women's Faculty Club? I am, err, a man."

"I can take you."

"Perhaps I can return the favor at the 'Men's Faculty Club'?"

"That's the Faculty Club."

"For men?"

"No!" she said with horror. "The days when faculty were gendered are long over."

The path to the Women's Faculty Club ran slightly uphill beside the stream. It curved through huge redwoods to a pleasant lawn, surrounded by flower beds. Simon wanted to walk the lawn, until he saw dog turds, between which squirrels navigated expertly to come a-begging. Ahead, two women were descending the steps from the upper lawn to the lower lawn; a third anxiously stopped at the top. Simon dithered while Hattie pushed on. He drew the attention of the leading lady, who turned to the others: "Careful, you're going to get run over in a moment. Careful, watch for it!" Simon jumped onto the lawn, on tiptoes, then flitted into the dining room, where he saw Hattie at a small table, looking around impatiently.

He sat down. Hattie handed him a menu, took up a menu, then said, "I am going to take you off the course."

"Oh!" said Simon, dropping everything.

Hattie said nothing further; her gaze switched busily back and forth across the menu.

"May I ask why?"

"Well, for one thing, you scheduled Confucianism. Janet teaches Confucianism."

"I didn't know that. It was in the previous syllabus."

"Yes, but Janet taught it then."

"I don't mind her teaching it again."

"No, she's teaching it in political science."

"So, could we both teach it, in different courses, different departments?"

"No, she teaches Confucianism," said Hattie. "Also, you removed the classes on Japanese literature and Indonesian dancing."

"I didn't think they were relevant to a course on Asian relations."

"Asia is a culture, and all cultures are by definition understood through their art."

"That's not how I was taught political science."

"Art comes before science." She continued without looking up: "We had experts on these topics from other departments when we created the course."

"I am happy for them to teach the same classes again."

"No, they don't need to: they're tenured now."

"Would they let me borrow their syllabi, so I could educate myself?"

"No! That's their intellectual property. That reminds me, make sure you file a copy of your syllabus with Alison."

"I am struggling to foresee how I could write this syllabus now."

With one hand she took up a filthy band of cloth around the other wrist. "Whenever I am uncertain what to do, I finger this bracelet – look!"

Simon read out faint characters amid frayed fibers. "W.W.F.D.?"

"What would Foucault do?" She looked at him expectantly. Disappointed, she pulled the bracelet up her forearm tightly: "Nothing can be ascertained until we break free of what society wants us to think."

"You mean, critical thinking?"

"Knowledge comes from denying all knowledge."

"I don't understand."

"Why isn't that enlightening?"

"It contradicts itself."

"That's what society wants you to think!" she said with triumph.

Simon sat still but attentive. Hattie leaned back with her hands behind the chair, and looked around.

Simon stood up: "I am going to leave now."

"Fine," she said casually, and picked up a glass of water. He had turned his back when he heard her voice again: "How arrogant are you?" Simon felt his hair rise, but nobody else seemed to be affected.

"You deny Foucault!" The chatter succumbed to shocked silence.

Simon returned down the hot trail, through a red mist of fine particles kicked up by somebody ahead. He watched them lift into the sunbeams and linger at chest height. They spattered his shirt, and rose towards his nostrils, while he bobbed and weaved from shadow to shadow near the stream.

He returned to the cubicle of humility to pick up his bag, then unthinkingly sat down to check his email. Guillaume Juncker had confirmed his appointment to teach Asian relations.

> The University of Sunshine and WISP are fortunate in being able to attract a number of qualified persons like yourself to hold temporary appointments and to lend variety and enrichment to our instructional program. I look forward to having you as a colleague at Bayside this semester, and I hope that your service with us will be stimulating and rewarding.

The email directed Simon to various "online resources for instructors," classrooms with audio-visual technology, videos in the library, and instructions on how to avoid being racist and a sexual predator. These long, early paragraphs were pasted in different fonts, before a large negative space and a new paragraph:

> On a delicate point: I have received a complaint from a student who heard you use the phrase "ladies and gentlemen" in a class. As you know, many find the term "lady" offensive for perpetuating submissive gender roles, and many find the term "gentlemen" offensive for perpetuating the myth that only men can be "gentle."

> Please do not persist in using these terms. I realize that such prejudices may be normal where you come from, but at the University of Sunshine and at WISP we strive to be non-judgmental.

> The student has chosen to remain anonymous for fear of harassment. Please do not attempt to contact the student. You are in a position of power over this student and such a dynamic can cause significant stress. Any communication on this matter should be passed to me directly.

> Call on me at any time with any concerns. My door is always open.

> Best wishes, Will

Simon replied that he was coming straight over to the geography department, but found the door marked "Guillaume Juncker, Professor of Human Geography" closed, with a sign declaring one office hour per week, on Wednesday afternoon, during Simon's class.

10. Smart Sisters

Simon shifted into the center of the bench to fit the blast from the air conditioner, took off his tie, unbuttoned his shirt, and held open his jacket, until he felt cool enough to put them together again. The shuttle turned off the street through an automatic gate onto a steep, short, and abrupt concrete ramp. He alighted on a footpath, which was even shorter, but snaked through the landscaping pleasingly. Between potted palm trees he found a heavy wooden door, with no knocker, no windows, just a single button, marked "Duty Sister." He pressed it: he heard a click, before a voice said brightly, "Welcome to Smart Sisters Sorority."

"I am Simon Ranald – the, err, professor."

"Welcome, professor! Please push the door."

His eyes rose from the step to a pale carpet flanked by a receiving line of smart sisters in colorful dresses. They started to clap, smile, laugh, and shout encouragement: "Welcome to Smart Sisters Sorority! Yeah, professor!" He stepped on the deep carpet delicately. He half-nodded, half-bowed, as he moved along, wondering what to do with his hands – clap, suppress their clapping, or shake their hands.

Their reception snaked up a curvaceous stairway, down which rushed Aurelia, in the only black dress in a bloom of other colors. He thought she was barefoot, until he noticed shoes like socks. She came to a sudden stop and replaced her hair behind her ears, breathless, and uncertain what to say.

"Was that reception really for me?"

"You're the first to arrive, so, yes! As sisters drop out to escort their professors, the later arrivals won't see much welcome."

"So, what happens now?"

"Do you want a tour?"

"I do."

"I can't take you upstairs – only sisters are allowed up there."

"With stability comes studiousness."

"Yes – that's why I joined: only two to a room from your sophomore year."

"Is that good?"

"I have seen sororities with five to a room – no library, no sunroom, no garden, no staff. We have cleaners, and kitchen staff for lunches and dinners, and a resident Big Sister. You'll meet her, she's a retired school-teacher."

"What if you're on campus during a meal?"

"Most of us are, for lunch or dinner; then we snack on campus or wait until we get back. We share a kitchen – one fridge, one microwave. Somebody ate my hummus this week – I emailed the list-serve, and said I was sad."

"And what else do you do here?"

"I do most of my work in the library."

"Can we see that?"

"Yes!"

Simon gazed around the dark red shelves, toffee-colored tables and chairs, and soft yellow lamp shades. He stopped moving when he saw the backs of students sitting at the end. He started to whisper: "Why aren't they dining?"

"They're new sisters – they'll get to invite professors next semester."

"I hate to disturb them."

"They were advised to be out tonight."

"Yet they preferred this to campus libraries."

Aurelia led him into the next room, bright with natural light, filtered by trees beyond the glass doors. The seating plan was written in calligraphy. They stood at their seats, discussing the garden outside, as the buffet table filled with food, and the other tables filled with people, until Aurelia suggested they serve themselves before peak demand.

Their table received three other couples of professor and student – biologists, linguists, and engineers. Everybody tried to find a professional connection, but failed. Most of the time, each couple was internally engaged. One student's voice rose until it captivated all others: "The best professors learn from their students, don't they professor? They help students realize what they already know. The most important thing for teachers is to have enthusiasm – enthusiasm for the whole idea of education, just for the opportunity to be with students. And they must have enthusiasm for student engagement. Students need a professor to teach them intellectual curiosity – the intellectual confidence to unleash their minds. Good professors lead students to their own enlightenment. Don't they, professor?"

"Yes," said her professor, meekly.

From the top table, a girl rose, called their attention, and introduced herself as the President of Smart Sisters Bayside. She begged their attention to the sorority's own acapella group. Six smart sisters in matching blue dresses filed in confidently. They sang six songs, in which each singer sang a solo. They filed out quickly, and took less applause than they deserved.

The President rose again, to invite the professors to introduce themselves by name, department, and specialty, and to share any courses or internships that might interest smart sisters. The names evaporated before anyone could decide whether the name was worth remembering. Most of the speakers were fringe adjuncts, new hires, or on exchange, like himself. All the predictable departments were represented, and the predictable departments had predictable courses. Simon had the sensation of being stuck in a nightmare where something indeterminate repeats, while the dreamer strains to realize what. When his time came, he articulated his courses carefully, certain that they would strike the audience as memorable – but when he sat down he realized that nobody cared.

On the next table, a man started speaking with a British accent, so distinct and emphatic that Simon felt like a foreigner. The man wore an ambiguous expression between genuine agony and mock whimsy: his face seemed inhumanly mobile; his lips, cheeks, and eyebrows were prominent; they twitched and pouted to accentuate his verbiage. "My courses are boring, unless you would be perversely entertained, watching me trying to lecture to an auditorium of a thousand seats that I can barely see. Then ponder the fact that this course is capped at 2,000 students. You may ask: Where are the other thousand? I do ask! And the course is over-subscribed! So much so, that I'll be forced to teach it again next semester. Why, you may ask? You should! Boring it may be, but it's a requirement for all mathematics and physics majors before they can declare. You don't need to be enrolled to share the fun, because I record all my lectures, and I post the videos online, just so you too can see how boring they are. Feel free!"

Nervous laughter built to appreciative applause.

He waited for quiet, then lent his fists on the table: "Now, my research: seriously, I research multiple dimensions. You think we live in four dimensions, but there might be a fifth, another ten, another hundred! And perhaps other beings inhabit these extra dimensions without us ever knowing! Perhaps they inhabit some of ours and some of their own, which means, right now, they could be observing us in ours, while we are oblivious to them in theirs!" He pointed in all directions.

The audience gasped.

"So, if that interests you…" he said quietly, stimulating a further murmur of appreciation. He lent forward on his fists again: "If you want to join the project as an intern…" He paused dramatically, while another murmur built. "Then take my intro course, declare a physics major, double-major in mathematics, and preferably get your doctorate too." He sat down heavily, before a roar of laughter. He rose, bowed with mock solemnity, sat down, crossed one leg over the other, hugged the knee with one hand, put the other hand to his chin, and considered the ceiling as if he were navigating the stars.

Simon felt sorry for the professors who followed. Most professors made their excuses, despite the arrival of desserts. Aurelia reminded Simon that she wanted him to meet her friends. They introduced themselves as seniors in political science, sociology, economics, psychology, and anthropology, unwilling to take the methods courses offered by their own departments. Aurelia turned to Simon. "What they want is something that their departments would approve, but which is useful in the real world."

"Well, I do aim to teach practical skills. I can't see why any of your majors would deny credit for social scientific methods." As Aurelia prompted him, he reassured them that he never taught narratives, self-discovery, meditative exercises, listening exercises, or emotional self-expression.

"What about life skills?" asked the student.

"Well, in addition to the social scientific skills, I teach hard work, focus, planning, and self-discipline."

"I've heard of discipline, but I've never heard of self-discipline!

What else don't I know?"

"I don't know. Try me."

"Is the glass half full or half empty?"

"Both."

"What came first – the chicken or the egg?"

"Neither – they're in a cycle."

"Why did the chicken cross the road?"

"One side must have looked better than the other."

"If a tree falls and nobody is there to hear, does it make a noise?"

"I fail to imagine how the presence of absence of a hearer makes any difference to the physics of noise."

"What's the meaning of life?"

"Whatever your genes and formative experiences dictate."

"What's the secret to losing weight?"

"Eat less, exercise more."

"What's the secret to a happy marriage?"

"Find a good partner and be good to them."

"What's the secret to happiness?"

"Be honest with yourself."

They fell silent, exhausted.

Simon felt shamefully presumptive, so he reiterated that they should come to class, and he would do all he could to support their petitions, as long as they were sure they wanted to learn what he was teaching. Then he asked them to excuse him. He walked over to the other Briton, who was pretending to escape from a gaggle of appreciation.

"Hello. I'm Simon, from London."

"Marcus, Oxford."

"You made me wish that I had chosen a real science."

"The trouble with a real science, Simon, is that in theory everything is solvable – you can't escape the pressure. It drives you mad!" His attendants giggled.

"The trouble with a social science, Marcus, is that practically nothing social can be scientific. The insolubility drives you mad."

"Touché! Don't be fooled by my obscure mathematical models of little practical utility. I am a reformed mathematician. I take an interest in practical things." He looked at his attendants appreciatively and smiled. "For that much I have Bayside to thank."

"I have London to thank for pushing me here."

"Oh, you're much better off here. Britain is dreary, while we remain colorful. Living in Britain is like living in Bayside's climate for only part of the year. I still enjoy British summers though."

"Actually, I have started to dislike the summers most – London is so hot and busy."

"Oxford too! I was told that it was a university town. But now it's more town than gown."

"Oh, that's a shame."

"Living in Britain is like watching ancient Romans turn into modern Italians."

"Aha! Yes. Now I think about it, living in London is like watching ancient Rome turn into modern Rome."

"Then there's no hope," he said, with a despairing look at the ceiling. His attendants giggled. He looked at Simon, then said casually, "I suppose this is your first semester."

"First here, yes,"

"This is my third. My advice to you, Simon, is: don't talk about your research except with potential interns. The people who hired us, they want us to teach so they don't have to – unless it might contribute to their research. My goodness! If you both teach and research, well then, you'll only make them look bad. And they'll give you more teaching."

Simon was fascinated, but Marcus restarted for the alcove under the sweep of the staircase. "I must go. The Big Sister will kick us out soon, and I want to play the grand piano." Marcus sat down heavily, tried several chords, then looked up and said, "Now, ladies – tell me what you like."

Simon stood back, with both admiration and inadequacy, until Aurelia appeared beside him. "Do you want to see the garden?"

"I do."

They reached it through the dining hall's glass doors. In the spaces between trees, low stone walls formed squares, lit by lamps in each corner. Simon bent to identify the vegetables therein, straining, stooping, and shuffling, until he ran into smart sisters sitting on a herbaceous border in almost silence. He begged their pardon and turned back to Aurelia in a hurry: "Thank you. That was all very nourishing."

"You're welcome." She looked up and stuck out her chin while nodding and smiling vigorously. "I told you it was a smart sorority – smart in mind and body."

"I would have joined it – if I were a girl, I mean. Oh dear! I mean, if I were a girl, I would have chosen this sorority."

"If you had said you want to be a girl, you would have done better."

"Aurelia – I appreciate and respect your mature guidance."

"You don't need to leave yet – we can sit. I normally come out here at this time of night to smoke some weed, before the night's work, to calm me down. Don't worry: these sisters are here for the same thing. But don't tell the Big Sister – she knows, but she shouldn't know."

He turned to the plants again, caressed the leaves of a tomato, and brought the scent to his nostrils, then took a pinch of compost, rolled it between his fingers, and sniffed.

"No, I should go."

Aurelia escorted him to the front door. On opening, it dragged hot smog and smoke. On the front step, three smart sisters amiably shuffled their posteriors to make way, and tapped their cigarette ash on the potted palm trees.

Simon turned to Aurelia: "Please, don't come out, stay inside. Think of your shoes!" He reached across the threshold to shake hands.

"Thank you for coming."

"Thank you for inviting me. You were right in everything you said." The shuttle bus was waiting for him with its door open and an interior as fumigated as the street. It looked lonely, and the cottage loomed lonelier still.

11. Guest lecturer

Simon rose ever earlier, in pursuit of the cooler hours, but found himself wakeful late into the night, until he felt ragged. He sweated through each walk home, cursed the cloudless dawns, and stayed later indoors.

Simon started his fourth week as he had started his third: reading what his students were supposed to be reading before class. He was interrupted by an email from Will of the WISP.

Dear Simon:

I am following up on news that you visited the Smart Sisters over the weekend. I would have followed up in person, but I am sitting in the geography department.

As I am sure you realize, you should avoid privileging any group. I have received many complaints from students. Remember: privilege is divisive. You should, of course, mentor students, but no students in particular.

You should have consulted me on this issue in advance – my door was always open.

Best wishes, Will

By reply, Simon corrected the record and begged for a meeting. He walked to the geography department, and found Juncker's door closed.

On Wednesday, he taught the students of methods how to specify their topics. In the cottage that evening, he found an email from DAFI granting extra time to a student with "acute indecisiveness."

Waking up on Thursday, he found an email from Hattie Maddux, asking him to assist Janet's course on the political science of Asia, by speaking to a class on European-Asian relations. Simon replied that he had no expertise on European-Asian relations. Her next email told him to telephone her immediately. She answered the call as if continuing a conversation: "You're European! Of course, you're an expert on European-Asian relations."

"But I'm not Asian."

"The instructor is Asian."

"Yes?"

"Yes."

"I see."

"It meets at the same time you would have been teaching the Asian Relations class."

"Ah."

"So, I know you're free."

"Yes."

"Don't get there on time – give her an hour to get settled."

"What do you want me to prepare?"

"Nothing: just support her. Add something interesting whenever she seems to need help."

"Where's the classroom?"

"I'm sending you an email."

Simon spent the rest of the morning researching the topic. After a quick lunch, he walked on to campus, where he adjusted his speed according to each glimpse of the clock tower, so as to reach the classroom at five minutes before the hour.

He stood at the doorway, one hand on the handle, the other steadying the bag on his shoulder, immobilized by the possibility that he was at the wrong classroom. It was full of students, talking to each other, settled in their seats, busy with phones or sharing computers.

Simon suppressed his dissonance, until he realized that the students at the front were holding their phones in the air. He sidestepped through the door to get a better look at their target, but the whiteboard was clean. Then he recognized an upturned shoe on the floor between the table and chairs. In the shade of the table he noticed another shoe, on a stockinged foot, connected to a trousered leg. Simon took another step, horrified and fascinated, to trace the leg to a torso, under which the arms were trapped. He stepped around the table, grabbed a shoulder, pulled out a hand, and found the wrist, while looking for the face. The head seemed artificial – a mop of straight short hair, falling either side of the median. He drew back a curtain of hair to reveal an open mouth pressed against the floor. One corner was slightly raised above a pool of drool, whose surface tension rippled. Bits of paper and fluff shivered, without travelling. Concern drove him closer while disgust held him back. The ripples were in rhythm with a squeaky rasp that accelerated and dropped away with soothing predictability. What had been inaudible to Simon, while standing, was full of conviction and character once he was on his knees. He let go of her wrist without ever finding a pulse.

"What is going on here?"

"She's wasted again!" said the nearest student.

Her neighbor turned with alarm: "That's prejudicial! She's just as empowered as a male drinker. Why not? Good for her!"

"Have you called for help?"

"She never asks for help."

Simon looked around, while reaching in his pocket for his phone. "Why are you all just sitting there?"

"We're waiting for someone to verify that we're here, so we get A-grades when the course is cancelled. Ain't you someone?"

"That's not how it works!"

"That's how it works every semester!"

"Help me get her into the recovery position."

"I'm not getting sued," said the nearest student, folding her arms.

"Nor accused of sexual assault," said the male student in the far corner, with surprising consideration.

Simon's hands were already on the woman's hip and angle. There he paused, awkwardly, feeling caught in the act. He pushed the hip upwards and the ankle inwards, until she was braced on her side. She let out a grumble that became a sigh, deep enough to make her lips flap and the drool to lengthen, before her rhythm returned. A stench of wine and whiskey rose into his face. He stood up. He pressed 9-1-1 on his phone.

"Ambulance – for a colleague, err, female, middle-aged. She's collapsed, unconscious and non-responsive, but breathing freely." Simon paused, straightened up, and turned his back on the door. "Intoxicated, yes."

He put his phone away. "Go home, all of you."

"Not until you've got our names," said the nearest student.

A curiously memorable face passed, on the way to the door. Simon recognized a similar departure from his first class on Asian

Relations: "Yeah, professor, like, you remember me name, coz I'm from London too, that's why I took your class." Boyan's facial ticks were alarming: every word triggered some part of his face to realign, squint, twitch, or sneer. The face was unmistakable second time around. "You've got my name, yeah? Yeah, shame, init? I thought I'd take the class, because I was, like, born in Eastern Europe, which is closer to Asia than London, you get me?" Simon felt so exhausted with the visual cues as to be relieved when Boyan said he needed to run to play soccer.

The other students lined up to write their names and student numbers on a piece of paper. He telephoned Hattie: "She's drunk."

"Are you with her?"

"Of course."

"Then she's not conscious?"

"No." They both paused indignantly. "I've called for an ambulance. I think she'll be alright."

"Of course, she'll be alright – she's tenured."

"I meant, her physical condition."

"Careful! Are you with students?"

"Yes."

"Can they hear you?"

"They told me she's drunk. That's my assessment too. And I've told the emergency services."

They both paused indignantly again. "Tell them we have to discontinue this course for unforeseen circumstances beyond the program's control, and they'll get A-grades."

"But I'm here. I could finish the class, while you find someone to finish the course."

"That's not how it works."

"How does it work?"

"Don't worry about it. You're not needed."

They both paused again, until Simon realized how it works. "I want my own course, on Western-Asian relations."

"Fine."

12. Gatsby

On Friday, Simon went to the library to browse for readings on Western-Asian relations. He satisfied himself with ten topics to fill the ten remaining teaching weeks, but lost confidence that Hattie would approve them, so went to see Joe.

"Print me a copy, leave it with me, so I can say I've seen it, then release the syllabus to the students."

Simon sat still and uncertain.

"Was there anything else?"

"No. Well, I prepared myself to persuade you."

Joe smiled: "That won't be necessary. What are you doing at weekends?"

"Well, I've done nothing so far except look for somewhere to stay and work on syllabi."

"What are you going to do when you run out of syllabi?"

"Explore Bayside some more, I suppose."

"Have you thought about going beyond Bayside?"

"What is beyond Bayside? I mean, the other cities of the Bay seem the same."

"Come over to the Peninsula. It's got some different neighborhoods: cooler, older neighborhoods. And we've got trams."

"Ah."

"Come over one weekend. My husband would be pleased to meet you. We could point you to the parks, the museums, similar places to those in London."

"I could use a different society."

"We have a literary society, which meets in the local museum."

"Does it attract a lot of academics?"

"It does."

"No, thank you: I really meant a different society."

"There is a British community on the peninsula."

"No, that doesn't seem right. I'm here to see America."

"Somebody might be useful to you, as one British-American to another."

"That's a strange term – British-American."

"It just came to me, literally."

"But literalness is not a good guide to how people speak."

"No."

"Does the peninsula have a literalness society?"

"Ha! No."

"Oh dear." Simon slumped sulkily, staring into the canopies of the redwoods beyond Joe's head.

"How about a local history society?"

"Yes. I have found myself often fantasizing about the Bay Area before Bayside."

"I do remember a funny group that meets at an old house that I like in South Bay. Everybody dresses like the 1920s. I'll look it up. Here: the 'Flappers and Go-Getters'; their annual Gatsby Picnic is this weekend."

"I'd better get my skates on."

"Spats on."

***

On Saturday, Simon ran to the library, where he searched the shelves on the clothing, thence the art, and eventually the development of the university in the 1920s. The photographs showed concrete being poured to form the clock-tower, the stadium, and the life sciences buildings. The paths and ramps conformed to the meanderings of the stream and the redwood groves. Everywhere looked cool, damp, green, and lush. The students smiled into the camera, in tall trousers and short sweaters, or long skirts and short blouses. Some were dressed as equestrians. Some really rode horses to campus, to wooden-slatted stables on the south side of the stream, where Jimmy Pons now had his office.

Simon walked back to the cottage with books deserving more consideration. He consulted Vonessa, who excitedly showed him a closet of costumes.

In front of the mirror in the cottage, Simon combined his slacks, a linen shirt, the jacket from his summer suit, and a cravat, which the Flappers and Go-Getters called an "Ascot." He topped off with a Panama hat.

He had second thoughts when he stepped into the full glare of the next morning, shielded by no cloud, mitigated by no breeze. Simon opened the door of the taxi, wiped his hand on the handkerchief in his pocket, took off his jacket, folded it twice over his other arm, and slid along the forward edge of the seat to its middle. The driver looked in his mirror, nodded, and said, "I am supposed to tell you that state law requires all passengers to wear seat belts, but this is the City of Bayside, so, you know, whatever."

He drove down the hill, turned right into the chaotic traffic of University Street, and screeched to a stop as a pedestrian stepped into the gutter from the sidewalk. She was barefoot and half-dressed, but as energetic as a race walker: she swung her arms high, and strode with her feet turned outwards like a ballet dancer. As the taxi overtook her, her eyes wildly fixed Simon's, as if she were a super-heroine who could melt steel with a gaze.

The taxi struggled to the freeway, where traffic raced from one inexplicable bottleneck to another, merged from either side, sometimes from both sides at the same time, and sometimes crossed all the lanes to join freeways flying overhead or underneath. With relief, Simon saw a sign for the 1920s' house.

The exit curved into a small street alongside the freeway, with just a chain-link fence and concrete blocks between them. The street ahead was blocked by a vintage car, diagonal across both lanes. On the nearest running board stood a mustachioed man with a fake Tommy Gun held at an angle oblique to the broad stripes on his shirt and suit. On the other side of the car was a tall skinny man in dark blue tunic, trousers, and cap, leather belt and strap, and shiny black boots, holding a weighty truncheon across his buttocks. From the far side came a skinny woman in a brown uniform. She had added two big rosettes one for suffragettes, the other for suffragists, but no knowledge of the difference.

"You can't park here! You're blocking the intersection. Taxis should drop off there." Simon was none the wiser, because her hands fired everywhere, except to adjust her spectacles. Nothing seemed to bother the driver, but Simon jumped out into the heat and glare. He paid through the window, and turned to find the officious young lady on his heels, bursting with indignation. "You're blocking the way!"

"I'm sorry, it's my first time."

"You should have got out back there." Her hands fired in opposite directions.

"Where do I go from here?"

"There's only one hill." She folded her arms.

Indeed, there was, and up the steep road he walked. He caught up with pedestrians carrying picnic hampers, rugs, bottles, children, and dogs. Simon turned to re-consider the way he had come. The roadblock was permitting vintage cars up the ramp, while directing other cars to find parking in the residential streets. The vintage cars turned through a gate into a shaded, tree-lined avenue, beyond a stationary line of pedestrians, standing under peak sunshine on the roughly poured asphalt, outside a chain-link fence. There Simon waited, struggling to make conversation with people who were too restless to converse but too proud to sit in the dirt. After lunchtime, the line filed slowly past a ticket-seller. From there, they walked up the avenue, although many fell out in the shade.

Simon strode ahead, unencumbered, connecting the shadows, until the driveway curled leftwards, around a big oak tree, to reveal an enormous house. Simon stepped up to the veranda, and looked out over a lawn. It fell away to a stream, before rising steeply to mature trees: chestnut, hazelnut, walnut, and maple. In their shade, cars were parked side by side, facing the veranda. On the lawn, other cars were crowded and flashing with glare. Their white-walled tires seemed proud from each shadowy chassis. The dazzling chromed spokes and rims seemed prouder still. The many colors of their bodies were blindingly difficult to discern.

Simon retreated into the cool mansion, sliding softly over the parquet floors – devoid of furniture. A curvaceous staircase beckoned him upstairs. From the balcony, he could see over the trees to the hard edges of buildings on the peninsula.

Simon procrastinated in the many rooms. He exited down the back stairs, loitered in the lee, then resolved across the bright lawn towards the cars on the other side of the stream. Each car was the main prop to a group of people, in deck chairs or on boxes, around tables on which they played with lunches or cards. In the shade, Simon slowed to read the brands on the faces of the cars, until brought short by a golden Rolls-Royce, flying a Union Jack pennant.

"Hello. Is someone here British or is the car just celebrating its heritage?"

A serious man looked his way, sitting in a chair too small for him, with his back to the car. His braces strained over a striped blue and white shirt; the sleeves were rolled up; and a broad silk tie was painted by hand with a speeding, streamlined car. "She's British alright," he said gravely, with the sullen mouth of a mournful Basset Hound, but the busy eyes of a Spaniel.

"And she's a girl," said the lady sitting opposite in a blue silk dress.

"She's a sexy, sexy girl," said the man beside her, with a twirled moustache, red jacket, cream waistcoat, white trousers, and white shoes. He lifted a glass towards the car, toasted, and sipped.

"Cars, like ladies, look sexier with each drink," said the woman in the middle, soberly.

"I bet."

"Oh, we've been at it since eleven," said the provocative lady. "We're Flappers and Go-Getters; that's when we start."

"Lucky you."

"You can be lucky," she invited.

"Lucy!" said the other woman.

"If you become a member."

"Lucky Lucy," said the man beside her, without reproach. "Recruiting she is."

"I meant lucky to get in at eleven, before the heat and the hordes."

"You know, every year, the Gatsby Picnic falls on the hottest weekend of the Fall."

"It's the last concourse of the year," said the mournful Basset Hound.

"So why not earlier or later in the year, Mr. Vice-President for Events?" asked the woman beside him, reproachfully.

"Because I need every other weekend to show this beautiful girl at every concourse through the summer."

"No," said the woman in the middle, as soberly as before, "We need an excuse to drink once the season ends."

Lucy cut in: "Well, as Vice-President for Recruiting, I demand that this young man is recruited." She gave him a leaflet from a lace-gloved hand. He took it uncertainly, lightly shook the hand, then felt it rise, so he bowed to kiss the air above it.

"Charmed, I'm sure," she said, quieter than before. "And pray tell me, what might your name be?"

"Simon."

"Jock," said the Vice-President for Events.

Simon pictured a jockey on the back of a Basset Hound, then decided he should go. "Thank you. I must complete my tour and find somewhere to sit in the shade. I am charmed to have met you all." He touched the brim of his Panama. "Good afternoon."

Simon completed the cars in the shade and ventured into the crowded hollow. It rose and narrowed to a level crowded with awnings, tents, and flags planted by first arrivals. Different groups had decorated with a fringe here, a velvet rope there, a handsome leather chair, a pile of plush cushions, picnic blankets, gramophones, portable writing desks, travelling cases, trunks, and perambulators. He proceeded considerately, until the bottleneck opened on to a dance floor, bedecked with colorful flags, lanterns, and lamps, and surrounded by deck chairs. In the back of a vintage truck, under a canvas sunshield, the band started up. The shiny floor unsympathetically lit the dancers' sweat from below. Couples staggered into the shade. Simon asked other lonely spectators at the corner, but none wanted to dance.

A young woman did approach Simon. She wore a large brimmed hat and a white dress of lace over silk, tight over the hips, flared from the knees down. She asked him to take photographs, with her camera. She had no friends with her, she said. She wanted to be photographed alongside a cream Rolls-Royce. She posed like a bride, with an umbrella over her shoulder, pointing at the sun. Simon kept taking photographs, while she tilted her head back and forth, until she took the camera to review the photographs. "They're perfect – I can go home now."

Simon climbed towards the ridge until he was under mature trees, level with the house. He sat on a dusty log. He was distant enough to appreciate the whole spectacle, but close enough to discern the curves of each car, the ripples of each dress, and the sway of each musical instrument. He waited for rest to turn into restlessness, but the glare remained antipathetic.

A couple sat in the sun just below. The woman adjusted her attitude constantly, but without rearranging the skirt. She found one uncomfortable position after another, until she lost control and ended up on her back with her feet up the slope. She squealed with delight, and stayed there, so her companion lay beside her, closer still. Simon dispassionately considered the authenticity of her underwear. Nobody noticed his lonely self.

Simon watched pedestrians walk on to the lawn, heavily and wearily, with ever more observable skin, jewelry, burlesque, and electronic devices. Suddenly, the smell of a barbecue wafted up.

At 4 p.m., the band stopped. The cars started to drive out of cover. By 5 p.m., the sun was definitely losing its harsh glare, and the departures were constant. The shadows of the tallest trees reached across the stream. The spectacle was bathed in golden light that soon developed a reddish hue, and the cars' true colors glowed in dignified contradistinction. Jock strode on to the dance floor, still in his striped shirt and braces, at the head of a group of incongruously clothed people. They took up the tiles of the dance floor, stacked the chairs, and collapsed the tents. Modern trucks arrived to receive the loads.

Simon stood up, dehydrated and empty, turning over the leaflet in his hand and the scene in his mind.

13. USOP

On Tuesday, after lunch, Simon started his first class on Western-Asian relations. He had been assigned a classroom on the top floor, on the sunny side. He opened the windows, lowered the blinds, and jammed open the door with a sign that he found on the floor: "Fire door! Do not prop open!" Cooler air was sucked in, but once he turned on the projector, he lost the battle.

He started by promising to request a new room, and that students would still earn a full course unit even though nearly a third of the teaching weeks had passed. A student informed him delicately that as a dual major in environmental sciences he knew the room was hotter than permitted under state law for the transport of animals. Simon considered his liabilities. The student added that the state was unlikely to prosecute a state institution. "How wise you are," said Simon. "I hope you take the course." Simon showed the syllabus and taught some theory before the class wilted.

"Hi! I'm Nicole, from your methods course, remember? This course is going to be great for my English literature major. You're so right about narratives. That's why I plan to write a counter-narrative."

Simon was correcting her, when Boyan came by. "Yeah, hello Professor, it's me, Boyan, because, like, now I'm American, I thought I should learn about Western relations with Asia."

"Let's get outside in the fresh air. This heat is making us both twitch."

Simon hurried outside, trailing students from his class, dodging students from other classes, desperate to find the shade. Aurelia was leading the trail. She introduced Judiciary, one of the smart sisters to whom he had sold his methods course. Judiciary was sharp in features and diction, business-like in dress and manner. "Aurelia persuaded me to take all your courses. She said you'd need two of us to stop you saying the wrong thing!"

"Probably true."

"She's kidding!"

"Really, I'm glad you and Aurelia persuaded me."

"I'm glad too," said Simon, "but really, I would have preferred if you weren't kidding."

"Well, we don't need to kid, do we, Aurelia? No. We don't want to lose you – we're running out of useful professors. We'll coach you. For a start, try to use a term for 'Western' that isn't so Western. Yes, really, I'm serious – that kidding around, it was out of character."

"Judiciary, tell him who your father is."

"No, that wouldn't help him. And don't encourage him to use paternalistic terms."

"Oh dear," said Simon. "Are you serious or kidding? Yes, well then, please hold my hand through this."

"That metaphor is either sexual harassment or micro-aggression, as convenient. You really do need our help."

"No, I didn't mean it literally. Yes, you're right. I do need help."

"Metaphors are not your friend."

"Unless," interjected Aurelia, "you're over-compensating. The easiest way to get over being male is to stereotype males."

"Thank you, I see the logic in that, but no, that's dishonest. I doubt the justification outweighs the dishonesty."

"It's a bit like what you said in the class on research ethics," said Aurelia, more to Judiciary than Simon. "The subject of your research has a right to know about your research even though we prefer the subject to behave as naturally as if they did not know."

"So you want to survive without being dishonest," pondered Judiciary quietly. "You're not making this easy for us. For now, just don't mention human beings, at any time, in any context, ever."

"That's difficult for a social scientist."

"Yes, now I think about it. Sorry, I got excited."

"At the least," mused Aurelia, "he shouldn't draw attention to his own attributes, while discussing society's attributes – somehow."

"He should apologize for his attributes, before he discusses society's."

"No, that's dishonest again."

"What's the worst-case scenario?"

"Other than a micro-aggressive sexual harasser? Naturally, he's going to be accused of being pale, male, and stale."

"Oh, Judiciary, how could you? That's harsh."

"You asked me!"

"I did."

"He could say he prefers to self-identify as a person without identity."

"He's a person without color or vagina."

"He's challenged by a shortage of melatonin and estrogen."

"There you go! I think our work here is done."

"I don't think the professor agrees."

Simon looked down despondently. "I am challenged by a grounding in reality."

At the yellow gothic building, the door was open, the heat was venting, but the cheap carpet was melting. "Ladies! Please mind your shoes, please don't follow. Oh dear! Did I genderize your shoes?"

"Yes, you did. And that's acceptable only if you're empowering us. We're not different, only superior."

Simon resigned himself inwards to his musty cubicle, where his mood was hammered further by an email from Guillaume Juncker:

Dear Simon:

I am following up on your new course. I would have done this in person, but was told that you are changing the classroom.

First, please keep room changes to a minimum. Room changes are very stressful for students, particularly in this weather. You are in a position of power over these students and this can cause stress given this dynamic. Because of your power, a student escalated to me, rather than confront you directly.

Second, please don't confront the student directly.

If anything I stated above is incorrect, please do let me know. Happy to chat in person as well. My door is always open.

Simon found Guillaume Juncker's door closed, then forwarded the sent emails to which Guillaume Juncker had not responded.

On Wednesday, he took the students of methods to the library to learn how to find sources. That evening, he found an email from DAFI excusing a student from the library due to an allergy to books.

On Thursday, as announced by email, the new President of the University of Sunshine System, Mary Metro, was scheduled to hold a "town hall meeting with the Bayside community." Simon was committed to see an American town hall meeting of any type. The grey plaza was enlivened with poles flying alternately the flag of Sunshine University and any of a series of inspiring images and questions:

"Do you remember when encyclopedia meant books?"

"Do you remember when people were forced to write by hand?"

"Do you remember when face-to-face meant meeting in the real world?"

"Do you remember when speech wasn't free?"

"Do you remember when education wasn't fair?"

He saw ahead the glass of the lobby, against which plastic plants were pressed tight and bleached by the sun. Insufficient light bounced from the lobby into the auditorium itself; and the small globular lamps high above were more like stars than suns. Still blinded from outside, he stooped as he carefully descended the central aisle. He took a seat towards the rear, once he saw on the stage that Mary Metro had started: although the classes were on Bayside time, she was not.

"I can't communicate how much I have benefited from listening to these students," she waved her arm to the five persons seated to her left, "who give up their time to represent all of you," she waved to the audience, "as selected by my office from first-generation students from under-privileged cities of this great state."

The students on the stage cheered themselves.

"I can't communicate how proud I am to be starting this listening tour at this special campus."

She paused for appreciation. The five students urgently coordinated, then flung their arms in the air. They pointed at the audience to encourage a wave that died behind the first row.

"I remember partisan critics – and, frankly, sexist critics."

She smirked, while her cheerleaders boo-ed.

"They complained that I lacked experience when I was appointed as United States Secretary of Internal Security."

"No!" shouted her cheerleaders, pointing their thumbs to the floor.

"But a listening tour taught me everything I needed – what those Beltway insiders had never learnt sitting in their offices. And, yes, after four years in government, I am still proud to be an outsider!"

She chuckled through the cheers. "Critics said I lacked experience when the Trustees appointed me President of this great university system." She paused for cheers. "But I will not be intimidated by prejudice!" The cheering interrupted her again. "I blazed the trail for all women. Secretary of State Trixie Downer is not just our nation's Secretary of State, she's a candidate for President of the United States. I am proud to have made her candidature possible. And I am proud to support her. And I am proud she has promised that I can replace her as Secretary of State once she wins the Presidency. Smash the ceiling!"

She held out her hands as if surfing the roars of approval.

"My visits to this university have moved me in ways I cannot describe. I am still learning how awesome this system is. This is the best public university in the world! Because it is the most enlightened university in the world! I have enlightenment on my side! I have you on my side! You are the enlightened educated! How can I fail?"

Then she ran out of practiced sentiments. She walked slowly back and forth across the stage, mumbling, paraphrasing herself, with a slight cough between clauses, which she directed into the little microphone on her lapel.

Simon leaned towards the faint breeze from the door, away from the hot air rising from the stage. Students straggled in, but the rear two-thirds of the auditorium remained cavernous with spare capacity.

Simon's attention drifted until the speaker's voice suddenly strengthened and quickened: "Now, I've heard enough from me. I want to listen to you. First, however, I want to remind everybody of what I have said." All that Simon could discern to write down was that she "could not value everybody more," that she was "inspired and awed every day by the responsibilities entrusted by the trustees," and that everybody should feel free to email her "anytime" with any concerns or advice. "My email account is always open."

Simon sent an email to let her know that none of the classrooms allocated to his program were air conditioned, and that a student had measured the temperature as above state allowances.

He received an immediate reply from the University of Sunshine

Office of President: "USOP and Secretary Mary Metro value your email, but regret that she cannot respond to all emails while she is out of the office on her listening tour."

At that moment, he heard the first question over the microphone: "How long is your listening tour?"

"Well," she coughed, "I'll be visiting all the campuses across this great state, except when I'm campaigning for Secretary Trixie Downer for President, and campaigning overseas for our endowments,so after about nine months I'll be back in my office, and as you know that's just up the hill, so I'd be delighted to return to speak to you then."

Then she remembered something. "I intend, after my listening tour, to develop a plan for this great system, a short-term, ten-year plan, to make this great system even greater, so great it will be an inspiration for repressed universities everywhere, around the world – and not just universities, but every sector, from industry to immigration."

At that point, a woman walked passed Simon, half-way down the aisle, and made a motion in front of her body.

"I am so sorry, but I need to go to a meeting with the trustees. Please email me with your other questions."

Behind two campus policemen, she swept up the aisle, as she looked high and waved higher, with one assistant speaking in each ear, half-a-dozen assistants behind, and a couple state troopers bringing up the rear. As she rose into the ambient natural light, Simon realized the yellow dye in her grey hair, the black plastic studs in her ears, the brassy chain around her neck, the dandruff, the padded shoulders, the ill-fitting jacket, and the stripy t-shirt underneath. From the stage, the five students cheered – punching the air and clapping above their heads, as photographers crowded around them, in the only area of the auditorium bright enough for photography.

In the gloom, Secretary Mary Metro's eyes met Simon's briefly, then she turned to an aide. By some sudden convection of hot air, and the respectful hush as she passed, Simon heard, as clear as if she had spoken in his ear, "The trustees must first reduce the pale, male, and stale."

14. The Hidden Chef

"Come on, Treasury!" said Judiciary. "You need to get up."

"Why?"

"For lunch."

"I don't get up for lunch."

"Lunch with Pappy!"

"Already? Lunch is next month."

"That's Pappy's lunch with political friends. This is Pappy's lunch with a new trustee."

"I hate lunch! And I hate Pappy's friends. You go – you're his favorite."

"No, I'm not. I told him I hate politics."

"Whatever. He named you after the department he wanted."

"He named you after the department he got!"

"But he got you first."

"But he got you last, and there his career peaked, so you're named after the department he always talks about."

"Ugh! I don't even remember that time. I've never even been there. I wish people would stop asking me about it."

"Please don't say that in front of Pappy again. You know it upsets him. Pappy likes to tell his guests that he gave up government for our education."

"If that were true, he would have taken a job at a private school."

"He could have done, but that wouldn't have looked good."

"I think he put the weather first."

"Well, neither of us complained about that. Otherwise we'd be fighting cold or humidity, except for one month at the start of the academic year and one month at the end. Where were you last night?"

"I can't say."

"I won't tell Pappy."

"It's not that – I can't remember."

"Can you even remember coming here, instead of your dorm? You're not a Smart Sister."

"I can't remember anything except cat kisses."

"Oh! How sweet! That's so last century – touching noses."

"No – other end."

"Ugh! Sick-making!"

"It's no different to Pappy's politicking!"

"You know, your date could have been just another pre-law trying to get to Pappy."

"Not a chance – I never told him my real name."

"That's dishonest."

"No, that's privacy."

"And what if he wanted to see you again?"

"That would be creepy."

"That's not fair."

"Fairness is a hair coloring. I'm empowered. Pappy always told us to be empowered."

"Yes, but he's a politician."

"Not anymore."

"Oh, more so! He wants to run for President again. First he hopes to be called to Trixie's campaign."

"He hopes to be called to Trixie's divorce."

"Well, think what he'll be like if she wins but doesn't recall him. She'll be on the news all the time, and he'll never be able to forget that he could have been First Lady."

"First Gentleman."

"She wouldn't let him call himself that."

"True. Neither of them is a lady."

"Nor are you. Come on Treasury – you're not even moving! Get up! We need to leave in thirty minutes. I'm going to turn on the shower and if you're not in it when I come back I'm going to tip over that couch."

"Where are we going anyway?"

"The Gourmet Ghetto, of course."

"That's miles away!"

"It's five blocks."

"Call us a cab, then I won't be late."

***

"You're late," said Tom Pinklewonk. "A politician is never late, except for the opposition. This is not the opposition – this is Director Daly, our newest trustee."

"Call me Neil, you lucky, lucky, ladies – if you self-identify that way?"

"There are no ladies here," said Judiciary, harshly.

"Except a potential First Lady," said Treasury, smartly.

"You lucky, lucky persons of no assumed gender. You know, your father never stops talking about his time in the Judiciary and the Treasury, and thence we're all reminded of you lucky, lucky persons of no assumed gender."

"Why lucky?" asked Judiciary, relishing her harshness.

"Why? Because your father is the newest trustee of Riverside University of London; and I am the newest trustee of Bayside. We aim to be the most enlightened colleges in the world, and that privileges you. Our colleges are no longer just strategic partners. Finally, the two most enlightened public universities are allies."

"What's the difference between partners and allies?" asked Judiciary.

"We're still working that out. But one thing you can sure of: no alliance will benefit humanity more, or your education."

"I want to do London sometime," said Treasury. "For as long as a semester, perhaps – although I could probably do it in a day."

"I would be happy to arrange that personally," said Director Daly. "Perhaps when your father launches the Pinklewonk Center for Liberal Regulation."

"We'll see what I am doing for the next four years. Now, let's go in."

The transition was dramatic from roadway to archway, from the luminous to the tenebrous, from sweltering to refreshing, from frenetic to ascetic. However, the immediate calm of the porch was disturbed by the noise inside the restaurant, as seen through the large plate glass windows on their left. Masses of men in white clothing pressed around long heavy tables and benches. Each group lurched and heaved with collective purpose. Occasionally, a roar rose above the general din. Suddenly, one group spewed a member to join another group.

Treasury pressed her whole body against the glass. "Mommy always said you can judge a man by his energy."

"Why are they all wearing white?"

Treasury turned to Judiciary with a hiss of delight: "They're martial arts students!"

Judiciary peered closer, quizzically: "Pappy! The Ku Klux Klan has taken your chosen restaurant for a convention."

"Never! Andy wouldn't allow it. He's working-class."

"Pappy, she's kidding! They're chefs!" said Treasury.

"Of course they are! Who else? Where else?"

"Are you sure we can get in, Pappy?"

"Of course we can! Andy knows me. I interviewed his kitchen staff to prove that the service economy promotes inequality. And I paid him out of my foundation. And I said I would name the restaurant in the acknowledgements. And I made a reservation."

"How does this restaurant work again, Pappy?"

"You describe yourself, then the hidden chef tells you what's best for you."

"Who is he?"

"Or she! You have seen female chefs! I have introduced you to many accomplished women, you know. It wouldn't hurt you to aspire to this." He swept his hand in an arc.

"This looks like hard work," said Treasury, wrinkling her nose.

"Pappy, Treasury made a normative assumption. Most chefs are men. So she assumed the next chef she met would be a man. It's a strong theory, as my methods professor would say."

"That sounds devious – an excuse to deny sexism, no doubt."

"No doubt," agreed Director Daly.

"Only if the assumption were prescriptive, Pappy, but Treasury wasn't proposing what should be, just what is."

"I wasn't?"

"And if the evidence shows that most chefs are men, then probabilistically the next chef we meet would be a man."

"The evidence? The evidence?! The evidence is that if most chefs are men, then the food industry is sexist."

"That's one theory, Pappy. But over-representation is not necessarily evidence for inequality."

"Who told you this?"

"My professor of methods. He's very good."

"A male professor! Of course he would deny sexism."

"Sexism is bad," agreed Director Daly.

"I don't think he would. He wants us to be 'evidence-based', he always says."

"Very devious. I've heard the same in court."

"Very sneaky," agreed Director Daly.

"He's not like that! He insists we consider all the evidence, but rank the best evidence. We also consider the arguments from all sides, but choose the theory that best fits the best evidence."

"Consider all the evidence! Consider all the arguments! How impractical! Can you imagine government like that? Or a trustees' meeting?"

"Not on your nelly!" exclaimed Director Daly. "We wouldn't eat!"

"That's why I became a lawyer: I have the skills to reduce everything to two sides, and only one can be right."

"He says his methods are useful in any domain."

"Bull! What's his name?"

"Simon Ranald."

"Never heard of him."

"He's from London."

"I've never heard of him," said Director Daly.

"You should meet him, Pappy."

"I don't need to meet him to know how he thinks. What is with you girls and male professors? I've made myself very clear that learning from male professors is reinforcing patriarchal norms. And I don't want any repeat of what we went through with Treasury last semester."

"Jimmy wasn't grading me at the time, Pappy."

"That's enough! I don't want to think about it. I used to think Jimmy Pons was a good mensch – but it turns out he's just a man."

"Such a man," whispered Treasury to Judiciary. They giggled.

"Judiciary! What did she say?"

"Pappi," said Treasury. "What are we waiting for?"

"That's very good," said Judiciary. "Ask a new question when you don't want to answer a question. You see, Pappy, we do listen to what you teach!"

"Pappy! Why are we just standing here? Nobody's here."

Once they shut up, they noticed that they had absent-mindedly formed a circle in the lobby. The floor was tiled with cork and teak. The walls were covered with the same wood shingles as the roof. Even the door proved to be clad in shingles, once it closed electrically behind them. Suddenly, the lobby became quiet and claustrophobic. In front of them rose a bulbous protrusion, obtrusive and obstructive like a buddha's gut, up to some hidden platform, two stories high. It was clad with thick bamboo that kept leading their eyes upwards.

"Are we supposed to climb up there? I can't see a way around, any doors, any windows, any bell."

"You wait for the hidden chef to summon you."

At that moment, as if roused, a disembodied voice boomed from the platform on high: "What are you?"

Tom Pinklewonk jumped forward with delight and presumption. "Why, I travelled from an impoverished upbringing in Bumbleff, New Jersey, to law school at Harvard, and to national government – where I championed the working-class. Now I hold the Chair for Liberal Interventionist Economics at Bayside."

"Lobster stuffed with steak."

"Ooh! I love both lobster and steak! You see how clever she is?"

"I think the voice is male," said Treasury.

"It changes. Andy loves women."

"Oh, good!"

Judiciary stepped forward. "While you two argue, I will speak to the electronic box. I am twenty years old, female, and a sophomore at Bayside."

"What major?"

"Undeclared."

"Pre-law!" interjected her father.

"Pre-no-more-school!"

They were interrupted impatiently: "Pizza salad."

"Salad – your mother would be happy."

"You hate Mommy."

"She didn't think I could be President!"

"My turn! I am also a student at Bayside, but the opposite of my sister. I am a team player, but I tread my own path. I am one of a kind, but I can fit in anywhere. I listen to everybody, but I have a mind of my own. I like everybody, but I like my own company. I love to travel, but I also like to stay home. Sometimes I like to get dressed up to go somewhere fancy, but sometimes I just like to veg-out in front of the T.V. I am the life of the party, except sometimes I prefer to people-watch. I like to eat out, but I also like to cook for myself."

"You don't cook for yourself!"

"No, but I like to! And I like sunshine, laughing, snowboarding, surfing, and birthdays – and eating chocolate cake in bed on cold evenings; and singing in the rain – but not cold rain."

"Oh, yawn, I'm starving to death!"

"And I'm a vegetarian."

"And she's a slut!"

The voice replied instantly: "Curried ice cream!"

"That's not true, Pappy – Judiciary was kidding."

"Number four – what are you?"

"I'm Director of Riverside University of London – champion of free and fair education, fighter against privilege, advancer of enlightenment."

"Jellied quesadilla," the disembodied voice boomed.

"What's a quesadilla?"

"Don't worry," said Treasury. "You'll love it – it's almost a state food."

"Is it a fish?"

The bottom of the bamboo tower swung open slowly and smoothly. They walked into riotous noise. They shouted at each other until exhausted, then they resigned to passivity, confident that everybody understood that nobody understood where to go.

Men in white careened around the heavy tables to their front, pushing plates around more than they were sampling, joking more than they were describing, drinking more than they were eating.

Treasury inclined to join them until her father stepped ahead in the aisle with his legs splayed. She fixated on the table that was reaching its climax: just as the plates stopped moving, the chefs stood upright, dusted themselves off, slapped each other on their backs, and made for the exit behind her.

"Let's get something to eat," said the leader.

"Yes, I'm starving," said the next.

"We can order take-out."

Treasury reluctantly made way, but her disappointment was

assuaged by excitement in the far corner. A huge television screen was showing a soccer game. The two nearest tables gesticulated to each other, sometimes with agreement, sometimes with ridicule. "So much passion!" she shouted involuntarily.

Her sister was drawn nearer: "What?!"

At that moment, one group leapt up with open hands to the ceiling. Its members jumped on the benches, rushed to slap the backs of their opponents, or took their joy to other tables. A huge American blocked their way down the main aisle and shouted, "Not here, pussy-feet, unless you want to see what football you should be watching."

One of them pushed on, looking to complete a circuit of high-fives, his right hand up, at which Treasury eagerly swung, only to catch his face. He never stopped, but contrived to look ecstatic and uncomprehending. He approached the next table steadfastly, but redirected into the aisle for the quickest return to base, when an American turned outwards and shouted, "Hey! Don't upset the sushi soup!"

Seduced by the immediate lull in the storm, Treasury shouted to Judiciary: "Between sushi, American footballers, and celebrating Italians, definitely not the place to bring a pregnant woman!"

Their father spun fully around. "Are you pregnant?"

Suddenly, they were dazzled by a light playing on their faces, from a mezzanine on the far side, directed by some person, shrouded in black from cape to gloves.

"Come on!" said Tom Pinklewonk over his shoulder, then swung his arm forward past his ear like a resolute explorer. They reached the mezzanine safely, just as the mysterious figure turned abruptly into a room, leaving the door open. They fell into the room, closed the door, and breathed in the relative quiet.

"You see, girls!" panted Tom Pinklewonk. "Andy wouldn't let me down. This is what championing the working-class gets you."

Their meals were sitting on a polished black table. In the far wall, a mirrored door trembled from the escape of their mysterious usher.

"Well, that was awkward!" said Director Daly.

"I agree," apologized Tom Pinklewonk. "That wasn't typical of Bayside, I assure you – out-of-towners. But you can't blame them – they need a liberal arts education, that's all. The poor souls probably have no education beyond culinary school."

Director Daly agreed with a tragic nod of his head. "If only they had read the newspaper this morning, front to back, as I did."

"Come on girls – find your dishes."

"What if we don't like what we're given?" asked Judiciary.

"The hidden chef knows best. Don't question the experts."

"Where's the bill?" asked Director Daly.

"Everything is on credit."

"How do you know the prices?"

"That's worked out later."

Tom Pinklewonk lent on the table, breathing deeply, before sitting down.

"You know, Pappy," said Judiciary thoughtfully, "I'd like to move somewhere really rural after school, to as small a town as possible – with no restaurants, no hotels, no conference center, no university – where everybody knows each other, people walk in straight lines, put their hands to their mouths when they cough, and keep their distance during a pandemic."

Tom Pinklewonk turned in horror. "You mean – inland?!"

Director Daly mirrored Professor Pinklewonk's face: "That sounds uncivilized!"

"Judiciary! I demand to know the professor who has put into your head all the nonsense you've been talking today."

15. Berk

Simon awoke on Sunday to a dawn as hot as the dusk. He ran to the pool instead of the ridge, but found it accommodating cultures that find mixed-gender swimming offensive. The men gathered on the bleachers, waiting for the women to finish, and the transgenders swam when they liked. Simon ran across campus to investigate the second pool, but found a handwritten legend: "Closed until further notice due to flooding."

He resolved to retry the main pool on the morrow, but awoke to an email announcing the closure of all recreation due to soot and ash, from wildfires in the high desert on the other side of the ridge. Then he opened an email from the Office of the Chancellor, scheduling "a town hall meeting to reassure the campus community of our emergency planning."

On Monday evening, Simon found the same auditorium, the same sultry gloom, the same under-utilization. He arrived five minutes before the hour, to take a lonely seat in the third row. Five minutes after the hour, the front two rows were sticky and noisy with people. A woman came to the microphone in the aisle to tell the "valued campus community" that "Chancellor Berk would be arriving on Bayside time." Berk stepped on the stage fifteen minutes later.

The white hair atop Chancellor's head was gathered in spikes of differing thicknesses and vectors. Occasionally, Chancellor Berk thoughtlessly touched a spike, cracked the thick gel, and withdrew his hand shyly but sharply, as if kicking himself for forgetting. He wore spectacles with thick black frames, proud over the untamed white hair around his ears.

"I am Chancellor Berk," he shouted grandly, before adding meekly: "But you can call me Dick." He stood still with his hands in front of his crotch, in the shape of a heart, or perhaps a vagina. "Colleagues and friends," he said solemnly; the corner of his mouth twitched into a crooked smile; and an eyebrow lifted jauntily. "I have come from a meeting of the emergency planning committee!"

He prompted awe, then he introduced every member of the committee in the front row, with such gravity that Simon felt obliged to take notes: Vice-Chancellor for Risk Sensitivity and Tolerance; Vice-Chancellor for Collective Liability and Individual

Responsibility; Vice-Chancellor for Change and Continuity; Vice-Chancellor for Conformity and Diversity; Vice-Chancellor for Multi-Culturalism and American Cultures; Vice-Chancellor for Elite Performance and Inclusivity; Vice-Chancellor for Disabilities Accommodation and Empowerment; Vice-Chancellor for Independence and Outreach. Simon could not keep up.

Chancellor Berk asked for a round of applause. "Allow me to speak for all of us, when I say we are fortunate that Bayside attracts and retains such incredible talent. These amazing people have volunteered to serve on this committee to make us all safe. Let's hear it for them one more time."

Berk clapped above his head, then punched the air with both fists. As the audience complied, Berk rocked side to side at the waist, then suddenly spread out his hands impatiently.

"I have spoken with University of Sunshine President Mary Metro, who wanted me to convey her best wishes to the entire campus community at this difficult time, while she takes her listening tour overseas. I want to remind you that no university president has more experience in emergency management than former Secretary of Internal Security Metro."

The audience cheered.

"She reassures me that she has spoken with her former colleagues in the United States government, and they have reassured her that the federal government is ready to assist."

The audience booed.

"Secretary Metro wanted me to remind you that no administration has done more to combat climate change than the administration in which she served, and she will continue that fight."

The front row started a chant: "Metro! Metro!"

"Her unwavering spirit of bipartisanship reminds me that only one party is responsible for climate change."

The audience booed.

"These wildfires are yet more evidence for climate change. That's why this university is redoubling its efforts to switch its on-campus energy plant to renewable timber." Berk confidently patted down the noise. Suddenly, he became fixated towards the rear.

A man skidded to a stop in front of the microphone, remained in a running position, and pointed like he was aiming a gun: "Global warming is a myth that kill jobs! Snow is falling in Canada!"

The man's stance transitioned from energetic and deliberate to puny and hesitant against the frenzy of gesticulation that rose from the seats around him. He decided to repeat himself, but soon stumbled backwards, waving fingers out of his face.

Berk's confidence returned. He brought the little microphone from his lapel to his lips and boomed: "I love free speech!" The audience cheered. He laughed. "Thank you everyone, thank you for honoring free speech. Let's get him out of here." He was cheered again.

"Okay, no more interruptions please. Now, let me tell you what we have done to counter this emergency. Of course, the Permanent Committee for Emergency Planning can't be expected to take responsibility. Oh no! We have appointed a Committee for Wildfire Emergency Response, which will draw on the special talents and skills of our community. Let me introduce them."

Simon continued his notes: a Professor of French Literature, who "brought special interest in narratives of tragedy"; a Professor of Feminist and Transgender Studies, who was "expert in speaking to vulnerable communities"; the Director of the School of Communications, "to help members of our community to express their feelings"; the Dean of the School of Social Work, who "would work to make all our efforts more social"; and the Dean of the School of Education – "an expert in telling people how to think."

He asked them to take a bow. "They will meet monthly to develop guidance on what we should do next time."

Berk returned his mouth closer to his little microphone and spoke quieter. "Now let me speak directly to faculty in the audience. As if an election year was not stressful enough for our students, now they must worry about a wildfire in the same state, only two counties away! Act now to encourage student engagement with the issues raised by wildfires. Be sympathetic when students need personal time. Assign narrative projects and feelings projects. Shift your assignments online. Postpone your deadlines. Lower your expectations. Suggest alternative forms of expression: give the students the opportunity to dramatize their personal experiences. Consider changing your final exams into field projects. Finals week would be the perfect opportunity to organize trips into the field! Of course, as a historian myself, I know the best way to teach awareness of wildfires is to take students into the most deprived urban areas."

He paused, clearly thinking about what he could say next. "If you are struggling to think how your discipline or field could incorporate wildfires, try cooperating with experts from fields of relevance – such as environmental science, risk management, operations management, and public administration." He could not remember any other useful disciplines. "Use your social networks – the experts are at your level, not mine!"

He squatted and squinted into the spotlights, swept a hand towards the audience, and knocked over the microphone stand. Amidst the crashes and waves of electric feedback, he strode off the stage: "I am Chancellor Berk! This is your university! You're wonderful!"

Berk skipped down the steps and paused in the central aisle to point at the front rows either side of him. Committee members rose to applaud. He stepped forward and pointed into the audience. "You're the experts! You! And you! And you! You too!"

Berk's index finger finished in Simon's face, just as Simon stood to leave. Given the sudden proximity, Berk's last word seemed encapsulated within a soundscape that was all their own. Given the intimacy, Simon felt compelled to reply. "Well, perhaps I could advise on methods, for analysis of the risk, or for investigating the impacts..." Berk liked neither intimacy nor proximity. His index finger remained frozen, inches from Simon's face. His smile melted into horror. Then he shouted, "Climate change is not a myth!" Simon was soon swept up the aisle at the points of a phalanx of fingers.

16. Creative grading

In the solitude of the cottage in the garden, Simon opened a long list of emails labelling him a climate change denier. For his new correspondents, any denial confirmed a denier, any silence confirmed a guilt. Since any reply could be copied, forwarded, or pasted online as evidence for misinterpretation, he chose silence, for efficiency not effectiveness.

Simon emailed some snap assignments. He wanted the students of Western-Asian relations to analyze the risks of war in the region. Simultaneously, he asked his students of methods to design an investigation of any risk except wildfires. One student's DAFI accommodation was immediately updated to specify that any deadline is inherently a violation of her accommodation for anxiety. The DAFI service excused another until further notice due to "acute agoraphobia," triggered when his noise-cancelling headphones stopped cancelling birds and trees.

At home, Simon printed out the submissions, took them up in both hands, and wondered how to begin. He tapped their bottoms on the table. He flicked through them. He laid them down as a stack. He picked up the top paper, but it wilted in isolation. He shuffled and spread them across the table – nothing struck his eye. They looked disappointingly consistent, except where students forgot to include their names. He started with the papers that were named. Even so, the selection looked sickeningly uninspiring. He gathered them all together between two hands. Suddenly he imagined throwing them down some stairs, before grading in the order found, because randomness is sometimes closest to absence of bias. Then he realized that the starting order would affect the ending order. Besides, he had no stairs. He felt helpless and unproductive. He sorted them in order of neatness, finessing one with another until he held a spread from the smartest to the messiest. On these prospects, he started to read.

The first paper delighted him; the second was better; a few belonged in their own league. Simon started a new pile in the middle. The next few papers slowed him down, so he separated them. Paradoxically, lesser papers demanded greater deliberation. The papers became less organized, less comprehensible, less sensible – and the evening dragged on. Gradually, laboriously, he filtered the papers into piles, from A-plus down.

The A-plus pile looked diminutive and noble. He went to write the grade on the top, but realized that it was so special as to deserve an explanation:

> This grade rewards your performance and reflects my relief that I can teach, because you produced as much as I could have. I don't always award this grade. Your paper and one other look exceptional amongst dozens. I imagine your first step was to choose a course that motivates you. Perhaps you just care to succeed at your choices. Either way, you clearly read what was asked, paid attention, started in good time, planned, revised, and polished. That process is easy to describe but difficult to execute. You are a rare executer. I have started to read "A-plus" as "applause."

Simon's hand climbed the A-grade pile.

> This grade makes me happy and should make you happy too. This isn't an A-plus, but you might not even realize that an A-plus was available. You did what I asked. The task is that simple, but simple isn't always easy. Whatever your endowments, you added the effort, so this is meritocratic. Take the honor and praise the system. What you deserve is what others should desire; and they should know that you deserve. In those senses, this "A" should stand for "American."

As he put his hands on the tallest piles, he typed up a single document, to explain all the grades, for issue to all the students.

> This is an A-minus. A little more could have topped the curve. I'm not complaining, I'm encouraging. I imagine you needed just a little more motivation or opportunity. Despite the minus, this "A" should stand for "assured," because I am assured of your higher performance.

> A B-plus falls one step below A-minus, but a change of letter implies more. You've earned the positive within the B-league, so you're above average, but still not in the first league. You're three steps from the top, and only one step above average. The explanations are impossible to generalize: perhaps you lacked effort or attention; perhaps this is your limit; probably you know better, and better awaits you, if you choose.

> You have two ways to look on a B-grade: it's supposed to be the average grade, so you're not below average; but if the true average matched the mid-point of the curve, it would be a B-minus or C-plus,

so you could think of your B-grade as inflated. An appropriate letter would be an "a" for average. Indeed, other professors give A-grades to everyone. You're average in an era of inflation – remember that before you satisfice. Average is normal, but also common, mean, and modish.

Your B-minus is already below average, but so close. There's hope in that, but also disappointment. Somehow you stopped short of the average. Likely you lacked the determination, rather than intelligence. As in so many arenas, what is scored on one scale as cognitive is mostly psychological. I hope you learn the difference.

As the height of the piles and the grades fell, so did his reticence, restraint, and resignation.

Your C-plus puts you at the top of the C-grades, but the C-grades are clearly below the B-grades, and the B-grades straddle the average, the median, and the mode. Look at each of your sentences and ask yourself – did this earn me anything? Probably not. Each mistaken, incomprehensible, irrelevant, or tangential assertion is a waste of your writing, and a waste of my reading.

The letter "c" could stand for "careless" or perhaps "clumsy." I start to think that it should stand for the "chore" that reading your paper became. Little of it was comprehensibly relevant to what I had assigned. You clearly regarded this paper as a chore to write, so don't be surprised that it is a chore to read.

Ironically, you could be receiving this C-minus with relief. At this level, the grades probably don't matter to you, either because you selected pass or no-pass, or you will now switch to pass or no-pass to escape the pressure for improvement. Thus, my effort to place your paper with such granularity is probably wasted on you, like most of what I do.

Getting down to a D-plus is dire, depressing, dispiriting, and debilitating. Every time I re-started a sentence, crossed out your repetitions, corrected your misunderstandings, explained your fallacies, or considered your plagiarism, I despised it more. Despising your paper inevitably leads to despising you too a little. I'm not proud to admit it, but I'd be lying to deny it, and I am too decent to hide it. Probably you deceived yourself about what responsibilities you could duck. Hopefully you won't choose denial.

What's the point of three D-grades given that I am supposed to give most students a B? I don't know; I'm really asking. The only reason I gave you the middle D-grade is because other papers were inconsequentially better or worse. You might realize something in the explanations for the grades above and below.

A D-minus is the lowest grade short of outright failure. You achieved this grade essentially by submitting something – the bare minimum, the blindingly obvious consensus that you've absorbed elsewhere from people who never attended my classes. I bet you've not attended most of what I taught. You're as good as a stranger to me. Perhaps the "d" should stand for "dead," as in "dead to me," "dead to education," or "dead last" – you choose.

I had twelve grades to give but you couldn't get on the first step. Other students fail because they chose not to submit anything, but you managed to submit something and still achieve nothing. This F is the thirteenth step, but don't take thirteen as unlucky, when it's all your own fault. Officially, the F stands for "fail," but here it stands for "fault."

I wrote F-minus on your paper because it went beyond failing: it flabbergasted me. You failed so foolishly that I needed to invent a grade just for you. I imagine you were intoxicated, riding unicorns through fields of poppies and mushrooms, while fantastic friends cheered your free spirit. If you weren't intoxicated, I would worry more. Please don't try to explain your paper: I am trying to forget it.

Finishing in the early hours of the weekend, swirling between admiration and futility, Simon made himself feel better by committing to join the Flappers and Go-Getters at their next lecture.

17. Art Deco talk

He dressed in his linen shirt, folded his cravat into one pocket, draped his jacket over one arm, and put his Panama on his head. He spent longer looking at his leather shoes. He looked at his hiking boots. He looked at his leather satchel. He put his shoes in the bag, but it bulged inauthentically. He put the shoes on his feet, then smeared them with petroleum jelly.

He had not ventured to the Peninsula before. He enjoyed his curiosity, but doubted his commitment, once he walked out, slower than usual, to avoid over-heating. He doubted his choice more on University Street, and most at Bayside train station, where every step felt sticky and stank of urine. Experienced pedestrians walked with intense concentration, watching for smeared feces. The distinction between human or canine was a question for those with the luxury of novelty. They navigated sleeping bags and camping cots, dogs and parrots, bicycles and carts, items for sale and items for hoarding, unremarkable crafts and remarkable expectations.

Under the arch declaring "Welcome to Bayside," he descended into rising stench and steam. On the platform, the smooth brick floor was slippery, the tiled walls were running with hydrated grime, his skin was clammy, and the way ahead was misty. The other travelers shuffled into whatever space was available, then resigned from activity and society. Above, the electric sign indicated trains at least twenty minutes apart, and all of them late.

The train descended for a long, stuttering journey under the Bay. Eventually, it bounced into a station of no differentiation except its name of "North Peninsula." Simon determined to walk novel streets rather than crawl through common tunnels.

The surface air was cool. Flabby fog flew briskly up the street, dragging oceanic smells through the pollution. A few stories above, the fog mixed with the cloud, which was still brightly lit from above. The buildings were taller and smarter than anything in Bayside, but appeared as stunted pillars and stilts to the white froth. Simon joined a shoal of pedestrians moving in the right direction. He looked for an opportunity to pass one shoal to join another, but was not helped by the sidewalk's crests and troughs, or its lists to port or starboard to accommodate each cross-street.

Simon counted twenty blocks before he remembered to watch for a cross-street named "Stella." He turned to a hotel of the same name – spelt in large white electric bulbs on a shiny black surface. He undertook revolving doors of chrome and glass. After the gathering dusk, the lobby seemed powerfully bright. He admired the white marble steps in each corner, with their sinewy aluminum handrails. Wearily and sensibly, he chose the elevator in the center. He pressed the button for the "Sky Bar."

The elevator opened opposite a cloakroom. Around the corner the whole floor was revealed, between three glass walls. A bar in the right rear corner was raucous with frantic drinking, under a sign declaring happy hour until 6 p.m. He preferred the circular dance floor. Atop a ring of black leather pads on chrome stands, furtive couples conspired in low voices. He headed to the shiny door in the opposite corner, where he found the little meeting room, of no remark except the view. He stopped at the glass wall, watching the cloud darken and slowly lift, until it settled around the pyramidal tops of the tallest buildings, and unveiled the kinetic art of the traffic below.

Simon was mesmerized and meditative, until the room filled with a rush. The last arrivals were least stable, but carried the largest cocktails and sought the least accessible seats. A lady in a blue suit and enormous hat fixed her eyes on an empty seat in front of Simon: she managed to sidle one step before sitting in the lap of the nearest gentleman, then she rolled into the aisle. Her friend sat down beside her, with equal squeals of delight, and motioned others to join them.

"They are a scream!" said a voice from behind. "Every lecture, at least one of them is on the floor."

"Not this early," said its companion.

"Well, they are late."

Jock stepped over them without acknowledgement. At the front, he turned crisply, called "Ladies and Gentlemen," and waited patiently for raucousness to decline to rambunctiousness.

"Welcome, welcome, ladies and gentlemen."

He waited for rambunctiousness to decline to randomness.

"I am delighted to see members attending our lectures as well as the picnic. And I am delighted to welcome a new member, recruited from said picnic."

Lucy looked over her shoulder and silently mouthed, "Charming."

"And we are delighted to welcome one of our own to speak about Art Deco architecture on the Peninsula – Teddi."

Simon heard the muffled patter of gloved hands. "Hussah!" exclaimed the men gently.

Teddi was clad in black from head to feet, except for a fabric white rose on top of the hat, and white stripes down a long skirt. At first, she seemed dour or stiff, until Simon decided she was thoughtful and unassuming. Each statement ended with her top lip finding its resting place beyond and over her bottom lip. Her gaze followed down to her notes, before rising for the next statement.

She was apt to complete her comments by drawing attention to a particular motif or material. A lady towards the front would let out a guttural "Ugh" – a noise between a voluntary expression of surprise and an involuntary expulsion of air. She gradually lent into the aisle, with her legs apart and her head peering around the shoulder of the man in front, until he turned to give her his drink. With each sip, she gradually reversed her process.

As Teddi explained where she had taken each photograph, Simon wrote in his notebook. Sometimes she pointed to buildings outside. She hurried to explain each image, to move on to the next, until Jock rose to interrupt her: "Alas, Teddi, although we could learn forever, our second happy hour won't last forever."

Simon remained at the window, studying the buildings, while his row cleared. He went forward, notebook in hand.

"Teddi? Would that be short for Theodora?"

"Yes, my grandmother's name. She shortened it the same way I do, although she pronounced it more like you do."

"Teddi?"

"Yes, and the other."

"Theodora?"

"That too."

"Do you prefer Teddi or Theodora?"

"Please call me both. Thank you for coming all the way from England for my presentation."

"Oh, I rested a few weeks in Bayside in between."

"Bayside isn't so far! Still, that's a hard journey."

"Yes. It was a first for me, rather like this group, and your topic. I say! May I see the images for which you ran out of time? That's what I meant to ask."

"Yes. I didn't expect to show them all. I collect them in case I write a book. I keep adding images to the presentation, without writing the book."

"I teach my students to try presenting before writing. It helps to settle the structure."

"It does."

"I mean, I didn't mean to suggest that you are not well structured – I mean, that your presentation is not well structured. That is: I didn't meant to suggest that it is not well structured. It was well structured. Oh, there are a lot of images here!"

"Yes, I find them in the books and magazines that come to my store. They don't sell well. Most people think antiques mean only furniture. They're not interested in context."

"Were you at the Gatsby Picnic?"

"I was! Were you?"

"I was. Where were you?"

"I left at lunchtime – I made the mistake of buying a black car, and wearing all black to match."

"Oh! I met a woman wearing all white."

"I should have been as smart as her."

"She had gone to a lot of trouble."

"I always dress vintage. I don't have any other clothes now."

"Even at work?"

"I sell antiques, so I look the part."

"What about at home?"

"I wear my finest clothes – the clothes I won't expose to the public."

"Then don't bring them to Bayside. I mean, I am not saying you shouldn't come to Bayside. Actually, I wish you could lecture there, on aestheticism, context, or clothes: they're all in short supply."

Lucy appeared between them: "Clothes separate grown men from toddler men – the men who dress like my children. Excuse me, Teddi, but this grown man is obliged to meet the other single ladies

– as if he didn't know. And if he wasn't told, he should have worked it out for himself."

Lucy led him to the bar. Simon was bewildered with new faces, at a proximity that seemed to bother nobody but himself. Friends handled each other easily, while he leaned and twisted and shuffled until his back hurt. He explained himself so many times that he started to say "Bayside" with the local slur. He nostalgized the Covid lockdown.

In the hope of stretching his legs and finding Teddi, he suggested the ring around the dance floor. A dozen took the invitation, led by a weak legged but strong voiced woman who spoke excitedly and constantly of the discomforts and joys of vintage clothing, which ended with her showing her pantaloons.

"They are real," she insisted, "Feel for yourself."

A man of her age, but much taller, sat sullenly at her elbow, looking out the window, except to replace her drinks. Simon asked the man for directions to the restrooms, which enlivened the man as much as it depressed the woman. At the elevator, Simon managed to coincide with the only person on his mind.

"Teddi Theodora! May I escort you down?"

"You may."

In the lobby, she led him on a tour of the motifs and materials that were frequent in her presentation, up to the entrance, where they were blocked by two men arguing.

"I say the lobby is where I will put on my hat. You, sir, will be improperly dressed on the street."

"And I say that a gentleman doesn't wear his hat indoors. So, you, sir, will be improperly dressed before you get on the street."

"You, sir, are no gentleman," said the man with the greasy ponytail.

"You! You, sir, are no gentleman," said the man with the chandelier earring.

"No! You, sir, are no gentleman."

"No, really! You, sir, are no gentleman."

Simon indicated the way ahead with his hat, then put it on his head as he pushed on the revolving door. Outside, they realized that she faced the way to the ocean, while he faced the return towards the

Bay.

"Would you like me to escort you home?"

"No, thank you, that won't be necessary, but be careful your way."

"Well, goodnight then. I was pleased to meet you."

"I hope to see you at the next event: last Saturday of each month."

"Indeed, I'll be there."

"Goodnight."

"Goodnight."

He was a few blocks into his hike, slower than before, scanning the skyline in recognition of Teddi's images. Simon jumped as a skate-boarder passed, riding with a relaxed slump as if falling asleep, except occasionally to straighten his hips and kick the ground. At the next block, the unmistakable slump was stationary, with the board under one arm, in a crowd of parallel people, all shivering in damp cotton hoodies, in front of the steaming aperture of a food truck. Simon empathized until he saw prices beyond his weekly grocery bill.

One of them stepped into his way: "Oh, you look fantastic! Look at you! Wow! You've got the hat to go with the suit. You know, I've just had great news! My brother just had a baby in North Bay, but I lost my pocketbook, and, I hate to do this, I just need fifty dollars to get a cab over to the hospital. I'd take your address and mail you a check tomorrow, I swear."

"I'm not carrying any cash."

"Sweetheart, this is the Peninsula! This is how we roll, we help each other, people are different here."

"I heard the same in London." Simon continued to the crosswalk.

"Then go home, you yuppy faggot!"

The skateboarders swarmed to her raised voice like floppy angels of vengeance, but gave up, exhausted, at the corner, after a dozen steps. They waved their skateboards in triumph and resignation. One threw his skateboard into the street, jumped on, hit a manhole cover, and lay in front of traffic calling for witnesses to sue the city. His peers expressed their support from the food truck. Simon watched warily from the other side, before realizing the status quo. He continued on his way, and quickly found anonymity in numbers.

Yet the dissonance between anonymity and alertness continued for nearly two hours, until he stepped inside the cottage late that night, after putting his shoes in a bucket of detergent.

18. Extremism

On Tuesday, Simon returned from his class on Western-Asian Relations to see an email from Joe, asking if he would be willing to take over the remaining classes in the course on "Right-Wing Extremism." Simon started to type his unwillingness to succeed another drunk, when he decided he should walk over to explain in person.

Joe took care to listen without interrupting, despite confirmation of what he would say: "I'm aware of what happened in that class. I approved Hattie's suggestion that you should teach Western-Asian Relations. The issue with Right-Wing Extremism is different: Walter needs more time with his family, no fault of his own. You should meet him – he may tell you more."

"I see. Well, I should add that Jimmy had not wanted me to teach my course on 'Counter-Terrorism and Counter-Extremism' while he had a course on 'Right-Wing Extremism'."

"I've told Jimmy that you're a WISP lecturer, which means you'll teach courses that must be creditable to all majors."

"Then can I set my own syllabus?"

"Of course. Any students who choose to drop the course can take a half-credit in 'Right-Wing Extremism.' The rest can stay to take a full-credit in 'Counter-terrorism and Counter-extremism'."

Thence, Simon found himself adapting another syllabus. He went into the library to check the availability of books, then he browsed aimlessly in the cool basement, waiting for the hour when he was due to meet the instructor. Simon walked across the darkening but still hot campus to the hotels and bars on the other side. He found "The Free Leech" – a faux Tudor frontage, cast from concrete and painted in two tones of brown, without hint of its purpose. Through a genuine wooden door, Simon found himself at the corner of a cloistered courtyard, full of tables and chairs under the open sky, but gloomier than outside. The only artificial lighting came from small lamps along the walls of the cloisters, and gas burners glowing above the tables. The courtyard was already alive with students, but it was also the sort of place where faculty could feel obscure.

Simon walked carefully along one cloister, comparing the faces with what he remembered of the photograph on WISP's website.

Since Walter had invited him to talk over a drink, Simon stopped at the bar, which emerged on the far side of the courtyard as a lonely and repellent place. The hot black vinyl on the stools made him think of soft tar; and the wooden top of the bar seemed to be sweating through its varnish.

"Hello – Simon?"

"Yes."

"I'm Walter Fontaine – I'm sorry, I am on Bayside time, when you were probably on clock time." The words came with a smile and a listlessness whose incongruity would continue to intrigue Simon. The smile seemed to fight against a face too gaunt and worn to accommodate it, too defensive of its vertical creases. Simon saw spectacles before eyes – round glasses in which the eyes seemed to float to the surface, beyond a large pointed nose, as if they were straining to arrive first, motivated by earnestness of communication. The eyes were almost everything, as the body sloped away from the neck to the hips, within a large black sweatshirt, over baggy trousers of the same material.

"Walter – how do you do?"

"I'm fine – how are you?" He sat on a vinyl stool. Slowly, Simon did the same. "Can I buy you a drink?"

"No, thank you – it's too hot for me."

"I wouldn't normally."

"Thank you for meeting before Thursday. I'll be glad for your advice before I take over your course."

"Thank you for taking it over. I never thought I would be in this situation, but it's best for the students. Joe tells me you know what you are doing."

"I'll be glad to release time for you to spend on more important things."

"There's nothing more important to me than this course." Walter recognized Simon's dissonance at such hyperbole. "I've been teaching it every year as long as there's been a PAX. I was one of the founders of PAX, you know. I am one of the few people who still gives peace a chance. But I need a break."

"Everyone is saying that around this time of the semester."

"Oh no, it's not that. This course energizes me – I just need to take

off more time than the course can bear. And I don't control when."
Walter turned to lean on the bar, diminutive and morose.

Simon felt both selfishly alarmed and selflessly sympathetic. "I'll
be glad for your advice."

"Don't get married in the State of Sunshine!" Walter's eyes and
head settled back. "Don't get divorced in the State of Sunshine." He
turned to Simon, with half a smile. "You meant the course, didn't
you? You hadn't heard?"

"No, I'm sorry."

"Don't be sorry, it's not your fault. Everybody else seems to
know." He smiled as pleasantly as a father to a trusted son-in-law.
"The course, then. What do you want to know?"

"Well, you see, I am more experienced in teaching about the
extremisms that tend to terrorism, and I would be most comfortable
continuing with that, but I don't want to repeat any of the 'right-
wing extremisms' that you've taught already?"

"That's easy. All terrorism starts with right-wing extremism."

"Such as?"

"The religious right."

"Which religion?"

"The Christian Right – anti-abortionists, campaigners against the
separation of church and state, those who segregate churches as
white spaces."

"What about the Christian Left?"

"What Christian Left?"

"I know Britain's Christian Left: levelers and egalitarians, for
instance."

"Egalitarianism isn't extreme."

"The point is: Christianity can be either left- or right-wing."

"Not in America. This semester we're looking at the rise of
Clashmore Hickling – the presidential candidate. He is the Christian
Right! Just compare him to his opponent – Trixie Downer. She's not
Christian or right-wing. So, there you go."

"What about the Christian socialists who aligned with
communism?"

"That sounds like political science. I'm an anthropologist; I teach
cultures. Don't forget that the students' field projects are funded by

the Centre for Right-Wing Extremism Studies."

"What about the Centre for Left-Wing Studies?"

"There isn't one."

"So, who would fund field projects into non-Christian terrorism, say?"

"All religious terrorism is right-wing, so you'd be alright there."

"Even Islamist terrorism?"

"Yes, of course!"

"Islamists don't identify wings, only religions. So far as their politics can be placed on the conventional spectrum, they seem collectivist, redistributive, centralized, and transnational – closer to left than right."

"Yes," Walter said agreeably, leaning forward with intent to please, "but their religion is right-wing."

"As for the secular terrorists, Soviet Communism has inspired most of them."

"Ah!" said Simon, raising his finger in triumph. "But Soviet Communism is a right-wing reaction against Marxism!"

"I'll be glad to take over your course, Walter, and to give you the break you deserve."

"Thank you, Simon, I haven't had a break in twenty years." He looked down again. "I've already given up my other courses for the year."

"Won't you lose your salary?"

"No – I'm tenured."

"Lucky you."

"Not really." He turned to look at Simon with a strained but earnest smile that was heart-breaking, then the whole story tumbled out like a purge. He was getting divorced: he had left the family home because his wife had asked for time alone: her only explanation was that she felt like she "was walking on egg-shells." He was glad to give her the time alone. She asked for a week. Then he found she had changed the locks. She said she did not want him back, but she did not want to divorce. She bombarded him with grievances one day, adorations the next.

"What were the grievances?" Simon asked.

"That I never loved her, I never respected her, I was just like every other man," Walter stuttered. Simon wondered whether her accusation hurt Walter more than his admission of what she had said. Walter paused, before he returned to his story. She had refused to buy him out of the joint mortgage or to return the money she had taken out of the joint bank account. Simon asked why he could not make it a criminal matter, but, as his lawyer had told him, "private property ceases on marriage." The money was community property – the quicker she spent it, the less would be subject to distribution, and the family court would order financial disclosure for no earlier than three months.

After a year of trying to negotiate personally, Walter filed for uncontested divorce, but she contested. "I understand what she was saying about the paternalist society, I was just hurt that she blamed me, so I lashed out by asking for a divorce. I provoked her."

Whenever they got to court, she raised new issues, so neither side could rest, and the judge was forced to schedule new hearings, months into the future. In between times, she would file new issues with the court by mail. Simon asked why the judge could not refuse the new issues as frivolous, but, as Walter's lawyer had put it, "the State of Sunshine allows everyone to have their say." Walter's mistake was to tell the truth.

Walter was spending more time writing legal responses than teaching, and most of his salary on his lawyer, who otherwise threatened to drop the case.

Walter admitted shyly that he retained a criminal lawyer too. His wife had said in family court that he had abused her. The judge refused to admit any such claim against Walter, but admitted her narrative of abuse "for the record." She had copied some of that narrative to his colleagues, and posted copies on his office door and in his classrooms, which were always discoverable on the university's website. He had consulted the University of Sunshine Police Department, which claimed it could not intervene in free speech.

Her visits to campus seemed to disturb Walter most. Simon kept asking why Walter could not spend more time off campus, until he admitted that he was sleeping in the office, to save money and to escape the neighborhood where he might run into friends. "As one of them said to me, 'She wouldn't be so angry if she were lying'."

With this final admission, Walter's nervous energy ran out. He slumped exhausted over the bar. His head, which had a natural drop to it anyway, settled horizontally. Simon was alarmed and uncertain: was this a clinical matter, psychological or physiological, or situational, or all things? He had no evidence from the other party, but he was in no doubt of the sincerity of this party. Walter spoke again, without moving: "I always thought: we're both so enlightened, so what could go wrong?"

Simon insisted on walking Walter back to his office building, but there Walter insisted on proceeding inside alone. "I don't want you to see where I sleep." With a flat smile and affectionate eyes, he took Simon's hand in both of his, wished Simon a good night, a good experience at US Bayside, and a rewarding experience with the rest of the course. His final words were: "Keep peace alive!"

Simon could not shake Walter's story. He calmed his subconscious by resolving to lecture in the methods course on observations, evidence, proof, hearsay, context, judgments, and interpretations. In the classroom, Simon was surprised to find a large box fan on the table: a student explained that she was lending it for the duration of the course. He placed it in front of a window, and directed it diagonally across the room. That evening, he received an email from the DAFI service granting to a student extra time on all assignments due to "physical assault by artificial airflow."

After class, he hurried through the sunshine and dawdled in the shadows, trading off the urgency to get back inside and the lethargy to keep cool. The WISP mezzanine was dark, except he found Joe in his office, with the door open. Joe turned his head to the side, his hands still on the keyboard, motionless, except for some facial quiver of recognition.

"You don't check your email during the day, do you? Walter was killed this morning, shot in the face, in the doorway of his office. His wife walked to the Police Department to turn herself in. She says she couldn't help herself given his refusal to release her from an abusive marriage. It's a good defense."

Joe turned to his computer sadly, then looked back sharply: "She couldn't implicate you, could she?"

19. FBI CT

Simon was early for his first class on Counter-terrorism and Counter-extremism. He connected his computer to the projector, as normal, then looked out of the window, with his hands behind his back, placidly self-aware. At ten minutes past the hour, he turned about, silently, and waited for the students to pay attention.

"Professor Fontaine should have been here, to help me to explain the handover of his course, but he was killed, before he could complete the course that he loved, which he had taught annually for twenty years. Please let us remember him, together, with a minute's silence."

Aurelia and Judiciary rose quickly; the other students followed quietly. Simon watched the clock, every tick, while the corridor reverberated with the crash of a sprung door, a phone call, the slap of a bag dropped on the floor.

"Thank you. This is where the new course begins."

"Professor Fontaine's death was terrible," said Nicole, "for me. It's only right that I speak first, because I'm an English lit. major, so I know how to express myself. And I already started a thesis about my struggle against extremism, to counter the conventional narrative."

"Not yet," interjected Aurelia. "We'll organize a healing circle later."

"I agree," said Judiciary. "Let the professor talk about the course."

"But we're all victims!" exclaimed a student to the rear.

Her neighbor reached to touch her hand: "Wait: terrorists are victims too."

Boyan stood up at the rear. "Yeah, I'd just like to say, I'm a victim of terrorism. You see, I'm from Europe, you get me? And Asia; and America. They all have terrorism."

A student put up her hand politely: "Is this when we all get A-grades?"

"As WISP has informed you all by email, everyone can take an A-grade for half a C.U., by declaring on your honor that you attended all of Professor Fontaine's classes." The questioner packed up and departed.

"Or you can continue through my course, for a full C.U., as graded by me."

"Unless you get killed too," said a student, somewhere between a proposition and a question.

"Yes," said Simon, "I suppose if I get killed, you'd all be entitled to A-grades for this half-CU too."

"Awesome," said the student, settling into her chair.

Another student raised her hand: "I've heard from your other classes that you have expectations."

"You'll find my expectations on this syllabus. See here: these readings are required, these assignments are mandatory. I will be taking attendance, as described here. I expect you to read the syllabus, in your own time, before next class, and the required readings for that class. Here are the readings for next class. The most important thing you should consider now is: Do you want to learn about terrorism in general, or right-wing extremism alone? If the former, please stay. I will lecture now, given a segue from my other course, on Asian terrorism."

"I take offense," said a student. "Not all Asians are terrorists!" She departed.

Simon came home to a DAFI email granting to a student extra time on all assignments due to post-traumatic stress disorder, caused by the realization that she too is a victim of terrorism.

The next morning, he opened an email asking if he could be available for a chat on campus sometime at his convenience. Simon had never heard of Martin Barmouth, and was moved to delete a typical academic presumption, except that Martin wrote with courtesy. Simon read down to see that the sender was a Special Agent of the FBI. He replied that he was free that day. Immediately, Martin Barmouth emailed to ask to meet at lunchtime, at a place of Simon's choosing. Simon suggested the Faculty Club.

Simon walked to campus, up the hill, alongside the stream, across the lawn, and into the Faculty Club. Simon knew this building as a landmark, but not a destination. It seemed like the origin of campus, in a hollow, surrounded by redwoods older than the city. The felled trees had become the log walls, floor planks, and shingles. Simon stepped unhurriedly along the corridor, enjoying each creak and crack. The planks ran past a reading room on the right, a dining hall on the left, which looked out through glass doors on to a wooden terrace, and thence – through a filter of maple trees – the lawn. Above each door frame, stained-glass filtered the otherwise unbearable midday sunlight, and splashed the colorful shields of the Ivy League on to the floor.

Two men came through the lobby, looking up and about, until they met Simon's estimation. They were dressed like they were ready to hike, and they moved like they hiked regularly.

"Professor Ranald?"

"I am! How did you recognize me?"

"Your face is online."

"Ah yes, and my department, office, classroom, and class times."

"I guess so!"

"Special Agent Barmouth, I presume?"

"Please call me Martin." Martin took Simon's hand, but motioned to the other man: "This is my squad leader, John Gard."

"Please call me John. We appreciate you meeting with us on short notice. We know how important your vocation is."

"Oh, I really can't say I feel comfortable being told I'm important at the best of times, let alone by the FBI."

"No vocation is more important," said John.

"I suspect you've got our vocations the wrong way around." Simon snapped to attention as the lobby door opened again. "Perhaps I should get you out of this corridor, and show you something more interesting. I was pondering that terrace out there. I haven't tried it yet, but we might find shade and space. I wasn't sure, but I hoped a Faculty Club would give us better options than we're used to on campuses."

"Absolutely! Looks good, sounds good, smells good. Please lead the way, we're in your hands," said John.

Simon continued down the corridor to the buffet. They took what they wanted, and paid by the plate. They escaped the busy dining room through the glass doors, to a cast-iron table in the far corner of the deck, flanked by maples.

Simon spoke up, as they were still taking their seats: "Actually, I am Dr. Ranald, not professor, just to be clear, but in any case, call me Simon, please. The titles are for students to use."

"Likewise," said John. "Please call us by our first names."

"Just so I know, what titles would I tell my students to use if you spoke to them?"

"'Special Agent' will do," said John.

Martin lent in: "Our titles are for the criminals to chew on when we first interview them. Actually, John is a Supervisory Special Agent."

"But it doesn't matter," said John.

"Because you command a squad?" asked Simon.

"Pretty much."

"May I ask how the squad is titled?"

"We do counter-terrorism."

"Oh! So you want to talk to my course?" Simon exclaimed eagerly, then sank embarrassed.

"No, we want to talk about your course," quipped Martin.

"Oh dear! You want me to give the FBI more time in the syllabus?"

"No, nothing like that," John offered. "Look, we wanted to get to know you first, but we're on point now, so we might as well get on with it." John looked at Martin, who lent in to speak.

"The thing is: you've been targeted, by a violent extremist group – because of your course." Martin let his words trail off apologetically, turned up his palms, and paused.

Simon rushed to reassure. "I am not unfamiliar with this sort of thing. I've had some anonymous threats before. I never thought to escalate any – as a criminal matter, because I could tell they didn't deserve to distract your good-selves. You can't teach counter-terrorism without upsetting extremists!"

"Right," said Martin. "But this is a local group, and it's personal: it's identified you as a 'fascist' because your scope is beyond right-wing terrorism."

"Words to that effect," said John.

"Most of the cases are neither left nor right, but religious."

"We don't doubt it," said John. "Don't over-analyze this, how this came to be, or anything else except what it is. You've done nothing wrong. You don't deserve this. But you're not going to persuade anyone beyond us. You can't reason with these people, and you can't change their incentives – that's our job. They're only interested in the interpretation that is most convenient to them."

"I started the course only yesterday."

"These groups – they spread misinformation through social media like wildfire."

"Yes, I know. I mean, everything you're saying I knew already – theoretically. How do you know this so quickly yourselves?"

"We can't tell you that yet," said John. "Have you noticed anything abnormal?"

"Well, a student did ask me whether she'd get an automatic A-grade if I were killed."

"Did you take that as a threat?"

"I took it as self-interest – it's normal."

"Don't assume an instigator that you know. One of your students – or colleagues – could have posted something praising what you're doing, but these people – whatever they find, they misrepresent."

Martin nodded: "Some of their comms were to the effect that you had shifted a course that had been against fascism into a course favoring fascism."

"Pretty much," said John.

Simon nodded, so Martin continued: "And that you had colluded to kill the previous instructor in order to take control of the course."

Simon remained motionless, except his eyes wandered aimlessly across the table. He felt them, but could not control them.

Martin started again: "Don't take it personally, this is just for your understanding. According to them, you're the terrorist, they're countering the terrorists."

"Who are they?"

"They call themselves the 'Fascist Fighters'; or 'FaFi' for short."

"Do they say 'Fascist Fighters' or 'Fascism Fighters'?"

"Actually, both."

"But they're different meanings."

"They use both interchangeably."

"How ironic."

"Right!"

"I've never heard of them."

"Keep behaving as if you've never heard of them. Don't call them out, don't refer to them – you'd only draw more attention. We want this to blow over."

"You said they're local – you mean Bayside?" They nodded. "City of Bayside or University of Sunshine Bayside?"

"Both," said Martin, "You can't be one but not the other."

"Then why haven't I heard of them?"

Martin looked at John and sat back. John lent forward, grimaced at the floor, placed his palms on the table, raised his eyes, and spoke softly. "Neither authority admits the FaFi on their lists of known violent extremists. The city says that if any FaFi exist in this area, they must be on campus, which is not a city problem. The university says no FaFi are on campus, so they must be the city's problem. Both have embargoed their intelligence."

"From the FBI?"

"From everybody. We can't speak for them or their intelligence. What we can tell you is that everything we've told you so far has come from our own intelligence."

"You mean to tell me that the city and university don't cooperate with the feds on counter-terrorism?"

"Not on counter-terrorism, not on counter-trafficking, not on counter-narcotics, not on anything – at least not until a particularly violent crime inside their jurisdiction."

Martin cut in: "Then they want a federal indictment."

"And FBI SWAT to arrest, search, and seize."

"These particular Fascist Fighters – have they perpetrated violent acts already?"

"They are perps, but intelligence is not evidence, at least not sufficient evidence to interest a federal prosecutor – yet."

"You've never arrested a Fascist Fighter?"

"Not in this area."

"Can I get a gun?"

"I can't advise you on that, but it wouldn't help you here: State law prohibits firearms on any site of education."

"What do you want me to do?"

"Just sit tight, but keep aware. Remember, the chances are that nobody you know is instigating this, but if you find someone suspicious, contact us directly. We'll give you our business cards."

"Thank you, I understand. Now, please eat; you must be frustrated, seeing it's right in front of you, without getting stuck in."

20. Optimists Club

Chancellor Berk was feeling optimistic. He always looked forward to meetings, this one particularly. He thanked himself that he had reached that step in his career when meetings were no longer run by people less effective than himself. He was determined to write a book on leadership, once he had time away from leading to think about how to lead.

All meetings are good, he reflected, but some are special. He had his weekly meetings with vice-chancellors, reports from exceptional sub-committees, emergency meetings of emergency committees, the monthly dinner at the university president's official mansion up the hill (even if Metro were out of town), the annual dinner with the trustees, the dinners with visiting speakers (if prominent enough), occasional delegations from the State Capitol, and receptions for national politicians reaffirming their liberal credentials.

The Golden Sun was a cooling, healing sun for those who had strayed. Chancellor Berk often said that he was enlightened enough to see everyone as equal, except the unenlightened. They could not see anything outside the dazzle of the untamed sun – the only sun their ancestors had known. Sure, they could feel warmed for a while, dazzled by brightness, pulled by mass, but inevitably its vicious core would lose its restraint, until, wham – a solar flare would reach out. They might as well be enjoying the warming tingle inside a microwave with a broken timer, or swimming in a pool pleasantly heated by spent fuel rods, or admiring the mushroom cloud between the flash and the blast.

Of course, a galaxy with only one sun is natural, but who wants natural? Progress is unnatural! Progress demands an extra sun, an artificial sun, a better sun. History is clear on the future: civilization is a struggle between the hot power we inherit and the cool enlightenment we create, and the future is cool.

That's why so many university chancellors are historians, he realized. (He reminded himself to remind his guests.) That's why he had chosen to stick with a public university. (He realized he should phrase this differently to his guests.) Other universities were more powerful, but his was the coolest. A public university is enlightened, because its private interests can be hidden. That's why his university was ranked as the greatest public university – as voted by academics. That's why he had stuck with it, despite inferior resources. (He reminded himself not to include the last clause in his story.)

Chancellor Berk most enjoyed the final hour before a meeting: he would unite his attention, and put his legendary free-spirited leadership skills to the task. He stopped fluttering with trivia in his office, and joined his staff in the conference room.

Underneath an enormous gilded sun on the ceiling, he pushed the papers around the conference table: his article on the progressions and regressions in American history ("If you're not progressing, you're regressing," he concluded); a summary of the "100 years of light" that Bayside had cast since its founding ("The only acceptable darkness is skin deep," he concluded); a press release on Bayside's ranking (selected years); the Institute for Government's warnings against "populism"; a survey showing the overwhelming opposition from faculty and students to "populism"; his own commentary on the current political trend to "populism"; and his own vision for a democracy in which popular choices are not so objectionable as to be categorized as populist.

He directed his staff to arrange the copies in front of each guest. Then he wrote on the whiteboard: "The Long View: The Historical Inevitability: Optimism: Progress: A Historian Leads."

This meeting was particularly special because it was his inaugural gathering of the region's most enlightened technology leaders and most enlightened education leaders, henceforth to be known as the "Optimists Club." Everything that Berk had rehearsed in his mind over the final hour he unleashed on his guests. "Fellow optimists! We cannot wait for Davos. We cannot wait for Sundance. We cannot wait for Secretary Metro to return from her listening tour. We need to discuss now, here, under the Golden Sun, how to save this country from pessimistic shadows. I have gathered the most enlightened faculty and tech leaders together – no scientists, just influencers."

Tom Pinklewonk was most prepared for this agenda: "We must shine the way to the election! We need to spread positive messages about Trixie. She's a very positive woman. I remember how positive she was at law school. She was positively frothing at the mouth against the right-wing."

"I am not be as old as you," said Aimee Pharisees, "but, let me tell you, I was more enraged at grad. school than anyone. I grew up in America! The sexism was something you men wouldn't believe. So I moved to the Middle East."

"Oh, nobody was more enraged by prejudice than me," said Hattie Maddux. "That's why I took up Asian Studies: I mean, there's no white racism in Asia. That's why I self-identify as Asian. I have always said that the only good white male was Foucault. Don't take any notice of his hyper-masculine behavior. We shouldn't judge a philosopher by his private life, otherwise we wouldn't be able to trust anybody. We should judge what he said rather than what he did."

"Hear, hear!" said Jimmy Pons.

Tom Pinklewonk rushed to usurp Jimmy. "We should judge Trixie the same way," he said.

"I hate white males too!" said Will Juncker eagerly. "I mean, growing up, I couldn't have been more enraged – I mean, Luxemburg is so white! And male! And poor Trixie: the sexism she has to deal with. Just watch any political debate: Trixie is always getting patronized, and ignored, and..."

"Manterrupted," said Hattie.

"Thank you," said Chancellor Berk. "Thank you, our five most enlightened educators. Now let me introduce you to our five most enlightened tech-leaders, who are also, I am delighted to announce, our five newest trustees."

Rob Partsome of BeLitter settled back into his chair, his hands hanging over the sides, as if normally he would be holding a cigar in one, a tumbler of whiskey in the other. He always knew what to say in these situations: "BeLitter stands shoulder to shoulder with all those oppressed by sexism and racism. Your enemy is traditional media. They focus on bad news. That's where social media is different. We encourage users to express themselves spontaneously, then we promote the Belitters that we like. Good news all around! And we ban anybody who says different. And BeLitter will give this university a million dollars in free ads., to promote whatever it likes."

Jean Cadhowling of SheepOnline jumped in. "Oh yeah, I'll give you just as many on SheepOnline. Sure – anything for progress."

Josh Chubfuddler of Tracebook nodded energetically with an awkward smile, before sudden reversion to pallid passivity. His audience continued to wait on him. Berk pushed a carton of juice his way, then opened it, then punched the straw through the top, then placed it in his hands. Josh Chubfuddler sucked. He looked up at his audience, opened his lips, closed his lips, swallowed, then spoke quickly. "At Tracebook, we don't want to interfere with the content that our users are sharing. We want to help our users share information, because a community is built on the sharing of information. We're not responsible for our users' content; but some of our users are hateful, and we'll declare their content unsafe; let us know if you see anything unsafe. We're in the education business too."

Rod Sorrie jumped in: "Education remains our priority. I couldn't have built MicroSorrie without educated workers. As everybody knows, I came here to find them. I walked into the engineering lounge and said: 'I left here as a freshman to join the computer revolution – so can you!'"

"We're so enthusiastic," said Jill Sorrie of the Sorrie Foundation. "What education needs is enthusiastic educators!" That line always made her most enthusiastic. "Rod knows how enthusiastic I am to spend his money."

"Before you spend any money, try our free ads.," said Rob Partsome. "You might be surprised how enthusiastically people spend their money while you appear to be spending yours. We'll help you configure the ads.: images of enthusiastic educators, hashtag 'enthusiastic educators'."

"At SheepOnline, we're encouraging images over text. And not just because I am an artist – I mean, I don't paint or anything, but I support the arts. A single painting can bear witness. Why explain that Trixie is the only female candidate when a picture of the candidates makes it obvious?"

"I prefer pictures of the female candidates," said Jimmy Pons. "They're empowering, for women too."

Tom Pinklewonk usurped again, but sounded somewhat desperate. "I like Trixie!"

Josh Chubfuddler unintentionally helped him out. "Yes, she has positive ideas about the freedom of social media."

"We're going to give this country a female president no matter what," said Hattie Maddux. "If women want equality, they need to vote for every female option. We are united! Anybody who disagrees is divisive."

"A Muslim president!" countered Aimee Pharisees.

"Let's get our first female President!"

"Muslim first!"

"We can't drop Trixie now," said Rob Partsome of BeLitter, imperiously. "Our analysis shows that users have Belittered more negative comments about Trixie than any other candidate. That proves she's leading the fight against sexism."

"It also proves," Chancellor Berk said, putting his finger on the articles copied on the table, "that she's leading the fight against populism. Populists manipulate popular concerns. We must beat them to it! My historic writings, and Tom's economic writings, are the most popular on social media. Now that's leadership."

"But what bothers me," Pons said quietly, "is that populism has become popular during your leadership, Chancellor."

Berk sat up defensively. "I believe in change!"

"At the top, Chancellor?"

"No! Not me, not us! We are leading the change, so we don't need to change. Everyone else needs to change."

"Hear, hear," said Aimee and Hattie.

"If we are not changing, how can we know we are not regressing? We need to make change normal!"

"What the public needs is enthusiasm for change," said Jill Sorrie.

"We're ready to invest in that enthusiasm," said Rod Sorrie.

"We'll provide the media," said Rob Partsome. "Hashtag 'change is good'!"

"Hashtag 'life is good if only you zombies would realize.'"

"That's too long, surely?" asked Jimmy.

"Hashtag anything positive," interjected Tom Pinklewonk. "Populists are exploiting the rise in crime to make people feel insecure, so we need to point out that crime is rising as people feel empowered to challenge the system."

"Agreed," said Aimee Pharisees. "All female prisoners are victims of domestic abuse. So, really, when you think about it, going to prison is empowering for women. I know because I studied them. They are more dignified, noble, respectful, and loving than popular culture admits. The evidence is in my photographs and interviews: I felt so loved."

"I would love that!" said Jimmy Pons.

Tom Pinklewonk interrupted: "I would love it more! I met a criminal once: she had been in and out of prison for most of her twenties and thirties on a dozen charges."

"What an ordeal!"

"The solution is to get more women into university. Their proportion still hasn't reached 60 percent."

"I've got a lesson from our police department," said Berk. "Put a trigger warning on all crime alerts – to the effect that they might contain information that some readers might find upsetting. Then people are less likely to notice crime."

"Take a different issue," said Rod Sorrie. "Take slavery – the news media keep reporting the rising costs of modern slavery, but not my Foundation's purchases of slaves out of slavery."

"I'm determined to use BeLitter to publicize the evil of guns," said Rob Partsome. "Just ask my bodyguards: I hate to see their guns."

"I've got a message," said Pons. "All immigrants are hot young entrepreneurs."

"I've got an idea," interrupted Pinklewonk. "Let's focus on what healthcare can do, rather than what it costs."

"Yes, focus on life expectancy, not ill-health," said Rod Sorrie

"Focus on fewer communicable diseases, rather than more avoidable diseases," said Jill Sorrie.

"In that case, the medical school should teach more communicable diseases, fewer avoidable diseases," added Rod Sorrie.

"I was alarmed to notice that the history department teaches wars," said Hattie.

Berk felt defensive, so he sought a collateral target. "Yes, but the political science department teaches the causes of war. That's just teaching people how to cause wars."

Tom Pinklewonk agreed. "We should be teaching open borders,

not wars. We should be focusing on the better angels of our nature. We should be desensitizing people to the risks."

"Yes," said Pons icily. He was upset to find himself agreeing with Pinklewonk, so he sought a collateral target. "Yes, Berk. Why is an enlightened university teaching criminology when the crime rates are rising?"

"Aha!" said Josh Chubfuddler with surprising vigor. "And why is the law school teaching more criminal law than entertainment law?"

"Why is an enlightened university teaching the exploitation of the working class?" asked Jimmy Pons.

Chancellor Berk rose to the challenge: "We're not!"

"You've got a business school!"

Berk sat on the edge of his seat, clutching the arm rests. "Oh yeah?! Well, you run a department teaching terrorism!"

"Counter-extremism!" cried Jimmy.

"And terrorism."

"Counter-extremism and counter-terrorism!"

"If you're teaching counter-terrorism then you must be teaching terrorism!"

"Yeah?! Well, Guillaume Juncker is Director of WISP, which authorized the course for all WISP majors!"

"It's nothing to do with me! I sit in the geography department."

"Oh!" said Jill Sorrie sadly. "I couldn't be enthusiastic about teaching terrorism,".

"Terrorism is a traditional construct," said Aimee Pharisees.

Hattie Maddux nodded: "Terrorism is what society wants us to think."

"Well, you can't blame social media, "said Josh Chubfuddler. "We provide a forum for the free flow of information: that's the best thing for terrorism."

Rob Partsome leaned in: "There's no money in information about terrorism, unless you mean to help the government, and we know where that would end."

"Yes, Jimmy," said Chancellor Berk, "You see? You're helping authoritarianism!"

"It's Will's responsibility!" said Pons.

"I'm not taking responsibility, but I am taking authority: I will cancel any course on counter-terrorism."

"That's so optimistic," smiled Berk, and everybody agreed.

21. ICE

By email, Guillaume Juncker instructed Simon to tell the students that the course on counter-extremism and counter-terrorism would end forthwith, and they would get A-grades. He added that Simon should consider returning home early, due to lack of demand for his courses. He noted that Simon's work visa was valid only so long as he taught.

Separately, Juncker emailed all of WISP's faculty to announce a faculty meeting for Monday. Simon replied that he would look forward to seeing him for only the second time this semester. Simon had not encountered his peers since the WISP reception six weeks earlier, except occasionally as one was coming in as another was going out, and all one could think to say was, "Are you going to teach?" or "Are you coming from teaching?" The answers left nobody much wiser.

Faculty meetings are scheduled on Mondays to minimize attendance. Faculty, like students, prefer their weekend to run from Thursday to Tuesday. A minority choose classes on Mondays because they expect smaller classes. Department chairs authorize classes on Mondays for the instructors they want at Monday meetings. Director Juncker chose this Monday because it was listed on a British academic calendar as "half-term," which, he was misinformed, was a quaint annual holiday observed by Britons to celebrate the mid-point of Queen Victoria's first pregnancy. He was not amused, so never realized the joke.

The sunshine was strong, like peak English summer, even though the sun ticked low and slow towards the shallow hump of its autumn trajectory. The city was unhurried, the campus too. Simon entered the conference room on time, to find it empty, except a side table colorful with food. He helped himself, before Earnest Keeper and Prisha Pradesh entered together.

"Oh, hello," said Simon. "Are you coming from teaching?"

"No. Are you?"

"No."

They were followed by Jewel Lighter, who walked in quickly with her shoulders back and her chin high. She sat down quietly with a bare smile, took out a little notebook, and sat still.

She was followed immediately by unfamiliar faces – insecure, young, erratic faces, approaching the salad like they were entering new pasture, at the bottom of the food chain, mindful of their backs.

Hattie Maddux never arrived; none of the major chairs arrived. On Bayside time, Joe and Alison arrived amiably but with occasional coughs and sniffles. Last to arrive was Guillaume Juncker, tall and stumbling with mock weariness. He had paused to permit Joe and Alison first, to sit towards the far end of the table, so he could sit magnanimously at its head. He socialized to left and right but did not mingle, as if he were too tired. He smiled through the pain, raised his eyes slowly, let them drop quickly, and rubbed them slowly one minute, quickly the next.

The schedule did not matter, until he sensed that Simon was approaching. He rapped on the table: "Far be it for me, as the chair, to get us back on schedule!"

He paused for laughter.

"Welcome to the middle of the semester. Nine weeks from today, we'll be turning in grades, and looking forward to a well-earned break." He smiled at one corner of his mouth, as if biting down at the same time. He looked up, looked down, and rubbed his eyes.

"So, it's time for our first meeting of this semester, so that you're prepared for the main half of the semester, now that the add-drop period is over. Now, you can start teaching for real, knowing that they can't escape!"

He paused for laughter, then cut it short with a look of despair.

"But don't forget that teaching is very stressful for students. They lost their liberty to drop courses just as you hit them with mid-term assignments, so expect a surge in mental health problems."

He paused for sympathy.

"Particularly encourage minorities to realize their special needs. The trouble is: they don't realize they're victims until you tell them. But if you advertise the accommodations, you'd be surprised how many admit them."

He paused wisely. Then, he told stories of how wise he had been in the previous year.

"Which leads me to relay the unpleasant news that we can expect undocumented immigrants to be particularly stressed this week.

The university has passed on intelligence that the Immigration and Customs Enforcement agency is planning to raid campus this week – possibly dorms, possibly classrooms, we don't know. So, sensitize all your students, encourage them to admit their stress, encourage them to miss classes. Every student will know an undocumented immigrant, so extend your accommodations to all students. Oh, and you should probably begin the announcement with a trigger warning, so the students can prepare emotionally or leave class before the rest of the announcement."

He paused for sympathy.

"If you see a truck labelled 'ICE' or any uniform other than campus police, you should call a new number in the campus directory. It's easy to remember as 'NOT NICE'. Just give your location. The 'Rapid Reaction Responders' – the 'three Rs' – will come immediately. Don't put yourself between the feds and the victim, let the 'three Rs' do it. They've received special training. They know how to exploit the situation."

He paused for admiration.

"Think about replacing your classes with self-directed learning, until our classrooms are safe."

He told stories of how he had let students stay at home to teach themselves in the way they know best.

"Wow! Look at the time. I must go to another meeting. No, don't thank me! Yep, another higher meeting, so you don't need to."

He paused for laughter.

"I'm sorry that again we don't have time for questions, but please bring them to me. Remember: my door is always open. No, Simon, sorry – I have no time for you. I will leave you in the hands of Joe and Alison."

Joe and Alison seductively introduced a new online system for reimbursing travel funds. Simon realized that everyone but him had a travel fund; and that everyone had backlogged miscellaneous expenses. Simon asked if he could get a travel fund. Alison said that Professor Juncker had ruled that no visiting faculty were eligible. Joe smiled apologetically. The collective sense was impatience to spend travel funds, so the meeting broke up without anyone declaring its ending.

Simon went home to ponder his options, but could not come up with any. On Tuesday, he lectured on Western-Asian Relations, while pondering the justification for a travel fund to take his students to Asia, once his work visa would be cancelled.

On Wednesday, he lectured on the skills of argument. A student wanted to argue about the skills. That evening, he received an email from DAFI excusing the student from class on the grounds of "low self-esteem." Simon wondered whether he could use a travel fund to send students abroad.

On Thursday, he wondered what he would do with a travel fund to study terrorism. His wonder was masochistic, hours before the terminal class of counter-extremism and counter-terrorism. In the stuffy air of the windowless corridor outside the classroom, his truculence boiled.

"Simon Ranald?"

"Yes?"

"You're a fascist," said the voice, matter-of-factly.

Simon's hand and gaze were still on the door handle, his mind in its normal routine. Alarm took over. He spun around, imagining a face to match the voice. Instead, he saw a mask, sunglasses, and a hood. A similar manifestation registered either side, along with a sense of movement, the movement of approaching, of emerging, of multiplication from one to many, from one to three, from his front to his fringes. Then there was surprising stillness, and in the quiet a word registered in his mind as if spoken with perfect diction in his ear: "ice." The false auditory sense continued to resonate like a bell, as his mind focused on the chest of the nearest hoodie, whose filth partially obscured the word "slice," below the smaller words "Pizza by the." Simon's mind was alive with a wild mix of puzzlement and striving, even after he confirmed his decoding.

"You're a fascist."

"I'm an educator."

"I wouldn't take your class."

"I wasn't inviting."

"I wouldn't accept."

"Actually, you should come in – we're debating extremism."

"You're not worth debating."

"And yet you're here."

"To fight your fascism."

Suddenly the mask to the right jutted forward: "Fight fascism!" This voice was female. She hooked a gloved hand into the pocket of the man at center. A female voice on his other side repeated the line, then the three of them chorused, "Not on our campus!"

"You're a fascist!" said the male.

"You're a fascist!" said the chorus.

"You're the fascists, hiding your identities, intimidating, interrupting education. No, you will not delay this class."

Simon still had his hand on the door handle behind his back. He turned it now and stepped backwards into the room, caught in a foolish dilemma between the selfish desire to shut them out and the good manners to hold open doors. Into that gap the leader stepped; the other two stuck to him.

Simon had nowhere to go when his bottom bumped the edge of the table gently. The leader had nowhere to go, with his accomplices tight beside him.

"Since you're in my classroom, why don't you join the class and learn something?"

"We're not here to learn!"

"Not on our campus!" said the chorus.

"You're a bigot – and a lousy limey."

"I'm not really British!" cried Boyan.

"You're a fascist and a foreigner, bringing foreign fascism to America, and we're going to drive you off our campus."

"Not nice!" said Aurelia, standing.

Judiciary also stood. She took out her phone. "I know whom to call."

"Yes, dial 'NOT NICE'," said her neighbor.

"It's a raid!" said other students hysterically.

"Not on our campus!"

"I'm calling!"

"Everybody stick together!"

"Not on our campus!"

"Fascists!"

Everybody kept returning to the same accusation, emphatic and clear, until everybody was in chorus, although not in agreement.

Then the invaders faded away, inconclusively and unjustifiably. The Rapid Reaction Responders arrived later, breathless and unready, unadmittedly and gratefully late. They rotated cameras, phones, and documents between their hands and the pockets of their special yellow vests, stamped with the legend "University of Sunshine," around the symbol of the golden sun, containing the letters "RRR."

Simon explained that the invaders must be "Fascist Fighters." The responders rapidly reacted, with refutation. Documents in hand, they rediscovered their purpose in reassuring and resolving. The students were reinforced and revitalized to speak with ever more imagination.

"They were definitely cops – they had mirrored shades."

"And bad attitudes."

"Yeah, arrogant and aggressive."

"They were racists."

"The leader was wearing a vest labelled 'ICE'."

"And they looked like pigs – oink, oink, under their disguises: prejudicial pigs."

"They racially abused the professor!"

The three responders urged the students to sit, compare their stories, and get their stories straight, in fulfilment of the scenario for which they were employed. The three responders then consulted their manuals, and read out another three Rs: rest, reflection, and renewal. After much reading aloud and turning of pages, the three responders, newly confident but still sympathetic, told the students to go home and practice the three Rs.

They turned to Simon to suggest that he cancel the course.

"No! They were Fascist Fighters, and I'm not letting them close down education. That really would be a triumph for fascism."

"You're so brave!"

"So brave!"

"So brave!" chorused the three responders.

"But really," said the first responder, "You should cancel the course; we don't want to run over here again."

"We don't," said the second responder. "Surely you wouldn't expose the students to any more stress?"

"Canceling courses," said the third responder, "is so stress-relieving! They automatically get A-grades, you still get paid for the course, campus is safe, everybody's happy."

"What if I want to teach this course?"

"Then you'd be in violation of policy," said the first responder.

"And personally liable for stressing the students," said the second responder. "Remember: you're in a position of power over these students."

"That reminds me!" said the first responder. "You're obliged to notify DAFI about what happened, so that DAFI knows to accommodate all the students against stress."

"You should go home now – manage your stress. Cancel all your classes."

22. Anti-fed hero

Simon sat alone in the little cottage in the garden, wishing for little Lola's company, while the squirrels scampered across the roof with inconsistent speeds, as if searching for a way in. He was unwilling to work, but unwilling to do nothing. He turned on his computer resignedly.

Hundreds of emails were waiting for him. The sight made him even more fatigued. He had turned to bed early, with books that failed to distract him, waiting for exhaustion to triumph over exertion.

Now bloody-mindedness rose to the challenge: he deleted declarations of admiration, invitations to speak to student organizations, requests to interview with The Daily Sunshiner, requests to tell his story to The Bayside Blab, requests to speak to local television, requests to sit on panels, and vaguer requests to meet a real-life hero.

He searched the local media. The subjects clustered around "Education versus Fascism," "Love not Fascism," "What Fighting Fascism Can Teach Us About College Success," and "The Role of Big Data in Countering Federal Fascism." Suddenly, he turned his gaze away from the screen into the reflective eyes of a motionless squirrel outside the window. "Why am I reading this?" he asked out loud. The squirrel twitched. "I want to know what Teddi Theodora might read."

The campus newspaper was patient zero to the pandemic of reporting. He clicked on the link to The Daily Sunshine's online edition.

Hero Prof. Stops Fed. Raid!

Federal agents raided a classroom on campus yesterday, targeting a new course on countering extremism, taught by Simon Ranald, an Exchange Professor from England.

Dr. Ranald declined to comment, but one of his students, speaking anonymously for fear of federal retaliation, told us how Dr. Ranald blocked agents of the Immigration and Customs Enforcement agency (ICE) from entering the classroom. He resisted them long enough for some students to escape out of the windows. The rest stayed to bear witness and to alert campus administrators.

Dr. Ranald was finally over-powered and person-handled into the classroom, where he continued to stand between the feds and the students. In a rare deviation from what his students describe as "his normally mild manners," he pointed out that feds are fascists. The feds fled, once administrators from the new Rapid Reaction Response Office came to Professor Ranald's aid.

The Rapid Reaction Responders were unavailable for comment, having taken indefinite sick leave, given the stress of the incident.

Campus officials, who declined to speak on the record, told us that Professor Ranald was the target of the raid after he complained about federal mishandling of his work visa. The Office of the Vice-Chancellor for Employee Excellence without Stress confirmed that he is a legal employee and a legal entrant to the United States.

Other officials, speaking off the record, said that none of the students enrolled in the course are undocumented immigrants. They speculated that the feds might have intended to terrorize students generally with a random raid.

The Chancellor of the University of Sunshine Bayside, Dick Berk, released the following statement: "Sadly, this incident proves that this university's prophecies were fulfilled. Federal agents violated the sanctity of our campus, and the sanctity of education itself, just as we predicted. Fortunately, this university was well prepared. I thank the brave administrators and the professor involved. We're just glad that our systems worked perfectly and nobody was harmed."

The President of the University of Sunshine System, Mary Metro, released a statement at the same time: "I am deeply troubled by the federal government's decision to end the norm, from when I was in government, not to pursue undocumented immigrants. This backward-thinking, far-reaching move threatens to derail some of this country's brightest young minds. I call upon Congress to pass bipartisan legislation to ban ICE agents from university campuses."

A spokesperson for ICE released a statement, saying: "ICE has never sent agents on the University of Sunshine campus, and has never had any plans to send agents."

On page after page, the newspaper continued with more eye-witnesses than Simon had students. It reported reactions from unaffected students on how they were affected. It quoted from his non-existent friends on campus. It speculated about how he must feel. He tried to email a correction, but it was returned as fraudulent. He tried to BeLitter a correction, but his BeLitters disappeared even as his followers multiplied.

Simon looked out of the window again. The day was Friday. He did not need to leave the little cottage. He looked forward to shorter days, the cat's desire to spend more time indoors, and the sanctity of his own little campus – uninvaded and unreported. He returned to the screen. He rebuffed, denied, and ignored strange correspondents, but the emails arrived faster than he could read them.

He turned off his computer and relaxed in irresponsibility. He read from the collection of travel books on the shelves beneath the little dining table. Occasionally, he turned on his computer to purge his inbox, just for the thrill. He settled into the cycle, until he noticed that an email kept reappearing, every time he deleted it.

The Office of the President of the University of Sunshine System and the Office of the Chancellor of the University of Sunshine Bayside have instructed me to liaise with you in their cooperative award of funds in recognition of your unique contribution to the University of Sunshine Bayside.

A teaching fund has been released to enable you to continue to teach your valuable and salient course on "Countering Extremism."

A research fund has been allocated for you to lead research into how to counter extremism on campus.

A travel fund is commensurate with the research fund.

Simon took notice of the following emails. Millionaires were offering to fund his fight for academic freedom, corporations were offering donations to his anti-defamation fund, academics were asking him to co-sign their research proposals, students were offering to intern.

He took his time over the weekend to consider all these offers. On

Monday, Clara Mudd, from the Budgeting Office, emailed to explain that she had started the budget process for him to sign on Tuesday, for approval on Wednesday, so that he could restart his course on counter extremism on Thursday.

Inside the Budgeting Office, everybody knew Clara Mudd, but nobody had seen her. Eventually, he was directed to the desk of Lee Green. As Simon approached, Lee Green was caught side-on, stationary but leaning forward, considering whether he could run one urgent errand before the arrival of the next appointment. As he met Simon's gaze, he straightened up and shouted across to the next cubicle: "No, put it in email, for the record. She brought her own furniture to her office. The university didn't pay her to bring it in, so the university won't pay her to move it home."

He spun around, sat down, and started collecting files, a little breathless, but earnestly focused, without looking up, except to smile once with acknowledgement.

"So, you're my most urgent visitor of the day?"

"Oh, I sincerely hope not."

"Dr. Ranald?"

"Oh dear, then I suppose I am. But please call me Simon."

"Simon Ranald, yes. My name is Lee Green. I did get everything ready, I hope, but let's take a look."

Lee Green neatly arranged the documents on the desk facing Simon, before selecting one for placement in the center.

"This one – is this one for you too? Clara told me not to write any explanation for this one. Were you meant to do it?"

"Max Mira Publicity Management? I've never heard of that before, although the name seems familiar."

"Yes, he's a big donor, got his name on several classrooms. Don't worry: if you don't know about it you weren't meant to fill it in. He manages publicity, so he must be managing yours – I'll just write that in." He took it in hand.

"Do you want me to sign it?"

"That amount is ninety-nine thousand, nine hundred and ninety-nine dollars, so, no, nobody needs to sign that one. Same for this one, for Max Mira Protective Services. And for Max Mira Talent Management. This one for you, though, goes over one-hundred thousand, so we'll need your signature, my signature, Clara's signature, then higher approval. So, let's work down the list: your salary for this course, twenty-seven thousand, three hundred, and eighty-seven, you see, sign here."

"But that looks like two courses' salary, and we're more than half-way though the semester."

"Yep, well, that's what she's told me to budget, so that's what you're getting, for two semesters – this one and next."

"Oh! Then I suppose I am staying next semester."

"Oh, you are – all the files say so. Now this one: twenty thousand, five hundred and sixty-two, your share of an administrative assistant, both semesters, sign here. And your research fund is five thousand; as is your travel fund."

"What about the rest of the pledges – the other several thousand dollars?"

"That's overhead, but you don't need to sign for that. You sign for what is for your benefit."

"Oh! How will I spend my research fund and travel fund?"

"You spend your own money, then make a claim online for reimbursement. That's the current system: but those sorts of funds might get devolved to you as cash next semester, like they were devolved to us last year, but they might be centralized again next year – probably, maybe. My advice: just spend them as quickly as you can, because if they get centralized again, then by the time you get all the approvals you would need, the system might change. Simon, seriously: watch the system."

23. Publicity

"Simon? This is Max Mira."

"Hello? How did you get my private number?"

"I need your private number – I'm going to handle your publicity."

"Yes, I saw your contract."

"You did? Keep that private."

"Yes! Please keep this number private."

"I can't do that! Journalists need to reach you, at any time."

"Why?"

"Interviews, of course. You can't have privacy with publicity!"

"I suppose not."

"Now, we need to get that rolling with a press release, today."

"I'd rather you arrange an interview for me, then I could speak for myself."

"The corporate media won't speak to you – the corporate media speak to the agents for people like you. People who speak for themselves speak to no-one. I speak for people like you."

"I really don't want any publicity."

"Everyone wants publicity! How else would anyone get anywhere?"

"I'd rather get there without publicity."

"You'll get there with my publicity or not at all. That's my specialty. I was once an academic myself. I was hopeless, before I discovered publicity."

"I'm already getting more publicity than I want."

"Listen, Simon, if you go quiet now, everyone will think you have something to hide."

Simon thought of Teddi Theodora. "People who know me will think I'm exploiting the publicity."

"Modesty suggests inadequacy."

"I'm not hiding my merit: I have published. And I am working on more publications. And my teaching rates well."

"Oh dear, I am starting to understand your difficulties now. Listen, grandpa: People today don't read articles of 10,000 words anymore – they're too enlightened. They don't need more theories and evidence. They can work out the conclusion from a blog – so start a blog; keep each entry to 100 words or less. Better still, post an image, with a catchy caption. Your job is to communicate the simplest version of anything – something so simple anyone can get it. People want to say to themselves, 'Oh yeah, I knew that all along; I just didn't realize it, until this professor put it that way; now I'll follow that professor.' You see? Why, I had a client, who spent ten years working on a unified theory of micro- and macro-economics, until he came to see me. Well, I got him posting 40 words or less per day about how climate change sucks. Now he's this university's first chair of environmental economics."

"I don't think I can follow his example."

"Alright, another example! One of your PAX professors: she started BeLittering about genocide in a remote corner of the world. Nobody else had ever heard of it, so naturally she looked like an expert. Then everybody started BeLittering about it. Soon enough, there really was a genocide! That's the power of social media for you. How many followers do you have?"

"About thirty – friends and family."

"Oh, you're killing me! I don't normally work with anyone with less than thirty-thousand. Alright, it's okay, I just need to adjust the schedule here: some promoted BeLitters, and a few hundred bots, you'll get to thousands of followers by this time next week, and tens of thousands by the end of the following week. Okay, this is what you need to do. First, delete every comment you ever made in social media. From now on, you post only aphorisms, affirmations, and affectations – the three 'As' – got it? Now, before you start to write anything, remember this poem: 'One of the As, or lose your say.' Yeah, write that down. So, before you write anything, think to yourself: Is this already a familiar aphorism? Aphorisms speak louder than words. That's the first 'A.' If you can't identify an aphorism, ask yourself about the second 'A.' Am I affirming something in the current consensus? For instance, Clashmore Hickling is an idiot. If you're not affirming anything, then, finally, ask yourself: Am I expressing some affectation with which nobody can disagree? For example, racism makes me angry. Then start commenting about what you hate about the federal government, constantly, every chance you get."

"I'd rather talk about my research."

"That's too complicated. Everyone gets one theme, and your theme is: you're the anti-federalist hero. Every time you see something in the news with any reference to the federal government, post a comment about what this proves about the feds, and remind your followers you know what you're talking about, because you're the anti-fed hero of Bayside. Got it? But make sure you don't sound like those other anti-feds, the right-wing anti-feds, because they're the wrong sort of anti-feds: the sort who don't want governments or academics telling them what's good for them. They're just ignorant trash. You're the right sort of anti-fed, that is: the correct sort of anti-fed, not the right-wing sort of anti-fed. You support the right sort of intrusion, not the right-wing sort."

"That doesn't sound fair."

"Life isn't fair."

"Or substantive."

"Academic success starts with style, not substance. That reminds me: you need to meet my photographer."

"Can your photographer not come to me?"

"Not on campus: she knows a more authentic academic environment – a public park, in an urban area, where you do your thinking, amongst the people."

"I do my thinking at home."

"Where's the style in that? Who would see you? Aren't you getting it yet? This is why you need me. Okay, let's get this done today. I've been sent your work schedule already, so let's see – you finish teaching today at five p.m. That doesn't leave much evening light, so run to the park by ten minutes past."

"You mean the park with the tramps?"

"The 'Homeless Sanctuary,' yes. Don't say 'tramps' in your interview. But make sure the tramps are in the background. Get her to take some shots of you from behind, looking over your shoulder, looking at you looking at them, thoughtfully and sympathetically, squinting into the sunset. Remember that. I'll tell her too. Don't wear a suit."

"What should I wear?"

"Hawaiian shirt, shabby sports jacket, scarf, pork pie hat that's too small for you. How big is your head? The bigger the better.

Let's practice your concerned face, now your mournful face. You're a natural! Now put them together. On the way over, practice holding that face while walking slowly with your hands in your pockets. Remember: you're a caring academic, with big ideas."

"I'd rather make a success of my writing and teaching."

"That's not going to work."

"No?"

"No. I've already explained this. Let's cut to the chase: If you don't cooperate, you'd lose your funding. I'm sure you were told."

"No."

"It's in the contract you signed. Right then: let's forget that nonsense and get back to it. Item eight: you're foreign, right?"

"British."

"We'll make that work: first-generation immigrant. Item eleven: why did you come to America?"

"Sunshine – and meritocracy."

"You escaped from provincial life, from suffocating tradition, from the little island to the big country, from the old world to the new world, from a monarchy to the free world! That reminds me: I've got a copy of your I.D. card. Under a bright light, you come out white. I'll tell the photographer to shoot into the sun and increase the contrast; and make sure the hat is pale."

"Do I have a choice?"

"No. The university will back my expertise over your creative differences: I write 'creative differences' into all my *pro forma* contracts; and I get to decide what 'creative' means. So then: next, item fifteen: Did either of your parents attend college?"

"No."

"Awesome: first-generation college grad. too. Item sixteen: how do you self-identify?"

"I don't."

"What's your culture? Your group?"

"I can't say I have one in particular."

"How can you have an identity without identifying with a culture?"

"I prefer to be myself."

"That's impossible. Okay, let me ask this instead: at any time, did anyone make you uncomfortable because of your race, ethnicity, gender, sexuality, or appearance?"

"Those are private matters."

"They're not! You put down 'male' on your confidential demographic declaration, right?"

"How did you know?"

"Have you ever felt uncomfortable being male?"

"Only on university campuses."

"That doesn't make sense. Your photo shows a funny hair color: is that natural?"

"Of course."

"So, that must have made you stand out, like an ethnic minority. Did you ever wear it long?"

"I've had it different lengths."

"Right! Gender confusion."

"No, that's not true. I don't want you saying that."

"Don't get hung up on what I say, think about what is heard. Wait! You're getting another call."

"How do you know that?"

"It's an app., on my phone. I need to track the attention you're getting. Yes, I know her, she's a journalist, so you need to take this one." Max Mira hung up.

Immediately, the other caller connected. "Simon, this is Christie Sheng of Bay Area Public Media. I'm hoping we can get you in the studio this evening."

"No, I really don't want to."

"Simon, we're public media, not corporate media. We're on your side. We're here to over-represent academics."

"You'll need to talk to the university about that."

Simon hung up. He opened a drawer, took out some business cards, and called John Gard. "John? The Fascist Fighters came to my classroom last week. Didn't you see the news?"

"Do you know their names?"

"No."

"Did you see their faces?"

"No."

"Did they perpetrate any violence or threat of violence?"

"They said they would drive me off campus."

"I'm sorry, Simon, that's not a crime. Frankly, you're mixed up in that fed-bashing over there, so I wasn't expecting to speak with you again."

"That's the same event! The fascist fighters came into my classroom, but the university reported them as feds."

"You're sure about that?"

"Yes! Now, the university wants me to start my own anti-fed campaign."

"I wouldn't do that."

"No. What should I do?"

"I can't advise you on that."

"I'm getting another call – can you hold on?"

"No, not without the other caller's knowledge."

"Oh no! Max is going to know about this call too."

"Max Mira?"

"Yes."

"I need to talk to you about Max Mira. Stop bashing the feds. Get yourself another phone, email me the new number, then I'll contact you. Don't be impatient: I'll need a week or two for authorizations. I'm hanging up now."

"Hello?"

"Professor Ranald? I'd like to interview you for The Bayside Blab."

Simon hung up. Then he turned off his phone. Then he took out the battery.

24. Yannis

Max Mira Protective Services arranged for Simon's classrooms to change every week, to protect him from federal retaliation. An app informed the students of the new classroom assignment within one hour of each class. That same evening, DAFI reminded him that DAFI students were entitled to three hours for every hour allowed to the unaccommodated.

Outside of classes, Simon spent practically no time on campus at all. In that fashion, Simon achieved aloofness from all hazards, from fascists to hero-worshippers.

This changed after his final class of the week, when he found a reporter waiting outside. "Max told me where to find you."

He spoke clear English, with a steady, reserved tone, except he emphasized most vowels as "ooh." He kept asking about "the US goovernment's relatioonship with Roosha and the Yoonited Kingdoom." He affected a short "eh" in place of the remaining vowel sounds – so short as to suggest he could not bear to prolong it. The "eh" came out like a cry of alarm, as if he had just grabbed something unexpectedly hot or the word hurt his throat. His face would take on a grimace while he coughed up the sound as quickly as he could. "Afghanistan" came out like the stutter of a machine-gun. Immediately after each sound, he looked confused between emphasis and regret. Simon could see him spelling out words in his mind before he pronounced them. "British Pooblic Broodc'sting is sooch a better place to woork, noo it has moved its nooz offices oot of Loondoon tut north."

"I hadn't heard that."

"Oh yes," he said crisply, "It's woonderfool." Simon could not work out his name from his pronunciation, so thought of him as Mr. Woonderfool.

Mr. Woonderfool talked mostly about himself before declaring himself satisfied. "I think I've goot enoof in Max's press release to read on the radioo as a hooman interest stoory. I'll file it to 'The Globe'."

"What's that?"

"A partnership between British and American pooblic broodc'sting. It always ends with a hooman interest stoory. It's all aboot international poolitics. Your stoory will coom at the end, after the cooltooral segment, which cooms after the moosic segment, which cooms after the spoorts segment, and that will coom after my oopening repoort on Roosha. My hook will be: the President might succeed, but he might face oppoosition. What do you think of that?"

"That's a tautology."

"We call it spot-nooz. Soom people think he might, but soom doon't. I've interviewed each side: that's two guests already; then I'll ask soomboody on the street what she thinks, for authenticity. Next time the nooz is terrorist, I'll call you. I always need a hooman interest stoory. You can tell me how the victims moost be feeling."

"You should go. Max doesn't guarantee the safety of this classroom beyond Bayside time."

"Are you rooshing to leave before that crazy fascist arrives from Loondoon? Max warned me aboot him."

"Yes, you should."

Simon dwelt to check his emails. The oldest was from Chancellor Berk, "to warn the campus community of the potential for disruption." The next promised an emergency meeting of the emergency committee. The next announced the re-titling of the Vice-Chancellor for Wildlife Emergencies and Planning as Vice-Chancellor for Hateful Emergencies and Planning. Chancellor Berk's final email went on so long that Simon was skip reading, looking for a cause for the emergency, between the repeated words "reassure" and "hope."

> Reassure your students by finding alternatives to teaching today, although of course the university cannot condone any disruption to classes...

> I hope that you will help to minimize concern by drawing attention to the breadth and depth of our response...

> I want to reassure the community that everything is being done to reassure everyone in the community...

> I hope that this hateful event passes without hate...

> I want to reassure you that my hope is that Adrian Yannis will agree not to bring his hateful, provocative, and intolerant speech on to our

tolerant campus...

A safe university needs a safe space from intolerance. Of course, free speech is valued nowhere more than on this campus. But sometimes we need freedom from free speech, although of course the university cannot condone any disruption to free speech....

Berk concluded by reassuring and hoping that nobody would encounter a "British journalist who has inflamed American political divisions as we approach national elections." Simon imagined the consequences of missing such a person, the puzzled questions that he would receive: "Why would you not listen to a fellow Brit?" "Does he live near you?" "Are you related?" "Have you met him?" "What's he like?" "Why do Britons like to inflate American political divisions?"

Simon wondered if he had time to invite Teddi Theodora, but the short notice would be unfair. Simon researched the visitor. "Adrian Yannis' Libertarian Free Speech Tour of University Campuses" was coming to Bayside's auditorium that evening. Simon walked out towards the plaza. It was blocked by a portable fence and two guards in yellow jackets. They asked for a ticket, until he said, "But I'm faculty."

"That's a good excuse."

The fencing continued along both sides of the plaza. On the left, atop a grassy knoll, in front of the Police Building, a crowd was protesting. The nearest group waved a banner from Bayside High School, under which an adolescent with a megaphone was shouting: "The whole school is outraged! Students and teachers are united against hate. Everybody is actively learning through activism. Boycott school!"

The "Students for Direct Action," "Students for Change," "Students for Direct Change" and the "Students for Change through Action" tried to out-shout each other, until one chant emerged dominant: "Support free speech! Boycott the bigot!"

The crowd contained more than a thousand people, faced by a dozen yellow jackets, whose high visibility was incongruous to their attitudes. At the other end, temporary fencing contained news photographers and reporters. Above, helicopters slapped at the air in lament at lack of progress.

Simon joined perhaps 100 persons, queuing up to the steps down to the auditorium's lobby. They seemed deaf to the tumult behind their backs. The silence of the group unnerved him; he blurted out a question: "Who is Adrian Yannis?"

The reaction was more muted than he expected. He heard a mild debate on how to categorize Adrian Yannis: perhaps he was a "shock jock," perhaps a "political commentator," perhaps a "political journalist." He was a "classic British satirist," said one. "No," came a reply. "He's American." "I think," came a softer voice, "he is properly described him as Greek-American." Simon recognized Boyan's reply, clear and confident: "He's Near Asian-British-American, like me." The latest arrival behind Simon turned to shout back at the crowd: "Who is Adrian Yannis? Does any of you know?" The crowd hurled abuse and milk shakes. The yellow jackets ambled out of the way and pulled up their hoods.

A couple of yellow jackets at the bottom of the steps opened the doors, went in, turned about, and beckoned. One repeated carelessly to each passing entrant: "The doors are opening late but the event is starting early." The wide lobby seemed to suck in the noise, until the doors crashed shut behind them. Then the doors into the hall were opened. Nervous coughs and chatter echoed on high. The attendees scattered as if socially distancing against the most contagious disease. Simon continued, politely, to the unattended front row.

Before everyone was settled, Adrian Yannis walked on to the stage, his arms out-stretched, each hand making the V-sign, his legs striding out in rhythm with the nod of his head, smiling broadly, wearing mirrored glasses and quaffed bleached hair. He seized the lectern and yelled into the microphone: "Yeah, free speech tour! Cheer if you love free speech! Cheer if you love free tickets! They're cheering outside! Make some noise if you love Adrian Yannis! Listen to that noise outside: they love me! Thank you Bayside for making this gig the most disrupted yet."

He pushed the sunglasses atop his head, looked either side, and welcomed the two uniformed police officers to the stage, even as they backed into the curtains. He tipped his head forward, rocked it from side to side, looked down and up, and batted his eyelids.

"Thank you all. You made it! Well done! Slap yourself on the back and call yourself a defender of free speech. Your administrators tried to ban free speech, they tried to discourage you, they discouraged attendance, they encouraged protest." He pointed with both hands to the back of the auditorium, cupped his hands behind his ears, and grinned.

He leaned in seductively: "Free tip, from the free speech tour: always point with both hands! If they photograph you pointing or waving with one hand, they'll claim you gave the Nazi salute." He straightened, pouted, and rocked his head. A few members of the audience gasped.

"Let me tell you what they won't tell you. They tried to dissuade me. They said I was risking my own safety, that I was risking your safety. Then they suggested I should cancel. Well, I don't cancel, because I'm not afraid of free speech. They're afraid of free speech!"

The audience warmed to him. The cheers grew.

"Then they told me to come out here early or have your safety on my conscience."

The audience jeered. His seduction contrasted with an intense frown that appeared whenever he started a new statement. He transitioned with an alacrity that made everybody tenser, until his next joke released them. Some audience members sat poised for a quick burst of applause, others to take notes. Everybody grew more attentive.

"Now, you," Yannis said quietly, closer to the microphone. "You made it. You get to enjoy the free speech of the free speech tour. But still thousands of your classmates are denied the opportunity!"

He pointed with two arms again, over cheers and jeers.

"What is your reward? Only you get to hear of my new scholarship opportunity – a scholarship paid out of my own money, but to be administered by the university, to my rules." He started to speak slower and deeper. "It can be claimed by anybody seeking to undertake any undergraduate degree." He paused with his mouth open expectantly. "At any university." He paused again and dropped his jaw. "As long as you're a white male American citizen!"

He stretched out his hands and raised the gasps and laughter.

"And that's not discriminatory! I'll tell you why, even though the liberals won't get it. For a start, it's affirmative action, right? Affirming a minority on campuses, that's right. White male American citizens are a minority on American campuses, that's a fact. Second, you can fake it like a liberal! So, all you women – pretend to be men! Pretend that you're transitioning to male, and if any administrator doubts you, call them transphobic! Moreover, tell them they're prejudiced for suggesting that anybody would fake it. Show them what you would do to them with a penis! All you persons of color – pretend you're just tanned! Say that you self-identify as white and dare them to question your right to self-identification! All you illegal aliens, pretend you were born here! Pretend you want secure borders to keep out those other scroungers!"

He laughed, dropped his eyes bashfully, bent closer over the microphone, and returned to the lower tone: "I love this country. I love it because the United States Constitution guarantees my freedom of speech. But I hate what the liberals have done to it. I am here to tell you to raise your free speech against them, and I'll show you how I do it. As the son of swarthy Coptic Greeks, I love that liberals don't know whether to call me white or a person of color. Then they get confused about my sexuality and my nationality. You know what I love best? They don't get that I am a first-generation immigrant. When liberals tell me how discriminatory the immigration system is, I agree with them, because it is discriminatory – against people like me who did it the hard way, the right way. That's right! I naturalized the legal way, the slow way, the responsible way. When liberals say illegal immigrants are only illegal because they're refugees, I say this: my parents were refugees. They escaped persecution in Egypt. But they didn't do it illegally. Wait, there's more, because I was born in Britain, a second-generation immigrant there, before I was a first-generation immigrant here. And liberals don't know whether I'm perpetrator or victim of British imperialism. Well, let me put them out of their misery: I would support the restoration of British imperialism wherever the authoritarians took over. Let's start with the progressive states of America!"

He stepped back from the laughter and applause, drank some water, then continued. "These progressives, these so-called liberals, they call me a bigot. But, as a sexual libertarian, I will shag anything

– any color, any gender – as long as they have the autonomy to agree, because that's libertarianism. That's what liberals hate! They hate that libertarians can reach their own agreements about what's right, without having values imposed on them. You see, the people who call themselves liberals these days aren't really liberals: they're bigots and authoritarians. Nobody could be less prejudiced than me. Yet, because I oppose privileges, they say I'm the bigot. Some people hate me just for being gay. They do! Can you imagine that. Then the gay rights crusaders hate me for being the wrong sort of gay, for opposing gay privileges. Then they misrepresent me as against gay rights. There's no such thing as gay rights! They're equal rights! And we've got them! As soon as you start issuing scholarships for gays only, that's gay privilege, not equality."

He held the lectern with both hands, and spoke again in a hushed, grave tone: "I'm a proud libertarian. I believe in individual liberty, the liberty to do whatever you want, as long as you don't infringe anybody else's liberties. Those liberties include the right to trade liberties with each other. That's what we do when we consent to live here in America, to benefit from American liberties, to take American responsibilities."

He raised his arms and his voice. "But those liberals out there want to tell us how to behave without our agreement! Those sorts of liberals threaten liberties!"

He let the noise from the audience peak, before he quietened down, with a smirk. "That's why liberty would benefit from fewer liberals like them, more liberals like me! Stop liberals killing liberty!"

He pretended to ride the audience's appreciation at the gallop, with suggestive leers and winks.

"Now, let's talk about the merits of my friend, Clashmore Hickling – candidate for President of the United States of America."

At this moment, a police officer strode on stage, and beckoned the other two. "We need to evacuate now! Please follow the instructions. Please cooperate. This is for your safety. You too, Mr. Yannis, for your safety too."

He handled Yannis back the way he had come, while Yannis gave the V-sign uncertainly, and shouted over his shoulder, "This is what your liberalism looks like, Bayside!"

The audience remained still and thoughtful, except a few who stood up in time to cheer. The two officers hesitated too, then sharply goaded the audience to the rear. Simon stood and looked in that direction: the yellow jackets opened the doors between the auditorium and the lobby. On the outside of the glass lobby, a roar erupted. He saw the crowd heave, push over the fencing, and rush across the plaza. Simon turned back to the stage: the officers were whispering at one side, like shy cats. Simon looked back and forth, then waved at them: "Stage exit! You need to open a stage exit!"

They met his eyes, then contrived to take more interest in the situation over his shoulder. Simon could see their mouths forming words, but by then the audience was loud with urgent conversation. Stung by their own ineffectiveness, the officers climbed down at the corner, waving everybody towards the lobby. Simon ran to the other corner, climbed the steps, and rushed into the wing: adjusting to the gloom, he realized a turn towards a metal staircase. At its top, he made out a fire door; he saw it shimmer; he rushed up, three steps at a time, and crashed through it, to find a glass corridor lit from outside by streetlamps. A police officer turned around: "You need to evacuate."

"You need to evacuate the audience – this way, any way but the front."

The officer preferred puzzlement. Simon looked left and right – the corridor turned at both corners of the building. He ran to one corner, to find the way ahead blocked with police officers, inhumanly bulky in riot clothing. Stones clattered against the glass walls, ahead of the happy fizz and whizz of fireworks. A louder strike caused a pane to vibrate a few times. Just as it settled, it cracked to the frame.

"You need to evacuate the audience this way."

"No civilians!"

Simon pushed on in the direction that dominated their attention, to the front corner, but everybody looked equally rank-less and irresponsible. Beyond, he could see the plaza swarming with people. Peaks of activity arrested his attention here, distracted his attention there. The grassy knoll looked incongruously bare. He pushed around the sharp equipment and unpredictable movements, looking for recognition, but everyone – including the carnivalesque celebrants below – was distracted by the disassembly of the fencing. The slapping and chopping of the unseen helicopters amplified, faded, and cycled again, as their searchlights converged.

The police officers rested their padded forearms and knees on the glass frames for comfort, except to make way deferentially to those armed with video cameras. Simon jumped behind the next cameraman, and thereby stumbled into the front corridor

He found Adrian Yannis, holding his phone high, and fighting off his escorts: "No, I'm not under arrest, so I'm not going anywhere! This is gold! I'm going to blow up social media with this." He turned his back on the window, held his phone in front of his face, and started to narrate the story since his arrival.

Simon watched a video camera being placed on the shoulder of another officer, who immediately crouched compliantly without turning around. Simon looked over the top at a section of fencing moving closer to the steps below. Then he noticed a large blob of black clothing, following, pressing, and directing with careless urgency. Searchlights revealed the primary colors of bandanas. Gloved hands pointed fiercely at whoever was needed to help the fence forward. Ahead of the blob, Simon saw an aerosolized mist appear, from which the crowd repelled and contracted. Some unmasked students fell out, coughing. The blob pressed into the crack, thrashing them with chains.

At this moment, Simon's former auditorium mates emerged from under the overhang, spewing into that same pulsing crack, the same gauntlet, the same crowd that was already recoiling. The crack enlarged. Television photographers suddenly appeared in the center, with more entitlement than anybody. The perpetrators in black stopped thrashing, turned to the cameras, punched the air, pointed at themselves, lifted their masks over their chins, and worked their mouths. They picked up a section of fence to batter the unseen windows below, smashing one after another, but without entering the building. The photographers tailed them unmolested.

In the background, the floodlights started to wobble, then came crashing down. The celebrants kicked in the lamps, then turned over the wheeled generator too. They climbed on its side, pointing into the crowd and the sky. Its roof was facing Simon, who read the stenciled legend: "Bayside Police." Suddenly, a small flame appeared. The crowd squealed with delight. The flame grew deceptively slowly, until it flowed around, rose higher, spread to the tree alongside, and belched dense black smoke. The crowd recoiled, leaving a circle of brightly lit but inanimate space.

The television photographers pushed into the space. The black blobs posed in front of the flames triumphantly, conferred, disaggregated, reconvened, then marched towards the street with their fists in the air, sometimes waving the crowd to follow. As the crowd synchronized, Simon could hear a chant: "We are the Fascist Fighters! We own the campus!" The chanters disappeared around the next building, but the chant could still be heard, until the smashing of glass.

To Simon's left and right, the police stepped back from the windows, deflated. An authoritative voice, too loud for the new quiet, directed them downstairs. "Almost the end of double-time, folks; time to earn it."

Yannis took up more space against the glass, made sure that the flames would appear in his background, then started to speak to his phone again: "The campus is burning with hate – hate for free speech, hate for liberty, hate for discourse, hate for debate, hate for critical thinking, hate for everything that our universities should stand for. This is what progress looks like. Goodnight America." He pocketed his phone, then asked brightly, "So, can we get out of here, or what?"

"No way!" said the authoritative voice. "We're not going out there with you!" He turned to his colleagues for amusement, then lent forward, and said, "For your safety, of course."

Yannis considered the situation, had an idea, then restarted his broadcast: "Campus is still so dangerous that the police have forbidden me from leaving the building. I don't know how long I will be held here. But let me reassure you, I am fine. And thank you for all your messages of concern and support." He batted his eyes, paused seriously, looked over his shoulder, turned back to the lens, and quipped, "I brought the house down."

Below, Simon could see police officers stepping gingerly outside through the broken windows. Some of the crowd pressed forward to film them, but most dissipated. The police milled around, called out to each other, then formed a line – three officers deep, across the plaza, facing the street.

The authoritative officer stepped alongside Yannis to have a look, then turned to take Yannis' arm, before looking up. "Hey! Who are you?"

"I'm Simon Ranald."

"Are you his boyfriend?"

Yannis was indignant: "Hey! I don't just shag anything, you know."

The officer looked at both of them, as if waiting for a double act to reach the punchline. "Well, you can't stay with us. Get down there."

"But FaFi hate me too!"

"There's no such thing as FaFi."

25. FBI CI

Next morning, Chancellor Berk blamed the violence on "black-clad ninjas from off campus and outside the city, who turned peaceful protest by students into an attempt to discredit this university." He wanted "to reassure the community that campus police and city police had successfully video-taped the perpetrators," and "to hope that the 36 students who had been hospitalized would see justice."

Next was an email from the chief of the university police, who asked for help in identifying the hooded, masked faces in a series of grainy still images, labelled from "Ninja 1" to "Ninja 21." She said that "crowd control is uniquely difficult," and that such violence was "unpredicted and unprecedented." She praised her "police officers for their tough restraint, and for making the hard choice not to engage, which would only embolden the protesters and escalate the violence." She praised both university police and city police for their "unprecedented cooperation and coordination," and thanked the "Bayside community for its tremendous support." The only criticism, she concluded, was coming from outside Bayside.

Berk forwarded an email from the Mayor of Bayside, who reassured owners of damaged businesses that they would see justice, as would the bystanders who had been hurt. The Mayor wanted "to reassure the community that city and university have pooled their resources and coordinated their responses." The Mayor regretted most "that the City of Bayside, with fewer police officers than protesters, had no hope of protecting itself." The Mayor closed by saying the violence was personal to him, because he had received threats for his unpreparedness. "Such threats are unacceptable and aren't welcome in Bayside."

Over the weekend, a joint statement was released by the city and university, announcing that their police forces would form a new joint quick reaction force, as the result of recommendations that had been scheduled weeks earlier, and had nothing to do with recent events.

On Tuesday, Simon introduced a class that had been scheduled weeks before, and had nothing to do with recent events: the Chinese Deputy-Consul for Political Affairs, and the United States

Diplomat-in-Residence, would speak on Western-Asian Relations. The American went first: she reviewed some international laws, and said that the government's role was to uphold these laws, indiscriminately. America's disputes with China were legal, impersonal, multinational – not bilateral. She ended by describing careers in the State Department. "We want to be representative – we want to look like you." All the questions were about the careers. Boyan was one of the applicants: "I would, like, stick to being American."

The Deputy-Consul said China's role was to uphold China's interests, discriminately. China's disputes were bilateral – the United States was interfering with China's relations with its neighbors. Her delivery was speedy and matter-of-fact. She said she was delighted to speak to students, it was a privilege. She wished she could have attended this course as a student, and she invited questions.

The first question was about how the Chinese President was selected. She described a "centralized democracy." The democracy begins at the villages, which elect representatives, who vote for representatives at higher levels. "Thus," she said, "the People's Congress votes for its President from candidates who have proven themselves inside the system. It is very like your university system."

A Chinese student asked in English how young people could become political representatives, given that politicians were supposed to offer decades of experience before promotion from local to national. She said that he should start now. Another Chinese student complained that he had never heard that he could vote locally. She said he should pay more attention.

After class, she dwelt as the students departed. "I wondered if I could sit in on your classes. I was pleased that a professor would want American students to hear the official Chinese version. I want to learn more of what the Americans learn."

"I always want students to hear the official positions. We appreciated hearing yours."

"Does anybody else teach both sides?"

"Not on this campus."

"Why is that?"

"Well, I suppose one way to avoid conflict in the immediate term is to pretend one side doesn't count."

"That isn't my way."

"I am glad to hear it. I suppose one side could hope that the other ruins itself while one refuses to engage it, but one wouldn't know what the other side is doing while one is ignoring it."

"Perhaps you would not mind if I consulted you again, after classes, from time to time, for a chat?"

"Please do: I was grateful for your help."

"I would pay you."

"That won't be necessary."

"I insist. I know your time at Bayside is limited."

"You do? How limited?"

"I didn't mean to be specific, but perhaps I could ask around, to be helpful to you, for next time we meet."

On Wednesday, Simon lectured on the fallacies and biases of argument. At home, an email arrived from Will of the WISP, reminding him not to challenge his students' free speech.

Simon left the classroom, when two strangers approached, stumbling with height and uncertainty of direction, on slippery, cheap black sports shoes. They looked alien – like potential graduate students who had lost the tour, yet somehow connected. He stopped.

"Simon? I'm Lief Kirk. This is Cooper. Sorry to interrupt you. We've come from the FBI."

"How do you do? I am glad you are here: John Gard told me more than a week ago that we should talk about Max Mira."

"Let's find some seats where we can talk some more," said Cooper.

"Of course." Simon took them across the lawn to the same table in the quiet corner of the deck at which he had sat with John Gard and Martin Barmouth.

"Actually, we don't know Max Mira."

"The FaFi then? If you've got more bad news, I am more prepared than last time."

"We don't do Fafi," said Lief apologetically. Lief leaned forward, with a look of childlike attentiveness on a large mobile face. Cooper sat on Simon's left, leaning away, with a look of amused skepticism on a square, boney face.

"Oh! I assumed John Gard sent you."

"That's a different squad – we do counter-intelligence."

"Oh! What did I do?"

"Nothing," said Lief.

"Did you want to lecture to my students?"

"We do sometimes, but this is about you."

Simon's mouth opened for a long time before he spoke. "My work visa is good for a year, and the university recently re-funded me."

"Yes, but no, that's not the issue. A Chinese Consul asked you to write some papers."

"She did. How did you know?"

"We can't tell you that. The point is, she's not interested in the papers, she's interested in what else you might do, after the papers."

"I committed to only one paper."

"You should! That's exactly what you should do. Write the paper, take the money, then when she asks for something else, let us know." Lief gave his card.

Simon looked at Cooper, who had fixed an expression and would not let it go until he had delivered his line: "We'd like to visit from time to time, for a chat."

"I am hearing that from both sides."

26. Marcus and Arjun

Marcus' prominent lips and eyebrows twitched with betrayal of his busy mind. He sat tall in the chair, elevated on the mezzanine at the rear of the Faculty Club, one elbow on a railing above the table below. A filthy woman, in an incongruous ankle-length leather skirt, dumped her stinking bags on the table, turned about recklessly, went to the owner, pointed to the table, feigned a foot injury, and accepted a free meal.

Marcus was not moved. His view was commanding; he could see all corners and all comers. After a few minutes of intense writing, he would search the room, then return to his mysterious scrap of paper. It could have been a musical score or a mathematical breakthrough, but was filling up with frivolous cartoons. Simon's arrival ended his persiflage; Arjun's arrival rekindled it.

"Arjun was at Oxford with me – except I stayed for my doctorate in a hard discipline, while he left to study business."

"I studied business management, to be useful, in the real world. Marcus stayed because he had nowhere else to go."

"I stayed for the highest and rarest of degrees, and I did not stay any longer than necessary. I took a post-doc. in the State of Sunshine, which is almost as far as one could go."

"That's right: after ridiculing my choice to study in America, he chose to come here too."

"I chose to work here, not to study here."

"You chose to join the trail I had blazed."

"I was offered a post-doc., which just happened to be in the same state."

"And you just happened to follow me to the same city."

"l chose another campus, before I was invited to Bayside."

"By then I was working here, which means that Marcus came chasing the only person he'd ever known with a useful degree."

"Arjun chose the most expensive degree he could find, then he started a non-profit."

"I started a business; I just chose not to give control to investors who would milk it for profit."

"Arjun would rather be skint than conventional."

"Like you academics."

"Like us academics, except with the risks of an entrepreneur."

"Both the risks and the rewards of an entrepreneur," Arjun corrected him.

"Risks of an entrepreneur, rewards of an academic. You're like an academic publisher: enough stress to feel like an entrepreneur, enough pretense to feel like an academic."

"Academic differentiation is part of my business model. You're just academic, without the business model. No offense, Simon."

"Careful, Simon. He'll be recruiting you to write too. I'll tell you how his online rag is differentiated: not academic enough to be a journal, not popular enough to be profitable."

"I publish thoughtful opinions. Would you like to write thoughtful opinions, Simon?"

"On what?"

"Not mathematics, I hope – Marcus has exhausted what little relevance he has to the news."

"Simon knows enough mathematics, I'll wager, to know that I can always make mathematics relevant. I could put 'big data' in any title to make it more popular than your idle musings on politics. I'll bet my article on big data is the only article bringing any corporate interest in your site. Now, that's my business model. Ooh! I've just thought up a title for another article: 'How big data proves the likely failure of start-ups'."

"I just thought of a better one: 'How the editor's big data proves the unpopularity of Marcus' articles'."

"Actually, my next project would be popular, profitable, and academic: 'The big data of dating.' You see? Two popular search terms in one article."

"Dating isn't as popular as sex – or self-help."

"Okay: 'Help your dating and sex life with big data.' Admit it! I'm right, you're interested."

"Yes, I'll admit it," Arjun said to Simon. "Marcus pitches something popular – but wait, Marcus doesn't have the ethos to write such a thing."

"Actually, I'm quite an expert now. I've tried all the dating sites and I've worked them out."

"That's a new approach for the man who used to say maths was more important than women."

"My time at Oxford," Marcus said to Simon, "involved a painful marriage and divorce, involving a posh girl from Gloucester, whose parents boycotted our wedding. A boy from London was not to their liking. Also, my table manners were not what they are."

"Well, what would you expect, when maths is more important than women?"

"That was then, but this is now, and this is America. And I've learnt by now that Americans love accents and intellects; and I've got both. Poor Arjun has neither – that's why he thought he should go into business. Yet he still has academic pretensions in case he fails at business as well as maths."

"As founder and chief executive officer of my own company, I have already succeeded at business and romance. I meet people far and wide, in the real world, while you're at home playing on your computer. Besides, I remain a serious academic; and I have an accent."

"An Indian accent doesn't count."

"That's for me to tell my Indian competitors – I've been to Oxford."

"Any American with a few thousand pounds and a few weeks in the summer can say they've been to Oxford! Who hasn't been to Oxford? No offense, Simon."

"I went to Oxford once."

"Don't be shy, Simon! You went to Oxford! You should slip that into every conversation. Here, let me give you a starter for free: 'When I was at Oxford, the colleges looked best in the dawn.' It works a treat. It's like my American colleagues dropping the H-bomb: 'Why, yes, I know Boston well, because I was at Harvard.' Ker-boom! All skepticism and preoccupation obliterated."

"An Oxford man can't drop the H-bomb."

"Could we say we're dropping the O-bomb?"

"No, there's no O-bomb. Maybe there's an O-ring – we're tossing the O-ring, as a lifesaver to that poor floundering girl, drowning in a sea of mediocre, indistinguishable men, and desperate for a lifeline."

"By the way, Simon, why were you in Oxford?"

"I went to meet a girl, a friend of a friend."

"Ooh! He tossed her the O-ring, in Oxford itself, no less!" said Marcus.

"No, that doesn't make sense," said Arjun. "Hush, Marcus. Let's hear Simon's story."

"Well, she lived in Northampton, I lived in London, so Oxford seemed like a fair mid-point. I paid for her dinner, because I had suggested the restaurant. Actually, a colleague had suggested the restaurant, I didn't know the place, but, anyway, she was there at my suggestion, so I felt obliged. That made things awkward, because she didn't like that, and a man never knows his obligations. I mean: Did I insult her egalitarianism by making her feel dependent on a man's wealth in the traditional way? Or would I have insulted her self-worth if I had suggested that we should split the bill? Either way, she could always call me ungentlemanly."

"Always."

"Indeed."

"Did she think that I was paying for her meal on prospect of seeing her again, when she could take turn to pay? Or did she suspect that I was trading money for sex?"

"There's an article to be written on that," suggested Arjun.

"That's easy: always pay the bill," suggested Marcus. "Americans expect to trade, except the feminists. But one shouldn't be making a date with a feminist in the first place."

"That's reductionist."

"Arjun, shush! I hadn't finished. The trouble begins once you find you're on a date with a 'fencinist' – she sits on the fence until the end of the date. If you pay and she fancies you, she'll shag you. If she decides otherwise, she'll walk away with a free meal but say you insulted her equality. It's a gamble, a game, a risk. Actually, you're right, Arjun. There is an article in that – a mathematical article. I'll write it."

"Not one I would publish. Mathematics is unpopular enough, without you upsetting most women. Hush, now: Simon hasn't finished his story."

"Well, in this case, she insisted that I must continue the date in a dance club nearby that she had heard about, so she could pay for that."

"Oh dear! That's even more confusing! Was she settling debts, so nobody is under any obligation? Or was she buying your obligation to shag her?"

"Then I walked her back to her car..."

"Ugh! So, you reintroduced traditional manners, or a trade. I'm not sure myself now."

"Because it was raining and I had an umbrella, so I had to walk with her under it."

"Both gentlemanly and patronizing."

"Yes, well, I don't think we had any choice: it was a small umbrella."

"That's a difficult signal – provocative but not deferential. A 'fencinist' could take it either way."

"I doubt she was thinking about it. I did ask if I could put my arm around her, so we could both get under it."

"That's sexual assault!"

"Wait," said Arjun. "He asked for her consent."

"Did she consent?"

"She did, with bells on."

"Whore!" said Marcus.

"Not necessarily," said Arjun. "She might have simply wanted to stay dry."

"Actually, I was the one getting wet."

"Then she consented out of consideration for you."

"I think so."

"Or she kept him dry to keep him sweet," interrupted Marcus.

"She sounds like a considerate lady, a considerate lady to a gentleman," Arjun insisted.

"Unlikely," sniffed Marcus. "She's clearly a whore."

"Marcus, Marcus, Marcus," said Arjun sadly. "You are no gentleman. And a lady is recognizable to only gentlemen."

"A lady is a disguise – a disguise in the first act of a play, in which the lead actress has a choice of roles and thence endings. The trick is to stay in the script until she takes on the role you want. It's a romance."

"Sounds more like a comedy of errors."

"It's a thriller. Nobody knows who she is, or how he will solve the mystery."

"More precisely, it would be a mystery, as they seek to discover each other's true selves – actually, a detective story, a double-blind detective story, in which both main characters are detectives."

"Arjun, you just made my case: it's mostly a thriller, as they try to outwit each other."

"Sounds more like a war story," said Simon. "They're maneuvering for advantage."

"Aha! Well interjected, Simon!" said Marcus. "You see, Arjun, Simon is on my side."

"No!" said Arjun emphatically. "Remember this: 'All's fair in love and war.' Ergo, Simon's suggestion was closer to my romance than your thriller."

"Poppycock! Simon's suggestion is closer to a murder-mystery, because everyone else gets bumped off, leaving only two survivors."

"Two survivors who fell in love along the way – so, it's a romance."

Arjun and Marcus paused, equally stumped.

Simon thought to summarize: "So now we have a romantic, comic, thrilling, murder-mystery, and a detective story, in wartime."

"Yes," said Marcus thoughtfully. "Now you realize how ridiculous romance is."

"Simon, please continue with your romance."

"Well, perchance, we found our cars parked nose to tail on the same street. Then she pushed me up against the wall and snogged me 'til my mouth hurt, right next to a food van, under its bright lights and with people walking past, busy on a Thursday night."

"Of course – big students' night out," said Arjun.

"She was a whore!" said Marcus. "I knew it all along."

"I don't think so. I think she liked me."

"So? What happened next?"

"She drove back to Northampton, I drove back to London, and we both had to work the next day."

"Is that it?"

"Yes. We remained distant."

"Why did you even tell us that story? I want a happy ending!"

"Well, that was my last date."

"You haven't dated in America?"

"Gosh no! I live in the same city as my students and colleagues."

"The same as London."

"Yes, that's true."

"You're missing out, Simon! Get your skates on, mate. This is the self-preservation society. Your competitive advantages are here, not there. Tell him, Arjun!"

"Actually, Marcus just gave me an idea for an article: 'Discovering your competitive advantages in dating.' I should get an economist to write that one. Simon, are you an economist by any chance?"

"No."

"So, what are you?"

"I don't rightly know any more. I left England a lecturer in international relations. I started here by teaching social scientific methods."

"Ugh! That's a bigger yawn than mathematics."

"Then I was asked to teach Asian Studies, then Western-Asian relations…"

"I am personally committed to Western-Asian relations," Marcus murmured.

"And now I teach counter-extremism and counter-terrorism."

"Aha!" said Marcus. "Simon could write on the big data of terrorism."

"I could, but I wouldn't, except to say that big data are not reliable. Terrorism is too adaptive, for periods longer than a few years, at least."

"Then please write something on the last few years, the most recent terrorism."

"Except, Simon, you would be well advised to integrate dating and self-help too."

Simon promised to think about it on the walk home, but instead found himself thinking about Teddi Theodora. More than three traumatic weeks had passed since their first meeting; he would need to wait more than a week before the next meeting of the Flappers and Go-Getters. Would an approach, this week, be enterprising or disrespectful? He could not find a dominant theory without gathering additional evidence, so he resolved to ask her.

27. Halloween

Simon came out of the class for counter-extremism to lock eyes with a man against the opposite wall. Alarm dissolved to calm: the man wasn't wearing black; he wore an over-sized, light-colored sports jacket; and he smelled clean.

"Simon, the elusive Simon! I've come to track you down."

"Max Mira?"

"You're a difficult man to contact, but not to track down. You've been missing calls. Have you kept your phone off? Look, I understand: stage fright, buyer's remorse, crisis of confidence. Whatever you call it, it's understandable, but you've got to come in, and I'm here to guide you in – to show you how it's done, how to make you a success. That's how important you are to me, my number one client, my one and only – for the rest of the day. Do you have your phone on you?"

"No, I left it at home. It's not working."

"That's no use then, is it? Look, we'll use mine. Here we go. Hello? Sarah, yes, I've got him. Go ahead, Sarah."

"Simon! It's a fascinating story – you are so lucky: struggling with your working-class disadvantages, against traditional English prejudices, and with your color. But you worked hard, got accepted for who you are, accepted into the Sunshine family, where – how did you put it? 'All peoples can feel a kindred sense of belonging without boundaries or identities.' Amazing! This story practically writes itself. But, for this exclusive, tell me something that's not here."

"My family wasn't exactly working class."

"Right, that's no longer the term. Let's go with 'hard-working family'."

"I came here for the sunshine..."

"Yes, the Sunshine community, I've got that. Give me something extra."

"Well, the truth is, my class was invaded by Fascist Fighters."

"Yes, the working class was invaded by Fascists, I quite agree."

"No, my classroom, invaded – invaded by fascists, in my classroom."

Max Mira took back the phone: "Sarah, Max, yes. Look, you've got the confirmation that your editor wanted, direct from the source,

I'll fill in the rest. Yes, he's very busy, for his own safety, you see. I handle that too. Yes, text me. I need to hang up now. No, nobody else, you're still exclusive. Yes, you're my one and only. Hanging up now. Look, Simon, you're not getting this. Let's walk and talk, this way. If you keep this up, you won't be keeping your funding."

Max texted while he spoke, often losing track of what he was saying. Viewed from the side, he seemed to have no neck, just an enormous unshaven prickly globe atop a larger globe, misshapen to one side more than the other. Yet his expensive and over-sized clothes smoothed much and hid more.

"Look, I can't keep chasing you down, holding your hand. You've got to work out this system for yourself. I've got other things to do, and I need to be sure you're the sort of man I can trust. Come on, this way. The Plaza is where we need to be tonight, and we don't want to lose our spot."

"Tonight?"

"Yes, it's Halloween weekend."

"Do you want me to get interviewed here? Photographed?"

"No, but get ready to take photos, and to interview. Let's see what you're made of. Prove to me I can trust you. Don't be so uptight all the time! Get that British stick out of your ass, let your hair down, wake up and smell the coffee. This is the best night of the whole academic year. Here, right here, right now."

Max Mira led up the grassy knoll towards the unmistakably furry, pregnant profile of Jimmy Pons.

"Hey Jimmy."

"Hey Max," said Jimmy, without giving up his survey.

"Hello Jimmy," said Simon. "Look, Max, I'll make this quick. What are the odds? There's one of my students. Boyan! Hey, Boyan! Happy Halloween!"

"Yeah, Professor, I'm not stopping. I don't celebrate American holidays."

"There he goes, Simon, and here we are. Jimmy and I celebrate Halloween."

"It's a bit early for me – I need to get home to prepare for the weekend."

"The weekend starts on Thursdays, Simon," said Max.

"Well, yes, I was thinking that myself actually. I had plans for this evening."

"What sort of plans?"

"Actually, I have a friend, whom I meant to contact tonight, because she works all day."

"She's not an academic then. She sounds like a loser," said Max.

"Teddi's not a loser."

"Teddi's a great name: gender ambiguous," said Jimmy.

"Come on, Jimmy," said Max. "We don't want ambiguity on Halloween night."

"True, Max, too true."

"I really need to contact her."

"Not if you care for your funding, Simon."

"Really, Simon!" cried Jimmy. "Why worry about contacting one gender-ambiguous woman when you could just stand here and let them come to you! This is the spot; and we're on the spot; and we're here to be spotted; and we're the official spotters. We get to see the earliest offerings, staging here for the night. And most of those who go off campus will be back here at some point to finish off. It's a tradition, and we must support campus traditions, and guarantee their compliance with our values. Best to get in early."

"You see, Simon? Jimmy is the black belt at this."

"We can see everything from one end of the Plaza to the other, and the auditorium down the steps in front, where the freestyle partying will concentrate."

At that moment, a student came to the top of the steps, turned, and shouted to her friend at the bottom: "I love you, bitch."

"I love you, too, bitch," came the reply.

"That's the spirit, hey, Jimmy? Look, Simon, at the top of those steps: that's the sun sculpture."

"So?"

"New couples will be having sex under that."

"I can't imagine how – it's exposed underneath."

"It's a tradition. Who are we to question it? What a night! Keep your eyes peeled!"

"For what though?"

"Bitches, Simon, bitches! Jeez, why do you make me spell out everything. We're off the record now. This is the highlight of the academic year – bitches become sluts."

"Slutty cops, slutty nurses, slutty air hostesses," said Jimmy.

"Slutty cheerleaders, slutty witches."

"Slutty schoolgirls!" spewed Jimmy.

"Absolutely! What highlights are we expecting this year, Jimmy?"

"Well, my advisory went out: no cultural appropriation in general, of course."

"Of course."

"Specifically, nothing Native American – team mascots are no excuse."

"Of course! I don't like sports anyway."

"Except slutty athlete, any variation thereof."

"Goes without saying."

"No Hawaiian costumes."

"That's a shame."

"No cartoon characters."

"Not even the animals?"

"No, some are disguised racial stereotypes."

"Ah."

"No Cinderellas, Snow Whites, or princesses. They perpetuate white beauty, you know."

"I've always said so."

"I wrote so! My advisory is categorical: no excuse for racism at Halloween; irony, satire, or ignorance are not allowable excuses. The university reserves the right to judge for itself. Specifically, no idealization of white standards of beauty. Pumpkins too must be colored."

"Surely some colors could be offensive?"

"We take them on a case by case basis. And students should stand up to racism and alert authorities, which means us, right here."

"Well said, Jimmy. Campus must be a safe space."

"No Mexican costume."

"What if you're Mexican?"

"Not sure. All costumes are cultural stereotypes, so, no, I guess not, not even if you're Mexican."

"That's why you're the expert, Jimmy."

"Yep, I should have organized another social justice workshop – great way to meet girls."

"I'd have been there, Jimmy – there's always an excuse for bringing the publicity."

"You're the expert, Max."

"You should organize a workshop before Cinco de Mayo."

"Great idea! That will break up the spring semester."

"I suppose military costumes would glorify war."

"I'm conflicted on that – I miss the slutty sailor."

"I forgot that one! Have they put law enforcement under military?"

"No, it wouldn't be Halloween without slutty cops."

"What about politics?"

"Well, under military I specified anything Confederate, so that solves another problem."

"Clever!"

"But otherwise no restrictions on politics – so you can expect lots of caricatures of conservatives."

"Important work, of course, Jimmy, but conservatives tend to be men, so I don't think you should be encouraging caricatures of conservatives."

"True, Max, so we won't count them. I'm betting on slutty aliens."

"Immigrants?"

"Sci-fi aliens! I'm betting on green ones."

"I don't mind green."

"Yep – no color-prejudice here."

"I even saw a slutty Oompa Loompa, once. And it worked. You wouldn't believe it could, in orange, but, damn, did it work."

"All bets are in then - except Simon's."

"Is this normal?" asked Simon.

"This is a tradition! The best thing to look forward to, two-thirds of the way through the semester. We've been doing it right here, every year, since Max was still a failing lecturer. Now it's time for you to give us some youthful cover."

"Yes, let's see if you deserve those start-up funds, Ranald. Look up! Here's the first, don't embarrass me: look official, like you're meant to be here." Max put his hands behind his back and stuck out one foot; Jimmy put his hands in his jacket and stuck out his gut; and Simon recognized Prisha Pradesh.

"Prisha!"

"Oh! Hi!" She looked surprised, but then she always did.

"Are you coming from teaching?"

"Yes. Are you?"

"No."

"I just finished class. I let them go early, once they'd finished the candy. Look, two empty baskets – success! No point teaching kids at Halloween."

"You're a pirate," said Simon, "I mean, you're all pirate, you're a lot of pirate. You've got the triangular hat, the floppy boots, the gauntlets, the frilly cuffs."

"I forgot that one," said Jimmy.

"Hi Jimmy."

"You know each other?"

"Yeah, well, Jimmy hired me, of course. And Jimmy introduced me to Max. He invited me on the board for the women's rights fundraiser."

"I did. You brought a husband."

"I'll walk you back to the office," said Simon.

"No, Simon," said Max, "you're interning."

"I'm going straight home anyway. Look, take this basket. The kids took all the candy, but somebody may give you some. You look scary enough, in this lighting. Okay, I've gotta go, back to my real kids, you know. Okay, bye!"

"Husband and kids – what a drag," said Jimmy. "Great idea to take the basket though. Well done, Simon."

"Too right," said Max. "I was thinking: what an excuse to make contact. You're learning already, Simon."

"Look lively, you two, look up: we've got some, a whole group of them."

"Wow, they're big."

"I think that's ironic padding – fat fairies and fat princesses, you see: ironic."

"It's not padding."

"You're right. Still, ironic, I think."

"Difficult to say. Either way, disappointing."

"It's not ideal, Max, I'll give you that, but, remember: some bitches are better than others, but all bitches are good."

"Wise words, Jimmy."

"Hip-hop taught me that."

"It's my preferred philosophy."

"No prejudices here."

"Here we go, a bigger group this time."

The group dawdled, tightly, discursively, fussily. After adjustments, they emerged into the light with coats and caps of dark materials, emblazoned with "ICE" or "FED," holding plastic guns and metal chains, connected to dog collars around the necks of three men wearing ragged clothing and expressions. "Fight racism!" they began to chant.

Max and Jimmy watched them pass moodily.

"What good was that?" asked Jimmy.

"I know. The only ones in rags were men."

"What was slutty about the others? They could have gone for slutty cop, and stuck 'ICE' or 'FED' on top, and still made an ironic statement."

"A compellingly ironic statement, Jimmy."

"Absolutely, Max. I mean, I would have given them all extra credit if they'd been my students, but, come on, play the game, this is the one night to go for it, release the inner slut."

"These millennials are lazy. It's true what the conservatives say – on that only, of course."

"There's some truth to that, Max, some truth to that. But I also blame conservatives for bringing back puritanism. Students aren't as liberated as they used to be."

"Wise words, Jimmy, as always. You've always got your finger on the younger pulse. You know, Jimmy, you need to drop some hints in your classes about another slut-walk on campus. We haven't seen one of those for a while."

"I know. Students these days aren't as empowered as they used to be."

"Damned shame, Jimmy."

"Damned shame, Max. Wait, here's some more." Into the light

ambled two nondescript students in the nondescript uniform of white t-shirts, blue jeans, and tennis shoes, with their arms crossed and heads down in loud, indignant discussion.

"Girls!" hissed Max.

"Uninhibited girls!" hissed Jimmy.

Two tall men passed in their own uniform of red baseball caps, white t-shirts, and tan shorts.

This was the final straw: "Hey! Racists! That costume is racist. We know what's in your heads. Don't manterrupt us. That's the same costume the frat boys of Mississippi were wearing when they hurled racial epithets at the football game."

"They read my advisory!" squealed Jimmy.

The girls continued their duologue: "You're oppressing us! Yes, you are! Halloween should be a Day of Absence for white people – and men. You're both – both of you. You're a provocation – a double provocation, a quadruple provocation. And you know it."

"What big mouths!" said Jimmy with admiration.

The girls were too focused to hear: "Stop scratching your heads. Put your hands down – you're being aggressive!"

"Oh! They're masterly!" said Jimmy, even louder.

The girls turned to the three men on the grassy knoll. "You need to stop them! You're the university's safety ambassadors. You need to stop bigots! They're killing us!"

Max was indecisive, but Jimmy stepped forward without hesitation. He handed the basket to one girl, took the other girl's hands, patted them, and said, "There, there, my dear – you're absolutely right, they're typical white men, but we're here to reaffirm you, so you come right over here with us."

His soothing could have gone on all night, but everyone was interrupted by the sound of heavy boots from behind. Four policemen in body armor and helmets ran on to the plaza, but stopped, disorganized, looking about, looking to adapt to each other. They were surprisingly quiet, except that their other equipment thumped and clattered as they twisted this way and that, trying to keep their carbines pointing outwards but not at anybody.

Max put his hands up; he looked at his phone, then snapped a picture of the cops, then he snapped a picture of the two girls.

Jimmy put his arms around his girl and buried her head in his chest. She squealed, and her friend burst into life: "What are you waiting for?! Those two! That's them! They're killing us!"

The two men in red caps had not moved, when their hands suddenly shot towards the sky. "Hands up! Don't shoot!"

The nearest policeman looked at them awhile, then at the two girls.

"Don't worry officers," said Jimmy, "We've got his in hand."

The nearest policeman breathed deeper but continued to pant. "Shelter in place – active shooters – dressed like us," he said, then he turned to the two red caps, and said the same thing. "Did you see them?" The two young men dumbly pointed the way they had come. "Then get going, quickly." They did, like athletes. He watched them indecisively, then faced up the Plaza decisively: "Come on." The police ran on, in their cumbrous, deliberate, anxious way.

"Well," said Jimmy, "What a stroke of luck! I mean, hey girls? You coming up here, for your protection, just in time."

"You must have called them so fast," said the other girl, to Max.

"Oh, he did," said Jimmy, "He is lightning with his fingers."

"That's right," said Max, putting his phone back in his pocket. "Just like that – in and out, as quick as you like."

"Not like those vicious policemen," said Jimmy. "You don't want to be around men like that."

"I'm going to follow them," said Simon.

"Good idea," said Jimmy, "Bear witness to their abuses. We don't need you bearing witness here."

Simon was already running down the slope, when he heard Max remonstrate, and Jimmy reassure.

Turning up the Plaza, the quiet seemed so sudden that time seemed to slow. The way ahead rose gently, up pink and grey concrete slabs, past the patch of black where the generator had burnt out one week earlier. The crest of the rise supported a still mist, glowing orange under the artificial light, preternaturally distant. The scene rocked and jerked in rhythm with his jog. Suddenly, he heard shouts. He quietened his steps and breath, but kept running. He saw a flash of yellow beyond the orange mist. He saw several more flashes, before he heard the bangs. Simon kept going, the shots still discordant in every sense, amidst sudden, surprising quiet. Over the gentle rise he saw all he needed: a discarded placard, an untied shoe, three policemen in an arc, the fourth trying to resuscitate a body on the floor, one leg rocking unnaturally with each compression, the compressions getting more frantic, the leg getting more frantic.

Closer still, Simon heard the leader talking on his radio: "Fake guns, fake body armor, fake holster, and a cell phone. But they came at us."

Cars drifted down the street in the background, under bright white streetlamps. A camera flashed from an open window.

"You need to close the street," said Simon automatically. He welcomed clarity. He wondered why he had clarity. He realized a new self in crises, a best self, a self he wanted to develop, given a more selfish situation than now.

"Yes," said the leader diminutively, utterly spent.

"I'm your first independent witness. and I saw the victim, before you did. I'll stay here through your handling of the evidence, your closure of the scene – from plaza to street."

The leader roused himself, provoked: "Street is the city. I'm waiting for backup."

The rest of the students in black emerged from cover and started to wail, just as distant sirens started to wail, like urgently pressing routs of wolves.

28. Protests

Protests started on Friday morning and turned to riots and looting by the evening. No police were there. On Saturday morning, the protesters declared the campus a police-free zone. Campus buildings were looted, including the Police Department. No police were there. A collection of statues in and around the Police Building were toppled, collected in a heap on the plaza, and burnt. No statues of police were there.

In the afternoon, the protests were coordinated with Riverside University of London. In solidarity, Director Daly and Chancellor Berk appeared by video link.

"We don't want to prejudge what happened this week," Chancellor Berk began, "but clearly the police made a mistake."

"I speak for the whole Riverside community," said Director Daly, "when I express outrage at what the actions of the Bayside Police prove about systemic racism in Britain."

"Academic freedom starts with solidarity," said Chancellor Berk.

"Pluralism begins with consensus," said Director Daly.

"In solidarity and consensus," said Berk, "I am renouncing all statues on campus. So, do what you will. True, some of them might represent people of color, but since the statues were cast a long time ago in dark metal, let's assume the worst."

"Yes, let's!" said Director Daly.

Chancellor Berk invited the delegation from Bayside High School to speak. Its self-appointed leader brought a prepared speech: "We need to solve the problems that the older generation has not. So, we'll protest, and we'll keep protesting, every day, until everything changes. If you're not protesting, you support the system! If you don't abolish the police, you support police violence! You're either with us or against us!"

The microphone was open for anyone to identify with the victims by talking about themselves. The voices of the traditionally under-represented were encouraged to come forward. The leader of the high school student delegation was first to the microphone. "I was a victim of police brutality years ago; I didn't tell anyone then, but now I feel brave enough to do so." She was heartily applauded for her bravery.

Aimee Pharisees stepped up to remind everybody that all the troubles in the world are due to traditional constructs: "Policing is a traditional construct! Abolish the police! Racial difference is a traditional construct! Smash racial difference, except minority racial difference!"

Jewel Lighter came up to the microphone, did not know what to say, and was applauded for her bravery.

Hattie Maddux explained what Foucault would do. "He would tell you, if he were alive, that nothing can be ascertained until we break free of what society wants us to think. Always ask yourself: 'What does society want me to think?' Then think the opposite."

Tom Pinklewonk took the microphone off its stand with one hand, and pointed wildly into the sky with the other. "The victims here just wanted to fight fascism – and for that they were murdered. They wouldn't have needed to be protesting at all, if fascists had not invaded this campus pretending to be students. Why didn't the police stop that invasion? Why aren't the police hunting those imposters? Instead, they're killing students! You do the math! Vote against police brutality! Vote Trixie!"

Jimmy Pons wrestled away the microphone and took the same stance: "Don't stop loving each other. Without love there is only hate. That's why your vote is so important! Vote for love, not hate. If you don't vote for Trixie, you're a hater; and a sexist, if you're male; or a traitor to your gender, if you're female; or both, if you're transgender; that is, if you self-identify that way. I am always available for advice. I am the expert."

By Sunday, the Fascist Fighters were in charge, to "police the police-free zone to prevent the police from policing it," as one of them told a journalist. The FaFi grew bored with the peace of campus, so marched into town, chanting, "We own the streets!" They smashed the same windows they had smashed a week earlier, and sprayed the walls with the legends, "Protect the people!"

Early on Monday, everybody heard from Chancellor Berk by email. He excused the riots as legitimate anger against the militarization of police. He said no students were involved. He blamed police behavior on lack of education and suggested that all police candidates need an undergraduate degree. He abolished the University Police

Department and renamed it the Let's-Talk-It-Out Building. The Mayor quickly announced the renaming of the city's police department as the Department for Perpetual Peace.

Simon found personal emails urging him to join the protests as a proven opponent of authority, as a bridge from Riverside to Bayside, as a bridge from young to old. He deleted everything except the official request to meet in the Let's-Talk-It-Out Building. He walked to campus that same morning. A tramp had taken residence on his street corner, displaced from the city center by disorder. He denounced authority with lucid vehemence. On the last block before campus, Simon walked through the pleasant cloisters and lawns of the first city church, where a clear plastic box on a post held books beneath a sign "Free Library." A tramp held a book in both hands: his expression changed from burning confusion to realization and back again, while he turned a page, tore a page, turned a page, tore a page.

Simon walked on to campus, through the protesters, into the Let's-Talk-It-Out Building, without comment. Within the hour, the campus newspaper published online a photograph with the caption: "Anti-fed hero protests police violence."

***

"Professor Ranald, thank you for coming in. I am Special Agent Ryan Topping."

"How do you do? I'm Dr. Ranald; or Simon."

"Please call me Ryan. I've taken over this case."

"Which case?"

"Surely you haven't forgotten?"

"I haven't forgotten any of them. Do you mean John Gard's case?"

"How do you know John Gard?"

"Or do you mean Lief Kirk's?"

"How do you know him?"

"Well, probably I shouldn't say. They had other business, I think you would say. What's your business?"

"The university and city have asked the FBI to conduct the investigation into the homicide last week, since they no longer have police forces."

"Oh, that case."

"Well, let's stick with one case at a time. The university's let's-talk-it-out officers have turned over your contact details as first independent witness."

"No doubt: I volunteered as such, indeed."

"We appreciate that attitude, Simon. I have to warn you now: this will be a long investigation, if only for procedural reasons – identifying witnesses, psychological reports, medical tests, imagery analysis, compassionate leave, discovery, that sort of thing, possibly a year, or more, if our investigation results in indictments, so be prepared."

"That sounds positively speedy to me. Back in London, Professor Sir Barry Liddle's war inquiry took a decade."

"If you intend to leave the US, we ask you to notify us."

"Of course, but I suspect I will be forced to leave the country much earlier than that. You see, my visa is valid only so long as I am employed here, and I don't really know from one week to the next whether I will stay or go."

"I have to warn you that we could get an injunction forbidding you from leaving the country."

"Oh, please! That would put my mind at rest."

"Who is in charge of your employment?"

"Well, I can't rightly tell you that either: Jimmy Pons seems to have been the one who accepted me on exchange, but then Joe Karolides asked me to move onto his floor, but he's not the ultimate boss of that program – that's Guillaume Juncker, and he sits in the geography department. He doesn't like me at all. Then Clara Mudd issued extra funding through next semester, but Max Mira takes charge of whether I keep it; and I abandoned him on the night of the homicide, so he's probably even unhappier. Actually, you really should call John Gard on that: he said he and I should talk about Max Mira, but he's probably still waiting for authorization. Events have moved so quickly that the cases just keep stacking up."

"Let's clarify those other cases in a moment. In the meantime, let's just confirm the statement you gave on the night. And let's confirm that you can't talk publicly about any of these cases until further notice."

***

"Simon, good man, there you are: always in the classes you're supposed to be, always on time."

"Of course, Max, that's my job."

"Your job! Yes, I never thought of it that way. Absolutely, let's add that to the list of reasons why Bayside would be wise to keep you. My job is to make things known."

"I agree."

"I heard that you were a witness to that horrible murder last week. I'm in charge of the change management relating to that, so let's see what we should be saying."

"Well, isn't that a conflict of interest, Max? I mean, you were there that night too."

"More reason to appoint me! I bring a personal perspective – subjective experience is the best experience. Now, I have a great idea for this. We'll make the university look good and influence the elections next month. We'll use this killing as further evidence for the University of Sunshine's long-standing policy against illiberal policing, with a personal plea for conservatives not to politicize the event – you see?"

"I do. Don't you think you should have volunteered that subjective experience to the police?"

"Subjective experience isn't for other people to own – that's how you get competing narratives."

"Well, I have already volunteered my subjective experience."

"You have? What have you said?"

"I'm under instructions not to say."

"I hardly call this collegial, Simon. Academia is built on loyalty, Simon – loyalty! When does your statement start? It better start after you ran away from Jimmy and me."

"I'm not allowed to say. I'm also not allowed to leave the country until I've testified, so I'm afraid you're rather stuck with me for a while."

"The country might be stuck with you, but the university won't be. Now, this is what I'm allowed to say! Get me a copy of your statement, or your funding is over!"

Bruce Oliver Newsome

29. CVE

Chancellor Berk was glad to be distracted by the second meeting of the Optimist's Club. This one promised to be more special. Showing great leadership, he would bring together the region's most enlightened educators and techies with national government servants. Possibly somebody else had achieved the same already, but nobody could do it better.

Yet it presented him with his sternest challenge: the optimists always met in the Academic Senate Lounge, with comfy chairs, candy, and laptops, but public servants expected a conference table, coffee, and a big screen. He called a meeting of the staff. Heroically, he led them to an agreement that had been in the back of his mind all along: they would dismantle the conference table, bring in the comfy chairs, arrange them in an arc facing the screen, place laptops everywhere on trolleys, and serve candy and coffee at the same time. He pinched himself to remember this achievement for his book on leadership. He plotted a follow-up book on politics – not just any politics, but hopeful, audacious politics, across history, as demonstrated by great leaders. Then he would be on course to lead public servants in government, not just academia.

Thus, Chancellor Berk was in the best of moods when his special guests arrived. He let them mingle spontaneously, to introduce themselves in that free-wheeling, unstructured way for which he was known. He let them make their own choices of candy or coffee, and to settle into comfy chairs of their own choosing, before he invited them to hear why they had come. Nobody was better at de-structuring, so he reassured them that he had not prepared anything, except one sentence: "We're not just an enlightening golden sun. We're a bridge between government and technology." Then he invented a personal conclusion, as all great free-wheeling leaders do: "And as a historian of science and technology, I bridge the humanities and hard sciences. That's why we don't need any scientists here."

Kyle Fistbumper posed as an old-hand, confident in command of his team, as if he had joined them years ago and was jaded by the burden. He appeared heavy-eyed, square-jawed, and wrinkle-mouthed; but inside he was awed and insecure. He was still getting used to his new title. He had hoped that Berk would extend the unstructured phase, so that he could introduce himself to everyone individually as Under-Secretary of State for Countering Extremism. He had practiced how his conversation should go from there: "Yes, I do work closely with Secretary of State Trixie Downer. Why, yes, the Secretary is an inspiration. She is an outsider, definitely – she's never enjoyed living in the capital. Yes, she is a lawyer; but she's also a specialist on the issues of our time and this state. Oh, you didn't know? Her undergraduate thesis was on racism in the farming of Agave Tequilana during the Wild West of the Nineteenth Century. Yes, not many people know that. Of course, it was the ideal foundation for a future leader of American foreign policy. Because, hey, what today isn't socio-economic, right?"

As Kyle fitted new inquisitors into old precogitations, his mind raced to adapt his script for academics: "Yes, I love sushi, as long as it's not culturally appropriated. I still have an SUV, but my other car is electric. I live inside the beltway, but my long-term plan is to go coastal. Recycling is very important to me – as important as the planet. I wish I had more time to volunteer – I would do it all the time. I love to travel – the less developed the country the better."

Alas, creative writing couldn't be completed in his head while other people were polluting it. He needed time to make the speaking-vector look cutting-edge by word-combining for alertness-making of the zombie-audience. He called this particular skill the attention-grab by comfort-bump.

Twenty years ago, working for government seemed so simple: every political appointee needs a speech-writer; every diplomat needs an audience-specialist; every analyst needs an editor; every briefer needs a communicator; every department needs a public affairs officer. He was the true origin of policy. Substance begins with style.

Suddenly, the government's priority changed, from hopeful visions for American society, to changing the minds of potential extremists. Never mind which extremists, this was a job for the creative writer, because all dissuasion and persuasion combine to the same tautology, all human beings are interchangeable, all stories are reducible, whatever the culture. And stories are the only things people remember, whatever the facts.

Kyle Fistbumper's one rule was to avoid satire, because, frankly, it always confused him. "I mean," he once exclaimed, when his creative writing teacher allocated 30 minutes to satire, "how does the reader know if the writer is condemning or condoning? Satire is grey in a world that should be black and white. If a novel does not clarify that racism is black and white, it shouldn't be published." Then he decided that extremists tend to satire, or tend to see satirists as extremists, one or the other. As he wrote in the inter-agency manual on creative writing for policy-makers, "Satirists are too nuanced for either fact or fiction."

Kyle Fistbumper advocated tragic, comic, romantic, epic, and erotic turns in every story, but no satire. Any story has villains, heroes, victims, lovers – all he needed to do was label the extremists as villains, his political administration as the hero, and everybody else as a victim. The only role left was the lover. He drifted from the stories to the story-maker himself. Once his personal story could be told, he would become the hero, and to heroes come the lovers; and nobody would be a victim. Life is so easy in the humanities.

He suddenly knew what to say – so suddenly that he almost cut off Chancellor Berk: "And as a creative writer, I am a bridge from the humanities to the professions!"

Once he had said it, he felt it needed something extra. A favorite mantra flashed across his mind: all single-sentence biography-pegs are short-falling, so don't be ambition-cowed from embellishment-making. Then he knew what to say: "And as an Under-Secretary of State, I am a bridge from government to academia."

He still felt a need. When in doubt, he reminded himself, go back to first principles. Logos? He had said the word "academia," so he must have come across as logical. Ethos? His ethos was clear: he was a creative writer. Pathos? He realized a crying need! He strained his creative talent, then decided to tell his own story: "I started out twenty years ago from university – a small liberal arts college, near the coast, a long way outside the beltway, learning to eat sushi for the first time, travelling far from home, volunteering to help the writing-challenged. Now the story has come full circle – I am returned to academia today!"

"But why are you here?" said Aimee Pharisees, chair of Middle

East Studies, looking up from her book for the first time.

Aimee's quick question ruined Kyle's attempt to re-acquire the pose with wrinkled mouth. Now he chewed on his cheeks with self-reproach for a narrative incomplete. He felt his team shift in their seats either side of him. "Why, I am Under-Secretary of State for Countering Extremism – err, I work for the government."

"'Government' is a traditional construct," she said with disdain. "'Extremism' is Islamophobic. I like 'countering,' though." She returned to her book.

Tom Pinklewonk had been relaxed, while Jimmy Pons remained inexplicably absent. Now, he realized, he had been complacent. His presumption to reply first had been usurped by a new rival. "Let me jump in, as the only one here who has served both government and this university. When I was Treasury Secretary, I bridged business and labor. I can't tell you how many labor disputes you never heard about because of me."

"Thank you, Tom," said Berk. "You were part of such an enlightened administration – a bridge between two bad administrations."

"If I may speak for the World and International Studies Program," said Guillaume Juncker. "International relations are bridges between nations; just like me, bridging from Europe to America. Of course, bridging is easier for me, because I am so tall – little joke. Hello! Please call me Will. I'll be here throughout the meeting. Please call on me again."

Kyle took a note from his subordinate on his right. "To clarify, we're really trying to build a bridge between government and technology companies, in order to counter violent extremism online."

"That's definitely the government's responsibility," said Rob Partsome of Belitter.

"We already know how to counter-extremism," said Jean Cadhowling of SheepOnline.

"We've been committed to it, for, like, forever," said Josh Chubfuddler of Tracebook.

"Microsorrie has been there since the beginning of forever," said Rod Sorrie.

"The Sorrie Foundation is committed to building bridges between educators, technology, and government," said Jill Sorrie. "With enthusiasm!"

"That's good to hear," said Under-Secretary Fistbumper. "But how should we proceed?"

"What have you got for us?"

Kyle's head rocked backwards with frustration. He did not like a speechwriter to look speechless, so he blurted out what he had agreed not to say until after everybody else had offered funds. "Well, I have a million dollars to develop a solution." His team shifted uneasily in their seats.

"Oh, that's not enough," said Rob Partsome.

"We've got billions – of users," said Jean Cadhowling. "One million won't make a difference."

"The Sorrie Foundation doesn't match anything below ten million," said Rod Sorrie.

Rob Partsome leaned forward in his chair, placed the palms of his hands together, and locked Fistbumper with a piercing gaze: "Nobody wants to get BeLitter involved in countering extremism. Social media can't be expected to navigate between stopping malicious activities and stopping freedom of speech. The solution to extremism is more communication, because eventually extremism will be drowned out."

Jean Cadhowling nodded vigorously: "We're just focused on our mission, helping people share their information. We believe, really deeply, that if people are sharing more, the world will be a more open place so that we can understand each other. Whether users love each other or terrorize each other, we just need to help them to connect, because, in the end, connections breed understanding."

Josh Chubfuddler leaned forward in the sunlight, unintentionally highlighting his curiously unhealthy complexion on top of an infeasibly boyish face: "This is just the beginning of where this could go. There are still billions of people in the world yet to connect through us to everyone else. Everyone, all over the world, has friends and connections, and can use social media to share valuable information, and we just hope that we can provide that for people all over."

"Okay, but how could we partner for the benefit of all of us?"

persisted the Under-Secretary.

"We'd like to bridge that issue," said Jean Cadhowling,.

"We've wanted to build that bridge for years," said Rob Partsome.

"Bridges are incredibly important," said Josh Chubfuddler.

"Jill and I are spending money on building bridges," said Rod Sorrie.

"How do we build that bridge?" persisted the Under-Secretary, with a squeak of exasperation.

Aimee Pharisees looked up. "The government would build a bridge just to blow it up later. I think you're arrogant to presume you can build bridges." She returned to her book, before adding: "By the way, I build bridges from the Jewish to the Muslim worlds."

In the tense silence, Hattie Maddux realized an opportunity. "I am the bridge from Asia to America; and the bridge from philosophy to society."

"That's so important," said Jean Cadhowling.

"That's incredibly important," said Josh Chubfuddler.

"That's super incredibly important," said Rob Partsome.

"I am interested in the difference between what society wants people to think and what people should think."

"So are we!" exclaimed the Under-Secretary.

"And I'm thinking that social media must have the data."

"So am I!" exclaimed the Under-Secretary.

"I'll dump you the data," said Josh Chubfuddler. "Anything for education. I've dumped in this school before."

"How?"

"I'll dump it in the Optimist Club's private Tracebook page."

"We all share a mission to share the truth," said Jean Cadhowling

"That's what we are!" said Rob Partsome, "Truth-sharers! More information equals truth."

"Jill, we should change the title of our foundation."

"Yes! The Sorrie Foundation for Enthusiasm for Truth!"

"Yes," said Jean Cadhowling. "And the government can give you some of that million to fund your research."

"I can broker that money," said the Chancellor.

"We'd need some guarantees," said Kyle hurriedly, "such as…" He took a piece of paper. "What about privacy?"

Josh Chubfuddler was prepared for this: "Privacy is incredibly important to giving people the ability to share. We give users complete control of their privacy, while creating a safe space, which enables them to share more information."

Kyle took another piece of paper. "Some part of the funding needs to be devoted to teaching. I would suggest creative writing for counter-extremism through social media."

Jimmy Pons walked in, late and already disturbed. "There's a great shortage of women in here," he sniffed. "At any truly enlightened institute of higher learning we'd be knee-deep in women." He looked at Pinklewonk and Berk accusatorily and slumped in a chair. "You seem to be abandoning the great Bayside tradition of Bayside time."

"No, Jimmy, but our guests are on government time."

"Nobody told me."

"My email to everyone did say 2 p.m."

"That means 2.10 p.m.!"

"Jimmy, let me introduce you. Everybody, Jimmy. Jimmy, everybody. Jimmy directs the program on Peace and Extremism Studies. Why don't you tell everybody about it?"

"My program has offered a course on extremism for twenty years."

"And I approved it for all the WISP majors," said Will Juncker. "I did. I knew it was the right thing."

"So," Kyle Fistbumper said uncertainly, with a piece of paper in each hand, "you have a course on counter-extremism already?"

"Not exactly," said Jimmy. "It's a typical story really. You see: the instructor was killed. So we gave it to a new instructor, who struggled to keep terrorism out of counter-terrorism, so we defunded him." Jimmy paused his story, thought for a second, then added, "Didn't you, Chancellor?"

Dick Berk rose to the challenge. "But in the next week, after the federal invasion of campus – no offense, Kyle – we funded a relaunch. So, you see, we've always had a course on counter-extremism."

"You're out of touch, Berk."

"What?"

"Yeah, well, Max Mira has defunded him again."

"What?"

"I knew nothing about it," said Will Juncker. "I sit in the geography department."

"I know everything about everything," said Jimmy happily. "The instructor wasn't prepared to support the University of Sunshine's new policy against policing. That is your policy, isn't it, Chancellor? Yes, so Max has already redirected the money to a new course on counter-policing. And he has already appointed the most extreme counter-extremists from off campus as Professors of Practice." Jimmy Pons turned to Berk and cocked an eyebrow.

Berk thought quickly: "Well said Jimmy. Jimmy is absolutely right: resources are always so tight at a public school. We need funding to counter extremism. Don't you agree, Under-Secretary?"

30. History Society

"First, I noticed an email restoring my funding, so I went through my past emails, trying to explain it, then I saw your email, so, good things really do come in pairs."

"You were lucky I emailed you after all these weeks."

"Yes, I was."

"I was expecting you to look me up."

"Yes, I planned to, when things calmed down."

"But I had to email you."

"You did; and I'm sorry about that, but I'm glad you emailed. When we said our goodbyes, I should have asked when I should reach out. I was uncertain of the etiquette around here."

"That's not easy – and we didn't clarify anything."

"It was a strange evening."

"We're here now."

"I'm glad."

"Me too."

"I often thought of contacting you, but events here kept getting in the way."

"I wasn't short of reminders. Everywhere I looked I saw news of you."

"Not willingly, I assure you! I mean, yes, willingly, that you should see me, but not willingly that I should be the subject of the news."

"Then you made a mess of that! Three weeks ago, I recognized your headshot on television as the anti-fed hero of Bayside."

"That report was not accurate."

"The week after that, I saw you on live television joining a protest against Adrian Yannis."

"I wasn't joining it."

"And last week you were protesting police violence."

"Again, not accurate."

"You surely got my attention, although I didn't know what to make of you. That's why I emailed; but apparently you weren't paying attention."

"I'm sorry: I haven't been checking my email much lately. I get too many emails! You were lucky I recognized yours."

"I'm honored."

"Oh dear, that's not what I meant! I meant, you put 'from Teddi Theodora' in the title, so it stuck out. Otherwise I might have deleted it, amongst so many others. You see, I've got in the habit of deleting emails. This campus – it's been unstable."

"It looks unstable."

"You look very nice."

"Thank you – so do you."

"You look as vintage as on the night I met you."

"Except I'm wearing all white today. I don't normally wear white outside the house. I wear black because, after all, clothes get so filthy around here, don't they? But it's so hot and sunny, and I wanted to be cooler than last time I left the Peninsula."

"I'm sorry we didn't meet then."

"We're here now."

"I'm glad."

"Me too."

"I'm sorry to make you come so far away from home – and to expose your white dress."

"This isn't vintage – and I made it washable."

"You made it?"

"I make most of what I wear outside."

"Then you must be an expert on the craft as well as the art."

"I practice. I pick up vintage designs, tools, and machines"

"Like an experimental archaeologist."

"I often think I am as close to a time-travelling historian as one could be. I don't imagine I live in the past, but I imagine what it would be like if I did. I read history to learn how to live authentically, and I learn history by living authentically. I'd like to write up my discoveries one day."

"I hope you do. You're a historian. That's why I thought to invite you to this."

"Where are we?"

"I'm not sure. I thought the invitation was to a visiting speaker, but we seem to be in a dining area."

They had taken seats across a table, facing each other. The tables were arranged in parallel at the rear of the hall, on a large mezzanine, from which the auditorium's seats descended in two pincers towards the podium. Here the speaker was introduced with more solemnity than dignity. The diners continued to munch and babble. The seats in the center were dark outlines before the large bright screens.

"Fellow historians! The Bayside History Society welcomes you to its annual visiting lecture and no-host brown bag dinner."

Simon and Teddi sat still and quiet, focused on the podium as if their eyes would help them hear, while closer voices provoked distracting imaginations. A group rushed to join their table, without curbing conversation.

"I know, I know: I'm late and I didn't bring the hummus, but my course on the Second World War is on the other side of campus."

"I've added a book on that war to my holiday reading list."

"I'll save you the trouble: Hitler lost."

"History sucks: it's got Hitler in it."

"I know: history is racist, and so last century."

"Yes, let's get back to current history, like the presidential campaign."

"Fellow historians," came the shout from the podium. "The History Society, with the generous support of the Max Mira Talent Management Corporation, inaugurated the annual lecture to bring radical perspectives on traditional subjects…"

"Try the falafel – it gives a radical perspective on Middle East traditions."

"It's so authentic. It's made only a block away."

"Our speaker this year is not a traditional historian," interrupted the shout from the podium.

"I'd like to write the history of falafel."

"You should: cultural history is so non-traditional."

"But is it radical enough? Give me some radical titles."

"Falafel and the struggle for cultural heritage."

"Falafel and the immigrant experience."

"The immigration of falafel into America."

"No, that sounds Western-centric."

"Our speaker," came the voice from the podium, "is probably best known for his reporting on Brexit extremism, or Brextremism, as he so creatively calls it…"

"I was thinking of writing something on the Iran-Contra affair."

"That sounds traditional."

"Yes, but the Reagan library isn't far away."

"And it's a pretty place to spend a couple years."

"But it's off campus – and it's rural."

"Yes, but I could still live here."

"But you wouldn't be here during the day. A social historian should be social."

"Actually, I was thinking of a political history."

"But that would be traditional."

"You can make any political history into a social history. Here, check out these titles: Iran-Contra's impact on society; Iran-Contra and the Iranian immigrant experience."

"Our speaker," came the shout from the podium, "was for many years based in London..."

"I'd like to spend a couple years in London. That's a very social city."

"Does London have a Presidential library?"

"Our speaker," shouted the podium, "has taken a break from his important vocation with the British public broadcasting corporation..."

"Broadcasting! That's the way to go. A historian working for a broadcaster, and broadcasting history: that's non-traditional, isn't it?"

"No: he's British for one thing, and corporate for another."

"But it's a public broadcaster, which is almost as good as a public university."

"Now, as I invite our speaker to the podium, please join me, in the tradition of the Bayside History Society, in refraining from any traditional show of applause, which may trigger anxiety and confusion, particularly in listeners with sensory issues. Please use silent jazz hands instead – it's like a wave, yes. Some of you have got it. I know, it is difficult – not that I am shaming anybody with learning disabilities. Okay, let's get straight to our distinguished guest historian."

Mr. Wonderfool stepped to the stage, respectfully mimicking the jazz hands. His voice rose clear and pleasing over the rude humdrum of foreign voices, without a Northern accent that they would not understand. "Thank you, comrades, for that warm American welcome. History teaches us that before Americans were independent, they were revolting..."

"I've got my topic: Falafel and the American revolution in food."

"Iran-Contra and the American revolution in society."

"Tonight," Mr. Woonderfool shouted imperiously, "I want to shatter the orthodox view that Churchill was a conservative. Traditionalists have got Churchill all wrong. Churchill was a radical! Yes, he joined the Conservative Party, but he also joined the Liberal Party. Yes, he was conservative compared to radicals of today, but he was the radical of his time. I'm here to counter the orthodoxy..."

"I wish I had thought to counter that orthodoxy. It's so hard to find an orthodoxy."

"That's right!" continued Mr. Woonderfool. "Churchill was a non-traditional historian, like me! He was a journalist and autobiographer. He made history, before he wrote about it. Then he revised the history. He was a revisionist! He opposed traditional orthodoxy – as well as orthodox traditions…"

"I want to be a revisionist!"

"I'd like to revise Barry Liddell's history of the Second World War."

"Yes, but his history has been well revised by many people already."

"Then I'd like to revise them."

"You should – everybody hates the orthodoxy."

"Which is the orthodoxy?"

"Just call the old revisionism the new orthodoxy."

"But be careful of orthodox revisionism."

"Churchill," cried Mr. Woonderfool, "was an internationalist. He first travelled internationally as a soldier – contrary to the British nationalism of his generation..."

"I'd study nationalism – if I could do it internationally."

"I've just realized another dissertation topic: The international appeal of falafel and Arab nationalism."

"The international clash between Reagan's nationalism and Iranian internationalism."

"Let us not forget," said Mr. Woonderfool, wagging his finger, "that, Churchill supported free trade! So, you see, he was clearly an internationalist."

"Free trade was good for falafel – there's a dissertation topic."

"Not just an internationalist," continued Mr. Woonderfool with delight, "Churchill was a socialist! I know he said he hated socialism, but the orthodoxy relies too much on what people say over what they must be thinking. He knew he could not win the Second World War without centralizing government, so he formed a coalition with the same socialists he had attacked in peacetime. He controlled prices. He conscripted soldiers and coal-miners and agricultural workers. He suspended elections. He rationed food. He provided free housing. He promised social services. If that's not socialism, I'll eat my beret."

"If my topic mentions socialism, could I call myself a social historian?"

"That's obvious."

"Like any good socialist," Mr. Woonderfool pouted, "Churchill fought fascism! And he chose to fight fascism in alliance with communism. Then he gave the communists half of Europe..."

"Did the defeat of fascism open the Western world to falafel?"

"Don't ask direct questions. Just claim that something has been over-stated."

"Or under-stated. It doesn't matter which, for a title."

"Right! The defeat of fascism has been over-stated."

"Falafel has been under-stated in Western history."

"Churchill," warbled Mr. Woonderfool, imagining himself at the despatch box in the House of Commons, "was a pro-European. When he spoke about the need to balance against Germany, he was speaking for European integration. When he spoke about Britain dominating Europe, he was speaking for European integration. When he spoke against the Iron Curtain, he was speaking for European integration..."

"European integration and the Iran-Contra affair: A relationship that has been under-stated."

"Falafel and European integration: now there's a relationship that has been under-stated."

"Churchill," Mr. Woonderfool asked his listeners to realize, "was a feminist. He married a woman. And four of their five children were daughters…"

"How about a feminist perspective on Iran-Contra?"

"You can't! You're a man."

"Yes, but Reagan was a man."

"That's another strike against him."

Mr. Woonderfool seized the lectern combatively. "Now, I turn to the most misunderstood accusation against Churchill: his imperialism. Yes, he talked about the British empire lasting for a thousand years. Yes, he argued against Indian independence. But he fought against German imperialism in Europe! He fought against Italian imperialism in Africa! He fought against Japanese imperialism in Asia! He supported Soviet counter-imperialism!"

"Falafel and the fight against imperialism."

"Falafel and cultural imperialism."

"The cultural appropriation of falafel."

"The cultural relativism of falafel."

"Humble as I am," said Mr. Woonderfool, reprising a delivery he had used to play Julius Caesar at college, "I hesitate to draw lessons from history. Lessons spoil a good story. But one lesson is very clear: international cooperation is important. And secondly: Churchill would have opposed Brexit. And whoever ignores history is condemned to repeat it…"

"Ignore my dissertation on Iran-Contra and you're condemned to repeat it."

"And finally," shouted Mr. Woonderfool, "history is too important to leave to the Generals."

"Falafel is too important to leave to the Generals."

Mr. Woonderfool was not finished: "Let's not give up on history. Stop the march of science. Condemn the past but not the historian. And remember this if nothing else: history proves that Brexit proves that history repeats itself."

The discussant leaped to the lectern to warn against any disabling applause. "Thank you for the jazz hands! Thank you to our wonderful speaker. Now I would like to moderate the questions. I'll take three at once…"

"Ooh! Ooh! Here at the back! Yes! Have historians under-stated Churchill's consumption of falafel during his many visits to the Arab world?"

"What did Churchill say about the Iran-Contra affair?"

"What did Churchill say about the current presidential election?"

"Wait, all of you, wait! What would Churchill have said about this breaking news: Presidential candidate Trixie Downer's supporters are counter-radicals."

"That's impossible."

"It's true – their correspondence has been leaked."

"I don't believe it."

"I've been on my phone the whole time. And there's already a podcast about it, so it must be true."

"She's right – Chancellor Berk's correspondence has been leaked, from within the Optimists Club."

"The Optimists Club is a populist myth."

"No, it's not. It's an orthodox center-left elite, keeping down the radical majority."

"It has a Tracebook page – a private Tracebook page; and it's been hacked."

"And it proves that the Optimists Club colluded to promote Trixie over a more radical candidate."

"Shame on Berk!"

"Bring back Churchill!"

31. Election

The plaza was chaotic with campaigning, but the office was quiet. Simon walked the circuit: only Earnest Keeper was in. His glass door was open, but, uncharacteristically, his other chair was empty, the benches in the corridor were empty, and he was bored.

"Simon!" said Earnest with enough desperation to encourage escalation.

"Good morning Earnest. Where is everybody?"

"It's election day, Simon!"

The realization of the presidential election hit Simon deep in his stomach, swam to the surface, and subsumed everything else that was on his mind. "Oh! Of course – so important a Tuesday that it's a holiday."

"Not really a holiday, but you've got the idea. Don't be ashamed if you forgot. I saw that you had other things to think about."

"Oh dear! That makes me sound self-obsessed."

"You're starting to fit in. You've been brave, here, Simon: to take on Jimmy Pons, then Hattie Maddux, Walter Fontaine's course, the feds, and now the police."

"Well, that's not accurate."

"You worry too much about accuracy. The trick is to get noticed as the authorities want you to be noticed. That's why I'm in today: less likely to get noticed. The best day to get work done in political science is on the most political day of the quadrennial."

"I didn't know you were a political scientist."

"I have an appointment in political science, actually. I took it once I got to know Jimmy. But it's the only department where faculty wear suits, and I don't like suits, so I chose to take an office in WISP."

"Really?"

"No, the chair didn't like me."

"Who's that?"

"One tenured faculty against you is enough. I took half-an-appointment here, so I can hope for a majority vote across two departments."

"Is the political science department weak in American politics? I mean, I really haven't seen any events about the election, other than student protests."

"You under-estimate the faculty. Those protests aren't organized by the students alone. Of course, the faculty write them off as field studies – after a few interviews, they've got survey results."

"Oh dear! That undermines my course on social science."

"The trouble with political science, Simon, is too much politics and not enough science."

Simon pondered Earnest's new-found confidences, then felt bolder. "Actually, do you know anything about a science disability?"

"Yes, a lot of students claim it. Easiest if you frame your assignments as opportunities to communicate their feelings."

"Well, that's just the problem: she won't communicate. She now claims both a science disability and a communication disability."

"Poor you! That's the worst. She can deny your communications and refuse to send any."

"Yes. I've never seen her, and I can't contact her. Is this like a writing disability, or a reading disability, or a print disability?"

"All of them. However, DAFI usually makes the student specify one form of communication as least disabled. Forward to me the email. Aha! See here, see this link?"

"You mean the word 'clink'?"

"Yes, that's the one. It stands for 'communications link'. Your student has put you in the clink, as we say. Let's see what happens here: it's a big download! Aha! She's got a disability for everything except talking."

"So, I could talk to her?"

"No! She's accommodated for misanthropy too."

"That's why she's never in classes."

"You're catching on."

"But I could still talk to her remotely?"

"No, she's a misanthrope in all media."

"So, how am I supposed to talk to her?"

"You're not! She talks to you. You're supposed to listen."

"Then, am I expecting an audio file? A video file?"

"No, you're not allowed to see or hear her. She's accommodated for anti-narcissism."

"What does that mean?"

"She thinks everybody else is a narcissist."

"So, how am I supposed to receive her talk?"

"Never fear! DAFI prides itself on accommodating all accommodations: a dedicated anti-narcissist student adviser provides a computer that is allowed to transcribe but not record. See here, the transcription has downloaded."

"Is that a test page?"

"No, those are her words. Look, I'll read it: 'You know, like, really, whatever, like, like, like…'"

Earnest read down silently. "She has a lot of 'likes'."

Earnest scrolled down a page; and another page; and another page. "Here's something! 'Like, like, like, yaha'!"

"What does that mean?"

"It's obvious."

"Is it?"

"No, that's what it means. She's saying, 'It's obvious'."

"What is?"

"I don't know." Earnest turned another page. "Then there are more likes."

He turned another page. "Here's a sentence! Oh dear!"

"What is it?"

"She doesn't like you at all."

"How do you know?"

"She rolls her eyes."

"The software can see that?"

"No, that's what she said." He turned another page. "In conclusion, she doesn't like you. This could ruin your funding."

"But I've never communicated with her."

"Yes, she blames you for that too. You really need to think of a good response to this one, otherwise it's not going to look good for you. You're supposed to respond within 24 hours. Now, look at the time! We're both due in empty classrooms. Let's go."

Only Aurelia and Judiciary showed up to his class on Western-Asian Relations. They wanted to talk about the election, but Simon said that as a non-American his comments would be inappropriate on election day, so he taught the class he had prepared. Thereafter, they volunteered to show him the polling place inside the lobby of the dorms. Rather than wait in line outside the door, they dropped mail-in ballots inside a yellow bag. Simon was repeatedly asked to pick a name for himself from the voter register. He settled for a sticker with the legend "I voted," except no slogan was available in any language except Chinese.

He walked home in a hurry, determined on an early night, but as he lay thoughtful in the dark, he heard periodical howls of protest from the neighbors. Eventually, he knew he could sleep, not as the noise abated, but as his curiosity abated.

The next morning, he rose late and caught up with the news. Downtown had been vandalized again – the same businesses on the same route. The freeway had been closed by trespassers during rush hour. Some protesters split off to the Bayside train station. Community Champions, from the Bayside City's Department for Perpetual Peace, formed a line to stop commuters from interfering. Journalists were allowed to pass freely. They distributed anti-narcissism communication apps in order to gather quotes without accountability. The Daily Sunshine pasted online the following list of quotes:

"Democracy is under threat! We will not accept the vote!"

"We did everything we could to silence Hickling, but he still won. That proves the election was stolen."

"He couldn't win an argument with us."

"What's the point of arguing with a bigot?"

"I demand a recount. Everyone I know voted for Trixie."

"Everyone knows that Trixie was rejected because she's a woman. Americans are sexist."

"As Trixie said, they don't even know you're prejudiced: they have subconscious biases."

"We will continue to act by any means necessary, because this election has left us no other choice."

"This election shows that protest is the only way left to the American people to show they're politically engaged. Get out the protest!"

"When their politics denies our candidate, we deny their politics."

"We're taking direct action against the ruling class, starting with commuters."

Chancellor Berk emailed:

Dear campus community,

The results of yesterday's election came as a surprise to most of us, regardless of our political views. It will take time for us to process and understand the meaning of the vote, both because we face a period of uncertainty and transition, and because the vote followed a deeply divisive and polarizing campaign. Thus, students are excused from campus for the next week, so that they may reflect and come to the same conclusion.

As a community, we must use this moment to reaffirm our values of respect and inclusion, while working together to preserve freedom, fearless inquiry, and diversity. We must support each other at this time, and express solidarity with all groups and individuals who fear for the future.

Above all, we must not lose sight of our commitment to the greater good, to our collective commitment to the improvement of our society and our world. I am confident that together we have both the will and the ability to rise above the rancor. Bayside continues to embody the best of what a free, open, and inclusive society should be.

Within ten minutes, Berk forwarded a statement from University System President Metro:

In light of yesterday's election results, there is understandable consternation and uncertainty among members of the University of Sunshine community.

The University of Sunshine is proud of being a diverse and welcoming place for students, faculty, and staff with a wide range of backgrounds, experiences, and perspectives. Diversity is central to our mission.

We remain absolutely committed to adhering to our "Principles Against Intolerance." As the Principles make clear, the University "strives to foster an environment in which all are included" and "all are given an equal opportunity to learn and explore."

We are proud of what the University of Sunshine stands for and hope to convey that positive message to others in our state and nation, despite the election of Clashmore Hickling.

The academics union promised an executive meeting.

We'll discuss when we'll protest, then we'll discuss what to protest. For those of you who are too upset to work, we'll discuss how to justify it to your line managers. In all communications, you should call this a day of outrage. If possible, staff should continue to be available at their desks for student healing. Teaching, however, would be a distraction.

Simon emailed Earnest Keeper to ask if they should be teaching. Earnest emailed back immediately, to relate that he had offered all his teaching and office hours for student healing. "It's great for course evaluations," he concluded.

Simon went to the cubicle of humility, on time for normal office hours. Boyan came by, fresh from Earnest's healing, but seeking more: "Yeah, I'm embarrassed to be American, but don't blame me, I'm not that American."

"I'm certainly not American, and I am not trained in American politics, so I really shouldn't distract you. Do you want to hear about what I taught on Western-Asian relations yesterday?"

"No, I'm not feeling Asian today."

Left alone in the cubicle of humility, Simon noticed an email from Marcus.

Dear students and colleagues,

As some of you may have heard, administrators are encouraging you to take the week to reflect on the election instead of study or work.

I want to let you know that I will be teaching. We have less than five teaching weeks until the end of the course. We've made good progress, but classes are valuable, and your education is important. Whatever the alleged issues of this election, I do not think you should be denied an education because of them. I say this with no disrespect for people who are affected.

I think we should reflect further on the broader relationship between politics and education. Normally I follow the old-fashioned etiquette to eschew discussing politics, money, and sex in public, but this university has not.

Politics, like most important things, including mathematics, are complicated. Mathematics can help. Do you remember learning about zero-sum games? You cannot avoid zero-sum outcomes in politics: some people will gain, some will lose. Education is no different: my teaching will suit some more than others. In this way, an education in anything, even mathematics, can teach you something about politics.

However, too many people are trying to persuade you that if you don't get what you want then the system is broken. Being younger, you're probably less cluttered with experiences, so your convictions are probably clearer, but clarity can overlap reductionism.

You and society are investing in your education so that you can help to solve these issues. Don't fall into the trap of thinking that seeking an education proves a lack of imagination or awareness. Learning proves humility.

That is why I am working. Your education is important to me, to you, and society as a whole.

See you in class.

Marcus

Simon forwarded the email to his students, confirmed that he too would be teaching all week, then went to teach the modelling of causal relationships. That evening, he received an email from DAFI warning him that the semantic frame "model" was associated with the employment of women as objects for male gratification.

"I really need to call Teddi," he thought, but the hour was late. He was still working through ambiguous emails from different university authorities on how to manage reactions to the election, when he saw an outstanding email from the FBI.

32. The Chase

"Simon, thank you for coming all the way off campus to meet us."

"This is my civic duty."

"That's the spirit. We know a visit to the feds can be problematic for your employment."

"I knew that too, but I didn't expect a trip to the federal building to be so hazardous."

"What do you mean?"

"Well, climbing up the steps from the subway, a glass tube came bouncing down towards me, followed by a man shouting, 'Don't touch my crack pipe or I'll kill you!' Just before I crossed the street there, a babbling woman rushed in front of a parked car to urinate on its bonnet. And somebody is banging on your lobby's windows demanding that you leave him alone. Nice building though."

"It's a new building. The city traded the land. You can imagine why."

"I imagine that local authorities sought positive externalities from your presence."

"Yes, I guess that's the academic way to put it."

"Oh, I was hoping not. How can I be more helpful?"

"Well, let's start with the case in hand. You remember Special Agent Barmouth."

"Martin, hello."

"I've added Special Agent Ryan Topping from the Halloween Homicide Task Force."

"Is this the Counter-Terrorism Task Force?"

"No, not this time – you're looking at the Counter-Trafficking Task Force. You see, Max Mira is a big deal: he's the subject of a dozen claims of sexual assault or trafficking in this jurisdiction alone, but he's locked up his accusers, colleagues, and officials with bribes, blackmails, and non-disclosure agreements."

"That sounds expensive."

"That's why he works so hard," said Martin.

"And we have to work ten times as hard. We need to prove his intent."

"That does sound hard – easier would be to assume intent."

"We can't assume anything."

"I know: you're not academics."

"Talking of academics, we want to prove his partner in crime – Jimmy Pons. We've collected numerous allegations from young women that Mira and Pons sponsored them as overseas students; and visited them overseas beforehand, when many must have been underage."

"Jenny Wren."

"Excuse me?"

"Many then."

"I'm afraid so."

"Then they weren't joking," recalled Simon.

"I'm afraid not."

"Then we need to stop them."

"Yes. You know them both professionally and personally, and you've informed us of their vulnerability. That's what makes you unique. So, let me bring my colleagues up to speed. Simon was with the two subjects on the night of the Halloween homicide. They didn't do anything illegal, but they might be worried that Simon's statements to the police include what the two of them were saying, and that public exposure would precipitate other revelations, bringing down the whole house of cards. They're living on a knife edge between omnipotence and terror. We need to wedge the crack in their omnipotence. Is all of that accurate, Simon?"

"You put it better than I did."

"We need to play our best hand. Mr. Mira is the bigger fish and most exposed, so he's our focus. What we need is audio evidence or imagery of Mr. Mira with somebody who will confirm abuse in this jurisdiction, before he buys them into a non-disclosure agreement, or gets them defunded or sent overseas. Phone records prove contacts, but not the nature of the relationships. Now, Simon agreed for the lab. to adapt his phone. Simon, here's your phone back. We've reversed Max's app so your phone will record whatever he says or shows to you. Otherwise, your phone will appear to be turned off. The warrant gives us just ten days to discover crimes of sexual abuse, trafficking, bribery, or blackmail. Simon expects the subject to be indiscreet and boastful. Is that accurate, Simon?"

"It's the most accurate statement I've heard since I arrived in Bayside. Now I just need to learn how to be duplicitous. Still, I've had many mentors."

***

"Max! Thank you for coming."

"Of course. You said you want me to manage your federal funding."

"Yes, it includes a budget for publicity."

"Still, your call was a surprise."

"I got my phone repaired. Now that I'm funded to teach counter-extremism with a focus on social media, I'd better stay connected to social media. And I remembered: you're the expert on social media. And I feel repaired myself, so, I realize I need to help my career along, distance myself from the horrible business of the Halloween homicide. I thought we could say that I was too distressed and confused to speak publicly before now."

"For the good of the university."

"Yes, for the good of the university. That's very clever. I'll hate the feds as much as you want."

"They're out of our control."

"That's accurate."

"Why were you in such a hurry to meet?"

"Well, I want a clear weekend, for once. I need to make time for a friend."

"Teddi?"

"How do you know that name?"

"I remember you using it at Halloween."

"You've got a good memory for names."

"It's a girl's name."

"You wouldn't like her – she dresses old-fashioned."

"Oh well. She's not needed. You made a good call to meet at the swimming pool, with the women's team. I might have suggested the athletic track or the soccer field, but you got the timing right here."

"Yes, I know my timing. First, I want to talk about my publicity."

"Me too. I had an idea for a shift in narrative: no longer about your present, but society's future: future technology for the advancement of social justice; you're combining new technology to solve old problems; a partnership between local tech companies and the university to counter extremism. For instance, the students could develop new tools for searching BeLitters and Tracebooks for the wrong sort of beliefs, and changing them."

"I did want to talk about my students' proposals for countering extremism. They're ready for implementation, so you could manage their publicity."

"If I manage their publicity, I need to approve their proposals first."

"I emailed the best three to you already. One team has proposed an immersive game that will challenge players to deradicalize a fictional student on a trajectory to terrorism."

"I liked the game, except the setting: a university campus! Surely, a military garrison, or a police station, or a federal office would be more realistic for breeding an extremist?"

"Well, who are we to disagree with students? The second team proposed an app to highlight fallacies in extremist arguments."

"Well, extremism is just obvious! An enlightened news source would have done the work already."

"And the third team proposed a similar analysis of the content produced by the Fascist Fighters."

"I don't understand what the Fascist Fighters have to do with extremism. I mean, they're anti-fascists! You're either a fascist or a fascist fighter. It's self-evident. Only fascists behave like fascists, you see?"

"Circularity is one of the fallacies they want to expose."

"What's circularity?"

"For example: 'Brexit means Brexit'."

"Exactly! Fascists are Brexiteers."

"Let's focus on funding these students."

"Oh, none of these proposals seem appropriate. No, I'm the expert in counter-extremist narratives. In the old days, we called them anti-defamation narratives. There is no better way to fight defamation than to compare our virtues with the opposition's vices. We'd produce a nice glossy book, with inspiring photos of the remorseless, optimistic trajectory to social justice: minorities fighting majorities, fighting power, fighting police, fighting the justice system, liberating the prisons, smashing capitalism, invading white spaces, evading borders, shocking the art world, educating the world, because education is power."

"A book – you're proposing a book, but the funding was supposed to support new technologies."

"Oh, a book is a euphemism. I wouldn't expect kids to read a book. We'll get those students of yours to build an app, linking to images and to audio files, with the inspiring stories behind each photo."

"What about the immersive game?"

"Tell the students to make it a first-person shooter: 'Shoot the Fascists'." Max breathed heavily with excitement.

"That's immoral."

"I don't see how."

"What about your stance on gun control?"

"Yeah, but the targets are fascists. Now, Simon, don't overthink this. Remember: I'm the expert on publicity. I tell you what: you award me the publicity contract, then I'll pay ten percent to you as honorarium."

"It's not about the money."

"No?" said Max with surprise. "What else interests a lecturer, on your lousy pay?"

"The students."

"We all care about the students."

"Yes, particularly the female students."

"Now we're talking! You see? We're bonding. What sort of female students?"

"You tell me."

"You've got the students."

"Yes, but I don't know whether they're good for anything."

"Good is what you step up to. You start with what's easy."

"What do you mean?"

"Everything is easy for the enlightened – just advertise that you're enlightened. You know! We're all feminist, we're all embarrassed to be male, we're all embarrassed to be American. Of course, that doesn't work as well overseas."

"I've come from overseas."

"Europe doesn't count as overseas. Overseas means south of the border, south of the United States, south of the European Union, south of Russia – but north of Australia."

"Only some of that is overseas."

"Whatever! The point is, that's where the easy pickings are."

"I don't know."

"Look at me! Look how fat I am – that's how desperate they are."

"I don't have your confidence."

"Confidence starts with money; and if you're in the right place overseas, you have the money of a king. That's how I started out when I was a lecturer. Now I have the money to be a king here, but it's safer to be a king there."

"What if I want to be a king here, on my salary?"

"Commercialize: set up a consulting business, for overseas students to get into American schools. Throw out the males. Ask the girls for a full-length photo – they'll usually make it sexy, and if they don't, then throw them out. Interview them overseas, in a hotel room, ask for a massage – they get the idea, and if they don't, you move on, because there's plenty of fish in the sea. If you've got the right attitude and persistence, you'd be surprised what you can achieve."

"I find this hard to believe."

"I'll show you."

Images started to roll across Max's phone, and to arrive on Simon's phone, from the other side of the world and back.

***

"Jimmy, I've got to bring in a new partner."

"Ooh! How young? How colored? How hot is she?"

"It's Simon."

"Is this a joke?"

"This is an emergency. My friends at the Capitol told me that somebody is making inquiries about my students. I don't know who, but somebody must be breaking her N.D.A., and I've got to find out, and slap her with a civil suit before a criminal case releases her."

"What's that got to do with Simon?"

"He's going to join you on the Thanksgiving run."

"You mean us."

"No, just you and him. I've got to represent 'Men Against Toxic Masculinity' in the Thanksgiving Day Parade. It will help to take the heat off. And it comes with a nice stipend."

"Who invited you?"

"Somebody from the law enforcement association. I've got to pump him for intelligence, so I couldn't say no."

"Why should I take anyone else south of the border?"

"We need to break him in. We can use him as a diversion, in so many ways. With the difficult girls, he'll be the young man with the accent, and we'll take the collaterals. We can throw him to the news media if they ask any questions. Look at him! He'll look more suspicious than us."

"Why him? He wasn't useful at Halloween."

"He's a convert! We broke him in. But he's still malleable."

"Typical man!"

***

"Simon, we need to talk."

"Yes, Jimmy, I feared that we would."

"You're coming south of the border, at Thanksgiving."

"That is Max's plan."

"Except Max isn't coming."

"No."

"That puts a lot of responsibility on you."

"I'm abnormally responsible."

"How do I know I can trust you?"

"I'm sure Max trusts you."

"Naturally!"

"You take the lead – I'll just follow whatever you do."

"Is that what he told you?"

"I'll do whatever you tell me. He told me to trust you."

"You'll have to, because he won't be there."

"No, so really all the responsibility is on you – and I trust that you'll do whatever you'd normally do."

"But I don't trust you."

"But you trust Max. He wanted me out of your program, so the heat would fall on WISP. He wanted me at Halloween, even to bear witness after you scored. Now he wants me south of the border. I hope you'll trust me by the time of the next trip to East Asia."

"How do you know about East Asia?"

"He showed me the photographs. You looked very happy."

"He showed you? I was – I was happy. The rule there, Simon, is the rule of ten: the whores can be negotiated to one-tenth of their asking price; and you don't need to speak Mandarin – you can display the numbers on your phone."

"Can you show me, on your phone?"

***

"Dr. Ranald!"

"Madame Deputy-Consul: I am particularly pleased to see you again."

"I am pleased to hear it. I was reminded to seek your counsel, when I saw your latest quote in the newspaper. Do you really think federal agencies and your university are at war?"

"No doubt."

"I hoped you could educate me. Who are these people who are at war?"

"Well, I'll tell you about one. Perhaps you can help me with him."

"I do hope so."

"Max Mira – he's very well connected in government – at every level. He tells me he's well connected with the Chinese government too."

"I don't know him."

"Not you personally. He claims that Chinese officials help him to bring Chinese students here, and he helps the officials who help him, and he helps the Chinese to stay here if they meet their promises."

"Who are these students?"

"I have photos, places, and dates for some. He claims to have confidential relationships with all of them. He certainly visits East Asia often, with Jimmy Pons."

"Can you write down the names of these two men."

"Certainly."

"Leave them to me, Simon."

***

Simon read out the names, then passed the list over the table. "I have evidence that each had a relationship with you."

"You knew that already. They're clients of my consulting business."

"But they didn't pay you any money. In return for sex, you wrote their college applications, you wrote recommendations, you signed their language proficiency, you counter-signed their loan applications."

"You're inferring too much from what I showed you. Every one of them signed a N.D.A. Everybody's protected."

"Actually, I have this information from outside this jurisdiction, so you're not protected."

Max's surprise turned to outrage. He took his hands out of his pockets, hunched his shoulders to his ears, inhaled deeply, and crunched his face, except to open his mouth. "How dare you?! Do you forget who I am, who you are? I run this campus. I run your account! I make the world a better place."

Simon watched Max grow tenser; he watched that tension build; he thought more about how it would be released. Sitting at the table suddenly seemed foolish, so he leapt upright. The chair fell behind him.

Max jumped, froze for a few seconds, then started to weep: "Please don't tell anyone. I've got a wife – she mustn't know. I'm only human – I was weak only once, with each of them. Please sign a non-disclosure agreement: I'll pay you half-a-million. Alright: a million. Please! Everybody deserves a second chance, right?"

33. Emergency

Chancellor Berk sat at his desk grumpily, rerunning the news about Max's arrest in his mind, while he tried to distract himself with play. He reminded himself to appreciate the fastest desktop computer on campus, the controls for minimum effort, the chair for maximum immersion, and the enormous flat screen that had been authorized for conferences.

He killed fascists on the battlefields of the Second World War, monstrous troglodytes in gloomy corridors that he imagined as fascist laboratories, and alien invaders that he imagined as the unenlightened and uneducated. He was sure he could have been just as good a soldier as a historian; he was already a leader.

This was not just play, it was work – a necessary distraction from the stresses of his job. It was research in popular culture: he was keeping in touch with the kids; and he was gathering anecdotes to keep relevant.

He realized that the news was still distracting him, so he added some music. Then he turned on the television. Then he opened his laptop, to see incoming emails. Then he placed his phone in front, to watch the texts arriving. It flashed an alarm about the imminent third meeting of the Optimists.

He returned to the game. He controlled the avatar's outrageous athleticism with slight twitches of his fingers. Vicariously, Berk raced up mountains without slowing, leaped over walls without upsetting his aim, changed direction in the air, threw grenades and fired a machine-gun at the same time, reloaded while sprinting, absorbed bullets without stopping, slaughtered all resistance on the final level, and kept up the destruction just to enjoy the gory rag-doll physics. The music soared – rapture! The alarm flashed – torture!

Berk walked in late, unchastened but chastening, unattended but attentive. Tom Pinklewonk had taken charge, but was being interrupted.

"I never liked Max," said Jimmy Pons. "I knew he was trouble from the start."

"He spent too much time overseas," said Guillaume Juncker.

"He was always trying to tell me about Asia!" said Hattie Maddux. "Me! About Asia! I spent a semester there when I was an undergrad!"

"He missed our meetings," Berk added sulkily.

"He was only as good as his money," said Tom Pinklewonk. "And I heard he was having money troubles."

"That's why he couldn't get bail," said Jimmy, happy to suggest Pinklewonk's ignorance, but abashed to betray his insight.

"I heard he has expensive tastes," said Rod Sorrie carefully. "At the Sorrie Foundation, we won't grant money to anyone with expensive tastes."

"We promote sustainability," nodded Jill Sorrie.

"His tastes were for vulnerable women," said Aimee Pharisees.

"I didn't know that," exclaimed Jimmy.

"Typical man!"

"Now, now, Aimee. We all hate men as much as you."

Berk's untypical gravity captured the conversation: "We were doing so well. Everything was perfect! Max is the victim of a vast right-wing conspiracy, fronted by the FBI – the 'Fascist Bureau of Infringement.' A man who spoke so publicly and gave so much money to feminist causes could never objectify women."

"You can't give back his money, Chancellor," said Pinklewonk. "We need everything for the political fight-back."

"I never give back money. That would compromise academic freedom. What we need is change – one big change to reclaim the headlines!"

"We need a change of culture!" Aimee Pharisees said. "It takes only one man to prove a collective problem."

"And one man to change it, starting at the top, hey, Chancellor?" said Jimmy.

"Or woman!"

"I know that."

"But you didn't say it!"

"Because Berk is a man."

"You just genderized the Chancellorship! You see! This university is systemically sexist."

"Sexism is bad," said Rob Partsome. "BeLitters are always saying so."

"Racism also is bad," emphasized Josh Chubfuddler.

"All 'isms' are bad," said Jean Cadhowling wisely.

Everybody agreed that 'isms' are bad, until Aimee asked, "What about feminism?"

Everybody agreed that feminism is good.

"You might agree," said Aimee, "but you're still men. You can talk the talk but not walk the walk. You're collectively guilty for the sexism that rejected Trixie as President. This university needs to draw a line! It needs to send a message. It needs to appoint a female Chancellor. Of course, I'm ready to be called."

"Aimee, I'd call you," said Jimmy.

"Aimee," said Berk. "I don't think you'd want to give up your important work at Middle East Studies to spend all day in meetings."

"Sexist!"

"Me? Nobody has done more to fight sexism at this university. My predecessor said he would do more than his predecessor, and I promised the same. Look at my record: all faculty and staff must complete sexual awareness training twice a year! It used to be once a year!"

"Twice is not enough."

"Well, I have more change for you," said Berk. "Just this morning, the emergency committee approved a new Vice-Chancellor. I have the announcement here, ready for distribution: 'The next Vice-Chancellor for Equity and Inclusivity will advance Bayside's leadership role in the field and practice of equity and inclusion by boldly establishing new paradigms and implementing new strategies and tactics that embed equity and inclusion principles into the fiber of the Bayside campus'."

"I'll do it," said Aimee.

"That wasn't...Anyway, a search must be made."

"But I already run the workshop on inclusivity and multi-culturalism! And sexism is a cultural problem – a culture that needs to be excluded from multiculturalism."

"You're quite right, Aimee, but I don't want to distract you from your workshop. Are inclusivity and multiculturalism not important to you anymore?"

"Then you should make me vice-chancellor for inclusivity, multi-culturalism. and equity."

"Three vague concepts would be too much for any person."

"So, give me just multiculturalism."

"We can't have a vice chancellor for one thing – that would be exclusive."

Everybody agreed that exclusivity is bad.

"I already have more cultural change for you, a new directive, so be prepared. You need to start using the correct language: if someone comes to you with a claim of sexual harassment, you are the 'responsible' person, the claimant is a 'survivor,' and the accused is 'the guilty party'. And you need to appoint a women's rights champion in every program, to be present at every meeting, to remind everybody how they might not even know that they've been abused. And make sure you specify in advance that attendance is mandatory for all, otherwise you'll get some clown arguing that since men can't be victims they don't need to attend victims' workshops."

Aimee interrupted: "We could make manterrupting a dismissible offence."

"This is just the beginning," said Berk. "Cultural change starts with the kids – here, today. And in a generation's time – well, anything is possible."

Aimee interrupted again. "A culture of consent begins with their parents. We should be teaching parents to ask babies for consent before touching them."

"That's the way," cried Guillaume Juncker. "I will make all WISP students consent to a course on cultural change."

"You won't need to make them," said Berk. "'Culture' and 'change' are already the most popular terms in new course titles."

"How about: 'globalization and cultural change'?"

"Even better!"

"I know what I should teach," said Tom Pinklewonk. "The triumph of working-class culture – globally."

"At BeLitter," mused Rob Partsome, "we know that 'human rights' Re-Litter well."

Juncker soared from his chair. "Then I will rename WISP as 'globalization, human rights, and cultural change'!"

"Well, I'll be okay: I teach Jewish and Muslim cultures," said Aimee Pharisees.

"We could teach a culture of peacefulness through the arts," said Rod Sorrie. "We're eager to fund the arts."

"Peacefulness through social media," suggested Rob Partsome.

"Peacefulness through virtual friends," suggested Josh Chubfuddler.

"Peacefulness through remote interaction," suggested Jean Cadhowling.

"No more teaching the causes of war," exclaimed Berk. "Instead, teach only war as depicted in the arts. No longer counter-terrorism, but terrorism in the arts. In fact, you could duplicate the courses: terrorism in literature, terrorism in film, terrorism on the stage, terrorism on canvas, defeating terrorism through art."

"Yes, Jimmy," said Pinklewonk with triumph. "See, there's change to be made in your program too."

"I've already decided my change: my introductory course on peace should become the cultures of peace," said Jimmy Pons.

"Yes, but you've still got a man teaching counter-terrorism."

"He is a man," said Hattie. "How is a man qualified to defeat terrorism through art? What about defeating terrorism through feminist art?"

"Yes, Jimmy," said Pinklewonk triumphantly. "Get your man off the stage."

"He can't be replaced, not now."

"Oh, why not?"

"He knows too much – about the subject."

"What he knows has nothing to do with what he should be teaching."

"I have an alternative," said Jimmy quietly. "I heard he has a friend, a mathematician. As you know, many people on this campus approach me for counsel, knowing my public fight for sexual equality."

"Yes, sexism is bad."

"My friends in the mathematics department have wanted to get rid of Marcus for a long time. He is unconventional. He teaches during stoppages. He mixes mathematics with politics. He is considered a tough teacher, but he's liked by the students. Now, he is advertising himself online on a dating website in Bayside. Clearly, he must be preying on students!"

"It's as clear as day!" said Aimee Pharisees. "Then we need to make an example of him. What we need is a single case to reveal what it's like to be a woman on campus now, where not only is rape prevalent but also there's this pervasive culture of sexual harassment. The scary truth is that if you dig deep enough in any campus, this is probably what you will find. It's not the exception. It's probably the norm."

"Finally, a real sexual predator," said Chancellor Berk. "I'll publicly censure this man and issue a statement of support for Max."

"At last, we'll get some real cultural change around here."

34. Scapegoat

"Marcus, you shouldn't leave: you've done nothing wrong."

"It's alright, Simon: this sort of thing is a hazard for people like us. This time it's me. It's inevitable these days. The only uncertainty is how long you can avoid it without jumping on the bandwagon."

"You should fight it."

"I can't – not now that it's become me versus me-too. My real name is part of hashtags and news articles and blogs – and comments on blogs. My name has been posted alongside terms such as 'predator,' 'criminal,' 'abuser,' and who knows what that I've yet to discover. Any search for me picks up them, forever. I could write a hundred books, leave the greatest treatise since '*Principia Mathematica*', cure cancer, and bring peace to earth, yet I'd still be known as Marcus the sexual predator."

"But there's no evidence. The university keeps claiming it's received complaints, but it won't disclose the accusers for their own protection; and it won't say how many, except to say 'several.' Nobody came forward until after it had announced publicly that it had suspended you, then it fired you given what it called 'the public record.' But you've been accused by people who graduated from this university before you joined it. Students who have never taken a course in mathematics have accused you of trading grades for sex."

"Social media have spoken; and social media cannot be expunged."

"But there's no criminal complaint against you."

"And no criminal law to protect me."

"What about civil action?"

"You can't sue academic freedom."

"You could still challenge the university's actions. You've been fired without due process, without disclosure, without recourse, without review."

"It says its human resource decisions are confidential."

"Surely your representatives could put pressure on your behalf?"

"The union says it can't do anything except request a review. The politicians have already picked a side. Tom Pinklewonk has led the way. I can't fight politicians as well as academics."

"You could correct the record."

"Nobody will talk to me. I'd need an expensive spin-doctor. Do you know an expensive spin-doctor?"

"Actually, yes, but he's on the wrong side of this."

"That's where most people are. So, in a sense, that's the right side."

"We just need time for supporters to volunteer themselves. Your students of mathematics loved your courses; and any of them could testify to no wrong-doing."

"They would be testifying to the absence of evidence."

"They could raise awareness amongst other students."

"No, Simon! Don't get yourself engaged in this. I don't want to drag you down with me."

"That's not going to happen!"

"Can you honestly say that your students haven't jumped on the bandwagon?"

"No, I can't. I received a DAFI email excusing one of my students from classes until further notice due to the shock of your predation."

"It's too late for me, Simon. It takes the best part of three decades to raise an academic, but only a weekend to ruin one."

"You're remarkably stoic about this, Marcus."

"Stoicism is the positive frame one can choose after realizing, 'Then there is no hope.' Once there really is no hope, one might as well accept it. Otherwise, I suppose one could deny it, fight it, or kill oneself. I've thought about each of those several times over, but I've decided I'm best accepting it."

"What will you do?"

"I thought about a change of career, but I still want to educate. I just want the education without the indoctrination."

"But where?"

"I think I'll teach abroad."

"We're already abroad."

"No, we're only abroad from Britain. We're not abroad from academia. It's epistemic, it's transnational, it's incestuous. It's dominated by bluffers, talking up each other, rewarding those who conform, punishing those who don't. I've got no better prospects at home than here. No, I need to go as far abroad as possible, to somewhere foreign to academia."

"That's not possible."

"Wait, you're thinking too conventionally! We need somewhere as unlike here as possible. I've seen what academics can do with academic freedom in a democracy, and it means freedom from democracy. If academia must counter systemic power and structural power, better to be contrary in an autocracy, don't you think? And if academia wants to be authoritarian, better that it's curbed by an autocracy rather than a democracy."

"That sounds perverse."

"But everything is turned upside down, Simon. If you want to be free, don't be academic in a free society: be academic in an unfree society."

"I'm not ready for that."

"I am. I have no choice. I'm already ostracized."

"Where will you go?"

"I think I'll go to Asia, China perhaps. Do you know anyone in China?"

"Actually, yes, and she was on the right side of this."

"What do you mean?"

"Come on, I'll tell you on the way – I know where she'll be."
***

The lobby was brightly lit by temporary floor lights, to encourage people to linger before the gloom of the auditorium. Trapped between the outside and the auditorium were the odors of incompatible foods, served freely from tables along the partition.

As they entered, Marcus was still discussing how to categorize "the near abroad" from "the far abroad." He interrupted himself. He pondered the national flags and cultural symbols scattered on the tables, the mix of national costumery and transnational insipidness, and the discord of parochial music and generic noise. After several abrupt changes of direction, Marcus came to rest and sniffed: "You brought me to international food day."

"No."

"International cultures day?"

"No more than any other day."

"International students?"

"I doubt more than a few."

"Study abroad?"

"Probably most of them will."

"Travel club?"

"That's the same thing. No, it's a bit of all of those: it's Bayside's mock international assembly."

"What's mock about it?"

"The students are role-playing."

"Where's the assembly?"

"Those suits – they're pretending to be diplomats."

"Who are they?"

"Probably politics students – who want to get into law school. And those unappreciated organizers over there, they need something useful on their resumé – they're probably humanities students."

"Where's the international?"

"Those PAX students are promoting world peace by eating each other's food."

"Where are the students who actually want to be diplomats?"

"They're probably too busy socializing."

"How do you know?"

"I'm betting. Mock international assemblies are unintentional mockeries of the same drama: different actors, same cast; different exposition, same urgency; different agendas, same inconclusiveness."

"By the way: where's the American food?"

"You'd need to go abroad for that."

"We can get Latin American food here."

A student looked up from behind the table with acceleration. "This is the South American Club." She tilted her head towards the next table: "The Latin American Club won't admit anybody born east of the Andes."

Her target at the next table piped up: "Yeah? Well you won't admit anybody born west of the Andes!"

"That's what the Central American Club is for!"

"Only if you're born south of Mexico!"

"You've got the Latino Club!"

"Only if you're born north of Mexico!"

Everybody was interrupted when Chancellor Berk and entourage cut through the throng like a sinking ship. Only his hand was visible, waving frantically in all directions, without attracting any responses. His trailing convoy was observable as a residual parting of the ways.

After he had disappeared into the auditorium, a disembodied voice requested that attendees should take their seats to hear the Chancellor's welcoming address at 1 p.m. The time was ten minutes past. The voice crackled into life again to add an invitation to hear the chancellor's "exciting announcement."

"I say," said Marcus. "Do you think he intends to announce his mistake about me?"

"No. He's brought the news media with him."

"Perhaps the mock international assembly would debate whether I should have been fired."

"You could make it a violation of your international right to economic security. You'd need the Human Rights Council to take it up, and for that you'd need to be championed by some members. Try the representatives for Iran, Syria, Russia, or Venezuela. They'll be sitting together somewhere. Go tell them the violation happened in America."

Two minutes later, the disembodied voice warned that the food stalls would be closing in five minutes.

"Quick," said Marcus, "beat the rush." He piled his paper plate with a dollop of food from every table, running with an expression of wild focus that intimidated any reproach, until he reached the descent into the auditorium, where a yellow jacket blocked him.

"There! What beautiful borderless cuisine." She smiled and made way.

They sat at the back and watched Berk conspicuously glad-handing the front row, without urgency. Students in suits were still on the stage, fussing around a lectern, snatching glances at the audience before withdrawing into the immediacy of their tasks. They re-adjusted the microphones, papers, water, and banner. Several minutes later, Berk mounted the steps, the suits scattered, and the audience barely hushed.

"My fellow global citizens. It's my honor to open this year's mock international assembly. International relations are important to this university, so important that we don't have an international relations program. No, we spread the subject over many teaching programs! Never have international relations been more important, never has this assembly been more important – but you heard me say all that last year. I want to move on to this year's exciting announcement. China's Consul-General and I have chosen this occasion to announce the opening of a Chinese Cultural and Educational Centre."

The audience hushed.

"Right here – we're re-purposing this building."

Berk looked up and paused, as scripted, but the audience was still.

"This whole building will be refurbished and renamed the Sun Tzu Institute." Berk paused again, confused by the silence. "Because international institutions are good."

The audience cheered and whistled.

"The Institute will host educators and researchers from both China and America."

The audience approved.

"The Consul-General has kindly consented that this room can continue to be used for the mock international assembly!"

The audience exploded with relief.

"The Sun Tzu Institute will incorporate the media center upstairs. For too long, local Chinese-speakers have been burdened with their own content. Now, China's government will take the burden."

He turned a page and read out some impressive estimates of the costs of refurbishment, operations, salaries, scholarships, and research funds, before he concluded. "More details will emerge after this work has started. First, I am delighted to announce the authorization of a new Vice-Chancellor for Yin and Yang, whom I will appoint during the vacation. Now, it is my pleasure to declare this mock international assembly well and truly open."

Over the applause, Berk could be heard shouting out his thanks. He waved, clapped, put his hands on his knees, and bowed. A suit took his place behind the microphone, thanked the Chancellor, called the assembly to order, and ordered out everybody except delegates, although everybody would be welcome to enjoy the institutional booths in the lobby.

Chancellor Berk went straight to the Non-Governmental Alliance for Democratization, on his way to China's booth. Marcus and Simon followed him, but were held up by the crowd at the United Nations. The booth was advertising the world's problems, under a banner with the slogan: "Do you want solutions? Pledge here!" A representative was filming. He beckoned two students. "Smile! Now hug each other! V-sign! Now say: 'We support the world's solutions'."

China's booths took up half the wall with jobs, partnerships, and scholarships. A spotlight had attracted a line of people waiting to have their photograph taken with a framed painting of China's premier.

"Let's do that," said Marcus. "We'll do it together, holding hands like in a prom photo. I'm getting kicked out of America without ever attending a prom."

"No, we're not doing that. Here's the woman I brought you to see."

"Hello Simon," beamed the Deputy Consul-General. "So, you decided to come after all – I thought you were too busy at this time."

"I rearranged my priorities; and I've come to introduce Marcus, from Oxford. He wants to teach in China."

"More and more people do. We have a Deputy-Consul just for them. Please allow me to introduce him to you, Marcus. What about you, Simon? Have you thought about teaching in China? We have good students."

"No doubt."

"Professors here often say to me that Chinese students are most dedicated, attentive, mature, and respectful."

"They're scholars."

"They prioritize learning."

"Indeed, they're foreign."

"You'll find China's students unused to all the extracurricular activities here, I'm afraid."

"I'm not afraid."

"You'd probably find it very different to what you're used to, but I think you would grow to like it."

"I would, but, alas, I still have commitments here and in London."

"Then would you think more about speaking to Chinese television?"

"What about?"

"I'd just ask you questions about what you wrote for me. We're using the television studio upstairs. Of course, I would pay you."

"Of course. But you know, I don't speak Chinese?"

"Don't worry – we will translate your words for the Chinese audience."

"But why not ask somebody Chinese to speak on China's relations?"

"The Chinese people are interested in what foreigners think."

Simon sat in the studio, looking at the robotic camera, feeling robotic. His reflection in the monitor below the camera seemed disassociated. Everything was within touching distance but seemed remote. The walls at front and sides curved around, covered with pyramids of foam. He leaned back to stare at the ceiling, and contacted the wall behind. He turned about, to ponder the mural of the campus, and wondered what part he would obscure with his head.

Song Chin's disembodied voice cut through his delirium. "Simon? We need a few minutes here to edit our last package for transmission to China, then we'll reboot the system for your interview. I'll ask questions based on your subheadings, to make them easy, so just retell what you wrote already. We're not transmitting this live, so if you make a mistake, just say so, start again, and we'll edit it later. Now, for the record, please state your name and affiliation."

"Dr. Simon Ranald, Lecturer in Peace and War Studies, Riverside University of London."

"And the title of your paper?"

"Western-Asian Relations in the Next Decade."

"Thank you, Simon. I'll speak again in a few minutes."

Simon drifted into consideration of what part of the world might be mapped by the blemishes on the ceiling, when the monitor jumped into life with a hum and a glow. Images were racing forward, partially concealed under banners and static. They suddenly slowed to show the talking head of Chancellor Berk, sitting in Simon's current seat, covering up the same part of campus with his head, speaking more confidently and smoothly than ever.

"On this anniversary of the world anti-fascist war, I send my sincerest sympathies to the Chinese people, from everybody in the Bayside community…"

Berk's speech was interrupted with static each time the film raced forward.

"The Chinese people have thousands of years behind them, thousands of years of history, so they can decide for themselves where their borders lie...And thousands of years before America, so Americans must learn where it is and isn't our place to be involved... As a supporter of China, and a friend of China, the University of Sunshine Bayside is playing an important role in improving that relationship...The Chinese Cultural and Educational Center of Bayside will serve as China's window on America, and America's window on China...Enlightenment comes through education, international enlightenment through international education..."

35. Fact and Fiction

"Simon? This is Clara, in the Budgeting Office."

"Clara Mudd?"

"Yes. I'm calling because your monthly assessment is overdue."

"Oh dear! Who should complete it?"

"Max Mira."

"He doesn't control my funding. He used to control my funding, then he took it away, then I got federal funding, which I control, except I gave him control of the publicity."

"Yep, the publicity; and a clause that restores his monthly approval of your status here. That's the contract you signed. If you didn't like it, you shouldn't have signed it. You need to chase Mr. Mira."

"But he's in jail."

"Then you need to go to jail. I can't go to jail."

"Oh! You mean: I need to see Max?"

"Exactly."

"For him to assess my funding?"

"Not your funding directly, but your performance this month."

"But he's been in jail most of this month."

"He still needs to sign the form. He knows how it works. I'll intermural you the form."

"Can't somebody else assess my funding?"

"No, only Max can do it. And I'll need it by the end of the next working work, which is Tuesday. 'Why Tuesday?' you'll ask. You will, because you're foreign. Thanksgiving is next Thursday. The university is closed on Wednesday for travel. The students will travel this weekend, so you might as well cancel your classes next week. Some will travel this week, so you could cancel your classes this week too. Otherwise, you would be causing intolerable stress. So, you see, there's no reason why you shouldn't be free to go to jail by Monday. And you'd better get the form to me in the morning on Tuesday, because I'll likely leave early that day."

***

"John, how can I get to see Max Mira?"

"You can't – you're a witness, he's the indictee. You wouldn't be allowed."

"Then, how can I get a form to him?"

"You could ask his lawyer to carry it in. She's allowed in anytime."

"I was hoping to surprise Max, in person, before he could say no. I don't think I want to forewarn his lawyer."

"I bet she would surprise him if you paid her. Although I bet she charges more than $1,000 per hour; and I bet she'd charge you for the hours she was carrying it each way. She'd probably charge you for the time she took to produce the invoice; and the time she was thinking about it too."

"Oh dear! I can't afford that."

"Why do you want to get anything to him? It sounds improper – it could prejudice our case."

"If I don't get his approval, I won't get paid this month, my job will be terminated; and my visa is conditional on employment – I'd need to leave the country."

"He's your supervisor then."

"I suppose so."

"I'll write that down – that will play great in court: you're appearing as a witness against him even though your funding is dependent on him. Doesn't he have a supervisor who could sign the form?"

"I don't think so. The contracting office says only he can get do it."

"That could be true. That's the advantage of contractual law. You can specify almost anything."

"What can I do now?"

"I don't know. If you were in government, I'd know the rules and regulations, but you're in academia. Well, it's a law unto itself, isn't it?"

"Then it's all over."

"Well, you've still got a criminal trial to look forward to."

"Two criminal trials actually – to which I'll be compelled to return, at my own expense, without a job or family or friends here."

"Oh, come on – surely, you've got friends here?"

"No, not since Marcus left."

"Cheer up, Simon. Look, it's Thanksgiving next week. I tell you what: I've got friends who have hosted my family for the last few years. I'll ask if they wouldn't mind you coming along."

Simon turned off his phone with a mix of gratitude and despair, then remembered his emails. First, he saw an email from DAFI, which granted to a delinquent student the opportunities to re-sit all classes and assignments, on the grounds of her anxiety over missing them.

He scrolled through dozens of emails until one resisted his dismissal. The University of Sunshine Press was hosting an open day for authors and publishers, one of which was promising an advance of a million dollars to be handed over on the day.

***

The auditorium's lobby had never seemed so quiet. It was full of tables decorated by different publishers, but they had not attracted students.

Photographers out-numbered faculty, and most of them were gathered in front of Chancellor Dick Berk, who was holding a huge mock-up of a front cover, much larger than himself. He was peeking around the side, grinning. The title was at the top, across two lines: "Leadership Lessons from Leading the Public." His name was below, on one line, in largest font. With his head on one side, his headshot appeared next to the word "Public," which was stacked above the word "Berk." When he moved to the other side, his headshot appeared next to the words "Leading" and "Dick."

The photographers zoomed out, then asked his agent to pose on the other side, with an oversize check held between them – an image for marketing to prospective authors.

"One million dollars!" shouted the publisher's publicist.

"One million dollars negotiated by my agency!" shouted the literary agent.

"One million dollars pledged for my name," whispered Berk, through a forced smile.

"Just you remember," she jibed back, without moving, "fifteen percent of this is mine."

"Not until I've written it."

"Not so loud. Haven't you found a writer yet?"

"I'm writing my own book."

"You're not."

"I am! I'm a great writer. My second book will be a guide to writing."

"If you don't deliver 10,000 words by the end of next month, this check will shrink by $100,000."

"You agreed a deadline?!"

"I didn't have any choice. They insisted."

"I don't do deadlines. That's bad leadership, that's pre-heroic leadership. I'm post-heroic."

"You've signed the contract."

"That's bad negotiating on your part."

"You're lucky they trusted you to deliver anything, after your last book fell through."

"You're lucky to be here, after my last book fell through."

"You're lucky I'm still here."

"I won't do it. I'm too busy being Chancellor. It's too much pressure."

"You will do it, or we'll lose $100,000 for every month you're late."

"You can't make me!"

From the rear, the voice of Jimmy Pons interrupted them, confident and looking for trouble. "Berk's book cover has no female of color!"

The publicist rushed to counsel. "But it has a male of color and a white female, which together make a female of color. But please do not think I am correcting you. I value your autonomy. Please send me your concerns. Here's my card. Thank you for considering our publications."

Professor Sir Barry Liddell was in the other corner, reading from his latest book: "Strategy: An Idiot's Guide."

"Professor Liddell will take questions now," said the publicist.

"I have a question for the professor!"

"Oh, please," said Professor Liddell, with a wave of his hand. "There's no need for titles. We're in Bayside! I've been visiting Bayside since I was a young radical, you know."

"Thanks, Barry!"

"Sir Barry," said Sir Barry firmly. Suddenly he felt uncertain: a semi-annual pilgrimage to Bayside sometimes left him feeling less culturally literate than he remembered from afar. Sometimes he wondered if Bayside did not represent America, or if the University of Sunshine Press did not represent America, which would be most inconvenient. He cheered himself up by thinking of Dorian

Floorman all at sea in the same situation. Tony Blair would know what to do. Sir Barry tried to lighten the mood: "I got this knighthood by being strategic, you know."

"Is that in the book, Barry?"

"No. It's in my memoir: 'Maverick at the Heart of Government.' Somewhere in there – I can't remember where. Wait – I'll find the page, and I'll read that too."

Simon passed within hearing distance, furiously waiting his turn with the representative from the University of Sunshine Press. Simon hastily introduced himself by his duties at Bayside, but was interrupted.

"Yeah. We don't typically publish people from the University of Sunshine. We prefer a diverse authorship."

"Well, I am a visiting lecturer from London."

"Yeah. We don't typically publish lecturers. There's little market for you – that's just the market."

"What if I published without affiliation?"

"Have you published anything already?"

"Articles, of course, and my dissertation, through my alma mater's press."

"Have you published anything popular?"

"No."

"Yeah. There's no point us publishing you until you're already published, you see?"

"No."

"What's your field?"

"Well, I have a proposal in counter-terrorism, and a proposal in social scientific methods, and another on Western-Asian relations."

"That's a lot of fields. If you had to tell me you had one discipline, what would it be?"

"If anything, I suppose, political science."

"No, Tom Pinklewonk does everything for us that is political – and legal, and economic."

"What about Western-Asian relations?"

"No, Hattie Maddux does Asia."

"Can I leave a sample with you?"

"No, I don't need to read anything to know what it says."

"Would you recommend another university press?"

"We don't allow other university presses into our open day."

Simon passed the many booths selling editing services, writing courses, workshops on how to get published, and agents, before he found the non-university presses. The first, in alphabetical order, was Aimless House, which advertised as the world's leading pulisher of both non-fiction and fiction.

"I wouldn't consider more than one book at a time," the Aimless representative said. "I might consider publishing subsequent books if your first is successful."

"Why don't we start with this one?"

"So, it's factual?"

"Yes, of course."

"But I don't sense any passion."

"I have passion for the work, for the facts, for factual work."

"But where's the book's passion? Where's its heart?"

"The facts are at its heart – after the theory and the methodology, before the conclusion."

"But is it emotionally compelling?"

"It's scientifically compelling – it refutes the conventional wisdom, it presents new evidence."

"Can you turn it into a history? A compelling narrative history, with an inspiring story, a beginning, a middle, and an end – an emotionally compelling climax?"

"I can't turn analysis into history."

"Don't let the facts get in the way of a good story."

"The facts tell a good story."

"Do you have a novel? Fiction sells better than facts."

"I know a fictional story about the sexual misconduct of a stoic young mathematician."

"That sounds too much like fact. You know, I wanted to be a novelist, but after a successful stint on the college magazine, I realized my passion was for other people's books. I must feel passionate about a book, or I can't represent it. I guess I'm just not passionate about any of yours. That's just the way it is. I can't explain it. Whatever it is, it should make me want to pick it up and not put it down. It should be a gem that I want to show off. Of course, let me know if another publisher wants to publish you – that would be different."

Simon went to see the representative from Pallan Press, whose tag line was a claim to specialize in non-fiction.

"Of course," she exclaimed. "We'd be delighted to publish you. Our minimum fee is $5,000. How long is it? We charge another $10 per page over 150 pages, so, best keep it short. And we charge $1,000 for any tables, graphs, or figures, so best to keep the data to a minimum."

Simon went to see Ruttles Press, which published thousands of academic books and journals each year. The representative listened expressionless. "I don't see a market for full-length books with those titles," he said, "but I could publish a chapter in each of our handbooks."

"That would be a start. How much would you advance me for those?"

"Nothing – authors contribute for the prestige."

Simon reached the end of the line, where he found the tiny booth for Powder Portal Press.

"Yes, we might be able to publish one of those, but we'd need a proposal for each."

"I have proposals with me – as well as drafts of the books, to prove they're almost complete."

"We'd also need a market analysis for each, a list of all the instructors who would teach with your books, and a list of all the competing books."

"What could you pay me?"

"We start at five percent royalties for first-time authors."

"Could I get an advance?"

"Why are you so desperate for an advance?"

"To help me to finish this academic year."

"Leave a proposal with me. But don't expect to hear from me for a year or so."

36. Thanksgiving

The billboards passed by in the contested territory between city and suburb. Trees appeared as sentinels, parks as bastions, the river as the front line, until the green predominated, increasingly bold and secure. When the large buildings of a school intruded, Simon realized how quickly he had normalized to a quiet country road. The school flew by. The valley's side reappeared, low and soft, except for the orderly rows of diminutive, jagged, leafless vines.Then the taxi turned right onto a track under an incongruous sign: "Dairy Lane."

The driver uncertainly kept the speed low, over mounds of dust, around a bend, between some outbuildings, up a rise, until a magnificent complex emerged below. Simon's eyes began at the peak of a tall, dark wooden barn. He traced the stone extensions on each wing, to small guest houses behind. After the taxi left him, Simon could hear nothing but the dust settle. Horses grazed silently at the far end of the paddock on his right. He turned to his left, with a slight crunch of the gravel, to recognize a raised vegetable patch, from where a bird fled with noisy alarm. He moved towards the barn, but paused to listen to the treetops stirring beyond. He heard a splash, and realized that their arc marked the far edge of a pond. He stepped slowly, as if each crunch might puncture the scene. Increasingly, the barn murmured and hummed with an infestation of humans: Simon sought their community even as he resented them.

Inside the cavernous gloom, the figures seemed surprisingly small and distant, seated on the far side, below the only windows, looking on to another field of vines, blessed with the setting sun. Tables ran down the center-line, tall with elaborate candelabras and decorations. He strained to recognize John Gard.

"Simon, you made it."

"Yes. Am I late?"

"No, we're both early. I just got here myself – I volunteer for the Samaritans these mornings. My wife should be here soon. She takes the youngsters to volunteer to feed the homeless."

"Where are our hosts? I'd like to introduce myself. Here I am, a stranger."

"Lucy doesn't like anybody in her kitchen, but Jock takes my help setting up the bar. We might as well take this way into the west wing – here, after you." They walked down a corridor of polished concrete. John opened a steel door into a storage room stacked with boxes of wine.

"No, not here, so he must be in the office."

John led through the far exit, passed a chicken coop, and rounded the end of an open barn, to reveal the gleaming chrome and aluminum body of a bulbous home on wheels. Inside the front window, Simon saw a face with half-moon spectacles staring intently at plans spread across a desk, busily annotating with a pencil, while the other hand held the plans fast. John rapped on the metal skin, the face looked up, and Simon remembered a jockey astride a Basset Hound.

"Jock! May I introduce you to Simon."

"Hello Jock. We've met before – through the Flappers and Go-Getters."

"You can drop the accent, my boy – we're not flapping and go-getting now."

"I don't have an accent."

"You do – an English accent: very effective."

"It's not my accent – I am English."

"Well, it's not my accent – I'm American."

"He is English, Jock. I've checked his credentials. He's come over to teach important things at Bayside."

"Really?" said Jock skeptically. "I met a Bayside student once – I found him in the stables having sex with one of my horses. He said the horse indicated consent with a wink. His defense counsel asked for leniency given the defendant's enlightened attitude towards consent. She also wanted the case to come to trial in Bayside, on the grounds that he resided there during semesters. Actually, she had graduated from Bayside law school, now I think about it."

"I never heard that one before," said John sincerely.

"That was before we met. Now I think about it, that was the final kick up the backside to persuade us to buy a second home near you – fewer horses, fewer horse-rapists."

"Fewer horse rapists, but more drug addicts. I interviewed a dealer this week – he said he was thinking of moving in, because we have the nicest buyers. They never haggle over prices, he said. They never ask for credit, always drive their own cars. 'Addicts, but polite addicts,' he said."

"That's a slogan for the cities on the ridge: fewer horse-rapists, nicer addicts."

"I suppose Bayside has the most enlightened horse-rapists and rudest addicts," said Simon thoughtfully.

"That dealer was trying to move out of Bayside," said John helpfully.

"I'm just glad my homes are on either side of Bayside. And I have a federal agent for a neighbor."

"I don't think I could have helped. I don't think horse-rape is a federal crime."

"I've got a federal crime for you: I received a letter, right here, hoping that I and everyone in my family gets cancer. It was anonymous, but I bet it was him."

"I'm sorry, but that's not a felony. Threatening to harm you is a felony; wishing that cancer harms you, that's not."

"He must have known that. Now I think about it, he was pre-law. I remember he got his charges downgraded so he wouldn't be barred from law school. And the judge said kids shouldn't be punished, kids should be allowed to make their own mistakes. Can you explain that one, Simon?"

"No. I don't teach law."

"What do you teach?"

"Well, nothing, as of this week – nothing ever again, probably."

"Simon and Bayside aren't getting along," said John with a mix of sympathy and apology.

"Glad to hear it," said Jock with a mix of detachment and glee.

***

Returning, they discovered John's wife with six teenagers – John introduced Simon to his wife, their daughter and son, and Jock's sons and daughters. Jock wanted only John's help with the bar, the women went to help Lucy, and the teenagers volunteered to entertain Simon.

In parting, Jock said: "Don't you dare convince any of them to study at Bayside."

"I wouldn't dream of it," said Simon.

The teenagers cordially interviewed him, respected his advice, and indulged his interests. They dwelt with the chickens, took feed to tempt the ducks, sat on the bench under the trees, walked amongst the horses, sampled vegetables and herbs, and instructed him on vines. A long time passed pleasantly, until the setting sun and cooling air persuaded them inside.

Simon was introduced to a couple dozen adults, whose names he would never remember, once he realized that one of them would be Theodora.

"Teddi! I didn't know you'd be here."

"I didn't know you celebrated Thanksgiving."

"Well, I didn't know. Nobody had mentioned it."

"Who invited you?"

"John Gard."

"The FBI man?"

"Yes."

"He invited you? You, the fed-basher of Bayside? Or is he investigating the Halloween killing? Or the abolition of the police? Or the riots?"

"No – I mean, I can't say."

"Oh."

"I'm sorry."

"I understand."

"No, it's not understandable, I know, I'm sorry. I meant to call you once events were more certain."

"This event seems certain."

"Well, I wasn't certainly coming, until the last couple days. I was still trying to get into prison."

"Prison?"

"I can't say."

"Oh."

"I'm sorry."

"I understand."

"No, it's not understandable. You must be thinking the worst of me. I wanted to be available these last few weeks. I was waiting for events to clear."

"When will they clear?"

"Well, they're clearing."

"That's good. So, you'll have more time."

"Yes, for a while – I mean, I'll have more free time from next week, but not for as long as I was hoping."

"Oh."

"I'm sorry."

"I understand."

"No, even I don't understand it. I came for a year, but I'll be compelled to leave at the end of this semester, except to come back, on official business, briefly, at some points, I don't know when."

"Oh. Well, that doesn't give us much time then."

"No."

"Not enough time."

"Perhaps enough time."

"I don't think so."

"No, you're right."

"I'm sorry."

"I understand."

The dinner did not smell as delicious after that, the sunset looked less spectacular, the barn less intriguing, the table settings less festive.

As the newest acquaintance, Simon was placed next to Jock, who sat at the head of the table, distracted by the future of his family and business.

"My youngsters don't want to stay around here – none of them, even here, where I've built their family home, as remote as I could, with a *casa* for each of them. All they can talk about is small towns, the smaller the better, as far away from the Bay Area as possible, where everybody grew up together and nobody moves far away, where the traffic is low, the crime is low."

"There's a lot to be said for that."

"Now that last part – crime, that's where Lucy and I must have influenced them. Things were different when we moved to the Peninsula. We worry about them taking up careers in the Bay Area now. It doesn't matter how good your job is, what money you make: everybody has to use the same communications. You could be dodging stabbings and tuberculosis on the subways, or intoxication and road-rage on the freeways. I've done it for twenty years – I don't want it for them."

Jock's neighbors agreed. Simon agreed. Simon's attention focused on Jock, although Jock was not talking to him. Part of his mind remained with Teddi. The crushing weight of acceptance stopped his gaze from wandering.

"We've got friends who have visited every year. They won't even fly into the peninsula, because they've seen the news. It's too dangerous – and filthy. 'Filthy utopia,' they call it. Lucy and I are giving up our roles with the Flappers and Go-Getters, because we just don't like going into the Peninsula anymore."

Lucy sat at the other end, except she kept walking around to give time to different guests, although she remained the least present, as she rushed hither and thither managing the courses. Throughout, she smiled enigmatically, habitually, naturally.

Returning hither once more, she stopped beside her husband and called their attention. "I am so pleased that you all have come to share Thanksgiving with us again, with some new arrivals this year." She glanced at Simon slowly and indulgently: "Charming new arrivals."

She restored her gaze down the table, without hurry, while she breathed in deeply and settled her smile: "This holiday was meant for people to come together to give thanks for the bounties and blessings of their year. Our new arrivals might not know that we follow the tradition of giving our thanks out loud, in turn, but don't worry, I will go first, as I always do."

She smiled. Simon could not tell whether she paused because she smiled, or smiled because she paused.

"As some of you know, I was diagnosed with something serious a few months ago. For those of you who don't know, it's rare and not easy to understand and not easy to cure. I don't want to go into details, just be assured that everything that can be done is being done. I've already passed through one round of treatment – a new, wonderful treatment, without losing my hair. A lot of you have said, you wouldn't even know, from the looks of me. I really feel fine: I'm blessed, truly. How wonderful to get cancer in this day and age, to see what modern medicine can do."

The silence was heavy with suspense and digestion. Lucy inhaled visibly, and everybody remembered to breathe.

She placed a hand on Jock's shoulder and continued: "I have spent twenty years with a husband of like mind and like heart. I have four wonderful children, who show me every day they have the values and skills to make the best of themselves and contribute positively to our world. I always fretted whether they would imbibe anything that I could teach. I have always thought of my children as little adults in development, and I am proud to have produced adults early, so I can rest easy."

The candle sparked and chattered in the pause.

"I give thanks that such inspiring adults have chosen to surround us. Now it's their turn."

Jock remained statuesque, looking ahead, as if any movement would crack his veneer. He spoke plainly: "I am forever thankful that I was persuaded to accompany a friend to an event that didn't interest me at all, that Lucy chose to do the same, that we met, that she became my best friend, that she agreed to marry me, that she has given me four wonderful children, and shared her life with me."

The sequence of speakers moved quietly and soberly along the other side of the table. Simon heard Teddi give thanks for brief moments with interesting people in hurried lives. Lucy's children thanked their mother for what she had taught them.

Simon's turn came last. As a fascinated listener, he had not prepared to speak, then was overcome with the sense of openness. He spoke without discretion: "I give thanks for spending my first American Thanksgiving with people so worthy of the tradition. As for my year prior, I give thanks for the opportunity to teach on the other side of the world to home – however that happened. I give thanks for surviving so far into the semester. I haven't been shot; I escaped terrorists and rioters; I was accused of being both a fascist and an anti-federalist. I've learned a lot about unfamiliar fields – such as human trafficking and law enforcement and marketing and publicity and public diplomacy. I've started and restarted so many courses I've lost count, but in the process I have confirmed how and what I want to teach. I've met the worst of people, but also the best – the best of Americans, the sorts of Americans I would want to be. I wish I had more time with such people, but my own semester runs out next week. Still, I am glad to be taking away the best and worst, because the one advantage of experiencing the worst is appreciating the best."

The quiet continued for a while, until Lucy spoke crisply: "Let's eat some more! Happy Thanksgiving."

John Gard passed by, leaned in, and said shyly: "I'd be delighted if you would give my children some advice about applying to Bayside before you leave."

"Please don't send them to Bayside – they're too nice."

Jock pricked up his ears and eyebrows: "They don't need to go to university. I never went to university; I set up my business before my friends graduated college; and they haven't caught up."

John persisted: "Bayside is still highly ranked."

"Over-ranked: I would put graduates of Bayside at the bottom of my hiring list. Chances are they're lazy, self-righteous, and indoctrinated, but not educated; at least, not educated in anything useful."

"I can't believe that," said John.

"Believe it," said Jock. "I once advertised for some entry-level staff, some recent college graduates who want to learn the construction business. I thought to ask at Bayside's career center. After all, that's my tax dollars at work, that's my local community. Well, it sends me a history major who said he had insight into the American way in business. His transcript showed he had studied nothing but witchcraft, slavery, and comics. Next, I interviewed a data scientist. He said he could use big data to transform my business, but couldn't tell me what data he would collect. I received a geographer who had studied nothing but politics, an economist who was sure that micro-financing would replace big business, an inter-disciplinary studies major who couldn't explain the major."

John was eager to cut in: "Perhaps Simon could explain it."

"I can't."

Jock would not be curbed: "I had a student who said she was studying peace and extremism. She said she was an expert in conflict negotiation and conflict resolution, but her answer to every industrial scenario I gave her was for both sides to keep talking. I asked her what other majors were in her program – she said development studies, which I thought would be relevant to urban development, so I asked the career center for one of those. Well, it sends me someone who insists that all development starts with deconstruction of the dominant structures. Then I asked explicitly for anyone with expertise in urban development. Now, I did receive a major in urban studies, but her concentrations are in alternative sexual identities, the contest for white spaces, and global inequality."

"I think Simon teaches in that program."

"I do teach in the World & International Studies program, but not in particular majors. Anyway, those majors are being abolished."

"To be replaced by what?"

"They're becoming concentrations in a single major to be called 'Globalization, human rights, and cultural change'."

"Why?"

"Well, the announcement says that it will better combine the traditional disciplines of philosophy, politics, and economics."

"Then it's stealing PPE's thunder."

"PPE has been in decline since so many graduates were exposed as politicians."

"What is the difference between PPE and 'Globalization, human rights, and cultural change'?"

"Just the cultural studies."

Jock raised his palms in triumph.

"It won't admit that it's cultural studies, because of complaints from anthropology."

"I interviewed an anthropologist. He promised he would make an excellent manager of human resources. 'How?' I asked. He said he would take blood from every one of my employees to prove that we're all descended from a common ancestor, then I'd have no more discord."

Jock's rising volume was attracting a crowd. His satisfaction improved with his memory.

"I remember an English major, who promised good communications skills, but she had managed to take courses that did not require her to write anything. She did persuade me that an expanding business could use a specialist in communications skills, so I asked for a communications major. Well, she smugly told me that she had concentrated in ethnography online, identity and representation in women's sports, and rhetoric in forgotten cultures."

John leaned back, defeated.

Jock was encouraged: "From my perspective, the University of Sunshine is only good for spending money. I've taken millions from the university every year, but not anymore – it's too much hassle. I kept raising my prices – most of my competitors did, but we won't make any more bids. So, now, when Bayside says that it gets quotes from three bidders to promote competition, you'll know the three bidders are the only bidders, because they're not busy enough. And they've fixed the prices sky-high. They subcontract to each other anyway, whatever the winner."

Jock leaned in and lowered his voice: "I'll tell you my last job for Bayside: I was refurbishing twelve floors of offices, rehabilitation suites, and classrooms for physical education, a lot of plumbing required. We get to the plumbing – suddenly, the foreman tells me the specifications don't provide for a step-down from the mains, so I forwarded this information to the project manager. She replied that I should comply with the specifications. So, after I re-tried a few times, I did what she kept telling me to do, thinking she must have made arrangements for another contractor to complete the job. We finished ahead of schedule. Somebody turned on the mains on a Friday, ready for the official opening on Monday. All twelve floors flooded over the weekend. Everything needs to be re-done, but I won't take the job."

"The building – was it the building with the swimming pool?"

"On the ground floor, yes."

"Nine weeks ago, a swimming pool was closed for flooding."

"Nine weeks ago, yes. That was the last straw for me. I can't have that sort of liability. It doesn't matter that it's not my fault: state politicians get involved, then they twist the story so that it's my fault. They talk about criminal charges for wasting public money. They don't need to make a legal case out of it; they just want the publicity, to look tough on big business, to look pro-education. Then Tom Pinklewonk will jump in to say big business always fleeces the public purse because of the way the economy is structured, and that government needs to hire him to restructure it. But the publicity will cost only me. I'll need to hire lawyers to correct the record. Protesters will picket my offices and the job site. I'll have to pay for the extra security. And when the police close the road for a protest, the city will make me pay for that too. That's why the contract managers are so arrogant. I told Clara – someone Lucy and I have received at Thanksgiving every year until now – I told her, I'm not bidding any more – not even on the buildings I raised."

"Clara Mudd?"

"You know her?"

"I've never met her. She runs the Budgeting Office, or at least the part that initiated my funding."

"Then I pity you! You can't trust her, unless she's in your pocket. Look, if you ever have any trouble with Clara, all you need to say is, you know who's really responsible for the flooding."

37. Last class

"How do you know about the flooding?"

"I'm just telling you that I know."

"Did Max talk about me?"

"He did mention you once or twice."

"I knew it – I knew he would, once his crimes came out. He was bound to start naming everybody he's ever worked with, just to spread the blame. Take it from me: Max Mira is no angel."

"I think I know everything there is to know about Max Mira."

"I knew it. I knew he couldn't be trusted. He said he could be trusted with everything. He said nobody was better at pretending to know everything while being able to deny anything."

"He was an academic."

"You're right! He was an academic, not an administrator. You can't trust an academic to do an administrator's job."

"I agree with you there."

"Right! Simon, you and I have a lot in common, if you think about it. Lecturers deliver most of the teaching, administrators organize everything, and middlemen like Max take most of the rewards. Do you want to be an administrator? I could fix it – a senior position, triple your salary, inside my department."

"No, thank you. I just want to finish my semester – without any more changes."

"But change is in our mission plan! We administer lots of changes – whatever you want."

"I just want my funding restored, so I can fulfil my obligations."

"You're easy, Simon."

"You can do it?"

"I can do it today! It's the end of the month."

"So, should I consider myself a lecturer again?"

"Until you want to become an administrator."

"No, I meant: should I consider myself authorized to instruct?"

"There's no need to teach. We can terminate your courses now, citing administrative contingencies – everybody gets an A-grade."

"No, I should finish what I started."

"You're an odd one, Simon."

"Thank you."

***

"Earnest, I'm back teaching."

"I heard you were in jail, with Max Mira."

"No, I never went to jail – he's in jail."

"He's not the first."

"He stands accused of sex crimes."

"How careless! I mean, that's why we have mandatory sexual awareness training."

"He forgot to approve my teaching."

"Damn him! That undermines all of us."

"I hadn't thought about it that way."

"Well, welcome back to teaching. How was your Thanksgiving?"

"Thanksgiving itself was very interesting. Then the rest of the holiday was like a respite, a real rest, a blessed relief. Campus was like a holiday camp. The libraries were quiet, the swimming pools were calm, the walkways were quick and easy, no protests, no office hours, no teaching. If only campus were always like this."

"We'd still need administrators though."

***

On Wednesday, Simon lectured on evidence. A student objected that "evidence should not trump feelings, if the feelings are very strong," and that "an evidence-based approach invalidates people with feelings." That evening, DAFI granted extra time to "students with excess feelings."

On Thursday, Simon taught his last class of Counter-terrorism and Counter-extremism, by holding a simulation of terrorism and counter-terrorism. All went well, until the terrorist side said it was unrealistic, because the list of fictional hostages did not include any children to kill. DAFI excused a student from any evaluation, given the trauma of being denied a realistic opportunity to kill children.

Boyan was absent all week. Some students said he had gone home to Britain, but some insisted he was in Asia, and others swore his parents lived in the Bay Area. DAFI excused him given the trauma of Adrian Yannis' imminent second appearance on campus, as acutely felt by a fellow British-American.

***

Simon's way back to the cubicle of humility was blocked by staff gathered around a radio. Simon dwelt, on promise of clarification about Yannis.

Alison was leading the preview: "She's such a good interviewer, because she's so good at interviewing. So skilled in leading the interviewee to say what she wants!" Alison turned up the volume. "That's the end of the news. Now, we should pay attention!"

Simon heard a manic jingle linking to the next program. "Welcome to Hot Air!" said the remote voice, emphasizing the final word like the answer to a stupid question. The speaker continued to read a script, in a memorably affected way. She liked to drop her tone through each clause, before ending with a deep "umm" – like she was sounding a tuning fork at the bottom of her scale. She would pause, to let the resonance take effect, before starting another clause, rushing and climbing the scale, as if asking a question in expectation of an exciting answer.

"Welcome to the award-winning weekday magazine of contemporary issues, umm, one of public radio's most popular programs. Each show features intimate conversations, umm, with today's biggest luminaries."

As she turned from the preamble before every show to the script for this show, her reading became looser.

"As you may have heard, umm, on the news just there…"

"Oh, what the hell!" said Alison. "We're listening to the news again. Wait, wait, wait! It's the news we want to hear!"

"The University of Sunshine has cancelled Adrian Yannis' second visit, umm, scheduled for Friday. The University of Sunshine released a statement today, umm, by President Secretary Mary Metro herself: 'Adrian Yannis' first visit to campus was marked by unprecedented violence, umm, but Mr. Yannis has failed to offer the University of Sunshine any guarantees against further violence. Chancellor Dick Berk of our Bayside campus, umm, had no choice except to cancel the event. He did so in the interests of public safety, umm, and I had no hesitation in approving his decision.' Secretary Metro there, umm."

The speaker coughed. Alison clasped her hands under her chin.

"Adrian Yannis has BeLittered a response, umm, a very angry statement, as follows: 'I had agreed to ridiculous demands to keep the venue secret to the last minute, umm, and to hold the event late in the day. The Left is absolutely terrified of free speech, umm, and will do anything to shut it down.' Adrian Yannis there, umm. So what did President-elect Clashmore Hickling say? Well, he has defended Adrian Yannis many times, umm, in his own Belitters. He re-Littered Yannis' BeLitter, umm, then he added the following BeLitter: 'The University of Sunshine does not allow free speech, umm. Yet it allows violence on innocent people. I will withdraw federal funds, umm, until it allows Adrian Yannis and all other speakers to speak.' President-elect Hickling there, umm."

The speaker coughed again. Alison gasped and sat down exhausted. "I hope my mother remembered to listen to this!"

"So, with that introduction, umm, let's welcome Secretary Metro to the studio."

"Thank you for having me."

"What would you like to add to your statement, umm, which I read just now?"

"It was quite unreasonable that Yannis should expect to speak on Friday evening – the evening of the last day of classes this week. And there are the security concerns."

"Can you tell us, umm, more about the security concerns?"

"No, I can't."

"Of course not, umm. So let's talk about some good news. I'd like to point out, umm, that all the contracts that Max Mira cannot fulfil, while he is indisposed, umm, as we reported on this program three weeks ago, have been transferred, umm, to women or men of color. Incidentally, all of them have been praised by former presidential candidate Trixie Downer, umm, as have you Secretary Metro!"

"That's right. Please call me Mary."

"Thank you, Mary, umm, that's such an honor."

"I'm sorry, I need to leave for a meeting now."

"Of course, umm. Thank you, Secretary Metro. Thank you for taking time out from your busy listening tour, umm, to explain this complicated issue."

"Wow!" said Alison. "She's tremendous. Isn't she, everyone?"

Everyone agreed.

38. RRR

"Earnest, what's R.R.R. week?"

"It's this week."

"Yes, but what is it?"

"Haven't you been told?"

"Nobody tells me anything."

"Isn't it in the monthly email from the Institute for Undergraduate Gratification?"

"No. That email was about making lectures as gratifying as episodes in a television series."

"It did?"

"Yes, you must remember! Start with an exciting vignette that isn't fundamental to the subject. Develop the characters to make them relatable, but both generic and representative. Build the drama, but relieve the tension with a joke. Repeat that cycle a few times, before reaching a cliff-hanger ending, then reward the attention with a long break."

"I can't remember any of that."

"The email prospects less content in each lecture, so we could stretch one course into several courses.:

"Right! I remember that bit – good selling point."

"It didn't mention R.R.R. week."

"That stands for reading, recitation, and review."

"Am I supposed to give them some reading?"

"No, they're too busy reading whatever you assigned them for classes."

"What's the recitation?"

"I don't know – I suppose they're supposed to recite to each other whatever they read."

"Then what's the review?"

"Ah, well, that's where you could do something: you could offer a review."

"A class?"

"Not a class! You're not allowed to teach anything: if the students catch you, they'll complain and get A-grades."

"So, what I am supposed to do?"

"It's easy, just show up to answer questions, and preview the exam."

"So, I should show up to classes, same as any week?"

"Hell, no! That's a sure-fire way to ruin your course evaluations. Students don't want any more classes. They call it resting, recreation, and relief week. It's for the kids to recover from what you've taught them already."

"Then, should I just announce that I will be in the classrooms at the usual times, if they want to ask any questions?"

"Warmer, but no, not like that. They tend to misinterpret announcements as expectations, and then complain about the stress, and get A-grades."

"So, I should just show up to my classrooms without announcing anything?"

"No. If they find out that you were there, but didn't tell them in advance, they'll complain and..."

"And get A-grades."

"You're getting it."

"So, I need to announce a review session that doesn't seem like a class."

"Exactly."

"So, I should schedule a review session, but not in my classroom, or at the time of my class."

"Very good. Whatever you do, you yourself shouldn't schedule it. You'd need to canvas the students to see when they want to do it, then find a room at that time. But don't use the university's own tool for that – it doesn't work. No, use social media. Best to let the kids do it, they know best."

"Oh my!" exclaimed Simon, leaning back with his eyes on the ceiling. "I know: I'll ask Aurelia. She's in all my classes."

Aurelia soon reported that nobody needed a review class, as the previous classes had been clear enough.

Earnest took the news reproachfully: "Nobody around here will like you for that."

***

The city was never busier than during resting, recreation, and relief week. Local businesses counted on their most lucrative week since the first week of semester. The students organized end-of-class parties, senior proms, graduation parties, fraternity parties, sorority parties, morning-after brunches, off-road convoys over the ridge, and sunset cruises around the bay. Thereabouts, they fitted in sit-ins, rallies, demonstrations, and marches against privilege. They met to discuss what issues they had missed. They met to discover what else offended them.

The industry that normally receives the least business during RRR week is journalism. Journalists, like students, use RRR week to catch up with the research they should have been doing during the semester. In Bayside, independent journalism (independent of the university and the public purse) had reduced to The Bayside Blab, whose editor suddenly thought of Simon. He stood up and wrote on the board for prospective investigative articles: "What is the anti-fed hero and protester against the Halloween homicide doing now?" Then he emailed Simon with an invitation to meet. The editor sincerely promised to pay for lunch, to keep everything on background, to keep all parties honest if Simon ever needed his story told, and to publish topical excerpts from Simon's research.

Simon was making his first attempt to visit when a crowd smashed the windows of the military recruiting center, on the ground floor below the offices of The Bayside Blab. The walls were sprayed with three propositions: "We are the Fascist Fighters! We own the streets! Fight white supremacy!" A witness pointed out to a reporter that the attackers were white, while the recruiters were not. A letter to The Bayside Blab accused the witness of being a fascist stooge, who could not have been there, because every Fascist Fighter was wearing black clothes from crown to sole. The Bayside Blab's staff analyzed the photographs, and found that the visible skin around their masks and gloves looked white. That evening, the newspaper's office was firebombed.

A letter arrived the next day, delivered via the hands of the Community Champions at the Bayside City's Department for Perpetual Peace, from the Fascist Fighters. The letter committed to an amnesty on further attacks, so long as the burnt lobby would be used as a safe space for white students to explore their whiteness, acknowledge white sins, and begin the journey of solidarity with the less privileged.

The Bayside Blab printed that letter in its next edition, without comment. The lobby was soon overtaken by repentant whites. The newspaper reported the scene in its next edition. The editor received an anonymous letter complaining that the blackening of the lobby and its participants by soot were hate crimes. The newspaper printed this too without comment.

The editor received another letter from the Fascist Fighters, refuting the implication that attacks on white privilege amounted to hate crimes. Their argument concluded: "It can't be a hate crime if it's true."

In the same letter, the Fascist Fighters suggested that the newspaper should turn over its offices as a reservation for privileged white people, which would be financed by taking spectating fees from tourists.

The letter further suggested that the reserved residents would like to make money for themselves by staging historical re-enactments. "Hell!" concluded the paragraph. "Some of the people in your photographs are so white, they already look like historical re-enactors."

The Fascist Fighters signed off as usual, "Down with capitalism," but added a postscript. "We demand ten percent of all revenues from our idea."

The Bayside Blab's executive board would debate any idea for turning around a loss-making business except honest reporting. The executive board refused the editor's plan to print the latest letter without comment, the editor resigned, nobody else would take the job, the board announced the closure of the newspaper, and the Fascist Fighters celebrated another victory against hate speech. As they reminded the reporter from The Daily Sunshine, "hate speech is free speech."

39. Exam week

Simon had set his deadline for final papers on the last working day of exam week. His office hour was on the first working day of the same week. Aurelia came by, as she did most weeks. "Today I've come for career advice."

"I'm really not an exemplar for career advice."

"Yes, you are. I have decided that I want to become an academic, like you."

"Oh no!"

"Why not?"

"Why would you want to take that opportunity cost for so little reward and so much risk?"

"But I have decided I don't want to be a lawyer, or a politician, or an actor."

"Take any of them – I've changed my mind too. I would respect you more if you took any of them. But don't do all three, then you'd add up to an academic."

"What should I do instead?"

"Anything more practical and applied."

"I thought about taking a certificate in creative writing."

"You should! But now I think about it: that's another qualification for academic."

Aurelia's puzzled indecisiveness was forced out by an impatient stranger: "Hi, Simon. Could you, like, tell me what I missed, before I do the paper?"

"You're not a student of mine."

"I am – I added, at the last minute. It sounded interesting."

"But I haven't seen you in any classes."

"Yeah, well, I don't do well in classes. But you could tell me everything I missed, so I could write the paper."

"You missed everything."

"Yes, everything I missed."

"You missed 45 hours of lectures, and more hours of readings."

"Yes, but I don't need the boxed set – just the stuff on the final exam."

"I don't set final exams."

"Even easier."

"I set final papers, which you would have known if you had looked at the syllabus."

"I don't ready syllabi – on principle: because, you know, a lot of trees die to make syllabi."

"I post my syllabi online."

"You never told me that."

"I didn't know you to tell you. You should have followed the link when you registered."

"I didn't know that. I'm a first-generation college student."

"You've already failed – on non-attendance alone."

"But I have a disability."

"What disability?"

"You're not supposed to ask about my disability."

"I cannot know how to accommodate an unspecified disability."

"The specifications don't matter. Papers are still assignments: I should get extra time on assignments, for my disability."

"You've had fifteen weeks, since it was announced in the syllabus."

"Then it's a fifteen-week assignment, isn't it? I'm entitled to at least time-and-a-half on each assignment, so that's, like, a lot."

"Twenty-two-and-a-half weeks."

"Probably."

"By then, the next semester will be starting."

"Yeah, agreed: by next semester. I'm entitled."

"I'm obliged to submit all grades next week."

"That's unfair! I need to graduate next week."

"Then you need to complete the assignment, by this Friday."

"Okay, next Monday then – I'll take the weekend."

"No."

"No? You can't say 'no'!"

"I've become really good at saying 'no'. I can say it repeatedly, I can say it by email or in person, I can repeat it to every repetitive question. It's easy – you try. One syllable, without nuance. It's so easy, I don't know why everyone pretends it's so difficult. Go on, you try."

"No, I don't want to."

The next day, DAFI emailed all instructors to warn that so many new disabilities had emerged during the week that instructors should assume every student has a disability, unless DAFI notified otherwise.

The next email was from Guillaume Juncker:

An undisclosed number of anonymous students have complained to me today that your final assignment is unreasonable. Don't forget that these students graduate a week from tomorrow. Our job is to make sure everybody graduates on time. The responsibility for any failure to graduate ultimately rests with the instructor. You should accommodate these students this weekend so that they can graduate on time.

You should have come to see me for advice on your final assignment – as you know, my door is always open. By avoiding this issue, you have left too little time for us to meet. I am sorry to see another Simon issue. You should avoid creating issues.

Simon replied: "I'm not passing any student who doesn't pass all assignments on time as specified in my relevant syllabi."

Will of the WISP copied Simon on an email to all students:

Due to problems with the final assignment, Dr. Ranald's courses will close forthwith. Everybody will receive A-grades. As a first-generation college instructor and foreigner, Dr. Ranald has struggled to adapt to the high standards at Bayside. I am sure you will join me in wishing him well as he moves on to his next position.

Aurelia was first to reply to all:

Dear Professor Juncker and the Wider Body of Those Who Care:

I just saw this; I had to reply immediately, even though my concerns may be read as emotional.

I have to say that I would be dumbfounded if everybody were to get A-grades.

As you know, I pay good money as a consumer of this for-profit institution. I find it insulting and hurtful that everybody gets A-grades without doing the work, by finding problems in the final assignment that I cannot see. This situation is a result of this institution's lack of true care and consideration for those who want to be educated meritoriously.

Should a single soul residing in WISP not see this, then their understanding of education is tragically myopic.

I need this institution, built upon the honorable task of educating the future generation, to respond in a human way to a human need. If you have further issue, I am willing to listen, and I am also willing to take this as far as necessary.

Judiciary Pinklewonk replied to all that she agreed with Aurelia, and added that she was copying her father – former Secretary of the Treasury Tom Pinklewonk. He mistakenly replied to all:

Judiciary – So this is the limey who has been leading you away from politics, and here he is exposed as a bad teacher, yet you want me to intervene on his behalf. I hope this is a lesson to you.

P.S. When you reply, be careful to reply to me only, not to all.

Simon replied to all that he would grade papers from students who wanted to complete the course that he had taught. Juncker instructed them to ignore Simon's "wrong-headed" email.

Simon searched his options. He went to see the university's ombudsman, who apologized that he had taken the position only six months earlier, so did not know what to do. He had previously managed a building. He liked to listen, but Simon kept asking for advice, which disturbed him, so he eventually suggested the University of Sunshine Office of the President.

Simon filed a list of complaints to USOP through its online form. Within the hour, a reply pretended that his only complaint was that he was being pressured to graduate students without qualifications, and ruled that "the claim could not be supported."

The next day, the college newspaper posted that Dr. Simon Ranald had been asked to move on, after posting impossible final assignments. On the following day, some strangers organized a "healing circle to attempt to heal the pain caused by Simon Ranald." In their welcoming remarks, the organizers focused on how to approach professors to suggest an extension on all final assignments due to the stress caused by Simon Ranald. Then the organizers invited the healing to begin.

"He's a Nazi. I heard he drew a stick figure on the board that looked like a swastika. And he drew it with chalk, which was white, so he's clearly racist."

"And he's a sexist. I heard him say that he enjoys Shakespeare. Remember the 'Taming of the Shrew'? Taming! Of a woman, nicknamed after a rodent."

"If he supports Shakespeare then he's a racist. Most of Shakespeare's characters are white."

"Othello is one of Shakespeare's few black heroes. That's racist."

"Othello was a flawed hero. That's racist."

"I bet Simon Ranald dates people of the same color."

"Racist!"

"I saw him bring a woman to a history talk."

"Racist and hetero-centric."

"I heard him illustrate a theory with the American Founders. It was all, like, 'he said this' and 'he said that'. Oh sure, he occasionally referred to a woman, but not once did he include a transgender."

"I heard he speaks German – probably because he's a Nazi."

"He never signed any petitions or joined any protests. He was obsessed with objectivity."

"He taught me that normal is what most people do or are. That's discriminatory."

"He said in class that a single event is no guide to a trend. Then he gave the example of the hot weather – he's a climate denier."

Simon went to campus to return library books, passing large advertisements for the healing circle, with the text encircling his headshot. He was approached by two excited youths: "Professor Ranald? I have heard that you are bigoted and prejudiced, so we've come to hear you say something offensive."

"Please go away."

"Oh, thank you, Professor Ranald – such an archaic insult. Give us another one."

"No."

"Say something about the working class."

"I've never said anything about the working class."

"Oh, you're such a snob, Professor Ranald."

"Since I am one of the few workers around here, I cannot possibly be a snob about the working class. You're mistaking real workers with the idle privileged who champion the idle non-privileged. What they call the working class seems to me oxymoronic."

"Ooh, the working class are morons, that's a great quote, thank you, you bigot! Now, what do you think of the common person?"

"I've never met the common person. I have met many common people. Indeed, almost everybody I have ever met is so common as to be undifferentiated in my memory. A single common person is yet another oxymoron."

They squealed with delight, took a photograph, and ran off.

40. Deluge

Simon felt annoyed to be late to wake up to it, to enjoy it from the start, to enjoy the anticipation, from the opening act of the darkening clouds.

He remembered his first week in the cottage in the garden, when the evenings had been cold and damp. He had watched the sun sink between the mountains north of the bay, between clouds ruffled intricately beyond the capacity of any palette knife, colored beyond the sensitivity of any camera, within a background of purples and pinks that deepened and melded into darkness, every evening a masterpiece, at once both memorable and impossible to remember.

Since then, every evening had been white and bright, identically disappointing, both forgettable and impossible to forgive, commonly cloudless and colorless, except for a hint of bleached blue transitioning to a hint of sickly yellow, ending ever earlier and closer to the south of the bay.

Now he awoke puzzled, to see the dawn ruled with clouds arranged in parallel greys, indistinct from the bay, but distinct from each other. He counted fifty of them before he resented his own over-analysis. Fifty shades of grey had never before seemed readable.

Heavy drops tapped on the roof. Soon, smaller, quicker drops drummed. The squirrels chattered at the bases of the lower branches. The birds dropped to depressions in the hard, bleached lawn, extended their wings, opened their beaks, lowered their bodies, and shimmied, while the rain pooled around them without penetrating the ground.

Simon gazed out of the window, fascinated, until he realized he was holding clothes that he meant to pack. He placed them in his luggage, resented the reminder, and returned to the scene. The self-reproach returned, which clarified as hesitation, so he opened the door. Little Lola rushed in with a call of togetherness. Simon stepped out with a murmur of reassurance. He stood in the rain. He felt cool and damp. He wanted to be colder and damper. He did not want a coat or a hat. He wanted his clothes to be soaked. He wanted his hair to be wet enough to be slicked back with one hand. He wanted to fling the water from his outstretched fingers. He wanted to absorb the dampness through his shoes. He wanted to be chilled.

He bent down at the knees and scratched in the dust until he made a paste. He scooped it with his fingertips and wiped it over his hands until they were streaked with brown, then he watched it rinse away. He pondered the rain gathering at his eyebrows and falling in the direction of his gaze. He enjoyed blinking the water into his eyes. He wetted his lips by parting them. He rose refreshed and effaced, confident that portent was converging, focusing, and aggregating.

He stood unwilling to break the charm. He wondered how he could both pack his clothes and stay outside. If only library books and computers were as accommodating as he, if only all would fit under the garden's umbrella, if only Little Lola would take his lap outside.

The fresh breezes turned into vicious squalls, the atmosphere was heavy, his clothes felt leaden, and his feet felt sunken. He heard an unfamiliar splash when a car drove by, then the forgotten churn of steady flows. He walked out to the street to see water pouring along the deep channel between sidewalk and road, rising against the tires of parked cars, crashing angrily against the inclined wheels, thickening at the bend, and flooding the junction.

He remembered that Vonessa had shyly asked him to stay out of sight, given widespread publishing of his headshot within a circle that needed to be healed, so he returned to the cottage. He enjoyed the protection and the solitude, without reason to leave again, without obligations or responsibilities, other than his own research and any emails from students who cared for his opinion. He returned to the bedside window, opened it, pulled up a chair, looked out, breathed in, and intermittently packed and worked.

He foresaw leaving only to swim in the morning, in a pool depopulated, dimpled, and diluted by rain. Then he imagined the pool flooding. He went to check the news online. "Flooding advisory!" screamed a news banner. The drains in the districts between the Bay and the railway were already overflowing. The university, being on the inland rise, was safe from the storm drains, but a whistle-blower had gone to the city news station to warn that a dam on the hill might fail. Simon turned on the television.

"I've never heard of a dam in Bayside," said the interviewer.

"Yes," said the hidden whistle-blower. "It's one of the assets listed by the university and the state towards its environmental exceptionalism. It was built to provide hydro-electric power in replacement of an experimental nuclear reactor, when the city declared a nuclear-free zone."

"I've never heard of a nuclear reactor in Bayside," said the interviewer."

"Yes," said the whistle-blower. "It was built for defense research."

"I've never heard of defense research in Bayside."

"The separate campus on the hill was sponsored by the Defense Department."

"I've never heard of a separate campus on the hill."

"Yes. My point is: the dam is unsafe."

"How long has this dam been unsafe?"

"For years," declared the whistleblower. "Years of drought have weakened the earth around it. The university's own professors of structural engineering tried to inform state officials, but state officials kept siding with campus officials, because neither side could agree who should make it safe."

"You mean to say, state officials knew that this dam was unsafe, located above a city with hundreds of thousands of residents, but did nothing about it?"

"They had known for years. The Commission on Infrastructure Progress refused to inspect it. The commissioners wouldn't know how to assess it anyway – they're partisan-appointees, and the ruling party has never changed. They accept whatever the university tells them. And they characterize all critics as partisan ingrates, or lobbyists for the private sector. They were warned every year of the drought, that the dam was no longer proof against a normal rainy season, but the professors were moved on – denied tenure, accused of impropriety, defunded – or their silence was bought with promotion or a blind-eye to their own peccadillos."

"And you have known for years?"

"I have known for a year, since I handled the contracting for these people."

"Why are you coming forward now?" asked the interviewer.

"Because nobody would believe those former professors

unless I came forward. Their accusations would be dismissed as sour grapes. I've kept what I know to myself for too long, thinking that I was still putting two and two together, or I didn't know everything, or I wasn't sure, but I can't kid myself any longer. Then in the last few weeks I overheard another professor being bribed and punished for talking about flooding – not an engineer, but a social scientist – an expert in other things, a visiting professor from a foreign university, somebody who arrived only this semester, not somebody whose awareness could be explained, and I realized that this scandal is out of control."

"You have chosen to protect your identity, as state law allows, but are you prepared to name those you have accused of wrong-doing?"

"Yes. Chancellor Berk knew because he approved Max Mira to suppress the disclosures. Clara Mudd handled the contract with Max Mira. Both Clara Mudd and Max Mira handled the contract with the young professor. Now he's been canceled and subjected to a healing circle, even before he could be recognized as a whistleblower. I am blowing my whistle publicly, for state protection, before the organization does the same to me."

"Are you saying the young professor is Simon Ranald?"

"I regretfully confirm your supposition: Dr. Simon Ranald."

Simon recognized from the business-like pronunciation of his name the voice of Lee Green. He switched off the re-broadcast, unplugged the television, hid it beneath the table, and returned to the open window, with his books and hopes for a rescheduled flight to London. "Transport chaos!" screamed a new banner online. He checked his email, and found, sickeningly, that his flight had been postponed indefinitely. The backlog would take a day to clear, estimated the airline. Simon remembered advice to triple whatever an airline estimated.

In the morning, Berk and Metro released a joint statement, denouncing the anonymous whistle-blower as a coward, blaming partisan opponents in state government for putting him up to it, denouncing Dr. Simon Ranald as a disgruntled former employee, and urging friends of the university to show solidarity and faith by gathering on campus.

They did. Holding umbrellas they could not keep open, and

candles they could not keep alight, the university's most enlightened optimists took command of the grassy knoll. They stood in front of trees decorated with snowflakes in acknowledgement of the coming winter holidays, and overlooked the plaza on which they expected to face journalists. The journalists were stuck on the stormy waterfront or the windy ridge, ready to step outside their vans with a photographer, hold the hoods of their jackets, and shout breathlessly into their microphones during live broadcasts.

Few students were ready to displace their end-of-semester festivities for a protest, although a few walked about in the hope of seeing professors they could petition for extensions or inflations.

The Fascist Fighters guaranteed a safe space by loitering amongst the trees, padding silently behind anybody on the move, and looming over anybody at rest. In between their duties, they separated in groups to compare umbrellas with heavier handles or sharper tips. One had brought a vicious tool branded as an "Aufhammer" – too unbalanced to be of any virtuous use, but too deceptive to be banned for its viciousness. In the gloom by the stream, three Fascist Fighters were filling glass bottles with gasoline and rags. They fell out over whether to call them "Molotov cocktails," which both glorified the Soviet betrayal of Marxism and trivialized the consumerist promotion of alcoholism, or "fire bombs," which both appropriated an obscure culture's ritual beverage and trivialized Western aerial bombing. Growing despondent at the chances for using their weapons, they debated whether to construct flaming torches, but gradually agreed that fascists intimidate with torches, while anti-fascists heal with candles. Besides, candles are less polluting. Then they agreed that they should refer to their gasoline-rag-bottles as "candles." On that point of agreement, they returned to procuring two for every Fascist Fighter.

Dick Berk worried what the rain might do to his carefully gelled hair, so held his umbrella tight to his head, but inadvertently crushed the spikes. Confused and annoyed with himself, he fumbled in his pocket for his prepared speech, but pulled out soggy pieces. He rushed to speak to the loyal representative from The Daily Sunshine, despite counsel to wait for real journalists. "My fellow Sunshiners," he shouted. "We are victims of a vast right-wing conspiracy. Lee

Green and Simon Ranald are not whistle-blowers: they are agents of the right-wing, just like the agents of the FBI, and the basket of deplorables who voted for Clashmore Hickling. Stand with us! Stand against them! You're either with us or against us!"

Tom Pinklewonk had brought a megaphone and an umbrella. Now he handed the umbrella to a Fascist Fighter who was admiring its heavy steel shank tapering all the way to the end. Pinklewonk took the Fascist Fighter's candle to point up the hill. "That dam represents all that is great about this university – power and education. If they defame our dam, they defame us. Max Mira is a feminist hero. Clara Mudd is a tireless guardian of your tuition fees at work. Simon Ranald is a jealous partisan and a bad teacher. And he tried to steal my daughter. Vote for Trixie Downer in four years!"

Jimmy Pons still resented Tom Pinklewonk, but his ire was redirected at Simon Ranald for trying to steal a Miss Pinklewonk. Pons snatched Fascist Fighter candles in both hands. "Simon Ranald is a sexual predator! Justice for Trixie, poor Trixie, denied the presidency this year! Justice for Julie, poor Julie, denied funding last year! Justice for poor Bayside, denied rain most of this year! Fill the dam!"

Guillaume Juncker took his turn, claiming to be the next most senior: "I support this university's infrastructure – that's why I am professor of human geography. Simon Ranald doesn't support this university – that's why he's going back to Europe where he belongs!"

Juncker had urged Joe Karolides to show solidarity, but Joe offered a prior commitment with his husband on the peninsula.

Hattie Maddux stepped up. "Let me tell you what Foucault would do, because it's obvious. He would challenge what society wants us to think. Society wants you to think that this university and this state colluded to hide the risks of that dam failing. Ignore what society thinks!"

Aimee Pharisees took the megaphone: "Damming is a traditional construct! Respect the natural flow of water and menstruation! Justice for women!"

Jewel Lighter was passed the megaphone, did not know what to say, and was applauded for her loyalty.

Jimmy Pons sidled up to Jewel Lighter, thinking that a quiet woman was most valuable at this moment. He was delighted when she startled and asked with unprecedented passion, "Did you feel the earth move?"

"That's right, baby. That's what I do."

Then everybody felt unsteady on their feet. The ground felt like a rug was being pulled one way and the other, so quickly as to keep righting them.

Jewel Lighter grabbed Jimmy's hands, then the quiet woman shouted so clearly and powerfully that everyone paid attention: "It's an earthquake!"

"Don't spread partisan pessimism," Pinklewonk commanded, but the earthquake disobeyed.

The lamps above the plaza and sidewalks cut out. The snowflakes ceased to glow. At the limit of their vision in the twilight, the most enlightened optimists could see only as far as the scaffolding and sheeting around the building above the flooded swimming pool. Silently, captivated by a shared focus for their first time, they watched it gracefully fold from the top downwards, until everything collapsed into a jagged skirt, revealing the moldy, stained façade. The sudden quiet relieved the ears while the eyes were still beset with dust.

The shock of silence was too brief, when a roar that all wanted to deny confirmed itself with amplification. The dam's collapse could not be seen but was uncontrollably imagined. The water emerged out of the darkness with more terrifying mass than its tardy noise could warn. By then, escape was impossible. The water crashed through the redwoods without effect, then washed the snowflakes, the optimists, the loyalists, and the Fascist Fighters down the greasy knoll, across the plaza, off campus, and through the broken windows of the military recruiting office, under stinking, cloying, suffocating muck.

The muck settled without witnesses or responders. Most personnel formerly known as police officers had quit. The remainder were serving as community champions at the public places protected for protests. The feds were still banned from the city. The ambulance services were on orders not to venture into Bayside without police protection. The fire services had been gathered at the dam to pump water out.

Most campus administrators were resting from the stress of

standing by for Yannis' second visit. Most of the students were off campus, off course, off line, or off planet.

41. Cruise

Simon knew none of this and could not be blamed, because that morning he had boarded a cruise ship, as arranged by Vonessa. She had been telephoned with an urgent invitation to succeed one of its entertainment staff for the Christmas cruise.

"No," she had replied, "I am expecting my family together for the holidays, but I know an articulate young man with a lovely speaking voice, who talks eloquently about foreign affairs." The Director of Entertainment did not jump at the opportunity as quickly as Vonessa had expected, so she added, with misguided parochial confidence, "He teaches at Bayside!" Fortunately, the Director of Entertainment was desperate, when Vonessa sealed the deal by adding, breathlessly, "He's perfectly comfortable with older people."

Simon had packed already. Lola remained asleep on his bed, so he left the door to the cottage ajar. Then he ran to Vonessa's car: she knew the safest way down to the port. Simon hid his sensitivity by urging her to return quickly uphill before the weather might worsen or he might be recognized. He backed inconspicuously towards the fringe of the hundreds of waiting passengers. Next to them, he realized that his computer satchel and wheeled bag looked inadequate. He held a jacket and tie sufficient for most occasions, but no evening wear. He had enough professional shirts and trousers for three lectures per week, but no certain capacity for daytime company. He was released from his dissonance by an invitation for staff to board immediately. He passed into the inorganic noises and shapes of the service deck. The passenger corridors were smoother, quieter, and tighter, his cabin more so. It vibrated and rattled with reassuring claustrophobia, without a window on his isolation.

The ship passed out of the bay that evening, timed to sail into the sunset, although everything it faced was misty, grey, cloudy, and blustery. Simon could not see from stern to bow, but the bow was where he imagined the crowds, while his bias was to face whence he came. He strained to make out the boundaries of the Bayside campus. He traced its largest landmarks to where the hill rose steeply. With careful imagination, he found the wooded ridge that obscured the dam, before the cloud descended again, and the bluster became blinding.

He turned his back on Bayside, and walked forward, to find only a few unsupervised children and callow honeymooners, all in shorts and t-shirts, running, squealing, from one exit to the next entrance. He could hear tapping against the windows of the Grand Lounge below. He paused to watch the gloomy cliffs of the bay's neck loom ahead and pass behind. The slow passage became indeterminable, so he went inside for an early and lonely dinner.

In the stuffy dawn, the ship's wake looked barely faster, as if, like him, it did not care when it arrived. He did not care to burden himself with its destination or schedule, until he returned to a note under his door from the Director of Entertainment.

She was keen to announce his first lecture for the next afternoon. On the wall of her office, she showed him the map of their journey, across Pacific islands to Asian peninsulas. She asked if he could speak on the current affairs of these countries before he visited them. "I think so," he replied. "Enough colleagues have shown me how."

"I don't want to tell you your job, but we've found that the evaluations rate well if you tell the audience whatever is closest to what they've already heard."

"Yes. Enough colleagues have taught me that too."

Simon found enough guidebooks and overviews in the library. Most of its holdings were fiction, but he had his fill of fiction at Bayside. He did not read there, because it accommodated more discussants than readers. He took his laptop to the "Quiet Room," but it was squeezed between the games room and the creche. He sat in the glass alcoves in the corridors along the upper sides of the ship, where passengers would rest legs but not conversations. He sat in the lounge until the teens club invaded. He sat in the theatre on excuse of preparing to lecture, until dancing rehearsal became dancers' squabble. He walked on deck to enjoy the chilly spray, struggled to read in the wind, and made notes as they occurred to him, which he transferred to his laptop in his cabin. Gradually, he organized his cabin as his only work area, as personal and likeable as a cave, cloaked in the hum and moan of the ship, uninterrupted, except for announcements from the soporific captain about course and weather, and from the manic cruise director about endless activities for endless relaxation.

He paid a small fortune to get online, to order gifts with reassuring messages to his parents for the holidays. They had emailed only news of their heir, and no inquiries about their spare. He revoked the outside world until foreign ports. Even there, he delighted in anonymity and dumbness. He visited governmental and historical sites of relevance to his work. In the dining rooms, he learnt not to presume the sort of person who would care for the company of the ship's lecturer, but to wait to be approached. He enjoyed the company of old couples who delighted in the humorous and profound, and of young families who expected children to participate in adult conversation.

At larger ports, he watched passengers depart and be replaced, until the ship prepared to reverse its journey. The Director of Entertainment offered him a flight home or opportunities on other ships. With her connivance, he plotted his passage westwards, through the Indian Ocean, the Red Sea, and the Mediterranean. After New Year's Eve, he lost track of dates, and thought only two days ahead, to the next lecture or change of ship. Most of January would go by before he returned to England, but he was in no hurry. He was ever deeper in his world of study, ever remoter to the world of academia.

Simon had no idea who might employ him after disembarkation. He sometimes wondered whether he could keep joining other ships, but his ethos as lecturer afloat was founded on his title as lecturer ashore. Sometimes the fantastic possibility entered his head of some part of academia ignorant of his decline and fall, but he resigned himself to being run aground in England. Beyond that, he cared not to imagine.

He did not even know where he would stay. He emailed Mrs. Hart, who agreed to take him back without worrying about when, because Jenny Wren was most anxious for his advice. His final passage berthed in Southampton early on a Thursday morning. By lunchtime, he was on Crimson Street, trying to imagine what had changed.

Only Mrs. Hart was home. She was anxious more than welcoming – most anxious about a series of letters that had arrived from Riverside within the month. "The most recent is in such a large and stiff envelope that it must contain an important invitation," she promised.

However, Simon started in chronological order, with six identical envelopes, all addressed from "The Director of Riverside University of London." On each letter, Sharon's hasty squiggle in lieu of the Director's signature was the same, although his name was unfamiliar.

The first letter informed all staff of a radical departure from the previous regime of Director Daly, but reassured them that jobs would be gained, not lost. The second was personal: it asked for news of his safe and prompt return from the fascist persecutions and tragedies of Bayside. The third invited him to be part of the new regime in some capacity that he might like to suggest. The fourth suggested a new appointment as Deputy-Director of Regime Change Implementation, or perhaps Deputy-Director of Radical Values Without Obsolete Virtues, or Deputy-Director of Cross-Fertilization Without Cultural Appropriation. The fifth letter promised to double his salary if he would accept within the week. The sixth stated that he would be appointed in absentia. The biggest envelope contained an invitation to his investiture as "title yet to be agreed."

Simon's sense of time was still befuddled, but, with Mrs. Hart's persistence, he was persuaded that the investiture really was scheduled for the morrow. Before then, he needed to apply his research skills to discover the relevant transpirations since he had last paid attention to the news.

42. Regime change

When American academia sneezes, British academia catches a cold sweat of inadequacy.

After the tragedy now known as the "Bayside Bogslide," the Trustees of the University of Sunshine urgently convened – remotely, from their private islands and tax havens. First, they agreed to postpone their emergency meeting until after the holidays. Second, they decreed that all final assignments would be cancelled and assumed to be worthy of A-grades.

In the new year, the Trustees ordered a review of the Budgeting Office by a special independent third-party investigative committee, to be appointed by three of their own: Rob Partsome of Belitter, Jean Cadhowling of SheepOnline, and Josh Chubfuddler of Tracebook. They appointed investigators from Gornorff Lab, which had been formed recently by all three companies to advise on how to protect their users' privacy. They were also the major shareholders.

Gornorff Lab reported quickly that Chancellor Berk had yet to pay his monthly instalment for the campus gym. The Trustees fired Berk posthumously for misappropriation of public resources, then scheduled their first emergency meeting on campus.

The Trustees laid a wreath inside the shattered military recruiting center, circled the water-damaged recreational building, threw sticks in the muck of the swimming pool, led a minute's silence for all victims, and – atop the grassy knoll – awarded the Jimmy Pons Memorial Scholarship to the youngest woman of color in the incoming cohort. From the plaza, they boarded helicopters for the one-minute flight over the site of the former dam to the sandy beach between the empty reservoir and the official residence of the President of the University of Sunshine.

There, they held their first emergency meeting of the new calendar year. Secretary Metro was persuaded to leave the Presidency, "given the growing demands of her political commitments, by mutual agreement and with mutual goodwill," as their press release explained.

Metro released her own statement at the same time.

Having proven myself as president of the vast and diverse university system of the great State of Sunshine for a whole semester, I am ready to be the next President of the vast and diverse United States of America.

Having seen fascism infiltrate even this great university system, and even the office of the chancellor at our flagship university at Bayside (Chancellor Berk's appointment preceded my arrival), I am more determined than ever to fight fascism in the White House.

Today, I announce the start of my listening tour of all the United States. I will be listening to all Americans on why they want me to stand against Clashmore Hickling in the next Presidential election. I want to become the first outsider to lead the free world.

The Trustees promised an exhaustive search for Metro's successor. After browsing the internal candidates, over the weekend, they appointed Trixie Downer. In their statement, they praised their brave and radical choice, noting that she was the second female (self-identified) to come second in the race for the Presidency of the United States, the second female appointee to the Presidency of the University of Sunshine, the second former cabinet secretary, the second out-of-state resident, the second pescatarian (except on holidays), the second law-school-graduate, the second proud mother of one, the second keen follower of baseball, and the second keen jogger.

Trixie released a statement, in which she set five goals for herself: "build community, enhance student experience, increase diversity, spread social justice, and chart a break from the past."

The quick appointment of a new President of the whole University of Sunshine system provoked fevered speculation about the next Chancellor of the University of Sunshine Bayside. Treasury Pinklewonk started a petition on SheepOnline for the posthumous honorary appointment of her late father, former Secretary of the Treasury Thomas B. Pinklewonk. Trixie Downer re-Littered with the comment, "Ha! Ha! University of Sunshine students welcome my appointment as their president with a good-natured hoax! #WhoisThomasBPinklewonk?"

Treasury Pinklewonk reoriented her petition to over-turn Trixie Downer's appointment as President of the University of Sunshine. Trixie explained by BeLitter that her BeLitter account had been hacked. Then she BeLittered that she was proud to fulfil the creative and enlightened idea of a posthumous honorary appointment. Third, she BeLittered that Treasury Pinklewonk would be the inaugural recipient of the Thomas B. Pinklewonk Memorial Scholarship at Bayside Law School, next semester, on expectation that she would complete her undergraduate degree program early.

After an exhaustive external search, Trixie appointed Guillaume Juncker as Chancellor of Bayside. He had been pulled out of the muck as the most senior survivor of the vigil, by virtue of landing on his feet, with the mud settling around his eyes. By correcting his posture for the first time in his life, he was able to hold his nose and mouth clear.

Jewel Lighter had survived too, but refused to talk about it. Trixie appointed her to a special committee of investigation.

Blaming a concussion, Juncker claimed no recollection of Chancellor Berk, the Optimists Club, the dam, or the Bayside Bogslide. He even admitted ignorance of human geography, although a re-reading of his prior BeLitters on the subject was sufficient re-qualification.

Trixie Downer's first instruction to Juncker was to appoint Kyle Fistbumper as Vice-Chancellor for Intolerance of the Intolerant, with secondary responsibility for Disregard of the Regardless. As a creative speech writer turned policy-maker, Kyle knew how to reach the intolerant and regardless – he called a press conference. He entertained the journalists to all the free food and booze they wanted, then tapped his glass, rose to his feet, waved away the microphone, put one hand on his hip, and raised the glass. "My friends," he said, in a quiet tone that relaxed him but reached nobody else. His eyes fell to the floor, his eyelids fell to his pupils, and his paunch fell to his belt. He pouted and swallowed laboriously to lengthen the pause. He imagined what the audience must be thinking: "Here is a creative writer who became a speech writer. Here is one of our own that is worth our undivided attention." The audience was spell-bound, because it could hardly hear him.

Kyle tugged on the lapel of his black silk shirt to relieve the tension from his paunch, pushed his tiny shiny trousers further down his hips, and started to speak from memory, while pretending that everything occurred to him spontaneously.

"My friends! We're gathered here today to talk about Bayside and you, but first let's talk about me. I visited Bayside a few weeks ago, as the government's expert, to help this university against a scourge of extremism, which I already knew was under-estimated, before I could tell anyone. Now, I can tell my story. Days earlier, I had been appointed an Under-Secretary for Counter-Extremism by Secretary Trixie Downer herself. After all, extremism-countering is synthesis-vectoring and concept-colliding by expression-messaging. Back then, neither of us knew we would be required on this campus full-time to fix this crisis. Clashmore Hickling – with his foreign hackers and populist lies – took over our government. We could have served longer in government, fighting extremism from the inside, but we've come to the other side of the nation, because fighting extremism in the White House begins with fighting extremism in higher education. Our future leaders are made here. And we need your help."

Gornorff Labs' final report to the Trustees concluded that "mistakes were made at all levels of the organization," although Clara Mudd was the sole handler of all contracts involving the dam and Max Mira. She was also the sole point of contact for the state government's Commission on Infrastructure Progress. "Big data don't lie," said a spokesperson for Gornorff Labs.

Clara Mudd denied being the sole handler of anything, but was solely indicted under state law for misappropriation of public funds, otherwise known colloquially as "scapegoat's law." During her arraignment, she too claimed to be a victim of Max Mira.

To replace her, Juncker promoted Alison from administration of WISP to administration of all the university's accounts, with the title of Vice-Chancellor of Leadership Partnering and Creative Restructuring. She purged anybody who had worked with either Clara Mudd or Lee Green. She replaced them with PAX students, on the grounds that counter-extremists were more urgently required than accountants.

Back at WISP, Joe Karolides was promoted to Director and asked to absorb Alison's responsibilities. He was desperate for Simon Ranald to re-appear, to replace Jimmy Pons as head of PAX. He needed a replacement for Prisha Pradesh too, who was food-poisoned by holiday gifts from appreciative students.

Joe reluctantly passed Jimmy's, Simon's, and Prisha's teaching burdens to Earnest Keeper, temporarily, pending a formal search for a more senior candidate. Guillaume and Alison called in Earnest to warn that they could find not fund Earnest's courses, due to unavoidable and impersonal budget cuts. They speculated but could not promise that he might be called back in more prosperous years, and that subsequent recalls might count towards the six years of teaching required for tenure. He was in his fifth year. Earnest went to see Joe with this news, just as Joe received authorization to hire new faculty on promise of tenure in six years.

The union objected that new faculty should not be hired to teach what current faculty could teach, so Will and Alison released a statement claiming that all courses would be new, given the switch from WISP to "Globalization, human rights, and cultural change." They authorized undergraduate students to teach their own courses "on subjects not addressed in the traditional curriculum." These courses would be branded as "Democratic Education," or "Ded" for short.

Simon's course on social scientific methods was replaced by "critical thinking." Joe asked Alison how to interpret "critical thinking."

"It's obvious: teach the students how to criticize."

"But they're expert at that already!"

Joe was persuaded to take early retirement. An undergraduate student of PAX was appointed to convert the former WISP courses to "Democratic Education" – to "Ded-en" the courses, in the new parlance.

Director Daly had joined the consensual condemnation of fascist infiltration of the University of Sunshine and state government. Speaking off the cuff to reporters waiting outside his favorite lunch venue, he said: "I know the great State of Sunshine well. I know the great university of Bayside well. Tom Pinklewonk was a great friend of mine, a tragic loss, a defender of the working class – a mission I naturally shared. I met Chancellor Berk a few times, although I did not know him well. In fact, I hardly knew him. He didn't seem working-class."

Stumbling, Daly sought to change the subject. "I am concerned also for the welfare of a professor, who, I have just been informed, was on loan from my own university at Riverside. He, or she, or ze, is a vulnerable, foreign transgender lecturer whose name is pronounced 'sinner' – that is: S-I-N-R, 'Sinner'."

Reporters in America could not find any lecturer of so unusual a name. British reporters bombarded the Riverside University of London's press office, which contacted Sharon. She was forced to correct the record before Daly returned to his office that evening from lunch.

Meanwhile, the Academics Union of Britain pressed the Trustees of the Riverside University of London to locate the vulnerable, foreign, trans-gender lecturer. Thence made aware of the discrepancy, the Trustees launched an investigation, under Dorian Floorman, because he was listed as the university's expert in Anglo-American, British-American, and European-American relations. He was still pondering whether to approach his American counterparts as a Churchill or a Blair, when journalists published a quote from Ricky Docker.

"Of course, I know Sinner!" said Ricky Docker. "I gave him the nickname – he's Simon Ian Nigel Ranald. I mentored him, you know, when I was editing a highly-regarded series of books. I would have gone to Bayside myself, if I hadn't been so busy here. By the way, I'm available to replace him this term."

Joan Moorish updated her online selfies, when her eyes were especially sleepy, knowing that her expression was as close to empathy as possible. Then she switched her BeLitters from feminist international relations theory to a campaign for "hashtag Simon come home." Speaking as "a close colleague and personal friend," she multiplied her followers hundreds of times.

Exhaustive investigation by the American reporters could not locate Simon Ranald in Bayside. Clara Mudd said she too had mentored him, as a close colleague and friend. Will Juncker claimed no memory of him, and forbade staff from commenting without going through his office.

The reporters satisfied their work-rate with long biographical reports, including hearsay on Simon's brave fight against fascists in the classroom, protests against Yannis, interventions against police brutality on campus, blowing the whistle on Max Mira, challenging Chancellor Berk, and even (according to Judiciary and Aurelia) teaching useful courses.

The reporters continued with visceral speculation of his demise in the Bayside Bogslide. By different accounts, he had been swept through a sewer into the bay, eaten by escaped pet alligators, sucked down an unmapped gold mine, rescued from the smashed military recruiting office by military personnel who then press-ganged him into military service, or washed up – concussed and amnesic – amongst the residents of the Homeless Sanctuary.

City authorities kept repeating that all victims of the Bayside Bogslide had been identified. The Fascist Fighters kept repeating that Simon Ranald had joined them to keep vigil against fascism on campus. Some went further, claiming that he was carrying evidence of a fascist conspiracy to defame the university, until sinister men in black carried him away, just before the dam was fracked from an unspecified location in the next state. Federal authorities confirmed that Simon Ranald had exited the country just hours before the Bayside Bogslide, but the feds already featured in the conspiracy theories. The British government could not tell whether Simon Ranald had returned to Britain, because it could not tell for sure who had crossed its borders.

A leaker revealed that Riverside University had not heard from him or attempted to contact him since Professor Sir Barry Liddell had written selflessly to Simon at the beginning of the exchange program to share his intimate knowledge of Bayside. A leaker at University of Sunshine Bayside sold Simon's most recent address, but Vonessa refused to divulge more than that Simon had left by ship when the feds said he did. Bayside's leaker revealed that Riverside had made no arrangements to receive Simon back from his exchange. Riverside's leaker revealed that Bayside had not informed Riverside of its intent to terminate his exchange early. Briefing off the record, both sides' leakers accused the other of conspiracy in a fascist plot. In the process, they revealed that they had not yet communicated with each other about Simon Ranald, provoking a new conspiracy theory in which they had colluded to cover up a vast right-wing conspiracy from America to Britain.

Chancellor Juncker got the upper hand by pointing out that Bayside was already engaged in a purge. At Riverside, the Academics Union and Students Union picketed campus against Director Daly. Their shared General-Secretary told reporters: "The Americans have purged earlier and deeper. The Americans! We demand that the Trustees should close the purge gap!"

The Trustees of Riverside University of London, citing a prior and unrelated internal review, dismissed Daly. However, under the terms of his contract he was entitled to full salary until his expected date of retirement, when he was entitled to 80 percent and to join the Board of Trustees.

43. Investiture

Simon's head hurt, so he went for a nap, expecting to wake for dinner. Instead, he woke to a cold wet morning, the comings and goings of landlubber traffic, and the Hart family's breakfast, without the cloaking hums and murmurs of a ship.

Downstairs, at his own late and lonely breakfast, he took up his correspondence. A package from the cruise line included statements on his pay, with advice on the number of days at sea he would need to accumulate to be non-domicile for tax purposes, a list of sailings he could join on a renewed contract, and a personal note from the General-Manager of Entertainment inviting him on any ship for immediate employment, given his popularity with the ships' Directors and passengers.

Simon's other mail included a large package from Vonessa, containing several letters, some of which she had interpreted rightly as official or urgent. Lief Kirk reminded Simon by letter, given his failure to respond to telephone calls, not to leave the country without an exit interview. The City of Bayside's Department for Perpetual Peace requested him to testify to the state of mind of Walter Fontaine before his death, and added an invitation to give a victim-impact statement against Adrian Yannis' return to campus. A federal subpoena ordered him to testify against Max Mira. Another federal judge subpoenaed him to appear at the federal inquiry into police violence at Bayside. Simon was copied on a circular from Chancellor Juncker's office that invited any staff or student to contribute to the oral archive of experiences of the Bayside Bogslide. The Smart Sisters of Bayside invited him to welcome the newest Smart Sisters. The Flappers and Go-Getters sent him their calendar of activities for the new year. The Trustees of the University of Sunshine requested donations to endow minorities, including the female student majority. The Sun Tzu Center offered him an international education and research fellowship. Marcus invited him to China. Jock and Lucy invited him to their Christmas party.

Overwhelmed, Simon spread their contents atop the dining table, then found himself moving between the chairs. He rearranged them as he read the details and considered the priorities.

Jock and Lucy had written a personal note on the back of their invitation. Lucy was losing the strength to maintain her homestead, and the children were struggling to maintain their grades, so she wondered whether he might like to join them through the rest of the academic year, since he had seemed interested in both the homestead and the children's education.

Inside was a smaller envelope, containing a card addressed simply to "Simon," wishing him a happy Christmas and New Year, from Teddi Theodora. He had never seen her hand-writing before. She signed her name with calligraphic flourishes; she dotted the "i" with a small shape that hinted at a heart; and she wrote her address in the corner.

He went back to the huge envelope from Riverside. A stiff invitation began with the word "Gala," embossed in gold, above the word "investiture." The date, time, and place glowed at center. At bottom, the fine print ended with: "No entry without this card. Donations to the 'Fight Against Exclusivity'." He returned it to the mantlepiece, where its old-fashioned smartness pleased Mrs. Hart.

He pondered his promise to visit his family as soon as he had established his situation at Riverside. He took in hand the calendar that Mrs. Hart had given him. With embarrassing labor of mind, he found the date that she had circled yesterday, reconciled today as Friday, wrote "investiture" in the same box, wrote "family" in the box for Saturday, and plotted the sailings out of Southampton from the following week.

When he rubbed his eyes again, he realized a smaller gilt-edged card clipped to the invitation. It was marked for executives only, with instructions for a limousine service, to be confirmed a week in advance. He thought it was handsome enough to put amongst Mrs. Hart's trophies. When she came in to admire them, she remembered that the company itself had telephoned Mrs. Hart for want of any response from Simon. Awestruck, she had confirmed her address and agreed its arrival time.

"Perhaps I should attend," he said.

"Of course, you must."

"I don't see the need, just me, amongst strangers."

"The invitation allows guests."

"My new friends are in America. Why don't you go?"

"Oh, I haven't been out in years. I don't like to go out."

"No."

"But Jenny Wren likes to go out; and she would benefit most. She wanted to talk to you about going to university this year."

Mrs. Hart foresaw Jenny gaining an easy introduction to her next transition. Simon foresaw Jenny mistaking this unrepresentative experience as her destiny in higher education. Then he imagined Max Mira beside her, shuddered, and insisted that Mr. Hart should chaperone. Mrs. Hart imagined Mr. Hart loose among buttery and creamy dishes, and insisted that she should chaperone. Then Mrs. Hart imagined Mr. Hart loose with the butter dish if left alone at home, so agreed that all four of them should go.

Jenny received the news excitedly when she came home from school, and rushed to prepare her prospective prom dress. Mr. Hart received the news distractedly, and complained that the weather was bound to increase the accident rate, and the company's reserves were already below plan. Mrs. Hart persuaded him by declaring that she had not prepared any dinner. She laid out his evening wear, but he was last to come down. She took up a tea towel and rubbed the surfaces of the kitchen, particularly around the door onto the little garden, while her jewelry creaked like a well-worn spring mattress, and her sequins fell like dandruff.

When the doorbell rang, Mrs. Hart turned on all the lights, then opened the door and stepped close to its curb, upright and twitching under the unnatural glow. She turned her face up the stairs and shouted with a gusto that Simon had never heard before: "Darling! Darling! We must go darling! We really must go, otherwise we'll be late."

Jenny Wren rushed down in a rustle of taffeta.

"Darling, where's your father? Never mind, take Simon's arm, dear. No, don't touch hands, over the top and drape it free. Yes, like that. Well done, dear. Follow Simon to the car. Mind the step, that's it. Darling! Darling!"

Simon helped Jenny Wren to the door that the driver held open, then let himself in the other side. Mr. and Mrs. Hart sat on the bench opposite, holding hands but silent and facing outwards, except occasionally to direct each other to a landmark from the days when they were young and walked London's pavements in their finery without ridicule or threat. At the halts, the rain beaded in great globules on the windows, before being dashed by the wind, and everything else remained unaffected.

Coming to a halt, the doors of the limousine were opened into the glare and warmth of spotlights normally used for outside broadcasting. Colorful searchlights played on the facade. Guests were guided half-heartedly by students in the costumes of footmen, except none were men, and all wanted to be known as actors. A red carpet pointed up the steps, under the carved stone pediment of the Dear Leader of the Holy Socialist People's Republic Business School, recently renamed, according to a banner hanging limply over all, as the British Public Broadcasting School of Mediocratic Management.

The seating plan showed Simon's party sitting with Professor Sir Barry Liddell (the new Deputy-Director of Strategy), Professor Dorian Floorman (the new Deputy-Director of American Partnerships), and Professor Ricky Docker (the new Deputy-Director of Research and Publishing). They regarded Simon like a younger sibling whose parental favor was intolerable but could not be challenged.

Mrs. Hart stepped ahead in her haste, with short steps, her hem held expertly off the floor behind her with one hand, a little purse clutched in the other. At the table, she dropped her hem with a flourish and shook each man's hand firmly. "How do you do?" she asked sincerely. Each man stood clumsily to attention. Ricky Docker held on to his drink, until she wanted his hand, when he put it down with a force sufficient to crack its stem. He poured the remnants of his drink into his water glass, dried his hand on the tablecloth, took her hand, and showed her to a seat.

Mrs. Hart waited politely for everyone to settle. She relocated Jenny Wren's gloved hands from table to lap, moved the butter dish to the opposite side from Mr. Hart, and started the conversation.

"The temperature is very pleasant this close to the stage, considering how frightfully frigid is the draught near the doors. The borders of my garden are very trying at this time of year. One wonders when the snowdrops might emerge so that one is reminded where one planted them in the first place, so that one might plant Easter bulbs in between, should the ground then be soft enough, of course. Then again, one wonders whether the ground might not be advantageously turned once more, so that the next frost might break it up further, before one drills anything further, but then, with climate change, the seasons are so awfully more difficult to predict, don't you think, Professor?"

The three professors blinked alertly, until Mrs. Hart's wandering eyes settled on Professor Sir Barry Liddell.

"That sounds like an interesting strategic problem," he said. Mrs. Hart tilted and turned her chin with delighted expectation, and remained silent, so he roused himself. "Your problem naturally reminds me of the situation before the First World War: everybody knew war would come, of course, but nobody wanted to be the first to mobilize – or the last."

"Oh, that is an awfully interesting!" said Mrs. Hart indulgently. "Please go on!"

"Well, the question of when to strike – well, that is the very essence of STRATEGY!"

"Oh, indeed, Professor Sir Barry, I so agree. A garden is proof of that. And Mr. Hart often tells me the same about the business of insurance, don't you darling?"

"Yes, darling, quite right, quite right. One must strike the reinsurer with an offer before the reinsurer has researched the issue well enough to standardize the risk, you see. Otherwise you might as well be buying bulbs at Easter."

"I see, I see," muttered Professor Sir Barry. "I know that very well from military history, when each side would like to strike in the spring, but doesn't want to strike too early in case winter returns, or too late in case the other side strikes first!"

"Quite so," said Ricky Docker, urgently. "I was thinking of writing a book on that."

"These reinsurers," asked Dorian Floorman, "are any of them American?"

"Most of them are American, indeed," said Mr. Hart.

"Really? Oh, that is convenient. Well, would you say they posture like a President Wilson or a President Roosevelt?"

"Which President Roosevelt?" asked Jenny Wren, helpfully.

"Well," stuttered Dorian Floorman, "I was thinking of F.D.R., obviously, but you could pick either, and I would still be able to tell you how to posture from the British side!"

They were interrupted by a Trustee's electrically amplified voice, introducing the new Director of Riverside. The Trustee read a biography of such detail that her wind faded midway through each sentence, and the broadcast came through as if censored.

"Born in the Midlands, in a constituency where the locals used to say that votes for the Labour Party were weighed, not counted…"

The General Union's representatives cheered.

"The great-grandson of a coal miner who died of pneumoconiosis and English capitalism…His first job was in a bakery making crumpets and tarts, which, in those days, were terms also used to describe women…"

The university's feminist monitor ticked a box on her check list.

"The first person in his family to go to university, he bravely left early to accept a job in journalism…"

The newspaper correspondents applauded.

"He is widely known for his impartial advocacy of social justice…"

His friends from broadcasting banged their tables.

"His journalism is known for his objective reporting on the need to lower the voting age…"

The Student Council's representatives yelled approval.

"He proved that most politicians are not as young as most people…He proved that young people have their own issues…He advocated for journalistic methods as academic methods…"

His friends from public relations cheered.

"He won the Young Journalist of the Year Award for his series of articles on women voting…He asked the radical questions that nobody else thought to ask…Do women vote? Do women care about female issues? Are young women interested in politics?"

The Dramatics Union's cheering drowned out all other unions.

"A journalist, broadcaster, and writer…A trustee of the Workers' Think Tank…A board member at the Royal Society of Arts and Enlightenment…A member of the Campaign for Soft Science…

A proven academic outside the constraints of traditional qualifications...The holder of a dozen honorary doctorates..."

The Academic Union's representatives cheered.

"He could not be more qualified to enlighten this university, whose history is otherwise many centuries old...Please welcome the next Director of the Riverside University of London."

The Trustees stood to lead the applause. The new Director walked up the steps on to the stage, in a white suit, black shirt, and white tie. He turned to the audience to wave, and Simon recognized Mr. Woonderfool.

Sharon followed him up the steps. She slipped in front to place his script on the lectern, then backed into the darkness with her lips pressed together. He had asked her to type his dictation in his dialect. She had looked at him blankly, until he added, "Standard English is cooltural coloonialism."

"That's an idea," she had replied.

"Standard English inhibits freedoom of expressioon."

"That's an idea."

"Just spell it the way you hear it."

Now Mr. Woonderfool looked down at the big type – no more than 16 words to a page – and started to speak: "This noo cent'ry is creating proofoond changes to oor soociety and oor ecoonoomy. We moost change quicker! Disciplinary boondaries are shifting and coonverging. So moost we! A yooniversity moost enhance oor lives soocially. A yooniversity moost create soocial change. A yooniversity moost make soociety moor joost. A yooniveristy moost prioritize stoodent well-being. A yooniversity moost serve everyboody. It moost offer noo approoches to edoocation – moor diverse approoches, moor diverse disciplines, fewer boondaries, moor participation, moor inclusivity, moor access – until everyboody attends yooniversity. A better term for our yooniversity would be diversity! Thus, I am annooncing that Riverside Yooniversity of Loondoon will be knoon hencefoorth as Riverside Diversity of Loondoon."

His friends from the newspapers, Public Broadcasting Corporation, unions, and councils applauded heartily.

"Nooboody wants to goo back to the past, oobvioosly. I doon't want to inflict the past on you, oobvioosly. Boot, in oorder to oonderstand oor footure, we moost coonfroont oor past. Now, let's watch the inspiring stoory of how this university has soorvived its past to get tut present."

Mr. Woonderfool did not like to strain his accent beyond a few practiced sentences, so he introduced a short documentary film, with his voiceover edited with his best efforts. The film began with a series of trigger warnings that he had learnt in British broadcasting, each fading to black before the next message appeared in clean white capital letters.

"Some viewers may find the following images upsetting."

"This footage contains flash photography."

"Historical soundscapes include discriminatory language that some listeners may find offensive."

"This footage shows white privilege."

"Historical film tends to under-represent the LGBT community. (This choice of label is not meant to split the unity of the GLBT, LGBTQ, LGBTI, and LGBT+ communities.)"

"This film features past political messages that some viewers might find conservative."

"Some of the following images depict abuse of alcohol and tobacco in non-working-class situations."

"The prevalence of lean body types in the past implies no 'fat-shaming' of the obese in the present."

"The language spoken in the following video is predominantly English."

"This footage shows traditional gender roles."

"Some products featured in past footage might not be available for purchase today."

"We have been unable to verify whether the babies shown in this footage were swaddled with their consent."

"This footage was produced before the requirements to provide subtitling, signing, and audio description."

"The persons shown in the following images are predominantly dead white males."

"Some images appear to show the handling of women by men without prior consent."

The moving pictures did not last as long as the warnings, or prove as alarming. The lights came up. Mr. Woonderfool returned to the lectern, wiped away a tear, and returned to his script.

As Mr. Woonderfool grew passionate, he remembered the gist of his script, stopped reading, and forgot his dialect. "I am pleased to announce that Bayside will be removing the remaining statues from its campus. You all have walked past the statue outside this hall, which depicts a man who once visited Rhodesia before it was independent of British imperialism. I will not honor him by speaking his name. I don't think we should be granting scholarships in the name of someone responsible for the political violence and economic chaos in Zimbabwe today. His scholarship will be renamed the Endowment for Zimbabwean Democratic Resurgence Despite White Imperialism. Another statue on this campus depicts a man who was the third-cousin by marriage of Queen Victoria, who was, obviously, an imperialist. And the third statue was erected as an abstract tribute to the working man, which is, obviously, both patronizing and sexist. Furthermore, I will be removing the busts of this university's founders from the corridor leading to my office, because white men are, obviously, intimidating to minorities. Two centuries of grime have done much to darken the marble, thankfully, but cannot disguise their hyper-masculine beards. Unfortunately, a lot of students just are not aware that this is actually a problem, so my priority in this academic year will be to make it a problem."

His friends applauded.

Mr. Woonderfool's eyes fell back to his script. "Noo, let oos meet my new Depooty-Directoors."

"Ooh, that's you," hissed Mrs. Hart across the table to Simon.

"I don't want to be a Deputy-Director," said Simon.

"What?" Barry Liddell spat with delight. Then his puzzlement got the better of him. "You mean, you'd rather go back to teaching?"

"No."

"Well, I wouldn't count on getting this rank by teaching alone, not for at least a couple decades anyway. And even then, you would still need to prove you can work with us – the senior Deputy-Directors."

"No, I don't want that either."

"Why on earth not?"

"For the same reason: I prefer the company of adults."

Mrs. Hart nervously laughed away Simon's riposte. Everybody's attention was regathered when the Trustee called the first of the new Deputy-Directors to the stage – the Deputy-Director for Change and Continuity. The next Deputy-Director was called – the Deputy-Director for Levelling and Promoting. Mrs. Hart turned to smile at Simon, but he was gone. The Deputy-Director for Equality and Selectivity was called. She started to panic.

"Jenny Wren!" she hissed. "Where's Simon?"

"He said he needs to reconsider his correspondence, and he may be some time, but not to worry."

"Mr. Hart!" she hissed. "Mr. Hart! You'll need to receive Simon's investiture, otherwise he'll lose it. They're calling him, go on, get up there – leave the desserts alone!"

That is how, with the mysterious and irreversible magic of academic investiture, Mr. Hart was appointed a Deputy-Director for nothing in particular, at Riverside Diversity of London, and all Mr. Hart's professional insecurities, and all Mrs. Hart's material worries, and all Jenny's educational dilemmas were resolved.